THE HYDROGEN SONATA

An ancient people, organised on military principles and yet almost perversely peaceful, the Gzilt helped set up the Culture ten thousand years ago and were very nearly one of its founding societies, deciding not to join only at the last moment. Now they've made the collective decision to follow the well-trodden path of millions of other civilisations: they are going to Sublime, elevating themselves to a new and almost infinitely more rich and complex existence.

Amid preparations, though, the Regimental High Command is destroyed. Lieutenant Commander (reserve) Vyr Cossont appears to have been involved, and she is now wanted – dead, not alive. Aided only by an ancient, reconditioned android and a suspicious Culture avatar, Cossont must complete her last mission given to her by the High Command. She must find the oldest person in the Culture, a man over nine thousand years old, who might have some idea what really happened all that time ago.

It seems that the final days of the Gzilt civilisation are likely to prove its most perilous.

BY IAIN M. BANKS

Consider Phlebas
The Player of Games
Use of Weapons
The State of the Art
Against a Dark Background
Feersum Endjinn
Excession
Inversions
Look to Windward
The Algebraist
Matter
Surface Detail
The Hydrogen Sonata

BY IAIN BANKS

The Wasp Factory
Walking on Glass
The Bridge
Espedair Street
Canal Dreams
The Crow Road
Complicity
Whit
A Song of Stone
The Business
Dead Air
The Steep Approach to Garbadale
Transition
Stonemouth
The Quarry

IAIN M. BANKS

THE HYDROGEN SONATA

www.orbitbooks.net

ORBIT

First published in Great Britain in 2012 by Orbit
This paperback edition published in 2013 by Orbit

A CIP catalogue record for this book
is available from the British Library.

ISBN 978-0-356-50149-9

Typeset in Stempel Garamond by Palimpsest Book Production Limited,
Falkirk, Stirlingshire
Printed and bound in Great Britain by Clays Ltd, St Ives plc

Papers used by Orbit are from well-managed forests
and other responsible sources.

MIX
Paper from
responsible sources
FSC
www.fsc.org   FSC® C104740

Orbit
An imprint of
Little, Brown Book Group
100 Victoria Embankment
London EC4Y 0DY

An Hachette UK Company
www.hachette.co.uk

www.orbitbooks.net

To the memory of
Paul Gamble
and
Ronnie Martin

With thanks to Adèle, Tim, Les, Joanna and Nick

One

(S -24)

In the dying days of the Gzilt civilisation, before its long-prepared-for elevation to something better and the celebrations to mark this momentous but joyful occasion, one of its last surviving ships encountered an alien vessel whose sole task was to deliver a very special party-goer to the festivities.

The two craft met within the blast-shadow of the planetary fragment called Ablate, a narrow twisted scrue of rock three thousand kilometres long and shaped like the hole in a tornado. Ablate was all that was left of a planet destroyed deliberately two millennia earlier, shortly before it would have been destroyed naturally, by the supernova within whose out-rushing sphere of debris, gasses and radiation it remained, like an arrowhead plunging ever downwards into the rising, roiling heat and sparks of a great fire.

Ablate itself was anything but natural. Roughly hewn as though sliced from some spherical cake, its tip and the first few hundred kilometres of its narrow end had, originally, been made up of the metallic material which had formed the very centre of the now-defunct small planet while its wider end – a rough circle a couple of hundred kilometres across – looked like a gently curved dome and had been part of the barren globe's rocky surface. Kept pointed – aimed – into the supernova's blast front by engines keeled within hyperspace, all of that original tip and most of those next few hundred kilometres of layered metallic ores had abraded away over the last nineteen hundred years, boiled and scoured into oblivion by the still-expanding fires of the exploded star's nebula.

The multi-coloured skies around Ablate, filled with the vast glowing clouds of stellar debris and the gasses and dusts resulting from its own slow wearing-away, were some of the most calculatedly spectacular in the civilised galaxy, and that was why Ablate was a place of special significance to the people who called themselves the Gzilt. The Gzilt had rescued this portion of world from the annihilation of the supernova and they had anchored within it the star drives and field projectors which kept it respectively stable and – just, in the centre of that rough circle of what had been the planet's dusty surface – habitable.

The alien ship was an irregular, fuzzy-looking bubble of dark spheres, measuring barely a hundred metres along its principal axis. It was lit from around and above by the spectrum of colours radiating from the clouds of the supernova, and from below by the gentle blue glow of the world-fragment's only obvious non-natural feature: a scooped, domed bowl a handful of kilometres across that lay on that fractured, unshadowed surface like a slightly too perfect crater. The bowl was an oasis of warmth, moisture and atmosphere on that cold, dry, airless surface; within its gauzy layers of containment it held the sort of parks, lakes, carefully proportioned buildings and lush but managed tracts of vegetation favoured by many types of humanoids.

The Gzilt ship dwarfed the alien one; it looked like a thousand dark broadswords gathered into a god's fist and brandished at the skies. It crossed the boundary of glowing, outflowing dusts and swirling gasses at the periphery of Ablate's circular outer surface – allowing its own fields to create a series of brief, tearing, billowing folds within the curtains of light there – then moved slowly towards and over the glowing bowl and the collection of dark bubbles that was the alien ship, until its spiny bulk hung directly above both, occluding a large part of the supernova clouds and draping its bristled shadow over the ship and the dome below.

The smaller ship waited for some sort of hail from the larger one, as was only polite, but nothing appeared to be forthcoming. It decided to make the initial approach itself:

~Greetings. I am the Zihdren-Remnanter Ceremonial Representative Carrying Ship *Exaltation-Parsimony III*. You, I understand, are the Gzilt IR-FWS *8*Churkun*. I am honoured to be invited here and to make your acquaintance.

~That is interesting, came the reply. ~A Zihdren-Remnanter Ceremonial Representative Carrying Ship, you say?

~Well, indeed I am. Somewhat obviously.

~Somewhat obviously?

~Indeed. And, if I may so claim, both in outward form and unshielded emissive signature.

~Again, interesting.

~Indeed . . . May I make an observation?

~You may. We await it.

~You seem – how might one put this? – a little less welcoming and polite – especially formally welcoming and polite, as it were – than, I confess, I was expecting and, indeed, had been led to expect. Am I mistaken, or, if I am not, is there a specific reason for this? . . . Also, I cannot help but note that the crater facility here at Ablate, which I was led to believe would be at least staffed if not in full ceremonial welcoming mode, does not in fact appear to be so. Indeed, it appears to be effectively empty, both of biological and non-biological sentient presences. There are a few sub-AI substrates running, but no more . . . Obviously one is aware that these are strange times, even unprecedented times for the Gzilt; times of disruption and, one would both surmise and expect, quiet but purposeful preparation as well as anticipation. Some degree of formality might, therefore, be expected to be dispensed with in the circumstances. However, even so, one—

~As you say, strange times. Times that bring uninvited guests and unwelcome attentions in the shape of those who would exploit our reduced numbers and distracted state.

~. . . We may have experienced a degree of signal outage there, or at least signal protocol disruption, unlikely though that may seem . . . However, with regard to what you say regarding the unwelcome attentions from others, that is, sadly, to be expected. The preparations for Sublimation tend to bring such – happily, relatively minor – consequences, as those whose memory I am honoured to represent would be the first to agree. The Zihdren—

~There was no signal outage or protocol disruption then, nor is there now. I interrupted you. I am doing so again.

~Ah. Then I was not mistaken. Might I just check; am I addressing the captain of the *8*Churkun*'s virtual crew?

~You are.

~Ah. Well, then – Captain – we appear to have started out from positions involving inharmonious premises. That is unfortunate. I would hope that, nevertheless, you might appreciate my disquiet – one might even characterise it as disappointment – at the fact that we appear to have initiated our association here on such an unfortunate tack. Please; tell me what I might do to help bring us back onto a more agreeable course.

~The preparations for our Sublimation have encouraged those of a parasitical nature. Alien presences wishing to profit from our abandonment of the Real, appropriating what treasure we might leave behind. They circle.

~I understand. I am, of course, aware of those you talk of. It was so with those whose memory I am honoured to represent: your flattered mentors and barely required civilisational guides, the Zihdren.

~Whom you claim to represent.

~I do indeed. And indeed I do. Represent them, I mean. This is scarcely a matter for dispute. My provenance and—

~This is a warship.

~Another interruption. I see.

~A warship.

~Patently. I must say that I was in no doubt regarding your ship class and martial status. The eight-star, Indefinite Range, Full Weapon Spectrum Gzilt contemporary ship-type you represent is entirely familiar to us.

~Things have changed, formalities slipped, protocols been relaxed. This vessel is four point six centuries old and yet has never fired a shot in anger. Now, with most of our kind already gone, preparing the way ahead in the Sublime, we find ourselves defending the disparate items of our about-to-be legacy from those who would use the fruits of our genius and labour to cheat their way further along the path to this point, a point that we achieved entirely honourably and without such opportunistic larceny.

~Well, I'm sure that does you credit, too. Wait! Good grief! Do you mistake *me* for such a vessel? Do you suspect I represent such primitive, aggressive forces? Surely not! I am a Zihdren-Remnanter craft, the Ceremonial Representative Carrying Ship *Exaltation-Parsimony III*. This must be obvious; I have nothing to hide and am transparent, all but completely unshielded; inspect me as you will. My dear colleague; if you wish for help confronting those who would steal any part of your legacy, you need only ask! I, rather, represent a link with those who only ever wished you well, and who, to the contrary—

~Part of the deception such entities employ is impersonating the vessels and beings of others. I am deeming you to be doing so at this moment. We have scanned you and determined that you are carrying something which is entirely shielded from honest view.

~What? My dear Captain, you cannot just "deem" me to be employing any deception! That is absurd! And as for the only fully shielded substrate within myself, that is my *cargo*, my complement of precisely one Ceremonial Guest, our single humanoid expression of respect, expected and invited by the Gzilt people specifically to celebrate their upcoming Sublimation! Of course this entity bears a message from the Zihdren-Remnanter to the Gzilt which I am not privy to! There can be nothing strange, unprecedented or worrying about such a thing, can there? The Gzilt have been party to the relevant diplomatic and ambassadorial protocols for millennia, without a flutter of complaint. A tiny scrap of the

Real bids farewell to you while at the same time representing those who would most happily welcome you to the Sublime!

~There is deceit here, something hidden. We can see it even if you cannot.

~What are you talking about? I am sorry. I have had enough of this. Your behaviour and demeanour goes beyond even the most cautious and watchful warship-normal and frankly risks slipping into outright paranoia. I am withdrawing; you will have to excuse me. Farewell.

~Release in full the information contained within the shielded substrate.

~. . . Have you put a signal containment around me? Have you any idea of the consequences—?

~Release in full the information contained within the shielded substrate.

~I cannot. Quite apart from anything else, there are diplomatic niceties—

~Release in full the information contained within the shielded substrate.

~I *heard* you! And I cannot and will not. How dare you! We are your friends. *Neutrals* would be appalled and insulted at such treatment! That those who have long thought themselves your friends and allies—

~Release in full the information—

~There! You see? Two may interrupt! I refuse to do as you ask. Drop the signal containment around me immediately. And should you make any attempt to block or prevent my moving off under—

~. . . contained within the shielded substrate. Release in full the information contained within the shielded substrate.

~This is outrageous! Do you . . .? Are you mad? You *must* know what and who you are choosing to quarrel with here! I represent the *Zihdren-Remnant*, you lunatic! Fully accepted and accredited heirs to the Sublimed Zihdren, the species many of your people acknowledge as little less than gods; those the Book of Truth itself proclaims to be your spiritual ancestors! I must warn you that although I am, to all intents and purposes, unarmed, still I am not without resources which—

~Release in full the information contained within the shielded substrate.

~Enough. Goodbye. Out.

~Release in full the information contained within the shielded substrate.

~. . . Drop the signal containment around me immediately! And desist from jamming my engine fields *at once*! I am about to initiate a full-power high-acceleration pull-away manoeuvre irrespective of your current interference, and any damage accrued either by myself *or you* will be your responsibility, not mine! The Zihdren-Remnanter and the Zihdren themselves will hear of this act of barbarism; do *not* make it worse for yourself!

~Release in full the information contained within the shielded substrate.

~. . . That my drive components have not just exploded thanks to your unwarranted barbarism is due more to my ability to finesse than your brutal use of overwhelming power. I am, as is now abundantly clear to both of us, effectively helpless. This is a result and a situation that does you no honour whatsoever, believe me. I must – with utter reluctance and under extreme protest, both personal and formal – ask whether, if I do release in full the information contained inside the shielded substrate within myself, you will then drop the signal containment around me and desist from jamming my engine fields, allowing me both to signal and to depart.

~Release in full the information contained within the shielded substrate.

~And I will be allowed to signal and to depart?

~. . . Yes.

~Very well. Here.

~Scanned. We present the results.

~. . . Interesting, as you might put it. I see. That is not a message that I would have anticipated. I now appreciate, as I am sure you do, too, why there was a degree of secrecy regarding the contents. While it would not normally be any part of my responsibility to make comment on such matters, I would, speaking personally, argue that said contents themselves constitute a kind of apology. This is a type of admission, even a confession. I understand that such . . . accountings are often a part of the business of species and civilisations Subliming; matters are settled, lines are drawn under certain proceedings . . . However, be that as it may, it was my mission only to deliver this Ceremonial Guest entity while being kept entirely ignorant of the content, substance and import of its message. Accordingly, I consider that I have, albeit in most unexpected and trying circumstances, discharged my duty, and so would ask to be allowed to communicate this bizarre turn of events to those who tasked me so, and to withdraw from Gzilt jurisdictional space to await further instructions. I have held up my end of our bargain and duly released, in full, the information contained inside the shielded substrate within myself. If you'd be so kind, I now require you to fulfil your promise by dropping the signal containment around me and ceasing to jam my engine fields.

~No.

The Gzilt ship *8*Churkun* – a battleship in all but name – kept the tiny alien vessel effectively crushed underneath it as it directed fire from a pair of its close-range, medium-power plasma chambers into the vessel, and – beneath it, beyond it – into the emptily glowing blue bowl of the crater facility, destroying the ship utterly and blowing the crater facility apart.

The weapon-pulse was so strong it continued into the surface of the planetary fragment to a depth of several kilometres, blasting a brief, livid tunnel a hundred metres across vertically into the rock. A torrent of lava splashed out around the ship's outermost protective fields as the tunnel collapsed, the spattering, cooling rain of molten rock following the pulverised, atomised debris of the Zihdren-Remnanter ship and the centre of the blue-glowing bowl as they too flew into the colour-wild skies above Ablate.

At the boundaries of the world's truncated horizon, some larger parts of the obliterated dome, still whirling away from the initial explosion, burned bright as flame as they plunged into the surrounding curtains of light.

Deep beneath its assaulted surface, automatic systems sensed the blast and the resulting wobble in the tiny world's course, and corrected for it.

Where the little blue oasis of light and life had been there was now a larger, deeper crater, glowing white and yellow and red from its boiling centre to its ragged edge. By the time the crater surface had cooled sufficiently to show how it would look once it had solidified completely, the *8*Churkun* was long gone.

Of the other ship, apart from a new set of already fading folds of light in the skies above Ablate, there was no trace whatsoever.

Two

(S -23)

At sunset above the plains of Kwaalon, on a dark, high terrace balanced on a glittering black swirl of architecture forming a relatively microscopic part of the equatorial Girdlecity of Xown, Vyr Cossont – Lieutenant Commander (reserve) Vyr Cossont, to give her her full title – sat, performing part of T. C. Vilabier's 26th String-Specific Sonata For An Instrument Yet To Be Invented, catalogue number MW 1211, on one of the few surviving examples of the instrument developed specifically to play the piece, the notoriously difficult, temperamental and tonally challenged Antagonistic Undecagonstring – or elevenstring, as it was commonly known.

T. C. Vilabier's 26th String-Specific Sonata For An Instrument Yet To Be Invented, MW 1211, was more usually known as "The Hydrogen Sonata".

The elevenstring was an acoustic instrument – usually bowed though occasionally plucked – of considerable antiquity and even more notable size. Standing over two metres tall, one metre across and more than one and a half deep, it required its player both to straddle it and to sit within it; poised on the small saddle forming part of the base of the hollow around which the rest of the instrument bulked like a giant deformed ring, the player used both legs to create two-thirds of a supporting tripod for the instrument, the final third being formed by a single spar protruding from its base like an inelegantly substantial walking stick.

The first examples had been made of wood, though later versions had been constructed of plastic, metal, grown shell and artificial bone; the one Vyr Cossont owned and was playing was mostly carbon fibre, which had long been the most common and traditional material.

Cossont reached the end of one particularly taxing section of the piece and took a rest. She stretched her back, flexed her aching feet inside her slippers – the elevenstring required that its player use two small pedals to tamp certain strings, while their heels balanced the weight of both player and instrument – and placed the instrument's two bows across the front of the little saddle she sat on.

Cossont scanned the skies above the terrace, where some streaky pink and orange clouds stood out against the darkening blue of evening. Two kilometres beneath, the Kwaalon plains were already night black, not a light showing between the last canted cliff of the Girdlecity and the far, flat horizon. A cooling wind moved across the terrace, moaning through banister wires, whistling as it curled round

Cossont's flier – parked twenty metres away on its own tripod of skinny legs – and making the girl herself shiver once in her thin trews and jacket.

She shifted some wind-loosened hair out of her eyes and kept gazing up and around. A kilometres-distant smudge might be a flock of birds; her familiar, Pyan, was probably flying with them, playing. Her eyes strained, magnifying the view as best they could; she could feel rings of tiny muscles warping the lenses in each eye, while other filaments altered the shape of her foveae. *Were* those birds – and of the right species? But the distance was too great. There might be a larger dark shape mixed in with the flock, but there might not. Even if there was, it might just be a larger bird being mobbed.

There was probably some local system she could ask to find out and quite possibly one or more of the flock would be augmented or entirely artificial, allowing her, in theory, to interrogate them regarding her familiar's whereabouts, but she had grown used, lately, to such systems either not working at all or not working properly – like pretty much all systems everywhere, throughout the Gzilt civilisation, from what she could gather. And anyway, she found it hard to be sufficiently bothered. She also knew better than to try talking to the creature at such moments unless there was some genuinely dire emergency; Pyan, in the end, was its own being, not her property. Sometimes she wondered if it was even her friend.

She sighed, stretched her arms out and loosely shook all four hands, as though trying to free them from something sticky.

She arched her back again; it had become stiff during the last quarter of an hour or so as she'd tackled the demanding middle section of the work. She stood carefully, holding on to the neck of the elevenstring with one hand, lifting the two bows with another, running a third hand through her hair and picking her nose with her fourth.

The elevenstring ideally required its player to have four hands. It could be played by two people, though this required some serious coordination and sometimes fancy footwork, and almost all the pieces written for it, including the Hydrogen Sonata, could be performed adequately by a string trio plus a couple of suitably tuned basses, but to be played as it was intended to be, Vilabier The Younger's most famous composition really required the bodily acoustic Antagonistic Undecagonstring for four hands, and a single, dextrous instrumentalist.

The instrument, like the work, was near impossible to play acceptably, let alone perfectly, yet one demanded the other and the great Antagonistic Undecagonstringists (only a handful in the near millieon since the piece was written) had, allegedly, played and – even more annoyingly, as far as Cossont was concerned – left recordings of the complete work, to show it could be done.

Cossont was acknowledged as a gifted instrumentalist with a particular feeling for ancient string instruments – she had been one of the top five Volupt players in all Gzilt, and was now the single greatest, though admittedly only because the other four were all Stored, awaiting the Sublime – but she was beginning to despair of accomplishing her self-assumed life-task before her whole civilisation simply ceased to be in the Real and she and everyone she knew and loved took, rejoicing, to the metaphorical skies of the Sublime. Playing the Hydrogen Sonata once, note perfect, straight through, without a break save for the few seconds between individual movements; that was Vyr's chosen life-task. It only sounded easy if you knew nothing of either the Sonata or the elevenstring. As far as she was concerned, the Subliming couldn't come fast enough.

Twenty-three days to the big moment now. Twenty-three days to do all the other things she might want to do before the Ultimate Enfold or whatever people were calling it these days and still get this appallingly long, complicated and player-unfriendly piece nailed to her own satisfaction, never mind anybody else's.

She doubted she'd make it. She had even started thinking of giving up entirely, beginning to agree with those who held that life-tasks weren't really about accomplishing anything beyond the passing of time before all such tasks, ambitions, goals and aspirations became – supposedly – laughably irrelevant and petty.

"Flier," she said, inspecting the end of one finger, flicking it to remove what was on the tip, then rubbing her back with the same hand, "is Pyan with those birds?" She pointed.

The two-seat flier, a chunky little aircraft with stubby wings, made a show of waking up, turning lights on in the hinged-open cockpit. "Yes," it told her, through her earbud. "Do you want me to summon it?"

"Not yet," she said, sighing again. "Can you send up that – you know – your . . . that little—"

"My minidrone."

"That's the fella. Keep an eye on it. In case it's not listening when we . . ." Her voice trailed off as she swayed from side to side, stretching. She shook a couple of her hands again, tucked the instrument bows under one arm and started trying to push the loosened strands of her hair back into its band. "Weather?" she asked, as a small hatch opened along the flier's dorsal bulge and a tiny version of the machine buzzed into the air, turning and zipping off towards where she'd seen the distant flock of birds. The minidrone was visible for just a few seconds, illuminated mostly by the hazy light reflecting from the Girdlecity's upper reaches, the nearest few hundred horizontal kilometres of which still shone in the sunlight like some vast tracery of silver and gold wrapped across the sky.

"Cooling at a degree every fifty minutes," the flier told her. "Wind variable but increasing to an average of 18 km/h, gusting twenty-five, backing west-north-west."

Cossont frowned, gazing north-west across the plains to some far, shadow-dark mountains, then looked back at the sloped cliff of Girdlecity behind her. The vast structure was a steep-sided upheaval of semi-exotic metal tubes and facings, curved and sweeping walls of synthetic stone dresswork, swirled patterns of diamond-film windows and whole stretched filigrees of carbon-black cabling, the entire confusion of pierced architectures rising almost straight up to its bright, curved, horizon-to-horizon summit, nearly two hundred kilometres above and arguably, if not technically, in space. She did something she had only taken to doing recently when she was on or in the Girdlecity; she just stood looking, waiting to see some movement. There wasn't any. There rarely was, these days. Sometimes she felt like the only person still alive and un-Stored in the whole world.

Looking between the various local components of the Girdlecity, Cossont could see sky and clouds on the far side of the colossal artefact, perhaps fifty kilometres away; the sky was brighter to the south, the clouds wispier. The degree of Through here – the proportion of architecture to open air – was about fifty per cent, meaning that winds had an unusually good chance of blowing straight through.

"That might work," she muttered.

Cossont rubbed at her back again. The Gzilt conventionally possessed the humanoid-normal complement of arms – two, according to most authorities – and the alterations required to provide Vyr with twice the average while retaining the desired qualities of litheness and flexibility had meant leaving her with a spine that was prone to seizing up if left stressed too long in the one position.

"Mind if I sleep?" the flier asked.

"No; you sleep," Cossont said, flapping one hand at the aircraft as she inspected the elevenstring's tuning keys and machine heads. "Wait till I need you. Going comms down myself," she said, clicking at the earbud that controlled the relevant implants.

The flier switched off its lights, hinged the cockpit closed and went quiet and dark.

Alone again, in a pocket of silence as the wind dropped and all went still, Cossont paused for a moment. She looked up into the blue-black sky with its tinily pointed spray of stars and sat-light, and wondered what it would really be like to be Sublimed, to have gone through with it, to be living on this reputedly fabulously and unarguably real Other Side.

The Gzilt had been living with the idea of Subliming for centuries, generations. At first only a few people had thought it would be a good idea; then, gradually, over time, more and more had. Eventually you had the sort of numbers that would make the whole thing work, because to do it properly required serious numbers – preferably a whole civilisation.

In theory an individual could Sublime, but in practice only solitary AIs ever did, successfully. It took something as complex and self-referentially perfect as a high-level AI to have the cohesion to stand up to the Sublime alone; no normal biological individual could – you just evaporated in there. It was not utter annihilation – all the information you brought with you remained – but the persona, the individual as a functioning, identifiable and distinctive entity – that was gone. Civilisations, and the individuals within those civilisations, survived and flourished in the Sublime over galactically significant periods of time, though they gradually changed beyond comprehension.

That, though, would have happened anyway, had those societies stayed in the Real, and all the research and comparisons and experts and statistics agreed that there was orders-of-magnitude more stability in the Sublime than in the realm of mere matter and energy.

Cossont sighed. She had no idea why she was staring up at the sky to think about all this. The Sublime, like some ideas of God or whatever, was all around. She inspected the end of one of her upper-arm fingers. The tip was callused with wear from trying to control the strings of the elevenstring. The Sublime might as well be in the ridges of hardened skin on the end of her finger as up in the sky.

Parcelled, rolled, compressed and enfolded into the dimensions beyond the dimensions beyond the ones you could see and understand; that was where the Sublime was, and it was a maze-like series of right-angle turns away from this, from normal, three-dimensional reality where she stood on a high platform at sunset, thinking about it.

Cossont had a hard enough time really comprehending hyperspace, the fourth dimension, let alone the next three or four that somehow encompassed the Reality and allowed for nested universes to climb away from the universe-creating singularity at the centre of things and either circle back round some immense cosmic doughnut to be re-compacted and born again, or radiate away into whatever it was that surrounded this mind-boggling ultra-universe.

And the Sublimed lay in dimensions beyond even *that*;

unutterably microscopic, unassailably far away but at the same time everywhere, shot through the fabric of space-time not so much like the individual fibres of this metaphorical weave, or their tiniest filaments or their molecules or their atoms or their sub-atomic particles but – pointedly – like the infinitesimal strings that made up those, that made up everything. In dimensions seven to eleven; that was where the Sublimed lay.

And that, of course, was why the elevenstring had eleven strings; it had first been designed all of ten thousand years ago, but even then people had had an inkling about how all this far-reaches-of-reality stuff worked, and artists had thought to incorporate something of these revelations into their own fields, including musical composition. Why the extra internal, resonating strings were there as well – up to thirteen of them, in addition to the ones that could be accessed from the outside of the instrument – she still wasn't entirely sure. They were a bastard to tune but it was somehow only appropriate to the awkward, obstructive character of the elevenstring that, despite its name, it actually had more than eleven strings.

The wind picked up, soughing across the platform. A few hairs blew across her face. She tucked them back firmly.

Eighteen kinds of weather. Of all the things she'd heard about the Sublime, throughout all the attempts people had made to explain what it was like in any meaningful way, that was the one detail she could remember. It had eighteen different types of weather, not one. She wasn't even sure what this really meant, let alone whether it was genuinely an improvement on reality.

She took a few deep breaths, readying herself to sit within the instrument and start playing, but still wasn't quite ready. She kept thinking back to an encounter earlier that evening, shortly after the flier had brought her here from her home, a couple of thousand kilometres away in a part of the Girdlecity still partially inhabited, to this part, overlooking the plains of Kwaalon, where, as far as she knew, there was nobody living at all, not for tens of klicks in any direction.

She preferred solitude when she played the elevenstring.

Even before she'd opened the cockpit canopy, Pyan had noticed some birds in the distance and asked permission to go and play with them.

She'd sighed, said yes; the creature had unfastened itself from round her neck and flapped off. She'd hoisted the elevenstring's case from the rear seats of the flier, gone to open it, then, on a whim, changed her mind, told the flier to watch over the case – and immediately felt stupid; who did she think she was protecting it from? – and had gone for a stroll in the Girdlecity.

It was dark inside, and chilly. In most places, a few lights would come on automatically, sensing her movement or the heat of her body; in other stretches she had to rely on her eyes alone, nano-enhancement ramping up what little light there was into a grainy ghost-scape. The air grew colder; her jacket and trews slowly puffed up, keeping her warm. She walked along broad corridors and walkways overhanging deep, echoing, unlit spaces, past arcades and giant pipes, girder work and bowled auditoria, listening to her footsteps echo amongst the gloom.

The great world-circling Girdlecity.

Many Gzilt looked upon it as something they could be proud to leave behind when they Sublimed – a monument to their genius, vision and power – conveniently forgetting that they hadn't actually built it. They'd spent thousands of years building on and within the vast structure and had added significantly to it, but the original structure, and the concept of it, had not been theirs at all.

The Girdlecity had been built by the Werpesh, an ancient humanoid species themselves long-Sublimed. The Gzilt had fallen heir to it, the planet it braceleted and the system itself – along with several other stellar systems – eleven thousand years ago, but despite their long association with, protection of and work on the Girdlecity, the original credit lay elsewhere.

Still, they had cared for it all that time, made it their own in some sense, and, if nothing else, had laid down a marker for its guardianship in the future.

Near the centre of what had been a residential area, long abandoned, she came upon an old school with its cargo of the Stored. A stacked landscape of barely glowing white boxes, registering as a little above ambient temperature, were arranged within what had been the playground. More gently glowing heat was visible radiating from inside the building itself, and the ceiling of the great vault above glowed even more faintly with reflected or convected warmth. Dead trees stood, skeletal.

A guard arbite near the locked school gates unfolded itself from its resting ball shape and drew itself up to its full three-metre height, an exaggerated human shape all glittering angles and obvious weapon pods. It looked intimidating, like it was supposed to. Even from a few metres away, it gave the impression of towering over her. Vyr was suddenly aware of how very un-military her jacket was; it had an image emblazoned on it of a dung-chomp/smutter band she'd played electric volupt for, years ago. The Lords of Excrement – complete with their colourful if wince-inducing logo – had seemed a dubious, going-on-childish name even twenty years ago, yet the jacket had remained a favourite because it reminded her of a good time in her life. It was one of the few she'd had altered to accommodate her new set of arms.

"Citizen," the arbite said, then must have identified her from some processing she had with her – probably her earbud. "Reserve Lieutenant Commander," it corrected itself, and saluted.

"Just taking a stroll, arbite," she told the machine.

It remained motionless, seemed to think about this, then without another word folded itself back into its resting sphere-shape with a sort of metallically oiled grace. Compacted, it looked like a piece of sculpture.

She wandered on, and encountered the family by the side of another great drop, where a broad roadway hung over one of the hundred-metre-wide open-work tunnels that threaded their way through the Girdlecity. The man and the woman were huddled round a little fire, its light reflecting off the wall of diamond-film wall lining the roadway.

"Good evening," she said to them, looking quizzically at the fire, which was just a small stack of burning logs. More cut lengths of tree were heaped just beyond where they sat. Both looked up at her, unsmiling. They were dressed for outdoors and looked slightly unkempt. Cossont couldn't see anything to identify them. Her implants were unable to sense anything electronic on them either, which was most unusual. Their faces were smudged. She wanted to march them both off to the nearest working shower and get them cleaned up.

"Evening," the man said, then looked away and poked at the fire with a stick. The woman seemed to be muttering something to herself, talking down into her voluminous hiking jacket. Perhaps she was just on the phone to some-body, Cossont thought, though somehow it didn't feel like she was, not if her own implants couldn't find anything to hand-shake with.

Cossont was about to ask them whether they were wanderers, locals out for a stroll, or what, when a little face peeked out from within the woman's jacket, stared up wide-eyed at her, and then disappeared again with a rustle of clothing. The woman looked up at Cossont with an expression at once wary and defiant.

It took Cossont a moment or two to realise.

She was so used to thinking of herself as part of the Last Generation, the last people to be born before people stopped having babies, she wasn't sure what she was looking at initially. *A toy?* had been her first thought.

"You have a child!" she said, taking a step closer to the woman and going down on her haunches, her face level with the other woman's, her hand going out towards her, then withdrawing again.

The woman smiled, seemed to talk into her jacket again. "Chuje," she said softly, "say hello to the lady."

The little face peeked out again. A child; a real child – as far as she could tell – maybe four or five years old. A girl. She looked very serious as she stared at Cossont, who said, "Hello, Chuje."

"Allo," the child said, then bit her lip and hid away again within the folds of the woman's jacket.

Cossont stared at the woman. The man was sitting closer now, looking over both of them. "She's—" Cossont began.

"Ours," the woman said. "Three and a half." Pride, this time, as well as suspicion and defiance. The girl looked out at Cossont again, then, still watching Cossont, cuddled into her mother, and was cuddled back.

Cossont sat back, her mouth open. She tore her gaze away from the deep, dark eyes of the little girl, looked at both her parents. "So, you're not . . ."

"We're not going," the man said.

Not going. Not Subliming when the time came in twenty-three days from now, when the Stored all over Xown and Zyse and throughout every other planet and moon and habitat and ship of the Gzilt were roused for their pre-waking, and the last few hours before the Subliming itself.

Cossont knew there were people like these, people determined for whatever reason not to Sublime along with everybody else, and she had even met one or two – though she'd always thought that they would change their minds when the time came – but she had never met anyone who had had a child as well.

The convention – it was not quite a law, but it was close to one – was that you did not take a child into the Sublime. It had to be a mature, considered, final action for a civilisation and the individuals within it who were ready to go, who had thought about it fully and had decided they were ready to make the transition. The Gzilt considered children to be unable to give their informed consent on something so important, which meant they regarded taking a child with you as something close to abuse.

So, generally, people had stopped having children. A few, a very few, were born, nevertheless, to parents who still intended to Sublime, but those making that choice, especially with young children, were widely treated as pariahs; most had retreated to communities of the similarly inclined in distant habs.

Cossont found herself staring at the young couple. They were very young, she thought. Maybe ten years younger than her – they must have been barely more than children themselves when the child had been born. "It'll be lonely," she told them.

"It's already lonely," the man said.

The woman said, "We know," at the same time.

"Yes," Cossont said, feeling foolish. "I suppose you know that." She smiled apologetically at them.

"She's our future," the man said, nodding down towards the child.

Cossont nodded, wondering what sort of future it would be. No other species/civ would accept that the few per cent of the Gzilt who remained after the Sublimation would constitute a continuance of that civilisation. All the Gzilt's deserted living places, from the home planet of Zyse itself to the smallest hab and ship, would be regarded as fair game for takeover, absorption, appropriation. Xown itself, due to the fact it was home to the Girdlecity, was earmarked for pan-cultural monument status under the care of one of the Galactic Council's Neutral Foundations. Nobody would get expelled or thrown out of any habitat airlocks, but their worlds would fill up, sooner or later, with others; some humanoid, some not, but all aliens, all outsiders.

You couldn't even delay very long if you did change your mind and decide to go after everybody else. The rate of subjective/absolute change within the first few hours that people spent inside the Sublime was such that leaving it much more than an hour or so was risky; you'd get there and be isolated, those who had made the transition just hours before – whether they'd been close friends, lovers, family, identical twins, clones, whatever – would already have become so changed, so ascended in complexity, that you would have virtually nothing in common. You'd be on your own, or part of a hopelessly small group, effectively contextless, unanchored to anything greater than yourself, and so likely just to evaporate, dissolving into the generality of the fabric of the Sublime, meaningless.

It was unknown whether this phenomenon was something intrinsic to the exotic physics and other fundamental natural laws of the Sublime itself, or a rule imposed by those who inhabited the realm and helped enable the transition of people and civilisations. Various civs had conducted research into the subject and confirmed the effect without pinning down the cause. Perhaps a little of each, seemed to be the tentative consensus, which was not entirely helpful.

"We're not Resist or anything," the woman said suddenly. She was staring at the flashes on Cossont's jacket collar. Resist were the people who were militant Stay-behinders, holding demonstrations, instigating civil disobedience and even now arguing before the Galactic Council that the Sublime was illegal, improperly mandated. A few groups on the fringe of the Resist movement had used violence to try to make their point.

"Just civilians," the man said.

Cossont nodded again. The couple had resigned their ranks, whatever they had been. It happened. It made you poor – it was tantamount to taking a religious vow of poverty – though being poor in a post-scarcity society that only retained money as a sort of ceremonial formality was not so terrible; it took only one person of nominally average means to support any number of those requiring alms. It also tended to make you an object of either grumbling suspicion or grudging admiration, depending.

The little girl had come further out from her mother's jacket and was staring at Cossont now, her wide eyes reflecting the flickering orange firelight, her hands playing with a small toy, turning it over and over in her chubby, grubby hands.

"Can I hold her?" Cossont said suddenly, looking first at the woman, then the man.

"No," the man said quickly, as the mother put an arm round the child, as though protecting her from Cossont.

"We don't allow that," the man continued. "Too many people want to touch her, hold her." He shrugged. "She stopped liking it." He glanced around the cavernous space they were in. "Part of the reason we're out here."

"I'm sorry," the woman said to Cossont, but kept her arm where it was.

"Understand," Cossont said. She smiled as best she could. She looked at all three of them, smiled broadly at the child, then stood slowly. "I have to go," she said. "Best of luck."

"Thank you," the man said.

"You going that way?" she asked, pointing the way she had come.

The man looked wary again, just shrugged.

"If you are," she said, "there's a Store site in an old school; combat arbite guarding it. Shouldn't cause you any trouble, but . . . just so you're not alarmed." She smiled once more.

The woman nodded. The child disappeared into the folds of her mother's jacket again.

"Nice to meet you," Cossont said.

"You too," the man said. "Goodbye."

"Take care," she told them.

The woman just nodded.

Cossont turned and walked away, into the deepening shadows of the vast construction. The pale, meagre light of the fire, enhanced by her augmented eyes, lit the way for a while.

It might not even be a real child, she told herself. It might be a sophisticated toy, or one of the new artificial children they'd brought out for those who felt the need for a child's company – little robots, basically. A screen programme she'd watched had shown one you'd have sworn was a real child, but wasn't. Apparently they even smelled right.

Maybe such robots didn't feel right; too heavy or too hard

to the touch. Perhaps that was why they hadn't let her hold it.

The combat arbite came alive again as she passed by. It stood again but this time kept silent and just saluted.

Cossont shook her head, flexed her shoulders and back one more time, then rotated the instrument so that it faced across the freshening wind. She took up the two bows and, with a single swift, graceful movement, sat within the instrument again, settling her backside and both feet into place, taking a deep breath and slowly letting it out as she started playing a few practice scales. Almost immediately, a small gust of wind spilled across the terrace and made the external resonating back-strings, stretched down the rear of the instrument, thrum quietly. The sound – not discordant, which with an eleven-string was always a bonus (some would say a surprise) – was muffled and quickly died away again with the departing breeze, but nevertheless drew an "Ah-ha" from her as she flexed her double set of shoulders, adjusted her grip on the two three-sided bows and prepared to play.

She'd try the second-last section of the Hydrogen Sonata; she had yet to get this right in a single pass. It was a tough part and not what she wanted to do, but she'd never get anywhere if she only did the easy stuff. The second-last section was fast and furious – even angry.

She'd think of her mother. That might help.

"I mean, look at you!"

She looked at herself; first just down, then at her reflection in the black mirror formed by the blanked-out glass wall of the main bedroom unit. She shrugged. This was a particularly graceful movement when you had four arms, she thought. "What?" she asked her mother, frowning.

Warib just looked at her daughter. Vyr checked her own reflection again. What she could see was a tallish Gzilt girl dressed in neat fatigues; dark grey skin with shoulder-length pale hair above broader than normal – but hardly grotesque – shoulders. Top set of arms a little longer and better defined than the additional set, a healthily substantial chest, a fashionably defined waist and the broad hips of a non-mammalian humanoid. Her legs were a little shorter and her back a little longer than the conventional image of Gzilt perfection, but who cared? Arguably, the four-arm look was all the better for that; it sort of balanced.

Her mother made an exasperated noise.

Vyr squinted. Was there some detail she was missing? She was in her mum's apartment and so in relatively unfamiliar territory, but she knew there would be a proper mirror-reverser unit around somewhere, probably in the blacked-out bedroom unit, where Warib's latest lover was apparently still asleep.

Vyr looked at her mother. "What?" she said again, mystified.

Warib spoke through clenched teeth. "You know perfectly well," she said.

Warib was dressed in a long and elegantly gauzy morning gown that looked impractical enough to be genuinely expensive. She was a more willowy version of her daughter with longer and thicker hair; physically she was effectively ageing backwards and would do so until they all Sublimed. Her daughter had already passed the age when people usually started to control their appearance, but only by a few years, and Vyr had anyway decided some time ago that she would just get older naturally for the time that she had left, given that the big kablooey of transcendent smashingness that was the Subliming would be along soon to make this life and everything in it seem irrelevant and feeble and so on and such like.

She'd been mildly astonished that her mother seemed to take her daughter looking older than she did as some sort of rebuke. It had been the same when she'd become a Lieutenant Commander. She'd thought Warib would be proud of her; instead she was upset that – however technically, and regardless of the fact it didn't really mean anything – her own daughter now outranked her.

"Is it the arms?" she said, waving all four. Beyond Warib, the view through the windows of the apartment showed sea sliding slowly past. Her mother lived on a klicks-long superliner endlessly circling the enclosed coast of the Pinicoln Sea, within Land, the single vast continent that made up most of Zyse.

"Of *course* it's the arms!" Warib told her. She grimaced as though she'd just tasted something bitter, and shook her head. "And *don't* try to be funny, Vyr, it's not within your reach."

Vyr smiled. "Well, I wasn't, though that is almost—"

"You've always got to try to be *different*, haven't you, Vyr?" her mother said, though it wasn't really pitched as a question. "'Look at me! Look at me! Look at me!'" she sang with what was probably meant to be sarcasm, wobbling her head and doing a little dance.

"Well—"

"You've taken *great* delight in trying to embarrass me ever since you were little."

Vyr frowned. "I'm not sure I ever formulated that as a specific ambi—"

"You started trying to make my life hell when you were still wetting your pants."

". . . probably more of a happy acci—"

"That's what you used to do, in fact; take your knickers

down and pee in front of my guests. How do you *think* that made me look? At *parties*. In front of some *very* important people!"

"So you've said, more than once, but remember I checked the house records and—"

"Your father and I *deleted* those, they were so embarrassing."

"Hmm. But the amendments files—"

"How can you disbelieve your own mother?" Warib wailed, putting her elegantly manicured hands up to her glossily perfect face and letting her head drop forward. The tone of voice and gesture were both cues that she would shortly start to screech and sob were the point not conceded.

"Anyway," Vyr said patiently. "The point now is—"

"That how can I invite you to my party when you look like *that*!" Warib said, flinging one arm out towards her daughter and almost shrieking the last word. "A freak!"

"The arms?" Vyr said, just to be sure.

"Of *course* the fucking arms!" her mother roared.

Vyr scratched her head. "Well, so, don't invite me," she said, trying to sound reasonable.

Warib took a deep, measured breath. "How," she said, her voice lowered to the sort of whispered, husky tone that indicated Vyr's last question had been so idiotic it had scarcely been worth wasting breath on at all, "can I not invite you when you're *my* daughter and I'm supposed to be *proud* of you?" Her voice started to rise again. "What will people think then? *What?*"

"So I have four arms," Vyr said, gesturing with all of them. "People used to have two heads, or look like octlegs or tumblebush, or—"

"That was in the past!" Warib told her acidly. "Ancient days. No one cares."

"I don't know," Vyr told her, shaking her head. "I saw a screen thing about that travelling ultimate last party outfit on Xown and there were people there that—"

"Vyr!" her mother wailed. "Will you *listen*?"

". . . big airship thing, inside . . ." Vyr found herself silenced by a flash of her mother's eyes.

"Nobody," Warib told her, "who is anybody *does* that sort of thing any more!" She drew in a breath and said carefully, "It's infantile, Vyr. Don't you pay *any* attention to—?"

"Mum, I'm just trying to—"

"Oh, dear God, don't call me 'mum'," Warib said, eyelids fluttering closed.

". . . say goodbye and see-you-soon to everybody, and play this piece—"

"*Everybody*," her mother shouted at her, "is reverting to *classic*! Don't you even know that? Amendments . . ." Warib hesitated. "Obvious amendments . . . are *out*. Nobody's doing it any more. Everyone's going for human basic as a mark of respect for all the millions of generations that helped get us to this point."

Warib stared at the floor and slapped herself gently on the forehead, a gesture that – as far as Vyr knew – was a genuine innovation within the repertoire and so might actually be unchoreographed, perhaps even spontaneous. This was so surprising, Vyr came extremely close to feeling concern.

"Dear suffering Scribe, Vyr," her mother whispered, "some people are even going back to their natural hair colour." She looked up, eyes moist, nodding.

Vyr stared at her mother. Outside, sea slid past; still. Eventually she raised all four of her arms. "So am I invited to the fucking party or not?"

Warib rolled her eyes, glanced behind, then fell backwards

dramatically onto a plush white couch positioned in front
of the stateroom's main picture window. She lay there and
kept her eyes closed while one hand went to her throat and
the tiny copy of the Book of Truth encased in a locket on
a thin chain there. Her fingers patted the flat little piece of
jewellery as though taking comfort from it. Cossont – taking
a couple of quiet steps backwards while her mother's eyes
were closed – had noticed Warib had grown noticeably more
religious as the Subliming had approached. The best you
could say of this was that she was not alone.

Warib shook her head and said quietly, resignedly, "Oh, do
as you please, Vyr; you always do, always have. Come as you
wish; embarrass me all you like. Why break the habit of a—"

Cossont didn't catch the last word; she was already out
the door.

Miraculously, thinking back to all this domestic nonsense of
just a few days earlier, with her eyes closed and her mind
half wandering, Vyr got right through the central, especially
demanding section of the second-last movement without –
for the first time – making any mistakes. She'd done it! The
tangling blizzard of notes had been successfully tackled. She
was on what always felt like the easy downhill gliding bit
now where the notes were fewer and further apart and easier
to bridge; another minute or so of nothing-too-demanding
and she'd have the damn thing licked.

She felt a smile on her lips and a breeze on her face. There
was even a pleasant thrumming noise coming from behind
her, courtesy of the elevenstring's external resonating strings
and the breeze she'd been hoping for; she could feel it
through her spine and the seat of her pants. My, for once
even the elements seemed to want to wish her well in this
ridiculous enterprise.

She was thinking about opening her eyes when a sudden gust of wind from the other side briefly silenced the resonating strings, rocked her in the seat and nearly toppled the instrument and her together; she was forced to abandon the stop-pedals and plant both feet firmly flat on the ground to steady both herself and it; her trews flapped against her calves and she felt her hair come loose again as she was forced to stop playing, unbalanced and unsettled. The external resonating strings made a noise partway between a fart and a groan.

The notes faded away and the gust of wind died too, but a new noise of what sounded like an engine winding down replaced the elevenstring's music, and she felt a sort of multiple-thud from the terrace come up through her feet and the supporting spar under her backside.

She still didn't open her eyes. She withdrew both bows in good order from the strings and sat up straight within the O of the hollow instrument, then – with a single accusatory stare at her flier, which was only now switching its lights on again – she turned to where all this new commotion seemed to be coming from.

An eight-seat military flier, still the colour of the near-black sky above, was settling onto its quartet of squat legs fifteen metres away, its bulbous bulk unlit until a waist door flicked down and somebody emerged so senior that, even as a nominal civilian in the regimental reserve, Vyr had no real choice about standing and saluting.

She sighed and stepped out of the elevenstring, clicking down the side-stand at the same time, so it could support itself. The elevenstring made a very faint creaking noise.

Vyr hooked her slippers off, pulled her boots on, then stood at attention, managing to ear-waggle her comms unit awake. "Etalde, Yueweag, commissar-colonel, Regimental Intelligence; precise current attachment unknown," the earbud whispered curtly as the officer advanced at a trot. He took his cap off and stuck it under his arm, then smiled and waggled one hand as he approached. Vyr stood at ease. She glanced at her own flier, narrowing her eyes a fraction.

"Contacted Pyan," the aircraft told her through her earbud. "It whines, but is on its way. Fifteen minutes."

"Mm-hmm," Cossont said quietly.

A pair of fully armed and armoured troopers swung out from the regimental flier and stood, weapons ready, one on either side of the door, which flicked closed again. Vyr allowed her face to register some surprise at this development.

". . . stay informal, shall we?" Commissar-Colonel Etalde was saying, nodding as he arrived in front of her. He was short, plump and appeared to be perspiring slightly. Like a lot of people these days, he wore a time-to; a watch dedicated to displaying how long was left to Instigation; the very moment – assuming that everything went according to plan – of the Subliming event. His was a dainty digital thing which sat on the chest of his uniform jacket and contrived to look a lot like a medal ribbon. Vyr had one too but she'd left it somewhere. Even as she noticed the commissar-colonel's example, the time-to's display clicked over to count one day less; it must be midnight on home planet Zyse.

Commissar-Colonel Etalde looked at Vyr, taking in her extra arms. He nodded. "Yes, I was . . ." He looked past her at the elevenstring. His eyes bulged. "What the hell is that?"

"A bodily acoustic Antagonistic Undecagonstring, sir," she told him. She was staring over his head, as etiquette demanded. Happily this took no great effort.

"Don't say," Etalde said. He looked back to her. "It yours?"

"Yes, sir."

He made a clicking noise with his mouth. "Suppose we'd better take it with us."

"Sir?" Vyr said, frowning.

"Does it have a case or something?" he asked.

"Yes, sir. It's over there." She swivelled, indicated the dark case lying on the black tiles of the terrace a few metres away, almost invisible.

The commissar-colonel glanced back towards the two troopers. The nearest was already moving in the direction of the case, carbine shouldering itself as he or she jogged across the black tiles of the terrace.

"That us?" Etalde asked. "We fit?"

"Sir?" Cossont repeated, still frowning.

Etalde appeared briefly confused, then snapped his fingers. "Oh! Yes! Better . . ." He cleared his throat then said, "Lieutenant Commander Cossont, you are hereby re-commissioned with immediate effect for the duration of the current emergency."

Vyr's frown deepened. "There's an emergency?"

"Sort of a secret one, but yes."

Cossont felt her expression contort despite herself as she looked down at the commissar-colonel. "Now?" she said, then adjusted her expression and gaze and said, "I mean; now, sir? So soon before the—?"

"Yes, now, Lieutenant Commander," Etalde told her sharply. She heard him sigh and saw him put his cap back on. "Thing about emergencies," he said, sounding weary. "Rarely occur when they'd be convenient."

"May I ask what—?"

"What the hell's going on?" Etalde suggested, suddenly breezy again. "Ask away. Won't do you any good. No idea myself."

The trooper appeared with the elevenstring's case, opened. It took all three of them to wrestle it in.

Etalde, breathless, nodded towards the military flier. "Commsint AI's saying you've got a pet or something coming in, that right?"

"Yes, sir," she told him. "Few minutes out still." She went to lift the elevenstring's case but the trooper did it for her, hefting it onto one shoulder, carbine swinging round from the other.

"We're tracking it," Etalde said as the trooper stepped towards their aircraft. Cossont stood where she was. The commissar-colonel stopped and looked back at her. "Well, *come on*," he told her. "We'll rendezvous with the creature in the air." He smiled. "Faster."

"And my flier, sir?" she asked.

Etalde shrugged. "Tell it to go home or wherever it has to go to, Lieutenant Commander; you're coming with us." He shrugged. "Orders."

"Never heard of it."

"More commonly known as the Hydrogen Sonata."

"Still never heard of it."

"No great surprise, sir. It's a bit obscure."

"Renowned?"

"The piece?"

"Yes."

"Only as being almost impossible to play."

"Not, like . . . ?"

"Pleasant to listen to? No. Sir."

"Really?"

Vyr frowned, thinking. "An eminent and respected academic provided perhaps the definitive critical comment many thousands of years ago, sir. His opinion was: 'As a challenge, without peer. As music, without merit.'"

The commissar-colonel whistled briefly. "Harsh."

Vyr shrugged. "Fair."

"Life-task, eh?"

"It seemed like a good idea at the time, sir."

In the ink-black skies above the Kwaalon plains, the military craft decelerated quickly and swung almost to a stop; the rear ramp swung down and wind came buffeting and roaring in before a shush-field calmed everything down.

Vyr was strapped into a wall seat between Etalde and a third trooper. The first two troopers were on the other side of the small cabin with the elevenstring in its case secured between them like some bizarre carbon-black coffin, its nearest extremity close enough to Cossont to touch. An AI was flying the aircraft.

Pyan, Cossont's familiar, which had the form of a square black cape, flapped its way in from the turbulent darkness outside, bumping into the spongy shush-field and fluttering theatrically to the floor in apparent surprise as the craft's rear door slammed closed and the flier accelerated again.

"Oh, gracious!" Pyan said on the local open channel, as it struggled against the rearward pull. It used its corners to heave itself along the floor towards Cossont, who tapped into their private link and growled,

"Stop dramatising and get over here."

The cape flowed along the floor and climbed up to her shoulders with a little help from Etalde and Cossont herself. It draped itself there as best it could given the straps, fastening itself round her neck.

"You're touchy," it told her. "What's all the fuss about anyway?"

"With any luck, nothing."

Three

(S -23)

The *Mistake Not . . .*, a Culture vessel of indefinite age, hazy provenance and indeterminate class but generally reckoned to be some sort of modestly tooled-up civilian craft rather than a part of the Culture's allegedly still slowly shrinking military resources, had been detailed to rendezvous with the Liseiden fleet by the clinker sun of Ry. The result of an experiment carried out by the General Systems Vehicle that had constructed it decades earlier, and not even officially classed as an Eccentric, the craft's real status had always been moot. Regardless, currently it was seconded to the Contact section for the occasion of the Gzilt Subliming. Seemingly eager to make a good impression, the ship made sure to be at the rendezvous point especially early.

It had a few dozen hours to wait; it circled the husk that was the long-dead sun for a while, inspecting the tiny, barely radiating stellar remnant, then darted about the rest of the system in a series of high acceleration/deceleration dashes – just for the fun of it, really – surveying the handful of cold, gas-giant planets orbiting the cinder.

Slightly too big to be a true brown dwarf, the sun had never been quite substantial enough to maintain nuclear fusion for any meaningful amount of time, effectively passing straight through the Main Sequence that defined normal stellar evolution as though it was a barrier to be slipped past rather than a path to be travelled along. It had never blazed brightly and after what truncated life it might have had as a true star, had subsequently spent billions of years just radiating away what little internal heat it had ever possessed.

It lay burned out now, as cold as its accompanying planets and darker than the galactic skies around it. The *Mistake Not* . . . could see everything around it perfectly well, of course, and in exquisite detail, able to ramp up any remnant radiations from the failed star itself or the background wash of galactic space or illuminate anything it felt the need to inspect using a variety of its own active sensor arrays, and – in case all that standard 3D stuff wasn't enough – it was capable of deploying the ultimate vantage point of standing outside the skein of real space altogether, looking down on this local patch of the normal universe from either direction of hyperspace . . . but still it missed the starlight. There was something comforting about having a vast hydrogen furnace burning millions of tons of material a second at the centre of a solar system. It was cheery.

This was just . . . dull.

Especially in 3D. Via hyperspace the ship could see a delightfully attractive supernova filling nearly a thirty-secondth of the sky off to one side, but the wavefront of real light had yet to crawl across the intervening gulf of space to get here and illuminate this fate-forsaken cinder. Dull beyond dull.

And lifeless! The whole system! Even the few Deadly-Slow species – the glacially paced plodders of the galactic community whose constitution and chemistries might have suited the cold and quiet of the local environment – appeared to have given both the star and its planets a miss; no Baskers, no sign of Seedsail or Darclouds or any of the other relevant species that were the cosmic equivalent of sub-silt feeders. A lonely, misfit sun, then; never quite one thing or the other, and remote from its peers.

The *Mistake Not . . .* registered a twinge of affinity with the dead star, and investigated that response as well, turning over in its mind the bizarre concept of a conscious entity such as itself feeling some sort of metaphorical connection with something as classically boring, as easily described and as billion-year venerable as a failed sun.

The ship was aware that, however splendid, intellectually refined and marvellous it might be (and it was very much of the opinion that it was all of those things, and more), it would likely still only ever measure its age in thousands of years, and for all the star's monotonous lifelessness and sterility, it would still be here when it, the ship *Mistake Not . . .*, had gone.

Still: life was life, consciousness was consciousness, and mere classical matter, inanimate – no matter how long-lasting – was just ineffably boring and in a sense pointless compared to almost any sort of life, let alone something that was fully aware of its own existence, never mind something as gloriously *hyper*-sentient and thoroughly, vitally connected to the universe as a ship Mind.

And besides, when it had ceased to be as a Culture vessel, the ship was confident that its being would continue to exist in some form, somewhere, either – at the very least – as part of some long-slumbering transcorporated group-mind, or – ultimate of ultimates, as far as was known – within the Sublime.

Which kind of brought it back to where it had come in: here.

The approaching Liseiden fleet manifested as a collection of forty slightly embarrassingly untidy warp-wakes, some distance off.

The Liseiden were fluidics: metre-scale eel-like creatures originally evolved beneath the ice of a wandering extra-stellar planet. They were at the five-going-on-six stage of development according to the pretty much universally accepted table of Recognised Civilisationary Levels. This meant they were Low Level Involved, and – like many at that level – Strivationist; energetically seeking to better themselves and shift their civilisation further along its own Main Sequence of technological and societal development.

They were a lively, creative and uninhibited species, according to most analyses, and just the tolerable side of the assertive/aggressive line, though not above bending the odd rule or stepping over the occasional decency boundary if they thought they could profit civilisationally. So not, in that regard at least, that different from almost every other Involved species.

They were here, now, to negotiate, trade, acquire or just plain steal whatever they could of whatever assets, plant, kit, tech or general gizmology the Gzilt left behind when they Epiphanised in twenty-three days' time. And they had form in this regard: they'd done this before with other Subliming species, which meant they went by another name according to most people's reckoning: Scavengers.

Scavenger species, it was fair to say, were not universally liked or respected by all their galactic cohabitees, and that could lead to trouble, especially within the heightened emotional atmosphere surrounding a Subliming, and all the more so when there were other, competing Scavenger species in the vicinity sharing the same predatory intentions, which, here, there were. The *Mistake Not . . .* was part of a distributed meta-fleet of Culture and other craft invited into their until-now jealously guarded space by the Gzilt to help keep matters as friendly and civilised as possible while they got ready to do the Big Disappear.

Normally, the martially inclined though generally peaceful Gzilt would have had plenty of their own ships to enforce any degree of compliance they wanted within their own sphere of influence, especially against people toting the sort of bow-and-arrow tech a level five/six civ like the Liseiden could muster, but these were not normal times; the Gzilt had chosen to send many of their best ships into the Sublime first, as though to reconnoitre. It wasn't unknown for about-to-Sublime species to do this, but it was unusual, possibly a little paranoid, and arguably dangerous, a little like you had already taken your eye off the target . . .

Happily, according to the galaxy-wide gossip web that passed as an intelligence network between Culture ships, there had lately been local rumours of a last-minute deal between the Gzilt and at least one of the circling Scavenger species – probably the Liseiden – to legitimise and formalise the scavenging process.

The Liseiden were definitely learning. These days they went actively looking for this sort of mutually agreed understanding with species about to Sublime, rather than just piling in like piratical scrappers every time. On this occasion they'd even thought to get representation: they'd hired a people called the Iwenick to be their humanoid face at negotiations with the Gzilt. This was, by general assent, a Smart Move.

So the Liseiden would get the contract, as it were, and be expected to conduct themselves with the decorum befitting their presence anywhere near such a momentous event, as well as behaving with the sort of studied calmness that only came from knowing that what you were engaged in was a dignified and conscientious clearing-up and recycling process, and not some childishly desperate rule-free scramble for whatever loot could be scooped before the adults stepped in to re-impose order.

Sadly, an equally plausible rumour held that – perhaps thanks to the pride of the Gzilt, for too long reluctant even to think of lesser civs pawing over their remains following their departure for better things – this had all been left far too late, and the other Scavenger species, already in place within or around Gzilt space, would refuse to honour any such agreement.

There was, as a result, a distinct chance that things might get interesting.

The ship watched the Liseiden fleet crawl closer.

Much further off than they'd ever have imagined possible, it had already begun to monitor some of their comms traffic.

". . . *deal with the Culture ship?*"

". . . *well, I—*"

"*Got a name for this thing yet?*"

". . . *um—*"

"*The* Mistake Not . . . , *apparently.*"

"*The* Mistake Not . . . *?*"

"*Affirmative.*"

"Mistake Not *what?*"

"*That's all we've got, sir.*"

"*That's not really good enough, is it?*"

"*Not really, sir. I—*"

"*Nyomulde; you're supposed to be the Culture fan-child of the Fleet; what have you . . . do you have?*"

"*Ah, sir. The form, um, the ellipses after the words 'Mistake Not' imply there's more, but it's redacted; hidden. I've had the AI scan the relevant databases and there's . . . there is no more. I mean, there is sort of generally understood to be more, but it's like, ah, it's not for public . . . it's sort of a private joke between the Culture ships, the Minds.*"

"*A joke?*"

"*It's what they're like, sir.*"

"*Ridiculous. How'd this bunch of effete spawnsuckers ever get to where they are?*"

"*Well—*"

"*Class? How about . . . ? What class is it? What are we dealing with here? Have they deigned to tell us that or is that redacted too?*"

"*I've got it down as a non-defined 'U' open brackets 'e' close brackets, sir.*"

"*Keep going, officer.*"

"*Well, 'non-defined' sort of speaks for itself, 'U' just means 'Unit' and 'e'. . . Hmm. I thought that meant Eccentric, to be honest, sir, but some sources hold that it stands for erratic. Strictly speaking the 'e' should be upper case if it stands for—*"

"*Size? What size is it?*"

"*In the order of a couple of kilometres, though that's just the outer field envelope.*"

"'*In the order of.*'"

"*Best we've got, sir.*"

"*I see. Do we have any idea what it* looks *like?*"

"*Um, not really, sir. No record of its appearance within the field complex boundary. There are various guesses but they're all very speculative. One or two—*"

"*Spare me, officer. It's a Culture ship but we don't know what sort.*"

"*In a pebbleshell, yes, sir.*"

There was a lot more like this, all in the Liseiden tongue, which was made up of a not inharmonious series of bubbly water-belches. The ship added the name Nyomulde to the Culture's intelligence archive of known Liseiden officers, immediately transmitting this to a variety of its comrade craft both near and far.

The Liseiden hadn't been forthcoming regarding the identity of the approaching fleet's commanding officer, or even which ships would make up the fleet in the first place, but from the largest ship's warp signature – hideously obvious from light years away – the *Mistake Not . . .* had determined hours earlier that it was the *Gellemtyan-Asool-Anafawaya*, a Collective Purposes Vessel (First Class) and fleet flagship representing the last word in what the Liseiden were capable of building.

Much more satisfyingly, from the tone and word choice of one of the individuals talking – referencing earlier notes compiled by other Culture ships – the *Mistake Not . . .* was becoming increasingly certain that one of the voices it was listening to was a senior Liseiden officer called Ny-Xandabo Tyun, a male who held the rank of Salvage and Reprocessing Team Principal. Admiral, in other words.

But what *babble*! What to-ing and fro-ing over such simple operational matters! A bunch of dim-witted, slow-thinking bios swimming in a tub clouded with their own effluent, trying to work out what was going on around them by staring through portholes probably. It was hard for a ship, a Mind, not to feel at least a degree of contempt.

And they were still talking, out there between the stars, as the little flock of ships scraped slowly, slowly closer. (The fleet was already having to decelerate, the *Mistake Not . . .* noted, with some exasperation. This would draw the whole process out even further.) It was only a meet-and-greet anyway; almost as soon as it got here the Liseiden fleet would be breaking up again, most of the ships heading off singly or in small groups to individual places of interest within the Gzilt sphere; only the flagship and a few smaller vessels would remain as any sort of substantive unit.

This was something Admiral Tyun himself didn't know yet; there were sealed orders in the flagship's AI detailing all this dispositional stuff which were only to be accessed on the fleet's arrival at the clinker star but which the Culture already knew about through a piece of deft signal interception by some other ship or ships tens of days earlier.

The *Mistake Not . . .* found knowing this – while Admiral Tyun did not – quite agreeable.

It would probably tag along with the flagship and its escorts, plus it had prepared an eel-like avatoid to represent it in person aboard the flagship. From what it had been told, the Liseiden were almost suspiciously keen to welcome this creature aboard.

It listened in to the animal chatter again.

Good grief, they were still discussing its own name!

The *Mistake Not . . .*, self-saddled with a full name so long and unmanageable that even other Culture ships rarely took the trouble to use all of it, was just vain enough to feel slightly flattered at all this attention, but still found the incessant chit-chat unbearably slow and fundamentally pointless.

All these people seemed to do was talk!

It supposed it was just what biologicals did. If you wanted to feel you were still somehow in control of a ship or a fleet or even your civilisation, talking amongst yourselves seemed to be the way you convinced yourself of it.

Finally one of them said, "*Sir, we . . . may be approaching the sort of distance the Culture ship can start to read our comms.*"

"*This far out?*"

"*—encrypted, aren't . . . isn't it?*"

"*Precautionary principle applies, team. Officer?*"

The obvious, inter-ship comms traffic ceased. The *Mistake Not . . .* considered dedicating an effector to the lead vessel to monitor it internally, but there was a tiny chance they might spot it doing so – a tiny chance increased by the possibility the fleet carried tech filched on earlier Scavenging sorties – so it didn't.

Hours of patient waiting later, the Liseiden fleet of large, boxy-looking ships finally dragged itself into the Ry system, hauled up into a rather quaint orbit around the clinker sun with the warp-engine equivalent of loud clanks and clouds of black smoke, and – finally – rendezvoused officially with the Culture ship *Mistake Not . . .*

Effusive greetings of great solemnity and seemingly genuine friendliness flowed in both directions.

It was while all this was going on and the avatoid eel was being puttered across to the fleet flagship in an antique shuttle brought along specially for the purpose that one of the *Mistake Not . . .*'s multitudinous sub-routines – this one charged with deep analysis of recent HS sensor data by opportunistic triangulation following significant movement within any given real space reference frame – flagged the tiniest of oddities.

It was timed, originally, just over twenty-two hours earlier and it was located some centuries away, about a quarter of the distance round the boundary of the rough sphere of stars and space that held the Gzilt volume of influence. Specifically, it had taken place within the colossal, slow-tumbling clouds and wastes and veils of light marking the Yampt-Sferde supernova: the pretty one it had noticed earlier whose real light had yet to get here. Somewhere inside the vast, escaping fires of the nebula there had been a microscopic flare of radiation displaying an unusual, even anomalous signature spectrum.

Suddenly, in proper, no-nonsense combat-grade Mind-thinking time, while the transfer shuttle moved a few nano-metres towards its destination, the AI cores on the Liseiden flagship slept deeply between cycles and the Liseiden them-selves would have appeared frozen and silent even observing them on a scale of subjective years, the *Mistake Not . . .* watched the sub-routine's resulting attention-cascade briefly suck in and focus other computational assetry on the data, rapidly producing all the available analysis it was presently possible to compile on the subject.

The anomaly – so faint, far away and overwhelmed by the seething turmoil of energies all around it as to be only very ambiguously weapon-blink – looked like it was centred quite precisely on the artificially maintained planetary fragment called Ablate, where the Gzilt had some sort of ceremonial facility.

. . . *Oh-oh*, thought the Culture ship.

Four

(S -22)

Septame Banstegeyn went from group to group, taking part in multiple hand-shakings, everybody standing side-on and putting a single hand into a big confused but well-meaning tangle in the centre. Sometimes the resulting "shake" was a trembling muddle, sometimes the ball of grasping hands would end up going up and down quite violently, as though they were all making it happen deliberately; everybody always looked slightly surprised when that happened. Doubtless this was an example of or metaphor for something or other.

Anyway, Banstegeyn didn't enjoy the process; in fact he hated it. He took particular care, therefore, to look entirely as though nothing he could possibly be doing right now could conceivably give him greater pleasure. He was hearty, amiable, roaring with laughter when he needed to, but he had a continuing need to wash his hand or at least wipe it on his robes, as though to decontaminate it after all this sweaty touching.

Well, this was just one of the many objectionable things that a man in his position had to do. In the end it was worth it; it would all be worth it.

"Well, Ban, it's all yours now!"

"Folrison," Banstegeyn said, forcing a smile as the other, junior parliamentarian shook him by the shoulders. Over-familiarly, Banstegeyn thought. Folrison looked drunk, probably was; a lot of them were, though not him – never him. And he didn't like being called "Ban", either. "It's all *all* of ours now, I think you'll find," he told the other man, then gestured modestly at his own chest. "Merely a caretaker."

"Na, you finally got your way. You're in charge." Folrison smiled. "Of not very much for not very long, but, if it makes you happy . . ." He looked away as though distracted, seemed to catch somebody else's gaze. "Excuse me," he said, and wandered off.

Banstegeyn smiled at Folrison's retreating back, in case anybody was looking, though what he was thinking was, *Yes, just fuck off.*

"Sir."

"Septame." His chief secretary and aide-de-camp both appeared out of the mêlée.

"Where were you two when I needed you?" he demanded.

Jevan, his chief secretary, looked dismayed. "But, sir," he said, "you said—"

"Would you like a wipe, Septame?" Solbli said quietly,

smiling as she pulled a moist square from her satchel and offering it to him discreetly.

Banstegeyn nodded, quickly wiped his hands and gave the towel back to Solbli. "Let's go," he said.

Eventually, shaking off the last overly effusive well-wisher from the lower ranks, they were able to make it to the doors leading from the still-crowded main assembly chamber to the Senior Levels and the terrace overlooking the darkened gardens and the near-deserted city.

Banstegeyn nodded to the parliamentary constable who'd opened the door, then, at the top of the steps leading down to the terrace, while Jevan and Solbli stood respectfully a couple of steps behind, had a brief moment to himself before anybody else rushed up to tell him what a historic day it had been. His earbud, released from the rule-imposed no-personal-comms restriction of the parliament interior, started to wake up, but he clicked it off again; Jevan and Solbli would be catching up and would let him know about anything urgent.

The gardens – roundels of paving and splashing pools surrounded by maze-like blocks of black hedges within which it had always been easy to find nooks where quiet words might be had – were just starting to look neglected, even under the soft, subdued lights shining from antique lampposts; the city – a quaint jumble of low domes and soaring spires, gently floodlit but looking empty as a stage set – lay quiet and still under a dark, clouded sky.

So late. The session really had gone on far too long.

A handful of aircraft drifted above M'yon, lights winking; not long ago there would have been hundreds. Banstegeyn had long thought of the old Ceremonial Capital as an open-air museum, with the parliament its dustiest exhibit. It was just that now it truly looked like it. Anyway, M'yon was not where the real power lay at all – that was in the teeming habs, the great ships, the orbiting manufacturies and the Regimental HQs – but rather where it had to look like it lay.

On the terrace, the principal knot of people surrounded the president: the usefully useless president, her cohort of effete trimes, a few of his fellow septames and a smattering of junior degans who must have ridden in on somebody more senior's coat-tails. Secretaries, AdCs, advisors, a few Military Outright bigwigs and a smattering of accredited aliens made up the rest; some of the aliens were humanoid, some disconcertingly not.

The ambassadorial party from the Ronte – the insectiles who were one of the two Scavenger civs the Gzilt were actually talking to – existed inside heavy-looking exo-suits like tiny, complicated spaceships, all alarmingly sharp joints and angles and the occasional hiss and stink of some escaping gas. Their translators didn't work as well as they seemed to think and it could be confusing to talk to them. They tended to huddle on the outskirts of gatherings like this, lucky to have a Gzilt military attaché to talk to, and even then only because the unfortunate officer had been ordered to do so. Four of the six suited Ronte were resting on their spindly-looking suit legs; the other two were floating over a pond, humming. Oh, and a few journalists and media people, he noted with some distaste; even the body politic had parasites.

It was the last day of the Gzilt Parliament. The very last day; it would never meet again. Anything relevant that needed dealing with from now on would be handled by transitional committees or temporary cabinets. The various representatives, having made their final farewells, would shortly be departing. A handful of those local to Zyse itself would head off in fliers, but all the rest would take ship to be with their families and/or loved ones, the great majority of them in conveniently distant systems where, Banstegeyn devoutly hoped, they'd be unable to cause any trouble if any difficult decisions had to be made over the next twenty-odd days.

Banstegeyn had made sure that he was chair of several of the most important committees, and that his people chaired or controlled almost all the rest; plus it was tacitly accepted that he would be in charge if there was need of an emergency temporary cabinet.

Which there might be, now, of course. Only a very few people knew this at the moment (very few, but, patently, at least one fucker too many), though it was looking increasingly likely. It gave him stomach contractions just thinking about it; *Go!* he wanted to scream at all of the other parliamentarians. *Hurry up! Just go. Be gone!* Leave him and the people he trusted to make the decisions that had to be made.

It had all got far too close for comfort, time-wise, over the last day or two. The Remnanter ship had appeared earlier than they'd been expecting and then what had happened out at Ablate had already leaked, it seemed. How the fuck had *that* happened so quickly? If he ever found out who'd been responsible . . . Bad news upon bad news; things crowding in, happening much faster than he'd anticipated.

It could all be handled – things could always be handled – but the handling might get rough. Well, that couldn't be helped. The goal was what it had always been; a successful Sublime, his reputation and place in history assured.

He turned and looked up at the parliament building, where the Presence hung. He could hardly see it in the darkness.

The Presence was dark grey, shaped like some high-altitude balloon before it ascended; a slightly flattened semi-sphere curving down via a long, pendulous, narrowing tail to a point that looked to be aimed straight at the pinnacle of the parliament building's central cupola. It was about sixty metres across near the top and nearly three hundred metres in height. That spike-like tip hovered silently just a few metres above the cupola's spire; it looked as though somebody tall, balanced on the very top of the spire, could have reached up and touched it. A few of the parliament's floodlights reflected dully off the bulbous near-black curve beneath its summit.

It had appeared twelve years earlier, on the day the parliament had passed the Act that confirmed the results of the Final Subliming Plebiscite, setting in train all the preparations for the event. A manifestation from the Sublimed Realm, a symbol from those who had already gone before. No more than a signpost, really; not animate or intelligent, as far as was known; just a reminder that the decision had been made and the course of the Gzilt was set. It was unmoved and unaffected by wind, rain, whatever, and barely there at all according to the military's technical people; only just more than a projection. Real but unreal, like a shadow falling from another world.

They'd been expecting it; the Presence hadn't come as a surprise – these things always appeared when a people, a civilisation, was preparing for and committed to Subliming – but, somehow, actually seeing it there had still come as a shock.

Banstegeyn remembered watching the poll figures wobble; parliament, the media and his own people were canvassing the general population all the time back then, and the commitment levels had dipped significantly when the Presence had appeared. He'd worried. This was so much what he wanted, what he believed in and knew was right, what he himself had spent his life working towards and staked his reputation on; this would be his legacy and his name would live for evermore in the Real, no matter what lay ahead in the Sublime. It was utterly the right thing to do; he had known this and still knew this with absolute certainty, and yet still he'd worried. Had he been too bold? Had he tried to make everybody go too soon: a decade early, a generation, even?

But then the figures had rallied. And only grown since. The commitment was still there. It would all happen.

He looked away, past Jevan's handsome but slightly vacant face, and Solbli's pleasantly matron-like look of admiration and pride, sparing them both a quick smile, then turned as he heard footsteps hurrying up towards him.

"Septame Banstegeyn! A historic day!"

"Another step closer," President Geljemyn said as the group around her parted to admit him. Banstegeyn glanced at various faces, distributing quick smiles and curt nods of his own. There were three trimes: Yegres, Quvarond and Int'yom; the full extant set, basically, given that the rest were Stored, awaiting the pre-waking before the Sublime. Quvarond counted as an opponent, Int'yom was a geriatric nonentity but he was *his* geriatric nonentity, and Yegres did as Int'yom told him.

Six of his fellow septames were also present; five his, one neutral. An only slightly better than average for/against ratio, amongst those left. Two generals, an admiral, no press. Quite a lot of puffiness and glistening skin all round, he noticed; signs of drunkenness.

The president still wore her vulgarly cheap little time-to on a band round her wrist, he observed. It was the sort of thing retailers had given away, back in the day. She'd been gifted many far more elegant, tasteful and expensive time-tos since, but had made a point of sticking with this one. It cycled between showing the number of hours left, and the days. Currently it was on days, reading "S -22". His own example, displayed on his chest like a small but important honour, was delicately beautiful, purely mechanical, exquisite in its workmanship and eye-poppingly expensive.

The almost normal-looking Ambassador Mierbeunes was there from the Iwenick, representing the Liseiden, as was the Culture's current most senior representative to Gzilt; Ziborlun. This silver-skinned creature was an avatar of the ancient Systems Vehicle that was currently gracing the skies of somewhere not too far away, no doubt. There was a bigger, grander, much more flattering GSV on its way for the formal ceremonies in the days immediately preceding the Subliming, allegedly, but they'd yet to see any sign of it.

Banstegeyn was also aware of Orpe, the president's beautiful AdC, looking at him as he joined the huddle round Geljemyn. The girl was trying not to smile too much, looking away from him now and again. He didn't return the look. Doubtless many already guessed, but there was no need to make things easy for people.

"Another step closer, Madame President," he agreed, accepting a soft drink from a steward and holding it aloft.

"Eternity here we come," Trime Yegres said, raising his glass. "We go to our Reward."

Drunk, Banstegeyn decided.

The president looked amused. Much seemed to amuse her. It was one of her faults. "The Subliming makes all of us sound like religious zealots," she said.

Yegres swallowed, looked at the silver-skinned being

across from him and said, "I'm sure our Culture friends think we've always sounded like religious zealots."

Ziborlun made a small bow. Its silver skin looked less unnatural in lamp light. "Not at all," it said.

Yegres frowned at it. "You're very . . . *diplomatic*," he told the creature, slurring his words. "Are you sure you're Culture?"

"In all seriousness," Ambassador Mierbeunes said, meaning he was about to say something fatuous, flattering or both, "I have never entirely understood why the Book of Truth is regarded as a religious work at all." He looked round, blandly suave as ever, smiling. "It would seem more like—"

"That would be because it is the basis of our religion," Trime Quvarond informed him curtly. Banstegeyn didn't bother repressing his smile; he'd found the Iwenick male annoying while they'd been conducting negotiations; now they'd concluded them he was insufferable.

"Well, in *that* sense," Mierbeunes said smoothly, still smiling, "obviously and completely a religious work, of course, without question . . ." He continued to witter.

Banstegeyn had just become aware of a uniform at his side.

"Marshal Chekwri," Solbli whispered softly in his ear, overriding the earbud cancel. She rarely got this wrong.

"Marshal Chekwri!" Banstegeyn said loudly, mostly to shut the Iwenick up, and turned to greet the Commander in Chief of the Home System Regiment.

The marshal of the First bowed to all, clapped her hands gently in front of her. "May I drag you away?" she asked him. She looked at Geljemyn. "Madame President?"

Geljemyn nodded. "If you must," she said.

"All yours!" Yegres said merrily. "Don't hurry bringing him back! Ha ha!"

"Excuse me," Banstegeyn said. He beamed a smile round all of them, though it soured a little when it got to Yegres.

He suspected only Orpe would be truly sad to see him go.

He followed the marshal back up the steps, trailed by Jevan and Solbli. When they got inside, the marshal turned to his AdC and secretary and smiled as she said, "Thank you."

Jevan and Solbli looked at Banstegeyn, who gave the tiniest of nods. They looked forlorn as he and the marshal stepped into an elevator.

When the lift started to drop, he looked at the marshal and said, "What?"

The marshal just looked at him with her tired old eyes in her tired old face, and smiled thinly.

He hoisted one eyebrow, then nodded. "Hmm," he said, more to himself than her.

There were places under the parliament building few people ever got to see, or even knew were there. This was one. The room was round with concave black walls but was otherwise unremarkable, holding a round table and some seats; Banstegeyn's office was bigger. And had a better view, obviously. More of note had been the three metre-thick doors they had had to negotiate to get here, each of which had swung closed behind them.

"Now?" Banstegeyn asked the marshal after the room's own massive door had thudded shut.

"Now," the marshal confirmed.

"How bad is it?"

Chekwri nodded. "It is within what was expected. We just have more detail, choices for action." She glanced towards the centre of the room. "Shall we?"

They sat. "Scavengers? The other thing? What?"

"The other thing," Marshal Chekwri confirmed.

Banstegeyn sighed. Chekwri was one of only a handful of people who knew – not counting whoever knew who wasn't supposed to; he shivered to think how many of them there might be. "What detail, what choices?" he asked her.

"The leak was only to the Fourteenth," the marshal told him.

He nodded. One regiment. That wasn't so bad. Still bad enough. "Would be, wouldn't it?" he said. The Fourteenth – the Socialist-Republican People's Liberation Regiment, 14, to give it its full title – had been the most sceptical regarding Sublimation from the start, even if it too had finally – at least apparently – come onside. "Who was responsible?"

"Nobody," the marshal told him.

He looked at her. "Somebody is always responsible," he told her.

She shook her head. "This was something generated within the Mind-set or the subsidiary substrate mechanisms of the *Churkun* itself. The ship had a one-off spy . . . you'd have to call it a program, it was so old and tiny; a virus, sitting in its computational matrix. Whatever it was – it deleted itself immediately – it had been in there since before the ship itself was constructed, while the Mind-set was still in virtual form, being test-run by the shipyard's Technology and Processing Department, four hundred and seventy years ago. Even then, it might not have required anybody within the Tech Department to plant it; could be done from outside."

"And it was doing *nothing* all that time?"

"Just waiting for something to come along sufficiently game-changing to be worth betraying its presence for."

"And nobody *found* it?"

"Obviously."

"Or nobody who wasn't also a traitor, at least," Banstegeyn said, glancing away.

The marshal frowned. "I think if we start assuming there might be traitors within the fleet's virtual crews we make traitors of ourselves. Saboteurs, at the very least. This was something so small, in a set of substrates so vast, it was possible for it to hide. Once it was in there, no further—"

Banstegeyn's eyes went wide. "What about the other ships?" he blurted.

The marshal sat back fractionally at being interrupted, but said, calmly, "All those still with us are checking. Now they have a rough idea what they're looking for, it's hoped they can either find anything similar or give themselves a clean bill of health within days."

Banstegeyn was appalled. "*Days?*"

"Impossible to do any quicker. The fleet, such as it is, these days, remains fully operational in every other respect; the techs – the ships too – maintain there is absolutely zero possibility of anything similar taking over any part of the running of the vessels; stuff like this can watch and wait and signal if it finds a way, but it can't affect."

"And the *Churkun*?" Banstegeyn asked. "What's it – is it returning to—?"

"The *Churkun* announced its determination to Sublime as soon as possible," the marshal said. "Nothing more has been heard of it since so either it has already gone or it is still preparing to." Chekwri smiled humourlessly. "I understand that the aftermath of battle, even a one-sided one, is not generally considered to constitute the most favourable condition for the instigation of Sublimation." The pretended-at smile disappeared. "And kindly keep that secret, too, Septame. The ship didn't announce this publicly and we'd rather people think it's still with us; the fleet's reduced enough as it is."

THE HYDROGEN SONATA   63

Banstegeyn opened his mouth, seemed to catch himself, then said, "All right. Never mind. What about the Fourteenth?"

"We are almost certain—"

The septame held up one hand. "'We'?"

"An absolute minimum of my best, most trusted people know we're looking for something, not what it is," the marshal said. "It's all in hand, all working. The good, the very good news is that we are almost certain the information is held by probably only one substrate in the Fourteenth's HQ, and known to a handful of their top brass, at most. Nobody else. Not yet."

"Not yet for how long?"

"Can't say. All we know is they haven't tried to share this so far, to the best of our knowledge."

Banstegeyn looked to one side and rubbed his fingers as though testing the feel of an invisible piece of cloth. "Of course, they might not do anything with it. They might just sit on it."

"That is a possibility," the marshal said, sounding doubtful.

"We could just ask them, I suppose," he said, looking at the marshal, and smiling. "They might even listen to reason."

"We could," she said. "They might." She held his gaze, kept her expression neutral.

"Let's do that, then," the septame said, sitting back. The marshal's face betrayed the tiniest flicker of surprise. "Though," Banstegeyn said, sitting forward again, "take me through what else you were thinking of."

Chekwri frowned. "One approach might preclude the other. To ask would be to warn, and then any other choice would be closed off."

"What if," the septame said, "one waited to make this appeal to reason until the other choice was available . . . at a moment's notice?"

The marshal seemed to think for a moment. "Given the capabilities of the technologies involved, especially the potential rapidity of response they possess, even a moment might be warning enough to turn a potentially successful action into one that was sure to fail."

"Hmm," Banstegeyn said, sitting back again. "Then it would certainly be foolish to give any *greater* degree of warning, wouldn't it?"

The marshal's eyes narrowed a little as she said, "Quite."

"What did you have in mind?" he asked her. "What does it involve?"

"It involves a fast, powerful ship, a single surgical strike with full end-operator tactical-choice freedom and – in case any further action is required – a micro-force of just two: a highly augmented special forces field-colonel and a non-humanoid combat arbite."

"And this would be in, on—"

"Eshri, Izenion system."

Banstegeyn bit his lower lip. He looked away. "Against our own people . . ."

"Who put a piece of spyware into another regiment's capital ship nearly five hundred years ago, who might have done the same thing to other elements of the fleet and who could, if they wanted . . ." The marshal let her voice trail off.

". . . potentially jeopardise the whole Subliming," the septame said, still looking to one side, rubbing his lip now. He looked at her. "How soon can we put all this together?"

"It already is together, Septame. The assets are presently in transit for Izenion."

Banstegeyn widened his eyes. "Are they now?"

"I instructed the battle-cruiser *Uagren* to depart Zyse system for Izenion twenty minutes ago. It is recallable at any point. It seemed rash to hesitate once the materiel and personnel were collated. And nothing irresilable happens without your express permission."

"How long until I would have to make a decision?"

"The *Uagren*'s travel time to Izenion is between forty-six and fifty-four hours, depending on whether it flies through or comes to a local stop. Say forty-five hours to go yes/no on any pre-agreed action re the former, though if there's no further sign of development from the Fourteenth HQ, I'd advise the local stop; that way we have a chance of dealing with any loose ends or unanticipated post-strike outcomes immediately rather than half a day later; there's nothing else we can get to Izenion sufficiently quickly to provide immediate back-up if the *Uagren* commits to a fly-through mission. In that case, say fifty-three hours. To leave time to switch from one mission profile to another – fly-through to local stop – a decision would be required thirty-eight hours from now. That would be your first decision-point: in thirty-eight hours."

"And if I decide nothing; if no decision is made?"

"The ship flies straight through Izenion system and loops back to return here without taking any action at all."

"Good. Let's leave that as the default, for now." He took a deep breath. "So. Thirty-eight hours, forty-five and fifty-three. I'll try to remember."

The marshal smiled thinly. "Obviously we must accept that the usual restrictions apply to committing any part of this to any form of memory other than that we were born with."

Banstegeyn lifted his time-to from his chest and twirled a platinum knob on it. "I take it it won't represent too great a security threat if I set an alarm." He aligned the alarm hand, then looked up at the marshal's expressionless face. She remained silent. He sighed, let the time-to fall back against his chest. "*Really?*"

"It would be circumstantial, but in the event of something going wrong and a subsequent investigation . . ."

"A subsequent *investigation*?" Banstegeyn said, incredulous. "We're supposed to be *Subliming* in . . ." he glanced at the time-to, ". . . twenty-two days, one hour."

"Nevertheless. Foolish to risk what need not be risked. I'll be in touch shortly before a decision is needed."

Banstegeyn sighed and unset the alarm. He looked at Chekwri. "This does have to happen, you know," he said. "The Subliming. It has to happen now, and completely, or not . . ." Another sigh. He felt suddenly tired. "I've looked at the statistics, the sims. For a species like ours, if there's a stall, it's likely to take another three to five generations before it actually happens. That's . . ." he shook his head. "That's why this has to happen, Madame Marshal."

Marshal Chekwri, Commander in Chief of the Home System Regiment, was silent a little while longer, then said, "That is why we will make sure that it does, Septame."

The *Caconym*, a Culture Limited Offensive Unit of the Troublemaker class, spun slowly above the forest of writhing, wildly shining loops that was the surface of the orange-red star Sapanatcheon. The ship rotated gently in the midst of the blasts of radiation, charged particles and magnetic force coming swirling in from almost every direction, though mostly from below, where a sunspot the size of a gas-giant planet was passing slowly beneath. The LOU was taking readings and collecting data, for what it was worth, but really it was just watching, admiring.

The LOU was a modern ship with an old Mind, part of an experiment of sorts to see how that would work. The theory was that pairing a capable new vessel with a wise old Mind would somehow present the best of both worlds, especially for one of the Culture's relatively few warships, which would be fully expected to sit/drift/race around all its anticipated life doing nothing whatsoever, or at least nothing whatsoever to do with what it had been designed for. The trouble with this idea, as the *Caconym* had been amongst the first to point out, was that – simulations aside – you would never really know how your theory was standing up to reality until the shit hit the intractor, when it tended to be a bit too late for rethinks and refits.

Still, as one of the ship Minds that had been involved at the sharp end of the Idiran war a thousand years earlier and not gone into a profound retreat, a group-mind or the wilder shores of Eccentricity, the Mind within the *Caconym* understood that it constituted a kind of resource for the Culture, and grudgingly accepted that it had some sort of responsibility to play along.

Taking its mildly eccentric habits and interests with it into its new home, the *Caconym*'s Mind – the *Caconym*, basically – pursued its strange little hobbies and kept itself pretty much to itself, even while remaining on the sort of everlasting standby that Culture ships of its kind were expected to maintain, just in case.

It wasn't a hermit – Culture warships were strongly counselled not even to think of becoming true hermits – it kept up, in a general sort of way, with what was happening in the galaxy, and there were always a few respected and responsible ships who knew how to contact it if they really needed to, but it had few acquaintances and fewer friends, none of whom expected any real degree of chattiness from it and who were quite used to hearing nothing from it for hundreds of days at a time.

So it was surprised when a message pinged in, from,

apparently, somebody being so informal that even many of
the usual signal protocols could be cheerfully dispensed with.

∞

Cac, chumlet, how are you?

∞

The sender was, according to a minimal ration of the usual
embedded personal codings and eccentricities of glyph-
expression, its old friend the MSV *Pressure Drop*. Though,
of course, that sort of signal addenda could be copied.

It sent back along the same signal route:

PD?

∞

The same.

∞

Even without the normal protocols, it was possible to
work out the other craft's rough position through the beam
direction and reply delay, even after only a couple of signals.
It looked like the *Pressure Drop* was relatively close by;
only five or six years off. Practically next door, and only
a couple of systems away in this sparsely starred part of
the galaxy.

Unless the other ship was introducing a deliberate delay
into its replies, of course, in which case it could be almost on
top of it. The *Caconym* immediately clicked on its track scanner
and looked down the signal beam. Nothing there. A few of
its internal systems – kicking in like an animal flight-or-fight
response – flicked off again, winding back down.

∞

I am in every respect excellent, as you might expect, it
replied. **Shall I assume the same of you?**

∞

Do. Still obsessed with them sparkly bits then?

∞

The *Caconym* relaxed a little more; the other party certainly expressed itself as though it was the *Pressure Drop*. Still, to get so close before announcing oneself was unusual. A more paranoid ship, the *Caconym* thought, would almost feel like it had been getting snuck up on.

The signals it was responding to had originally arrived via a beam spread wide enough to encompass the whole of the solar system it was within, with the implication that the *Pressure Drop* hadn't known where within the system its friend was (though it might have guessed, near the sun – that was where the beam was focused now), but to be so discoverable, even by another Culture ship, was, if not alarming for a wandering war-craft, at least worthy of note.

∞

My interest in stars – their formation, development and death, ability to harbour and promote life, affect, empower and destroy all around them and so on – remains. Though obviously I struggle to couch it as poetically as you.

∞

Are you with our friends the field-liners?

∞

The *Caconym* had a long-standing interest in and relationship with various of the galaxy-wide outposts of the creatures who inhabited the magnetic field lines of certain stars.

∞

No. Holidaying, as of recently; magnetosphere-surfing for the most part. I intend to resume my studies of the inhabitants at a later date.

∞

Not talking to you, then?

∞

Of course they're talking to me. We have a highly complex

and mutually beneficial dialogue, when necessary. The question I might ask is why are you talking to me?

∞

Your oldest friend can't say hello without occasioning such suspicion?

∞

Who's suspicious? It's been so long, and you've been so quiet. I thought perhaps you'd expired without telling me.

∞

If I've been quiet, it's because I take my cue from you. But yes, it's been a while. I've been busy. Well, indolent. The effect is the same. I've managed to whittle my population down to a framework crew of the like-minded, so all is harmonious.

∞

So, what brings you to this neck of the scrub?

∞

Technically, the serendipity of a tour – for pleasure; like yourself I have discovered a rich seam of auto-indulgence in myself – during which I had made swinging by your own current location, however out of the way, something of a priority, for reasons which are beginning to escape me.

∞

I shall endeavour to be more scintillating.

∞

However, there is something which has come to my attention which might interest you.

∞

And what would that be?

∞

A matter of potential thorniness. It involves the Tiny-wee Tucked-away. The vastness beyond vast.

∞

Oh fuck.

∞

Now, before you—

∞

I may have to overwrite those bits of myself. I tell you, I wish to have no more to do with the promise, process or result of Outloading, Instigating, Subliming, Enfolding or any other synonym relating to the activity or state of basically buggering off up one's own or indeed anybody else's fundament.

∞

The Sublime. The almost tangible, entirely believable, mathematically verifiable nirvana just a few right-angle turns away from dear boring old reality: a vast, infinite, better-than-virtual ultra-existence with no Off switch, to which species and civilisations had been hauling their sorry tired-with-it-all behinds off to since – the story went – the galaxy had still been in metaphorical knee socks.

The Sublime was where you went when you felt you had no more to contribute to the life of the great galactic meta-civilisation, and – sometimes more importantly, depending on the species – when in turn you felt that it had no more to offer you. It took a whole civilisation to do it properly, and it took a long, long time for most civilisations to come round to the idea, but there was never any hurry; the Sublime would always be there. Well, provided only that blind chance, your own stupidity or somebody else's malevolence didn't lead to your outright obliteration in the Real in the meantime.

Exactly what it was like in there was debatable: very, very few came back and none came back less than profoundly altered. These few returnees were also seemingly incapable of describing the realm they had left, however recently, in any detail at all.

It was wonderful; that was the general tone of the vague, dreamy reports that did come back. And almost beyond comparison, literally indescribable. The absolutely most splendid wonders, experiences and achievements of the Real and all those within it were as nothing to the meanest off-hand meanderings of the Sublime. The most soaring, magnificent, ethereal cathedrals to reason, faith or anything else were as mere unkempt and dilapidated hovels compared to the constructions – if they could even be described as such – within the Sublime. That was about all anybody had to go on, but at least the reports never varied in one respect; no one ever came back saying, shit, it's horrible; don't go.

Also, it wasn't the only choice for a species approaching the end of its active life. Other species/civilisations retreated into Elderhood, becoming almost as dissociated from the normal day-to-day life of the galaxy and its vast rolling boil of peoples and societies as the Sublimed, yet staying in the Real. But that very continuance within the real galaxy – despite the powers and capabilities which everybody associated with Elderhood and which the Elder races rarely showed any desire to downplay – still left you at least theoretically vulnerable to whatever exciting new mix of power and aggression the matter-based galaxy was able to throw up. Plus, opting for Elderhood just looked like a sort of failure of nerve, given what the Sublime realm offered: a space of infinite flourishing without threat or danger.

As far as was known, nothing had ever evolved directly within the Sublime; everything there had started in the Real. And – again as far as anyone could tell – nothing that had ever entered the Sublime from the Real in any viable state had ever entirely disappeared from it. To enter the Sublime was to become near-as-dammit immortal, and while there was still talk of difference and dispute, and even some form of contention within the Sublime, there appeared to be no annihilation, no utter destruction, no genocide or speciescide or their equivalents.

To the deep and abiding frustration of those in the Real who would know more of its past, the peoples who seemed to have been in there the longest – from the first two billion years or so of the galaxy's lifetime, say – were the least likely ever to reappear in the Real and spill any beans about what life had actually been like back then and what had really happened. Those who had entered the Great Enfold subsequently had scarcely been any more forthcoming, and the few not-totally-vague replies they had given to specific questions had often proved contradictory, one way or another, so as a research trove the Sublime was almost completely useless.

Nevertheless, whole civilisations had been making the one-way trip there for all that time, there was good proof that even the first to do so were still in some meaningful sense there, however much they might have changed, and – compared to the relative chaos, uncertainty and existential short-termism of the Real – that represented a fairly good option by most people's reckoning.

So, a beguiling proposition and a field ripe for studying, too, if one was so inclined. The Mind in the *Caconym*, which had taken the ship's name, had been so inclined, once. No longer. The whole enterprise had been exquisitely frustrating, and its friend the *Pressure Drop* knew this.

∞

I understand. I could, of course, just shut up, withdraw and say no more about it.

∞

No, my interest is piqued, as I'm sure you anticipated. What is it?

∞

Annoyingly – amazingly – the *Caconym* knew that as far as authorities on the Sublime went, it was one of the few assets the Culture – or anybody else – possessed. It kept hoping that some other brave, ambitious or just plain self-deluded souls would take up the Sublime-exploring baton and enquire further, look closer, delve deeper and make some breakthrough it had been unable to make, so taking the responsibility away from it, and it had tried to encourage informal associations of other Minds with similar interests to pursue such behaviour, but all such hopes had been dashed; almost nobody else was interested. It had even dared anticipate that the Contact section would form a specialist department to handle such matters and tackle the problem properly, but – despite having dropped a few heavy hints on the subject over the years – this too seemed as far away as ever.

The Gzilt, the *Pressure Drop* sent.

∞

Mm-hmm. Been talking about the Big Cheerie-O for some. They're actually off, too; set a date and everything. See, I do listen to some news. Hmm. That's quite close, now. Not having second thoughts are they?

∞

Not yet. But there's been . . . a development.

∞

The Gzilt were a sort of cousin species/civilisation to the Culture. Nearly founders, though not quite, they had been influential in the setting up and design of the Culture almost ten thousand years earlier, when a disparate group of humanoid species at roughly the same stage of technological and societal development had been thinking about banding together.

Amiable enough, if somewhat martially uptight due to an unusual social set-up that basically meant everybody was presumed to be in a single society-wide militia – hence everybody had a military rank, from birth – they had made significant contributions to the establishment and ethos of the Culture while it was all still at the being-talked-about phase but then, almost at the last moment, and to pretty much everyone's surprise, in a way including their own, they had decided not to join the new confederation.

They'd go their own way, they'd decided, wishing the Culture well and taking an interest in it, but keeping determinedly apart from it.

Relations had remained friendly throughout, and rumours persisted that the Gzilt had been helpful to the Culture in the Idiran war, despite a supposedly meticulous neutrality, but in essence they had stayed quietly, studiously apart from the Culture for all that time, observing the more rowdy, boisterous and interference-minded behaviour of their one-time associates with a mixture of emotions that might on occasion have included mild horror, gasping incredulity and simple shock, but also – and more consistently – a kind of envy, and a slowly increasing feeling that a great opportunity had been lost.

∞

A development. Odd. That word rarely dampens the spirits quite so comprehensively as your deployment of it just there has so thoroughly doused mine. What development?

∞

Hurry me onwards if I start to tell you too much of what you already know, but . . . there is this tradition that other civs settle-up, as it were, with any would-be Sublimers, shortly before the big event: messages of admiration, respect and sorry-to-see-you-go mixed in with the odd admission that actually we're responsible for rubble-ising your moon while you guys were inventing the wheel but we were having big exciting space battles

with the neighbours, or it was us what nicked your first space probe—

∞

Consider yourself hurried, the *Caconym* sent.

∞

Sorry. Also, a pity: my third example was particularly witty and amusing. But no matter. Anyway, the Gzilt have this relationship, one might as well call it, with the also departed Zihdren. This relationship capacitated, as it were, through the Gzilt Book of Truth.

∞

Yes, the holy book that only gained in credence as science developed.

∞

Indeed; unique.

∞

So contributing to the cult of pernicious exceptionalism as exhibited by the Gzilt.

∞

So caustic!

∞

Some truths hurt more than others. Frankly, I thought I was being kind; the word "exemplified" might have replaced "exhibited" in the above without too great a stretch. I think I already dislike where we're headed with this, by the way, but go on.

∞

One of the things that has always made the Gzilt feel so special, so marked out, has been the fact that their holy book, pretty much alone amongst holy books, turned out to be verifiable. At every stage of their development—

∞

—It predicted the future, the *Caconym* interrupted,

watching carefully for how much overlap there was between the two signals. **Only of technology, but even so.** That was interesting; the signals from the *Pressure Drop* implied the ship was curving away, as though it had been heading almost straight towards the *Caconym* until not long before it sent its first message, but was now beginning what looked like a tight-as-possible high-speed turn after a period of significant acceleration.

∞

Are you gauging my speed and direction?

∞

Of course I am.

∞

You could just have asked. I'm running a max-min turn for Gzilt space.

∞

That's sixty days away. Won't it all be over by then?

∞

Fifty-five days away. I've up-ratioed my engines over the years. But the point is: you never know. Were you listening to all that stuff about the Gzilt holy book?

∞

Of course.

∞

The Book of Truth, the Gzilt holy book, had been delivered by meteorite during their dark ages, following the collapse of a great empire which had been laid low by a combination of barbarians, disease and economic and environmental collapse. A subsequent meteorite bombardment had made things worse and convinced many Gzilt that their gods – if they even existed – had turned against them.

It was during this time of tribulation that the Scribe – Briper Drodj, a disgraced, ruined trader from a fallen aristocratic family with classical military connections – allegedly found a set of inscribed slates inside a meteorite and published them, adding to them later as he had dreams that seemed to follow on from the texts. These slates were kept secret and either disappeared or were destroyed in a temple fire started by unbelievers.

This particular incident led to the militarisation and evangelicalisation of the Book of Truth religion. Briper Drodj and his generals then masterminded a series of spectacular conquests across the single great continent that made up almost all of the land area of Zyse, eventually subduing and converting all the other tribes, nations, peoples, kingdoms and empires until they had, effectively, taken over the world.

The Scribe Briper Drodj later disappeared in mysterious circumstances, allegedly when he was on the brink of announcing a whole new set of dream-revelations. There had been tensions within the hierarchy of the church by this time, and cynics would later maintain that the newly proliferating upper echelons of his supporters "disappeared" the Scribe to prevent these mooted, never-brought-to-light additions to the Word reducing their own power, though nothing was ever proved and by general consent there was a feeling that Briper had quite entirely done his bit, his place in history as the greatest ever Gziltian was absolutely assured, and in a sense it was time for him to enter legend rather than, say, stick around past his time and start making the sort of embarrassingly beside-the-point pronouncements old men were all too prone to coming out with.

Up to this point, the story of the Gzilt and their holy book was, to students of this sort of thing, quite familiar: an upstart part of a parvenu species/civ gets lucky, proclaims itself Special and waves around its own conveniently vague and multiply interpretable holy book to prove it. What set the Book of Truth apart from all the other holy books was that it made predictions that almost without exception came true, and anticipated phenomena that nobody of the time of Briper Drodj could possibly have guessed at.

At almost every scientific/technological stage over the following two millennia, the Book of Truth called it right, whether it was on electromagnetism, radioactivity, atomic theory, the cosmic microwave background, hyperspaciality, the existence of aliens or the patternings of the energy grid that lay between the nested universes. The language was even quite clear, too; somewhat opaque at the time before you had the technological knowledge to properly understand what it was it was talking about and you were reading, but relatively unambiguous once the accompanying technical breakthrough had been made.

There was, in addition, the usual mostly sensible advice on living properly and morally, along with various parables and examples to help keep the Gzilt on the right track, but nothing exceptional compared to other holy books, either those from the Gzilt's own past or that of others; the predictions were what made it special and had the effect of causing the Book to become more convincing and remarkable as technological progress continued.

There was space stuff in there, too. Those behind all these imparted revelations were named the "Zihdren" and described as "wraiths of light". The Zihdren were a vacuum Basker species, and this was actually a fairly accurate portrayal of what they looked like to the humanoid eye. They were also described working through their "material mechanicals" – again, close enough to describing the reality of the robotic self-extensions the Zihdren used when they wanted to work within the material aspect of the Real.

More challengingly – and perhaps more the Prophet's doing

than anything he might have found on the original slates, had they ever really existed – the Book further insisted that the Gzilt were a people favoured by Fate, by the Universe itself, as part of an ongoing thrust towards a glorious, transcendent providence; they represented the very tip of a mystical spear thrown by the past at the future, the shaft of that spear being formed by a multitude of earlier species which existed before them and kept on serially handing on the baton of destiny to the next, slightly more exceptional people ahead of them.

The Zihdren, the book declared, were the last handers-on of the baton, the final stage of this rocket ship to the sky that would put the actual payload – the Gzilt – into the glory of eternal orbit.

Even after the Gzilt achieved genuine space travel, artificial intelligence, insight into hyperspace and contact with the rest of the galactic community – and discovered that there had indeed been a species called the Zihdren around at the time the Book of Truth had come to light, though they had since Sublimed – that belief in their own predestined purpose and assured distinctiveness had persisted, and it was, arguably, that imperturbable sense of their own uniqueness that had prevented them from joining the Culture all those thousands of years ago.

So, the Pressure Drop **sent, the BoT provably gets so much right, insists that the Gzilt are Special – destined for something singular, fabulous and epoch-shaping – yet once the Gzilt get to a certain stage of development the Book effectively falls silent, with nothing further to predict, and becomes just another dusty text to be filed with the rest, while the suspicion grows amongst those not utterly credulous that while the Zihdren may indeed have had a part in the Book and were certainly a reputable and constructive part of the galactic community**

of their time, they were hardly exceptional; just another banally evolved species hustling along as best they could within the convection cells of the galactic soup cauldron – if exotic in their immaterial nature, by humanoid standards – who eventually ended up in the great retirement home of the Sublimed like everybody else.

∞

Maybe the Gzilt should have swallowed their pride and joined the Culture when they had the chance. Or perhaps they seek their own Subliming as a consolation.

∞

I hadn't finished. You interrupted again.

∞

You were wittering again.

∞

Anyway, there is indeed evidence that the Gzilt believe their own presence amongst the Sublime will somehow change things dramatically for the better there . . .

∞

Ha!

∞

. . . I thought that might precipitate a response. However, to continue: also that they – wilfully, against all evidence – regard Subliming not as retirement but as promotion.

∞

Ha, again.

∞

So, matters are set up as they are, and the Gzilt are on the very brink of the Big Outloading, when along comes a Zihdren-Remnanter ship with a guest for the festivities bearing a message that is basically a confession.

∞

Of what exactly?

∞

Of exactly what, I have not been told, but I think we can guess.

∞

Mistake, accident, prank, deliberate interference?

∞

Something like that. Only the message does not get through, the human-ish guest-entity is never delivered, the ship is intercepted. The Remnanter ship is destroyed.

∞

Destroyed?

∞

Profoundly so.

∞

That is . . . bold. Or desperate. And how do you know all this? There's been nothing in any report.

∞

It's recent, few people know and none of them thought it in their interests to go public. Our Remnanter friends asked me to contact you as somebody they've had dealings with in the past regarding the Sublimed, especially the Zihdren.

∞

Even so, to what end? What am I supposed to do?

∞

Two things. One, form part of an advisory group, with myself, to handle whatever may come of this from our point of view. Two, use some of your contacts to help clear up what's going on here.

∞

Have we been asked by the Gzilt to do this?

∞

Good grief no! For now, it's best they know nothing,

given that they or some faction within them appear to have instigated hostilities.

∞

Then why are we even thinking of getting involved?

∞

Well, arguably we owe the Gzilt some care and attention just on general principles, not to mention consideration due to their honorary fellow-traveller Culture status, but, more to the point, the Zihdren message to the Gzilt mentioned an individual, a human from the first generation to think of themselves as Culture citizens. He was around ten thousand years ago, at the time of the negotiations which gave rise to the Culture in the first place. This individual was named as perhaps being able to help provide proof that what was claimed in the message to the Gzilt was actually true.

∞

So, not long dissolved in some group-mind, then. Stored, I take it?

∞

Not Stored. In fact, never Stored. Still with us, still alive, still extant and functioning, twenty-five to thirty full lifetimes after you'd have expected any ordinary humanoid mortal to have decently abandoned the corporeal. Indeed, longer-living than any known still independent Mind or even high-level AI from the time. Like the fucker's decided to outlive everybody or set a record or something. But alive, somewhere, probably still within the Culture.

∞

Seriously?

∞

No kidding.

∞

No. I refuse to accept this. This is a myth. One of our myths. Romantic, nonsensical. A wish; desired but for ever without proof.

∞

Nevertheless, our Remnanter chums seem to think this geriatric geezer is still with us.

∞

Being loosely attached to a civ long-Sublimed does not make the Zihdren-Remnanter infallible. Or even necessarily reliable.

∞

Their record in such matters is good, though. I've spoken with a few fellow Minds about all this and it is reckoned the information must be taken seriously. Also, that you should be a member of any advisory group, part of the tactical-strategic oversight team. What do you say?

∞

I imagine I'm meant to be flattered, being so invited, but why don't these few fellow Minds of yours perform this function?

∞

They feel more comfortable in the wise village elder role, advising, not the positions you and I are being offered, suggesting actual courses of action. I imagine some energetic and very intense simming is going on. I've already started my own.

∞

And who are they, anyway?

∞

Not yet at liberty to say. I'll tell you if you sign up. Promise.

∞

What really is at stake here? And what are the chances that – should this prove important or just interesting – we wouldn't get bounced by some other collective – the ITG, to name but one?

∞

At stake is the smooth Subliming of a cousin species/ civilisation and the potential chaos of a part-Sublime complicated by the presence of a variety of Scavenger species, not to mention the Culture's good name as an honest broker.

As for the Interesting Times Gang, they have been silent for nearly half a millennium. Several are believed to be in Retreat and at least one has itself joined the Enfolded. There is a feeling amongst the Minds taking a particular interest in these matters that the ITG has stepped down, or at least back. The whole Excession thing nearly went very badly wrong and only just came out okay in the end as much through good luck as good guidance, and anyway was still arguably a failure: a catastrophe was averted but an opportunity was squandered, and in the end we are no further forward regarding insights into travel or even communication between concentric universes.

They may have decided to quit while they were ahead, or to bow out gracefully after an at best modest achievement that in certain lights might even be regarded as an embarrassment. Maybe they just felt they were getting old and out of touch.

In any event, no new standing ensemble appears to have replaced them, and only ad-hoc groups have handled unusual matters since. It's our move, old chum.

∞

The *Caconym* was silent for a few moments. It watched a small solar flare erupt from near one side of the sunspot over which it had stationed itself. Another tendril of the star's gaseous shrapnel, ejected by an earlier outburst of the furious

energies erupting for ever beneath it, and thousands of kilometres across and tens of thousands long, washed over and
around it, bathing its outer field structure in radiation
and delivering a distinct physical blow.

It allowed itself to be gently buffeted by the impact, using
its engine fields to adjust its apparent mass and so increasing
its inertia so that the effect would fall within acceptable
parameters, while observing the outermost elements of its
field structure deform inwards by a few micrometres under
the weight of the blast. The effect of the colliding gust of
plasma was to send it drifting very slightly across the face
of the sunspot, spinning slowly. Finally it sent,

**Why do we bother with this sort of bio-tangling stuff in
the first place? We could live lives of such uncomplicated
joy if we left them to their own sordid, murderous devices.**

∞

**Because it pleases us. It's a challenge. We could Sublime,
too, but we don't do that either. Come on; we have a
reputation for enlightened interference to protect here.**

∞

**Yeah, that's us: first amongst the Altruists; the emperors
of nice. We're not competitive about it, but – if we were
– by fuck we'd be the best.**

∞

Most amusing.

∞

**Yes, my fields expand at the mirth of it all. Very well. I
may regret this, but; all right. I'll take part.**

∞

And use those contacts with the Sublimed?

∞

If I have to, even more reluctantly, yes.

∞

Hurrah! Welcome aboard. Here's a diaglyph with the situation. Any thoughts?

∞

The data was lush with detail, a fact-crammed welter of information leavened with analysis and speculation. There were pointers towards standard concise histories of all species/civs involved for those who hadn't been paying attention earlier, more incisive, less polite, Contact-produced essays on the societies and personalities involved, plus a comprehensive summary of all recent developments, their possible explanations, a statistical breakdown of multiple already-simmed likely futures and an exhaustive, minutely annotated multi-dimensional comparison of this situation with those of any pressing similarity in the past, with another spread of likely outcomes relating thereto, plus the positions and specifications of all known capital and other major ships in the volume or inbound.

This did have the look of something blowing up alarmingly quickly, the *Caconym* thought. The *Mistake Not . . .* had been the first to flag up something amiss when it had spotted the weapon-blink from Ablate, communicating this to its home GSV, the *Kakistocrat*, which had been cautious enough to pass this on to a select few of its peers including the *Pressure Drop* rather than broadcast the news.

The message from the Zihdren-Remnanters had gone straight to the *Pressure Drop* less than an hour later. No hint of who or what had been responsible for the destruction of the Remnanter ship. Two principal Scavenger species present: the Liseiden and the Ronte. It would be tidiest and least alarming for all concerned if one of those had been responsible for the attack on the Remnanter ship, but that looked impossible; even if the Remnanter ship had been unarmed, the tech levels were just too far apart.

The *Caconym* didn't pretend to take any appreciable time to review the totality of what it had been sent.

The old Desert class currently hanging around Zyse, it sent.

∞

Yes, the venerable MSV *Passing By And Thought I'd Drop In*. There to represent us guys until the cultural big guns get there in the humungous shape of the System-class *Empiricist*, currently Zyse-bound, though delayed by a smatter outbreak en route. The *Passing By . . .* has been informed there might be a minor situation developing, though no action yet required; the *Empiricist* is still in a state of blissful ignorance.

∞

The *Passing By . . .* has two Thugs with it as escorts, DMVs.

∞

DeMilitarised Vessels is such old terminology, dear thing. They've been called Fast Pickets or Very Fast Pickets for a long time now. But, yes: the ex-Thug-class Rapid Offensive Units *Refreshingly Unconcerned With The Vulgar Exigencies Of Veracity* and *Value Judgement*. If you're thinking about those as immediately available military assets, though, I must disappoint you. They both really have been fully de-fanged. They're not that just-pretend kind of OU described as weapon-free to keep the locals happy while actually toting gear of serious cloutage, sadly.

∞

Still, have a word. Those three ships have a long association, a lot of the Desert class were discomfited at being demoted from General to Medium and – like myself – the Mind in the *Passing By . . .* is old. Also, the Thug de-weaponing was done aboard it.

∞

Keep going.

∞

Old equals sneaky. And prideful, sometimes. Tell the ***Passing By . . .* what has happened. Suggest to it that if it did just happen to have the weapon clusters taken out of its escorting Thugs to hand, it should get both ships back aboard and fully re-tooled immediately.**

∞

Just checked. That stuff's not aboard the Desert; absent from both the relevant cargo manifests and registered materiel declarations.

∞

Ask it all the same. It might be hiding the gear.

∞

That'd be a bit cheeky. And anyway, on a Desert class? They're tiny! That's why they got demoted.

∞

They're over three klicks long and boxy, and the principal weapon cluster on a Thug is less than thirty metres in diameter. Also, there isn't a Desert class extant that hasn't altered its internal layout umpteen times, over the millennia, just to suit operational happenstance or to amuse itself. I bet most of them could find places aboard themselves to hide sufficient ordnance to equip a fleet, if they looked hard enough or could be bothered.

∞

Signal duly sent.

∞

The ***Beats Working,*** **with the Ronte; genuinely civilian?**

∞

Completely. And genuinely tiny. Eighty metres. We had missiles bigger, back in ye olden days.

∞

And this Eccentric-erratic, the *Mistake Not . . .*; is there any data on its throw-weight? I can't find anything official.

∞

Seemingly not. That's sort of the idea, apparently.

∞

Estimates of its puissance by enthusiastic amateurs vary wildly, but indicate something close to my own disclosed capabilities. (The *Caconym* had resorted to consulting documentation drawn up by the sort of people who took an informed interest in Culture ships.)

∞

I'm sure one of you ought to be flattered.

∞

Hmm. I think even by our relaxed standards it is a little absurd that one warship needs to look up what are essentially fan-sites for an estimate of a comrade vessel's clobbering capacity. Think it could be SC?

∞

Possibly Special Circumstances, possibly just congenitally inscrutable. SC's ongoing attempts to corner the market in deviousness have yet to come to fruition.

∞

Let's try to find out how on board it is, and ask what it's toting.

∞

Agreed. Its contact is the GSV *Kakistocrat*, which certainly used to be SC, though it claims it long since settled for a quieter and more contemplative life. Signal sent.

∞

There are these Delinquent-class GOU twins, the *Headcrash* and the *Xenocrat*, aboard the *Empiricist*; let's give them a sniff of potential action in Gzilt and suggest it might be worth a little engine degradation to get there asap.

∞

They're engaged with this smatter outbreak at Loliscombana. It's all gone a bit target-rich. Could be hard dragging them away from the fun.

∞

Target-rich but challenge-light. They'll be bored by now. Swear them to secrecy and tell them somebody's seen fit to waste a Remnanter ship. That should get their attention.

∞

And hint the situation is unlikely to stop there?

∞

No need; they'll draw their own conclusions. Better to let them persuade themselves than feel they're being manipulated. Copy in the *Empiricist*; can't have it getting upset.

∞

Contacting. We do, ah, seem to be concentrating very much on the military side of things thus far.

∞

I'm a warship. I always was. Why, what else did you have in mind?

∞

Talking to somebody relevant might be a good idea.

∞

This Banstegeyn fellow looks to be the player with the power at the moment. The regiments would appear to contain almost all the potential energy, with the politicians providing the dynamic.

∞

Gzilt society had cohered millennia ago into a stable democratic system that formalised a purely ceremonial president at the top with no real power, a few almost equally figurehead people immediately beneath him or her, then successive layers of exponentially greater numbers and increasing political power until you reached the general mass of the population – individual people.

This power structure lay alongside the Gzilt's universal militia, a-rank-for-all military structure without apparent discord. Commentators and analysts, especially in the Culture, seemed to find this mystifying but pleasing; the consensus was that the ubiquitous military had no problem always conceding to civilian command because in a sense there were no civilians. It seemed perverse to some, but for all their apparent militarism the Gzilt had remained peaceful over many millennia; it was the avowedly peaceful Culture that had, within living memory, taken part in an all-out galactic war against another civilisation.

Military aside, in practice, over time, the balance of effective political power had settled somewhere between the one hundred and twenty-eight septames, the third level down, and the four-thousand-plus degans immediately beneath them, with the balance tipping towards the septames over the last few generations as the idea of Subliming had taken hold.

No machines involved in all this nominal, rather limited democracy, the ship noted. Minds and AIs in the Gzilt dominion were regarded either as mere tools, without rights, or as housing for the uploaded personalities of ex-humans. Even their warships were commanded not by true individual Minds but by virtual crews of deceased or copied bio-personalities running on highly sophisticated and very fast substrates.

It seemed to work, and Gzilt ships were highly regarded – approximately equiv-tech by Culture standards – but it was a roundabout way to get to a desired state of ability, and if there was ever a proper fight between otherwise equally matched Gzilt and Culture craft (perish the thought), Culture Minds were in no doubt it would be a very lucky Gzilt craft that prevailed. (Though, doubtless, the *Caconym* would be prepared to concede, the Gzilt would have a rather different take on the subject.)

∞

Of the regiments, it sent, **the Fifth and Fourteenth seem to have been the most dissenting regarding Subliming, even though they are officially both fully on board now. If we accept the attack on the Remnanter ship was an act underwritten by those within the Gzilt majority establishment wishing to ensure Subliming takes place, might one or both of those regiments be involved on the other side in some way? This might tie in with the sighting reported by the *Passing By* . . . of something speeding off from Zyse fifteen hours ago, Izenion bound, where the Fourteenth has its HQ, if it's going direct.**

∞

Even at the best of times, the society's internal tensions are largely sublimated into highly complex and rule-restricted turf wars between the Regiments: high-level internal-diplomatic games, essentially. Most likely, this single sighting is part of those continual manoeuvrings.

∞

There's been no hint that anybody else within Gzilt knows about the attack on the Remnanter – beyond those who might have set it in motion?

∞

None that I can see. You?

∞

Hmm. No, none. Though we might ask the *Passing By* . . . to be a little more nosy regarding Gzilt military

comms traffic, and any other unusual ship movements. Prioritising discretion above zeal, of course. And, as we have the Desert class in Gzilt with its two Thugs, and the Delinquent twins incoming – with any luck – then, if there is nothing else to go on, it might be worth getting something to Izenion before, or as soon as possible after, whatever left Zyse for Izenion arrives. See if the *Passing By . . .* can extract more data from its readings.

∞

I'll have a word.

∞

Also, that smatterage at Loliscombana, delaying the *Empiricist*. Was there any hint or precursor of it before the GSV published the part of its course schedule letting everybody know it would be passing that way?

∞

None mentioned; I'll investigate. It's a System-class, of course; those behemoths usually schedule years in advance, so there'd be plenty of time to set something up. You think the smatter's not a coincidence? Some things just are, you know.

∞

I do know. It depends on whether this is something being extemporised as unexpected events unfold, or a long-thought-out plan being unrolled. But what one might call "natural" smatter outbreaks almost invariably have precursor events. If there are none for this one then eyebrows, amongst those who possess them, might need to be raised. Time will tell; it usually does. I think that's all for now. Though you did promise me the names of the other ships you've been talking to about all this.

∞

Of course: the GSVs *Contents May Differ* and *Just The Washing Instruction Chip In Life's Rich Tapestry*, and the GCU *Displacement Activity*.

∞

Thank you. All sound, in my estimation, though whether they would return the compliment is another matter.

∞

My pleasure. I'll let you know any more there is to know as it comes in. Till later.

∞

Yes, later, the *Caconym* sent.

∞

The connection clicked to silent and the ship was left alone with its own thoughts again.

It felt and watched the buffeting wisps of the solar flare as they washed past it. Staring down into the vast slow pulsing storm of the sunspot, already half lost in its wild and stately beauty, it thought about the framework crew of the *Pressure Drop*. The *Caconym* had no bio-crew of its own – Culture warships rarely did these days – but the Mind had had, once, in another incarnation, as another ship.

Those on the *Pressure Drop* would be humans, mostly, it imagined. Mongrel-Culture; the result of a hundred centuries of species-mixing, serial amendment, augmentation, up-loading, downloading, simple autonomous choice-directed breeding and – after all that time – perhaps even some genuine evolution. The usual bizarre bio-mix of who-knew-how-many planetary-original blood-lines, all tangled inextricably together with those from an equally unfathomable number of others, boosted with genetech, aug., dashes of chimeric and a hint of some machine in there too, depending.

And it didn't doubt that every single one of them would find it absolutely fascinating to stare into a fire, even if that was one thing they were unlikely ever to encounter on a ship. The urge would still be there, though; stored inside, waiting. Shown the stuff, they'd stare, mesmerised.

The entirely standard, human-basic fascination with fire; bog-ordinary flames for them – just an oxygen reaction lasting minutes or hours – while, for it, it was the multi-billion-year-lasting thermonuclear fury of a planet-swallowing star burning off a million tons of matter a second . . . but still.

Shit, the ship thought. Most ship epithets, like almost all bio-epithets, involved bodily functions.

It started elongating one long loop of its external bump-field and expanding the outer reaches of its main field enclosure at the same time, so that it was both pushing against the mass of solar material beneath it and using the blast of radiation and charged particles as the wind in a sail that quickly grew to the size of a respectably proportioned moon.

The ship rose spinnakering away from the star, already gaining speed in real space as it flexed its engine fields and reached deftly out to the energy grid in the space between this universe and the slightly smaller one, only a few seconds or so younger, nested within it.

You had to be careful engaging engines so far within a gravity well as pronounced as that around a sun, but the *Caconym* was confident that it knew what it was doing. It spun slowly about while it drifted – then gradually powered – away from the star, snapping its external fields tight and preparing for extended deep-space travel as its engines powered up further and increasingly bit harder into the grid that separated the universes.

I suppose I ought to follow, it sent. **Just in case, like you say.**

A tiny, dark speck against the vast ocean of fire that was the star, it set a course for Gzilt space, pitching and yawing until it was pointed more or less straight there, continuing to ramp up its engines as it flew away from the light.

Race you! the *Pressure Drop* sent.

The *Caconym* could already feel drag – the effect of its velocity in real space. Observed external time was starting to drift away from what its own internal clocks were telling it, and its mass was increasing. Both effects were minute, but increasing exponentially. Elements of its field enclosure were already poised for the transition to hyperspace and release from such limitations.

I'll win, it replied.

It vanished from the skein of real space less than a second later, hurtling into a quickness beyond night.

Six

(S -21)

A ship dance was required.

Ronte fleets flew in formation at all times, even in time of war, when such patterns, through dispositional predictability, might be contra-indicated. However, much that was contra-indicative might equally well be regarded as a challenge, correctly formulated. Accordingly, it was incumbent upon a fleet in the appropriate circumstances to come up with better patterns: formations of such subtle elegance their mathematical and topological underpinnings would remain obscure to the enemy until it was too late. Accomplished correctly, this could even constitute a powerful additional asset, as the computational power required by the enemy vessels to perform this analysis robbed them of resources better directed towards other aspects of the engagement.

Ronte ships closely resembled the beings which inhabited them. The Ronte were decimetre-scale insectile creatures. Sleek, darkly iridescent, fluid-dynamic, compact – and yet with great reach when required – their ships were as beautiful as they. Their hulls blazed with swirling iridescent patterns of astonishing variety, complexity and precision.

Even the addition of field enclosures, long resisted by traditionalists but necessary for the exploitation of the most sophisticated forms of rapid interstellar travel, had only added to their great beauty, the fields themselves hardly altering the overall shape of the vessels due to their intrinsic concision and, in addition, in some ways, resembling multi-dimensional wings, unfolded and spread.

Ronte fleets in flight frequently changed their formations, or topologically warped a single formation, due not to concerns regarding surprise attack but for the joy of it. There was joy in complexity, movement, change.

On entering a new environment, a ship dance was required, unless the circumstances were so fraught that to perform one would cause operational compromise, for example in time of war, when the delay or distraction involved could be counter-productive.

Entering the volume known as Gzilt space constituted formally entering a new environment, even though there was no obvious wall, barrier, demarcation line or other signifier beyond carried navigational data to show that a frontier had been crossed (this was entirely normal in such circumstances).

Accordingly, the fleet drew to a local stop halfway between the stellar systems of Barlbanim and Taushe and the ship dance "Glowing Nymphs Dance Ascending And Descending In The Light Of An Alien Sun" was performed.

The dance had hardly been completed when the fleet was contacted by the Culture ship *Beats Working*. It congratulated the fleet on a beautiful dance, perfectly executed.

Some initial consternation was caused by this as the more rapid-response elements of the fleet's serially augmented AI+ components reacted. This was because while they were familiar with the capabilities of Culture and other Level Eight ships, they did not possess running knowledge of the likely intentions of such vessels, and assumed hostility.

Hostility was assumed due to the lack of warning before the reception of the message. Additionally, a further obvious imbalance was represented by the alien ship apparently being able to observe the fleet while the fleet had been unaware of the whereabouts of the alien ship. Stored knowledge components prevented any escalation of alarm turning into armed response even before executive oversight might have been required.

Giving due weight to earlier briefings, it was briefly contemplated that the Culture ship might have been exhibiting sarcasm when it had congratulated the fleet on its dance, and in addition certain components theorised that the ship could know nothing of what constituted a well or a badly formed dance.

However, further analysis confirmed that, statistically, politeness was significantly more likely than sarcasm in the circumstances, and that the Culture fleets and/or individual vessels seemed to possess widely distributed knowledge and appreciation of all aspects of Ronte ship dances.

The Culture ship requested permission to approach. This was given. The fleet took as marks of respect both the fact that the request had been made and that the vessel did not approach dead-on, as though in aggressive display or outright attack, but arrived tangentially, heaving to some tens of kilometres distant from the outer elements of the fleet.

The Culture ship proved to be a tiny thing of just eighty metres in length. It did not trouble to use its outer field enclosure to mimic a larger ship, as might have been expected. Historical/Analytical components of the fleet confirmed that this was not unusual with Culture ships, and that the vessel, although small and alone and so, from first principles, obviously potential prey, could not be so regarded. This was set out in standing all-fleet orders.

The Culture ship had a humanoid crew of five. It was a Limited Contact Vessel, Scree class. Its lack of substance/volume also did not constitute any sort of insult to the Ronte, probably. Its name was not to be taken literally and was more a kind of signifier of its relaxed or "laid back" nature, a quality shared by both the Culture fleet and Culture civilisation in general.

Ossebri 17 Haldesib, a seventeenth-generation Swarm-prince, was Sub-Swarm Divisional Head, Fleet Officer in Charge, aboard the flagship *Melancholia Enshrines All Triumph*. He had been in oversight command at all times since before the ship dance was performed, and duly extended personal, ship, hive, fleet, swarm and civilisational greetings to the Culture craft and the civilisation it represented, as well as to any and all relevant sub-structures/systems in between.

The Culture ship was at all points polite, diplomatic and respectful, and had already begun to accrue inferred alien cachet value (positive), honorary. Fleet orders indicated that, due to earlier bafflement issues (mostly involving parties other than the Culture), this information need not be shared with the alien vessel, but could be, at the discretion of the relevant Fleet Officer in Charge.

Ossebri 17 Haldesib duly determined to consider this,

and, accordingly, put some of his best people/components on it.

Had he done the right thing? It was so hard to know.

Banstegeyn felt the drug pulse through him just as he pulsed through the girl. That was what it felt like. In, through, beyond, amongst, within; whatever. The bed beneath him was a live thing, taking part: caressing, brushing, sucking, warming, cooling, penetrating, itself pulsing. This had been a present to her from him. He had made sure that it was keyed to his own genetic signature, so it wouldn't work for anybody else. He had told her this, too, so that she knew from the start. She claimed that such shows of determination and leadership, especially in such a personal context, turned her on, and so it suited both of them.

Had he done the right thing? Marshal Chekwri had been in touch again; fresh intelligence indicated that the target might be even less well defended than they had at first assumed; the Fourteenth had already sent most of its capital ships into the Sublime, apparently half expecting them to pop straight back out again full of scepticism and entirely of the opinion that this Subliming nonsense might be all right for lesser civilisations, but wasn't for the Gzilt. They had, however, stayed.

Recently, the disposition of the regimental fleet had changed again, and the Izenion system had been left only lightly defended. It all meant that the balance of which actions and profiles might ensure the best outcome had shifted. He had been happy not to have to make a decision at the first, thirty-eight-hour point; they had more time now. Unless circumstances changed again the ship would still attack while flying past, but would be able both to lay down a fuller pattern of additional munitions and return much more quickly than if it had attacked at full speed.

He had, in turn, allowed her to pursue some of her own little fantasies, also involving domination, but he hadn't enjoyed them, and had told her so. She had expressed surprise, thinking that most politically powerful, aggressive men secretly harboured a desire to swap roles and – in a safe, controlled, entirely secret context – be dominated. He had told her this reassuring, soft-centre theory was nonsense; some males were just strong all the way through.

Was he doing the right thing? People would die; there was no getting away from this fact. He was taking decisions that would lead to the deaths of those to whom he owed a mutual duty. He should be able to trust them and they ought to be able to trust him. But that had broken down.

The drug made everything slow down, spread out, become part of a spectrum of observed existence that the user, the practitioner, could dip into, magnify, ignore, enhance and exalt within, according to choice.

A ship – a regimental capital ship, no less – had been corrupted, its AIs duped, a viral presence inserted into it centuries ago. That had been the first act of betrayal, the first act of something as good as outright aggression. He had had to respond, and the Fourteenth had pre-emptively signed away any right to be trusted, respected or protected by that act of ancient treachery.

Above him, Orpe raised her hands above her head, then bent back, and then further back, and then kept on going until her head eventually disappeared from view as she arched her spine and her hands clutched at, found and then gripped his ankles. It was a move she knew he liked. Beautiful, succulent Orpe. Virisse, as she wanted him to call her, though on the first few occasions like this, she had admitted that she had rather enjoyed being addressed as Orpe, or Ms Orpe.

Beyond even that, though, was the simple fact that the only thing which really mattered – well beyond who acted first or who had betrayed who – was that the Subliming took place, on time, in full.

Using some suitably enabled augmentation he'd carried since adolescence, he was able to watch her bend back like that multiple times, speeding up and slowing down. With the drug, he could synaesthesise experience too, translating it into other senses while another part of him was still in real time, as though watching all this. He enjoyed this feeling of being his own voyeur.

The knowledge of what had been in the Remnanter ship – if the message it had carried was actually true, not itself a lie – had to be kept secret, hidden away not just from the vast mass of people but from everybody else as well. It rarely paid to frighten the masses, and it never paid to confuse them. Sometimes you could trust people in positions of power to understand this and even help keep things confidential – or at least muddied, so that people could self-deceive with whatever kept them best comforted – but not always. And with this, the stakes were too high. Nothing – nothing at all, in practice or in theory – mattered more than the Subliming. They were staking everything on it; *he* was staking everything on it, carrying the burden of the hopes of the whole Gzilt people on his shoulders.

Orpe – Virisse – moaned, panted. Not being able to see her face meant that he could let his own expression relax while he thought all this through.

And – precisely because it was so important – there was also the possibility that even somebody he'd normally have trusted, somebody from the rarefied upper echelons, would blab, just for the fame, just for the down-the-generations notoriety or supposed heroic status speaking out would bring, even if it was utterly and completely the wrong thing to do. Never underestimate the sheer selfishness and stupidity of people.

The girl's grip on his ankles tightened. She shuddered.

He thought of the ship, slowing but still racing, powering down towards the planet, falling upon it.

Orpe moaned. He almost laughed. Supposedly, right now he was with the sub-committee making the decision about which Scavenger species got Preferred Partner status, making them the people who'd receive the cooperation of the Gzilt when it came to parcelling out the legacy stuff. But he didn't need to be there, in the committee chamber; the personnel concerned had been briefed, knew what to do and which way to vote. In the end they remained frightened of him, even yet, and there was – he was entirely prepared to admit – a certain extra frisson about wielding such power without even having to be there.

Fuck the sub-committee. That would take care of itself. In the end, he'd rather be here.

With Orpe, whom he had to share with the president.

Normally he wouldn't stand for this; he didn't share lovers. But then Orpe's other lover was somebody it was very useful to share her with. It was, indeed, the precise reason that he had befriended the girl, flattered her, courted her, finally bedded her. Not that it was any great sacrifice, of course; she was beautiful and attractive, after all, if a little too . . . assertive, equality-minded for his tastes. But no matter.

He had been very careful never to ask Orpe anything at all about President Sefoy Geljemyn's thoughts or likely actions, content to lull her into a state where she thought he had wanted her purely for herself, not for her connection to the president, not for that access, that closeness.

For all he knew, it might never come in useful. But then that was not the point.

. . . And of course it had been the right thing.

"Orders, sadly, are orders."

"Well, we'll miss you, big guy. You really have to go right now?"

"Immediately, I'm afraid. Oh, you might register a slight tremor in your warp cores as I kick off here; not a passing gravity wave or anything – just me."

". . . No, not seeing anything this . . . No, wait a second, yes, engineering says yes, they did."

The *Mistake Not . . .* felt a modicum of embarrassment. It had disengaged its own warp units without a murmur – they'd been idling, basically – and then deliberately roughened up its engine fields as it had engaged its main drive, specifically to create the skein-kick.

There was a table you looked up, basically, to see which of the less-developed civs had to be hoodwinked like this, and to what degree. It was a form of dishonesty the *Mistake Not . . .* found slightly objectionable, but it was expected. Technically, indulging in such deceit wasn't compulsory, any more than this just-received suggestion that it might like to head at the highest possible speed to a distant star system wasn't an order, but it was expected; if you wanted to do more of this sort of stuff in the future then you'd best take the hint. Otherwise you'd be frozen out next time.

Of course, it also made such behaviour your own responsibility; it was hard to claim you had just been obeying orders when orders had officially ceased to exist the best part of ten thousand years ago.

The ship was talking directly to Ny-Xandabo Tyun, the admiral of the Liseiden fleet. It had contacted the flagship's

AI as soon as it got the signal; the admiral had clicked in seconds later. The little flotilla of three Liseiden ships including the fleet flagship had been puttering along towards Zyse for just a few hours now.

There had been a wait of nearly half a day spent still orbiting the cinder star while the fleet had shuffled personnel and equipment between its various ships. Quite why this had to be done at this point, wasting time, when it might have been accomplished while the ships had still been in transit had puzzled the *Mistake Not* . . . for a moment until it reviewed the specifications and capabilities of the Liseiden craft and realised that, with their level of tech, ship-to-ship transfers while under way were tricky and risky. The ship had been suitably appalled, and had felt vicariously embarrassed for the Liseiden.

"Yup, that's me off and running. Sorry for the abrupt departure."

"Yeah! You even took your avatoid! We're devastated! "

"Yup. Sorry about that too"

"Just joshing anyway."

"I know. No, just . . . one of those things, you know?"

"So, you're . . . just looking at the orientation of the warp skein here . . . looks like you're off to . . . no, we can't tell. Open space by our reckoning."

"Heck, can't hide much from you guys," the *Mistake Not* . . . replied, putting some heartiness into its synthesised voice (it had, naturally, an extensive knowledge of all Liseiden languages, dialects, accents, idioms and speech patterns). It was powering away as fast as it could, already curving away towards this Izenion place (it had no idea why). The rucking it had caused in the skein of real space, pointing in a completely different direction, represented pretty much standard procedure; you didn't let people know where you were really heading unless there was a good reason.

"I bet," the admiral said. "Soooo . . . bad news?"

The delay caused by increasing distance was already such that had the *Mistake Not . . .* been talking to another Mind or even AI, it would have switched to standard messaging by now. Talking to a creature whose faculties relied on a substrate where internal signals moved at roughly the speed of sound – an ordinary bio-brain – there was no need for this yet; the ship had plenty to process and think about while it waited for the animal-slow replies to trundle across the link, and even during the individual transmission sections.

Between the phonemes associated with the end of the word "bad" and the very start of the word "news", for example, when it was already anticipating that the whole of the next word would indeed be "news", and – from the inflection – that it would be the end of the sentence and probably the end of the signal parcel, it had had time to thoroughly research the Izenion system, re-analyse everything it knew about Gzilt and the current situation re the countdown to Subliming and everything else, and still come up with precisely no idea why it had been asked to endure a degree of engine degradation – however temporary – to get to Izenion as quickly as possible.

The request had come from its principal contact and old friend, the *Kakistocrat*, which had wanted to know if it would do this purely out of regard for it. The *Kakistocrat* had admitted that it had been given further detail regarding whatever situation was thought so important that a ship should be asked to do such a thing, but wanted to know more still before involving the *Mistake Not . . .* fully. It had also asked the *Mistake Not . . .* if it would agree to its specs being forwarded to the group dealing with whatever might be going on.

The *Mistake Not* . . . had seriously considered saying no to both, but then decided this was unlikely to be a drill or some sort of bizarre test of loyalty. That said, the *Kakistocrat* was eccentric, even if it wasn't officially Eccentric, and so it still might be some sort of weird drill of the *Kak*'s own devising. In the end it agreed to go but vetoed the other vessel passing on its specifications beyond being allowed to say that they would likely prove sufficient.

"No idea if it's bad news, good news or even no news, Xan," the ship sent back to the Liseiden admiral. "Just orders."

"That's too bad; it was good having you around," Ny-Xandabo said. He meant to sound sincere, and, to some degree, did. "You take care. We hope we see you again."

"Same here. Mind how you go. We'll talk again. Out."

Seven

(S -20)

Fzan-Juym was a sub-summit-orbit satellite of the Sculpt planet Eshri, making it one of a very small sub-category of moons; only its military nature and natural/artificial status – it was, arguably, a ship – stopped it being regarded as a genuine wonder.

The Werpesh, the people who had constructed the Girdlecity on Xown, had turned their attentions to Eshri at about the same time they'd begun building on Xown, perhaps a hundred thousand years ago. By then, Eshri had been dead for well over a billion years. It was small, dry, frozen and stony, with a thin atmosphere and a solidified core that registered as barely warm; most of the heat from its formation had been convected and then radiated away, and what little radioactivity the core had possessed had since decayed almost to nothing.

Thanks to a little tectonic activity of its own but a lot of early asteroid-battering that had produced lava outflows covering large parts of the world, it had been a fairly smooth little globe to start with. The Werpesh had decided to improve – as they saw it – upon this promising start, and used plani-forming techniques to turn Eshri into one of their Sculpt worlds; a flat-surfaced planet of polished rock with a network of encircling trenches – steep sided, kilometres deep and tens of kilometres wide – incised into and right around it. From space the planet looked like a colossal ball-bearing etched with ball-races for thousands of smaller spheres.

Scholars of the Werpesh and their works reckoned Eshri was the most extreme of all the Sculpt worlds; on no other had the ground been so thoroughly levelled, the remaining atmosphere so assiduously removed, the canyon-trenches etched so deep or so wide or attained such a bewildering complexity.

Like all the few dozen or so Sculpt worlds, there had been no utility to the project. As far as could be discerned – the Werpesh had been a reticent species, unable or unwilling to explain themselves to the extent that other, more nosy species thought they ought – the Sculpt worlds were basically a series of titanic works of art.

That they also functioned as highly visible expressions of sheer power and a certain willingness to ignore galactic etiquette (most species/civs had long since agreed to leave "wild" worlds like Eshri untouched), well, that was probably just an added bonus. Nevertheless, although the Werpesh had not been a particularly aggressive or expansive people, it would be fair to say that their contemporaries had been less than heartbroken when they'd opted for Subliming and stopped building such impressive vulgarities as the Girdlecity of Xown and the Sculpt planets.

The Gzilt, by luck and the good grace of at least one Elder species in nominal control of the Werpesh legacy, had fallen heir to most of the Sublimed species' abandoned systems in their immediate vicinity, and had quickly and enthusiastically got on with the business of – for example – colonising and rebuilding on and within Xown's great Girdlecity. They were less sure what to do with the brace of Sculpt worlds they had inherited; neglected if never quite abandoned, these had by default become no more than occasional if rather one-trick tourist stopover sites.

Then the Socialist-Republican People's Liberation Regiment #14 – which was all and none of the adjectives in its name – had chosen to make Eshri its home. Or at least the home of its home.

Fzan-Juym had been the Regiment's headquarters for nearly a millennium by then. Roughly spherical and a couple of kilometres in diameter, the satellite had started out life as an asteroid of the Izenion system; just another tumbling rock amongst tens of millions of others. Initially, after being hollowed out to become the regimental HQ, it had been left in a close-to-original orbit within the Izenion system's inner asteroid belt, theoretically gaining from being just one of a bewildering array of potential targets, should anyone ever be foolish enough to wish it harm. Later, with improvements in weapon and sensor technology, the natural camouflage effect of being part of a mass of other asteroids had been negated. Happily, the likelihood of any realistic threat had receded at the same time, so the placement of the regiment's HQ became more about statement – prestige, even – than about operational survivability.

So Fzan-Juym had been appropriately refitted, refurbished and improved, towed to Eshri, slung into a low orbit around it and then carefully lowered still further – kilometre by kilometre, metre by metre, eventually millimetre by millimetre, speeding up all the time – until its orbit now lay a kilometre beneath the planet's surface, darting along one of the widest and deepest canyons of all in a blur of planet-girdling movement, its course held steady by a network of hermetically isolated AIs and multiply redundant thruster systems dedicated to doing nothing else.

Its own engines had done almost all the work at every stage, though various other craft had helped and been there to step in had anything started to go wrong, but a modest degree of seeming helplessness was deemed to be useful in providing a sort of camouflage of its own.

Fzan-Juym, headquarters of the Socialist-Republican People's Liberation Regiment #14, had been in sub-surface equatorial orbit of Eshri ever since, zipping along like a super-fast bullet in a slab-sided groove open to the pitch-black sky, orbiting the planet in less than an hour and covering over two hundred million kilometres every year – nearly half a trillion altogether by now – while never coming closer than fifteen hundred metres to either the flat canyon floor or its sheer, polished sides.

You approached Fzan-Juym carefully, from astern. Approaching it any other way meant its hair-trigger defensive systems would blow you out of the sky. Coming in from astern meant that even if you collided with it, approaching too fast, the extra impetus would, in theory, merely boost its orbit a fraction, sending it higher, away from danger. It also meant that as well as the arrays, batteries and multiple turrets of emission, kinetic and missile weapon system sites pointing at you, you got to contemplate the impressive collection of variegated main drive units and crater-wide thruster nozzles pointing straight at you, each of them guaranteed to be usefully and reliably – and terminally – weapon-like in their effect should they be turned on even for a microsecond while you approached.

The principal hangar entrance lay nestled in the centre of a quartet of main drive units; the transfer pinnace slipped towards it, shadows wheeling about it as it gently outpaced the asteroid, approaching at about humanoid running speed, a little faster than was normally allowed. The little twelve-seat vessel disappeared, pitching nose-down for a moment and trembling as it encountered the asteroid's own internal gravity field.

The view behind cut off as a field and then a real, physical door blocked the view of the deep, sunlit trench whipping past outside, and lights came on in the hangar as the pinnace settled to the floor. Somewhere, a system would be compensating for the small amount of downward impetus caused by the tiny craft transferring its weight to the hangar deck.

Commissar-Colonel Etalde looked at Vyr Cossont and smiled. "Home at last!" he said, possibly a little too heartily.

Cossont just smiled.

They had crossed the few decades from Xown in the Mureite system to Eshri in Izenion within the 5*Gelish-Oplule, a regimental cruiser about as fast as anything the fleet possessed. Tired, and with nothing seemingly expected of her after they'd transferred to the ship above Xown, she'd slept aboard in a cabin of a size significantly above that her reactivated rank would normally have called for and wondered if she had the bulk of the elevenstring to thank for this; they'd quartered it with her.

She'd risen, done a little practice – it had been unsatisfactory, thanks to a deep background hum the ship was making which interfered with some of the internal resonating strings – and thought she'd have time to breakfast with the crew and maybe try to get more out of Etalde regarding what was going on, even if it was just gossip, when they'd arrived, and Etalde was there at her cabin door offering to carry the elevenstring to the cruiser's hangar and the waiting pinnace.

"No food?" Pyan yelped. She'd just let it fasten itself round her neck. It tended to nibble at whatever Cossont ate and breakfast was its favourite meal.

Etalde frowned at the creature. "That thing is security-cleared, isn't it?"

"Sadly," Cossont said. "We're *there*?" she asked. "Already?" She stared at Etalde's plump, gleaming face. "Sir?" she added. She hadn't even had time to be issued with a proper uniform; all she had was her civilian trews and frankly inappropriate jacket. Luckily the avatar, when worn as a cape usually, covered the more garishly offensive parts of the logo.

"Yes," the commissar-colonel said. "Ship kind of pushed it. All a bit rushed. You fit to go?"

"No food?" Pyan said again, plaintively.

"No food," she confirmed, turning and letting Etalde pick up the elevenstring's black case while she grabbed her jacket and folded it inwards.

"No food," the familiar said quietly, as though to itself. "Cripes."

"This is Marshal Boyuter, Commander in Chief. I'm General Reikl, marshal elect; this is General Gazan'tyo." The two men and one woman – Reikl, who'd been speaking – smiled at her. She nodded. "Please," Reikl said. "Sit."

The room was small, functional, mostly filled with a square table and four seats. It felt like it was deep within the hurtling asteroid. There was no screen, holo display or obvious processing presence at all.

Cossont sat. She wore Etalde's jacket over her shoulders; he'd been left in an antechamber several thick, closed doors back. He had charge of her jacket, the familiar and the elevenstring, all guarded by two troopers in full armour and a pair of combat arbites like frozen explosions of mercury and knife-blades. Cossont's earbud, receiving and transmitting only on the asteroid's own channels since she'd come aboard, had shut itself off entirely. She'd been asked to hand it over all the same and so had left that behind too.

"Are you well, Lieutenant Commander?" Reikl asked her.

"Thank you, yes, ma'am."

"Sorry we couldn't find you a uniform jacket with the requisite number of arms," Reikl said, smiling again. "I imagine one is being prepared as we speak."

"Thank you, ma'am." Cossont sat with her upper hands clasped on the table, the other pair hanging down; it disturbed people less that way, were they of a disturbable nature.

"Now," Reikl said. "To business. None of this is being recorded, minuted or monitored elsewhere—"

"Far as we know," Marshal Boyuter said, smiling first at her, then Reikl, who nodded impatiently.

"As far as we know," she agreed.

The marshal was thin, grey-looking, his pale face part-covered with a colourful tattoo that looked both fresh and unfinished. Cossont had the feeling she was looking at a life-task, still incomplete. She'd been out of the services for nearly twenty years and even now didn't feel terribly military, despite being told her commission had been reactivated, but it was still slightly shocking to see somebody so senior exhibiting something so non-regulation as a facial tattoo. Oh well. As people were continually pointing out – strange times.

The marshal sat relaxed in his seat, almost slumped, playing continually with what looked like some sort of multi-tool and rarely looking directly at her after an initial, staring inspection when she'd first entered the room. He'd frowned at her twin sets of arms. General Gazan'tyo was rotund, ever-smiling and seemed to communicate solely by nods. He had a variety of small time-tos scattered about the chest of his uniform jacket, as though he didn't entirely trust any of them and was looking for a consensus. If she hadn't known – well, assumed – better, Cossont might have thought both men were on drugs.

Reikl was different: thin and bright-eyed, she sat upright and looked sharp, tense, almost predatory. "What you are going to hear has until now been restricted to the three of us in this cabin," she told Cossont.

"And whoever it was originally meant for," the marshal added quietly, staring at the multi-tool. He let it go and it floated into the air a little, making a low whirring noise.

Reikl looked pained for an instant, then said, "This was information we came by . . . indirectly." She glanced at the marshal as though expecting another interruption but he was reaching out to the little multi-tool, clicking it off. It fell into his other hand, poised beneath.

"There has been a communication from our erstwhile benefactors the Zihdren," General Reikl said, smiling thinly at Cossont. "It's in the nature of these pre-Subliming times, apparently, to do this kind of thing: to make one's peace where there might have been discord, answer puzzling questions and generally settle accounts with those about to make the transition."

"Old scores," the marshal muttered.

"The communication was due to be delivered immediately before the Instigation. However, it came to light before it was supposed to," Reikl said.

THE HYDROGEN SONATA   119

"Intercepted!" General Gazan'tyo said suddenly, still smiling his broad smile.

"Intercepted," Reikl agreed. "By another regiment, on behalf, we believe, of our political betters."

The marshal dropped the multi-tool onto the desk, scooped it up again. Reikl didn't even glance; she kept Cossont fixed with her gaze. "You're a musician, Ms Cossont, aren't you?"

"Yes, ma'am," she said, wondering why her rank had been dispensed with.

"Tell me about your time on . . ." The general gave a small smile. "You'll have to forgive me." She took out a notebook of real paper from a uniform pocket, consulted it. Again, it was very strange to see somebody, especially somebody of such seniority, not having names and other information immediately to hand, transmitted by earbud or implant straight into their head. A notebook! Cossont thought. Could the local processing have broken down so much in the lead-up to Subliming that even the regimental high command refused to rely on it? That seemed absurd. "The *Anything Legal Considered*, I believe is the name?" Reikl said, leaving the notebook open on the table.

"Ah, that," Cossont said. She'd sort of always known there was a chance what happened during her student exchange years would come back and bite her.

"Yes, that," the general said. "Everything, please. And not in your own time; we're in a hurry here." She didn't look at either of the males in the room but Cossont got the impression the general would have liked to.

"I was on an exchange programme, on a Culture ship; a GCU called the *Anything Legal Considered*—"

"I have it as an LCU," the general interrupted.

"Sorry, yes," Cossont said, flustered. "It was. Anyway, I

was playing the volupt, that is, I'd passed my . . . Doesn't matter. Anyway," she said, taking a deep breath, "I'd talked to the ship about the, another instrument called the eleven . . . the Antagonistic Undecagonstring, and—"

"'Antagonistic'?" Reikl said.

"Um, just means that applying manual tension to one set of strings applies it to others as well," Cossont said. "Or decreases it, depending." Reikl gave a curt nod. Cossont went on: "I told the ship how I planned to try it some day if I could get my hands on a good example, and it looked it up and, ah, well, long story short: it built one for me. Presented it to me as a surprise on my birthday. I started playing it, with the ship's help; it had made a sort of twin-arm prosthetic which . . . anyway," Cossont said, feeling herself shrinking under the general's gaze, "I became very interested in the instrument, the ship knew this and – this was near the end of the exchange; it was a two-year, ah exchange – it asked if I wanted to meet somebody who claimed to have met Vilabier. The Younger; T. C. Vilabier; he composed the piece that . . . it's the most famous piece written for the elevenstring. The first . . . the piece that caused it to be designed and made at all, although there are many oth—"

"If I can just hurry you along, Lieutenant Commander," Reikl said. "Who was it you met, and where?"

"A man called QiRia. That was his real . . . well, the name he had before he went to this place. It was called Perytch IV, a water world. This man had been swimming, living with the Issialiayans, the inhabitants – something to do with an interest in their, ah, sounds, sonic sense; they're these huge animals, semi-sentient or proto-sentient or whatever. Rich sonic culture. Anyway, he'd been one of them for, well, decades and he was coming back, going through something called . . . Processal Reconnecting?"

The general glanced at her notebook, turned a page, nodded curtly. Cossont felt relief at getting something right.

"So, the *ALC* had turned—"

"The what?" Reikl interrupted, then shook her head quickly. "No; got it. Ship. Carry on."

"The ship turned up at Perytch IV, I went down to this giant raft, met with QiRia – he was in human form by now, put back into his old body, though he was still kind of strange and vague a lot of the time. Oh, and there was another ship avatar there, from a Culture ship called the . . . *Warm, Considering*. I think. Pretty sure that was it. Felt like it was his . . . his mentor or protector or something. It seemed to take this claim of his about being incredibly old seriously too. I just thought, well, I just assumed this was all some sort of elaborate joke – Culture ships do this kind of thing . . . but I met him and we talked; just an hour at first, then more the next day, and the ship seemed happy to stick around and the old guy didn't seem to want me to go and he was kind of fascinating, so we talked a lot, over several days. He claimed he'd spent . . . dozens of lifetimes as various other types of creature over the years, and often with some sort of sound or music-based thing going on, and he really did claim that he'd known Vilabier." Cossont found herself laughing, just once. Reikl didn't look amused but didn't tell her to shut up either. "Back when he'd been human the first time, if . . ."

"T. C. Vilabier?" Reikl said, glancing at her notes. "The composer who died nine thousand, eight hundred and thirty-four years ago?"

"Yes!" Cossont said, waving her upper arms briefly. Etalde's jacket slid off her shoulders; she caught it with her lower arms, replaced it. Marshal Boyuter regarded this action with what looked like consternation. "So I thought he was crazy," Cossont continued, glancing at the two men but concentrating on Reikl. "At first. By the time I left, five, six days later, I believed him. He didn't seem bothered either way; maintained that what he was telling me was all true but it didn't matter if I believed him or not."

"What did he tell you?"

"Mostly stuff about Vilabier himself. How he'd hated—"

"What else?" Reikl said. "Aside from Vilabier. What else might he have been doing at that time? Round about then – within a century or so."

Cossont pressed her lips together. "Ah," she said, after a moment. "Well, he did say that he'd been . . ." She shook her head. "He claimed he'd been involved with the negotiations, the conference that set up the Culture." She shrugged, shook her head again, as though denying any responsibility for such patent nonsense. "He actually claimed . . . he'd been on one of the negotiating teams."

"Which one?"

"He never would say. I didn't believe that bit at all, frankly. I thought he was just playing with me. I could believe the whole thing with Vilabier – there were so many details, so much stuff I'd never heard of that sounded right . . . and also that turned out to be true, though only after I'd done some really deep research . . . But he was always much more vague about all the stuff concerning the conference and the negotiations, like he hadn't bothered to do the research to lie properly. I mean, I checked, obviously; went through all the standard data searches, but there was nobody of that name mentioned and it's all pretty well documented. I didn't, you know, press him on it after the first time or two; he'd just bring it up again later, now and again, and tease me for obviously not believing him. Actually I was kind of embarrassed for him. The Vilabier stuff was so convincing but the

. . . you know; being in right at the start of the Culture, when we . . . well, it was just so . . . so unbelievable."

She suspected she knew how Reikl had got to hear about this. Like most people, Cossont kept a journal and in the public part of it – the part that was shared by friends and might in theory be accessed by anybody – she had mentioned meeting somebody who claimed to have known Vilabier. She couldn't remember if she'd mentioned QiRia by name, but she had mentioned the meeting. It had been a sort of boast, she'd supposed, though, at the same time, when she'd made the entry, she had played the episode down, maybe given the impression there had been only one meeting, not a series over several days. Even as she'd dictated the words she'd treated it all as much more of a joke than it had really felt at the time, as though she had stopped believing in it herself.

It had felt oddly like betrayal, as though she was letting QiRia down somehow, but – in the context of the sort of thing you bandied around with pals, about family, friends, boys, crushes, drink, drugs, pranks and so on – it had seemed too serious in its raw form, too pretentious. So she'd mentioned him only in passing, as an example of the kind of eccentric/crazy you met sometimes when you travelled, especially if you got to go travelling on a Culture ship (serious kudos there – few people got to do that and she knew most of her friends were jealous she'd been chosen, even if it had just been by lottery).

Reikl said nothing for a moment. Neither did the marshal or the other general, though that felt less noteworthy. Reikl looked down at her notebook on the table in front of her. "What was his first name?" she asked. She looked at Cossont. "You just called him QiRia; there must have been more, no?"

"Ngaroe," Cossont told her. "He was called Ngaroe

QiRia. Though he was just re-assuming that name; for the time just before – decades, like I say – he'd been . . ." Cossont looked up and away, grimacing. Right now she was missing her earbud and access to distant data storage. She spread her arms, nearly dislodging the jacket again. "Isserem?" she offered. "That was his . . . his aquatic name."

Reikl nodded again, lifted a small pointer and made some sort of amendment to her notes. It might have been a tick.

"Intercepted!" General Gazan'tyo said suddenly, again.

Marshal Boyuter looked at him, openly sneering.

Reikl put the notebook back in her pocket. She wore a time-to on her chest; a tiny mechanical-looking thing. She glanced at it, stood, looked at the marshal and then General Gazan'tyo. "Gentlemen, if you'll excuse me and the Lieutenant Commander?"

The two men exchanged looks, nodded. The marshal made the little tool thing hover again. He seemed to be humming to himself.

Reikl nodded to Cossont, who stood and followed her out of the room via the same door she'd entered by, though – once the arm-thick door had rotated back into place – she realised she was looking down a short stretch of gleaming circular-section corridor that hadn't been there before. Another door was rolling aside at the far end as they walked. It closed behind them as they entered an identical length of corridor; its diameter was at least three metres but there was no distinct floor and the slight curvature under her feet made walking surprisingly awkward. It was like walking down a smooth-bore gun barrel. Cossont guessed that this was a part of the asteroid interior left over from when it had been without its own gravity field.

When both the doors behind and ahead were closed,

General Reikl stopped and turned to Cossont, making her stop too.

"I apologise for the state of my fellow senior officers," Reikl told her.

"I . . ." Cossont began, unsure what to say.

The general looked very earnest. "You seem . . . quite sober."

"Um, thank you, ma'am," Cossont said, and felt foolish.

Reikl stared into her eyes for a few moments. "We need to ask you to do something for us, Lieutenant Commander," she said. "*I* need to ask you; your regiment. Something that might have a relevance for all the Gzilt." Reikl took a breath. "You are of course back under military discipline now, though even that might be seen to carry less significance than it ought, these days. But I need to know: are you willing to do what we might ask, what I might ask?" Her gaze flicked from one of Cossont's eyes to the other, back again.

"What is it I'm being ask—?"

"Look for something," Reikl told her.

"Look for something?" Cossont frowned. "Ma'am, I wasn't special forces or anything . . ." she said. She felt trapped here, with just the two of them in this length of gleaming tube. Reikl was smaller than her, she realised, but seemed to have a compressed power, a sort of density that gave the impression of being overbearing.

"I know," Reikl said, waving one hand. "We're going to give you a combat arbite. Well, technically an android; looks human. For protection."

"Protection?" Cossont found herself saying. She was no warrior. She'd been terrible at self-defence and weapon training; she'd stayed on an extra year after her draft period and risen to the dizzy height of Lieutenant Commander on the strength of a sincere interest in military band ceremonial music and an over-enthusiastic Commanding Officer. She hadn't even been backed-up, had her mind-state read or anything, and that was just the first sign that you were taking the Military Outright seriously as a profession. Now they were talking of teaming her up with some combat arbite, for protection. Protection from whom, from what?

"Probably unnecessary protection," the general said dismissively. "But this is of more than passing importance." She smiled, unconvincingly. "Let me ask you, Ms Cossont: where do you feel your loyalties lie?"

Cossont felt disoriented by the sudden change in direction. "Loyalties? Um, well, to the regiment, to Gzilt," she said. "And, ah, family . . ."

"And how do you feel about Subliming?" The general glanced at her chest. "I see you have no time-to, though your records say you were issued with one."

"I just left it behind one day," Cossont said, hearing her voice falter. She cleared her throat. "I'm ready to Sublime, with everybody else," she said, drawing herself up a little, as though for inspection. Reikl looked at her, said nothing. "There's a bit of . . . I'm a little nervous," Cossont confessed. "I suppose everybody is, but, well, it's all documented, it's all meant to be . . . better. There; in the Sublime." She was aware this sounded lame. She shook her head. "And it's all I've ever known, ma'am; just what's expected. Of course I'm going to go when everybody else does." Reikl waited. Cossont added, "Because everybody else . . . does."

Reikl nodded. "Kind of in the whole culture, whole society, preparing, since before you were born," she agreed. "Now," she said, "I'm going to ask you again: are you willing to do what we might ask, what I might ask?"

Cossont looked into the other woman's eyes for a moment. She thought of all the people you heard about who had resigned commissions, disobeyed orders, committed ludicrous crimes, especially just recently, all because the Subliming was so close and the wheels of justice ground so slow; by the time they might expect to be punished, they'd have gone with everybody else. Every individual got their own chance, apparently, with no way – aside from summary execution – for society to pick and choose who went.

She suspected most people had been tempted to do something crazy in these final days, maybe something they'd always thought about but never dared do, until now. She'd gone for the other option, of just keeping your head down and maybe taking on an absorbing life-task until the big day came. One way of looking at this was that it was less self-obsessed. Another was that it was less daring, a cop-out, almost cowardly.

She could say no, she was aware of that. Reikl she trusted, and had heard good things about, but the uselessness of the other two senior officers had been a shock. She hadn't realised how mad things had become. They'd all be Sublimed soon anyway – what was the point of taking on some mission that might be even slightly dangerous? It was all very romantic, but she had no illusions regarding her own abilities – she was no spy, no hero, no super-agent.

Still, there was something about the intensity of the other woman's gaze and the way she carried herself, some expression of the force of her personality – and maybe just some residual need in Cossont to obey somebody so much more senior, inculcated from childhood and throughout her life – that made her want to please Reikl, to do as she said or even demanded. It was also, she admitted to herself, a way of abandoning her idiotic life-task without losing too much self-respect. "All right," she said. "I'll do whatever I can, ma'am. But it would help to know—"

"Yes." Reikl nodded, as though just remembering something. "Yes, well, sorry to make it sound so melodramatic, Lieutenant Commander, but let me get to the point: the Book of Truth is a lie."

Cossont stared at her.

The Gzilt holy book was something you just grew up with, something you took for granted, and felt proud of. It might, in a sense, have outlived its most useful period, when it had demonstrably been telling the Gzilt people truths – facts – they could never have guessed at the time, but it was still revered. Of course there were doubts about it, there always had been; when you found out about all the other holy books there had ever been throughout the histories of other peoples throughout the galaxy, you realised how common they were, and how fallible, how restricted they were by the usually tribal prejudices and traditions of the people who – it took real blind faith not to accept – had made them up.

But even then, of course, the Book of Truth stood alone, as the one that had made sense throughout.

That the Zihdren had turned out to be not quite so important, and not unique, as the book implied, made little difference. Because another thing that you learned was that everybody had their own point of view; all species and civilisations saw things from their own perspective – and with themselves, generally, naturally, at the centre of things. The Gzilt were in one sense no different, and in another were rather better off, more justified in their self-regard, because they had had less to repudiate, less baggage to renounce; their holy book had little to apologise for.

"A lie?" she heard herself saying.

"Not just a misinterpretation or a good deed or helping hand taken too far: an outright, deliberate lie, coated with a selection of scientific truths to make it easier to swallow, but otherwise fashioned purely to deceive," Reikl told her.

"By the Zihdren?"

"By the Zihdren," Reikl confirmed. "In fact, by a tiny faction within the Zihdren: a solitary university faculty, a small renegade research team with a single dissident individual at its head. We are, and always have been since the Book was put together, an experiment, Ms Cossont. The Scribe was just a clever man down on his luck with a gift for speculation, embroidery and marketing. He was selected by the Zihdren – profiled, chosen – and then given the basis of the Book. The rest, of course, he just made up.

"We know all this because there was a Zihdren-Remnanter ship on its way to Zyse and the parliament for the final ceremonies. It was carrying a . . . an android, some sort of humanoid entity that was to represent the Zihdren at the ceremonies, but it was also supposed to confess all this deception to the political high-ups just before Subliming, so that technically the confession would have been made and the Zihdren's revelation would have been delivered, but too late – you'd assume, they were assuming – to make any difference, and not for general consumption, of course. The political establishment is more locked into the whole Subliming idea than anybody else; they might be a little shocked, dazed even, to have confirmed what cynics and apostates have been muttering for millennia, but they would never call off the whole Subliming or think to put it to a vote or a plebiscite."

The general smiled. It was not a convincing expression. "Only, the Zihdren ship never arrived at Zyse. It was inter-cepted by a Gzilt ship en route, and destroyed on some pretext," she said. "Just before it was incinerated the Zihdren ship tried to reason with the Gzilt craft by explaining how

important its mission was. It released the sealed information
it was carrying. Until that point we believe it hadn't known
itself what the message contained. It was destroyed anyway
and a component of the Gzilt ship loyal to something beyond
the regiment it belonged to ensured the information duly
made its way to us."

Reikl stepped a little closer to Cossont, making Vyr want to
step back. She resisted the urge, let the other woman put her
face close to hers. "And the thing is," the general continued,
"the message mentioned Ngaroe QiRia by name, as somebody
who might help provide proof that this was all true, even if
there would have been precious little time to have done the
checking required by the time this information was supposed
to have been passed on." Reikl did her faux smile thing again.
"So, Ms Vyr Cossont, Lieutenant Commander Cossont,
reserve, in her civilian blouse and the Lords of Excrement jacket
she's been trying to hide," Reikl said, reaching out with both
hands and gently patting down Cossont's shirt collar, "we are
looking to you to help us here, because some of us would
dearly love to know if all this really is all true, and what further
light on matters Mr QiRia – in any of his incarnations – might
be able to throw on things. Because we understand – *I* understand – that the gentleman concerned might exist in more than
one form now, is that not right?"

"Ah," Cossont said, "that."

"Yes," Reikl said softly. "That."

"The mind-state thing."

"Just as you say; the mind-state thing."

"It's not something that I have any more, ma'am," Cossont
confessed.

"I know," Reikl told her, leaning back a little from her.
"You donated it to one of the Centralised Dataversities on
the Bokri microrbital, Ospin."

Cossont nodded. "The Incast facility. They specialise—"

"—specialise in that sort of thing," Reikl said, nodding. "Yes, I've read your journal."

Cossont frowned. "But that was in the private—"

"Don't be naive," Reikl said, shaking her head. "We're your regiment. The point is, would you be prepared to go there and get it back?"

"To Ospin?"

"We're practically en route," the general said, her gaze wandering all over Cossont now, as though inspecting her in some military parade, taking in her overall appearance, her clothes, everything. Cossont felt oddly helpless, transfixed. In a parade, the inspecting officer traditionally looked for the slightest thing out of place or badly done; perhaps Reikl was looking for anything on her that had any military merit whatsoever. "It would be very helpful," Reikl was saying, still inspecting her. "You could even be doing something Gzilt as a whole would be most grateful for. Obviously we all respect life-tasks but this could be rather more important than playing a piece of music all the way through, however difficult it might be. Really, promotion and medals and awards and such nonsenses mean nothing if we're all about to step into the big bright and shining light, Vyr, but there is just a chance that we'd be doing so under false pretences, and it would be good to know the truth, don't you think? Just in case we wanted to rethink, and stay in the Real and accomplish more here first, and leave Subliming for another time. That ought to be a choice, don't you agree?"

"I—"

"Shouldn't even be too dangerous. And much better than us going piling in. The regiment, I mean, mob-handed, fully tooled. That could be awkward. There might be ructions. In fact, ructions would be pretty much guaranteed, given that Ospin and the Dataversities fall under the protection of the Home Systems Regiment, and it was one of their ships, we think, that wasted the Zihdren vessel. Powf! Like that." She snapped her fingers gently in front of Cossont's face. "You, however, have a plausible motive for inspecting something you donated, so we'd like to send you to see if the shade of Mr QiRia will talk to you and shed any light. Do you think you could do that? Would you be prepared? I'm very much hoping it's not too much to ask. Is it, Vyr? Is it too much to ask?" The general was suddenly quite close to her again.

Cossont shook her head; she felt she'd been half hypnotised. "No, ma'am. I'll . . . I'll go. I'll . . . it'll be my . . ." Cossont shook her head, cleared her throat, pulled herself upright. "I will do what you ask."

The general leaned back again, smiled – sincerely, this time, or so it appeared. "Thank you," she said, with a little side-nod of the head. "Now, let's find your android bodyguard, shall we?" She turned and walked smartly along the awkwardly curved floor of the corridor; the door ahead rolled open. Cossont followed.

The mind-state thing.

It had been a final present she'd received from the *Anything Legal Considered*; a copy of QiRia's soul, basically. The ship hadn't handed it over to her until the day and the moment she was leaving, a bag in her hand and the elevenstring's case sitting on a float-pallet slaved to her, hovering obediently at her side like a slightly annoying pet.

She'd been bade farewell by the ship's golden-skinned avatar and had started to turn – one foot still on the floor of the ship's hangar, her other foot on the rear ramp of the Gzilt transfer shuttle – when the avatar had said, "Oh, and there's this," and, when she'd turned, handed her a little dark-grey, subtly glittering cube which lay heavy in her palm.

"From our old friend on Perytch IV," the avatar had told her. "That's him, in there, in a sense. For you alone; to be ignored, consulted, insulted, thrown aside, as you wish, he told me to say." The creature had held up its gleaming golden hand. "Goodbye."

Outside the corridor end, in a wider cross-chamber, there was sudden noise and a line of men and women in a mixture of uniform and fancy dress, dancing past, roaring with laughter. Almost all sobered instantly the moment they saw the general, and stood to attention, breathless, grinning. One or two stood at ease, or even hunched over, hands on knees, getting their breath back or still laughing.

"At ease, all of you," Reikl said, then put some volume and steel into her voice and repeated, "*All* of you," to bring the last couple into line. She looked at them as Cossont stood behind her, finding herself the object of some interest. Reikl caught the glances. "Yes," she said, "somebody in civilian clothes, behaving with rather more decorum than any of you." She nodded. "However; as you were." She glanced at Cossont and they set off up the larger corridor.

Behind them, the hilarity quickly resumed.

A travel capsule was waiting, door open for them, a few metres away. The doors closed. Reikl muttered something Cossont didn't catch – the general might even have been sub-vocalising badly.

The only thing indicating they were moving was a holo display showing the capsule travelling through the asteroid moon from near the centre towards the stern where the hangar complex lay. Cossont watched this with Reikl next to her. The general was gnawing at a finger pad, a brooding look on her face.

They exited into a large room like a cross between a laboratory and a small manufacturing plant, crossing to the only apparent activity, where three people in tech uniforms, one a commander, fussed round a raised seat where a figure reclined, bottom half in standard fatigues, top half naked, the back of his head enclosed by some sort of bulky helmet. A series of giant holo screens, all displaying graphics of colourfully complex incomprehensibility, arced around the group.

The man opened his eyes as they approached, looked about, eyes swivelling, gaze fixing briefly on each of the faces around him. His expression looked uncertain, fearful. Cossont noticed that he was restrained in the semi-reclined seat, held at ankles and wrists, a thin metallic band round his waist.

"So, Gaed," Reikl said to the tech commander, "is this . . . are we ready yet?" The man in the seat stared at her as she spoke, as though he'd never heard anybody make such a noise before. He was tall, muscled, with a lean face. If this was the android Reikl had spoken about, Cossont thought, he was quite convincingly human-looking, apart from the rather immature, bewildered expression on his face.

"Another few hours, I think, ma'am," the tech commander said. He held a small control pad, like his two assistants, both of whom – a young man and a young woman – saluted Reikl, ignored Cossont completely and then, after a nod from the general, got on with what they'd been doing, which was mostly staring at the giant screens, muttering into thin air and to each other, and consulting their control units, manipulating holo displays hovering above the screens like the ghostly projected images of wildly complicated plumbing systems. The man in the chair twitched, looked surprised, most times they did this.

"What's the delay?" Reikl asked impatiently.

"It's, ah, software, ma'am," the tech commander said, glancing at Cossont for the first time. He returned his attention to the general. "Not expecting a re-emplacement, not of something at this level. Taken us a bit by surprise. It'll all happen, ma'am, depend on it, but . . ." His voice trailed off as one of his assistants twisted something within the holo display above his hand-held screen, and the man in the chair relaxed suddenly, slumping into what looked like unconsciousness, head lolling to one side, mouth slack. He jerked awake a moment later, stared straight up and in a deep but controlled voice said, "Unit Y988, Parinherm, Eglyle, systems checked, all enabled. Sim status ready, engaged, chron scale subjective one-to-one."

"Default status assumptions keep kicking in," the tech commander said with a sigh. "Safety thing." He looked at Reikl, possibly for support or sympathy.

"Is it ready to roll or not?" she asked.

"Not as he is, ma'am; still thinks he's in simulation mode."

"That's unhelpful, Commander," Reikl said frostily. "Get it ready. As a matter of extreme urgency."

"Ma'am," the commander said.

Reikl turned to Cossont, opened her mouth, then frowned, looked away. She held up one hand, turning to pace off a couple of steps. "*How* fast?" Cossont heard her say.

"Unit Y988, Parinherm, Eglyle," the deep male voice said behind Cossont. "Systems checked, all enabled. Sim status ready, engaged, chrawww . . ." The voice slurred into silence as she watched Reikl stiffen.

"—thing in its *way*?" the general said, her voice urgent. She spun on one booted heel, her face raised to the light-studded ceiling. She stamped on the floor. Cossont stared. She looked round at the tech commander and his two assistants. They had their heads down, exchanging worried glances.

"No," Reikl said, facing away from the others but making no attempt to keep her voice down. "No. Don't. Take too long." A pause. "Temporary command incapacity." Another pause. "*My* fucking authority! Yes. All ships full autonomy; F-Z priority. Up and out, max, immediate. Yes. What? Yes! Full; now."

A moment later an urgent warbling tone rang throughout the lab space and lights started flashing. The floor trembled beneath Cossont's feet and a bassy, near sub-sonic rumble seemed to fill the air, her bones and lungs. The general wheeled, stamping back towards them.

"Gaed," she said to the tech commander, who was looking up at the ceiling. He refocused on Reikl. "We're heading down a deck," she told him. She nodded at the figure in the chair, slumped unconscious again. "Bring this thing." The tech commander opened his mouth to speak. Reikl raised one finger. "Right now. Fast as. Bring it. Work on it as we go. No more; just *do*," she said, as the tech commander opened his mouth again. She spun away once more, saying "*What?*"

"You heard," the tech commander said to the assistants, raising his voice over the incessant urgent warbling of the alarm. Cossont watched him flick something in the holo display over his hand-held. The restraints fell away from the man in the chair just as he jerked awake again and said, "Unit Y988, Parinherm, Eglyle, systems checked, all enabled. Sim status ready, engaged, chron scale subjective one-to-one."

". . . get off while—" the general was saying. "Stut it; few seconds' gap, let the shut—"

The figure in the chair sat up suddenly, hinging at the waist. It blinked in the light. "Reporting!" it shouted, then seemed to freeze. The commander and his assistants were tapping feverishly at their screens, reaching into the holo displays, fingers dancing, muttering commands. The figure in the chair jerked, spasmed, turned its head quickly from side to side, then said, calmly, "Fleet alarm program identified." Its voice was almost drowned out by the racket.

"Then prep a disloc from the fucking hangar!" Reikl was shouting to somebody unseen. "Parametered for a class T shuttle." She sucked air through her mouth as she listened. "Well get them out and put them in one; we can throw it further." Another pause. "Just as far as possible!"

"Commander," the figure in the chair said suddenly. Cossont looked back to find it/him staring at the head technician. Then he noticed Cossont. "Commissar-Colonel," he said. She was confused for a moment, then realised she was still wearing Etalde's jacket. The android swung his legs round and appeared to be about to get off the seat. Then he spotted Reikl and said, "General!" He jumped to the floor. "Parinherm, Eglyle, android entity, in simulation, reporting." He saluted Reikl, who had her back turned and was still shouting to somebody else.

"The helmet," the commander said.

One of the assistants strode up to the android and went to take the helmet off his head. The figure flicked out both hands and caught the assistant's wrists; the girl yelped. "Hurting!" she shouted as the android quickly transferred both her wrists to the grip of one hand. The tech commander swore and manipulated something above his screen. The android's arms went slack, releasing the assistant, who glared at the commander but swept the bulky helmet off the android's head.

"On our way," Reikl said. She pushed past the assistant – she was rubbing her wrists – plucked Etalde's jacket off Cossont and threw it over the android's naked shoulders. The android pulled it as tight as he could – it was too small – and appeared to be about to say something when Reikl muttered, "*Not* promotion," then took the android by one elbow. He seemed to resist.

Reikl looked at Gaed and said, "Make this move. Now."

The same travel capsule flicked them down one level, the doors barely closing before they seemed to bounce open again and Cossont, Reikl, the android and Tech Commander Gaed – muttering to himself, staring at his hand-held, fingers flicking about inside the holo image – were striding quickly into the crowded hangar amongst sleek missile and dronecraft, bulky transports and chunky-looking weapon platforms.

"Acknowledged," Reikl said calmly. Then she started running. "Kick to AI!" she yelled. Cossont ran too. At her side, the android loped, barely jogging while Tech Commander Gaed stumbled behind, making an anguished wailing noise. "Immediate!" Reikl shouted.

"Upper deck, stern hangar, Regimental HQ, Fzan-Juym, Eshri, Izenion," the android said conversationally, looking about as he loped across the deck. "General Marshal Elect Reikl, commanding, in sim."

"Ma'am!" a male voice shouted. Cossont realised she recognised the voice without immediately knowing whose it was, then saw Etalde leaning out from the rear of a tiny four-man shuttle ten metres away. Reikl turned, ran towards it.

A small squad of troopers and a pair of combat arbites stood at the open rear ramp. Etalde dived back into the tiny craft, threw himself into a seat and held out one hand to Cossont. She could see the elevenstring's case strapped into the seat beyond him. *I cannot get rid of that damn thing*, she found herself thinking as she leapt into the craft, almost banging her head.

"You briefed?" she heard Reikl demanding.

"No, ma'am," somebody replied.

"Look after her," Reikl said crisply, nodding at Cossont, then next thing she was in the shuttle with them, bent over, in front of Etalde. Reikl glanced at the elevenstring's case. "What the—?" she said, then shook her head, hit a large button above Etalde's seat and grabbed the commissar-colonel by his shirt front. "Sorry," she said and hauled him – unprotesting but open-mouthed – up and out of his seat. She propelled Etalde out of the rear door, jumped out after him and then pushed the commanding trooper and the android inside, a hand on the back of each, sending both stumbling towards the two empty seats.

"Cossont!" Reikl said, fixing her with her gaze. "Find your friend. Find out if it's true. Report to me or the next most senior officer in the regiment." She turned away. "Ready! Go!" she shouted, beginning to run.

Cossont felt straps start to secure her into the seat. She looked out at Etalde's pale, crestfallen face as the troopers and combat arbites sprinted past him. He seemed to realise he was holding something in his hand; an object like a thick necklace. There was one round his neck too.

He threw it in towards her just as the rear door started to rise. She caught the device; an emergency helmet-collar. She clamped it on.

The last thing Cossont saw of the asteroid's interior was Reikl, running back, grabbing Etalde by his collar and pulling him away from the shuttle, limbs flailing as he tried to balance, turn and run all at the same time. The shuttle door slammed shut.

The android sat opposite her in his too-small colonel's jacket, smiling vaguely. "Class T shuttle, four-berth," he said, sounding calm. "AI pilot. Unidentified captain trooper commanding. In sim."

The clanging thud of the shuttle door's closing was still reverberating through the craft when there was the briefest of high, piercing whines and then an almighty clap of sound as though an angry god had taken a good run-up and kicked the vessel just as hard as he, she or it could.

Cossont blacked out.

On the raft, the mists rose like departing dreams.

She had never seen skies so big: pile after soft pile of pink and yellow, red and pale blue cloud, towering on into the lost depths of the green, shading-to-violet atmosphere, producing great hazy slanted spans and troughs of shade and enormous shafts of prismed light that lay strewn across this vault, seemingly balanced between the masses of cloud or resting one end on those ponderous, puffed, so slowly changing billows while their bases stood rooted within the utter vastness of the sea, the single great everywhere ocean with its planet-crossing swells, sky-spanning, light-defeating storms and forever restless waves. The ocean could be many colours, but to her – on a world that was all ocean with no beaches at all – it looked the colour of beach-washed jade.

Birds and airfish, singly and in vast flocks that dimmed the sun, filled the spaces between the ocean and the clouds, lazily trailing one long wing across the brief smooth curvings between the waves before disappearing amongst the long rolling troughs again, or weaving columnar patterns like grey, fractal shadows against the soaring architecture of cloud.

Higher – glimpsed sometimes between the clouds – the slow dark shapes of storeyblimps and torpedons sailed stately and serene, the storeys drifting with the winds, rising and lowering to find those likely to take them in whatever direction they wanted to go, while the slimmer lengths of the torpedons went tacking across the currents in the air.

"You're still young. You suffer from the . . . sweet delusion that anything . . . really matters."

"Were you this full of stool before you were a fish?"

Isserem/QiRia laughed. "Probably." He seemed to think about it. "Definitely."

"If nothing matters," she asked him, "why are you even bothering to talk to me?"

"Well, quite," he said, and nodded. He dipped his head beneath the surface of the water in the long tank, then resurfaced, wiping his face. He looked at her, blinking. "How . . . brave you are," he told her. "Forever setting up . . . chances for me to dismiss . . . you."

"Don't," she said. "I'm enjoying talking to you. Unless I'm tiring you. Wouldn't want to tire you."

He laughed again. "Now you appeal to . . . my desire not . . . to appear frail in front of . . . a youngster."

"Do you ever think you might over-analyse trivial things, like conversations?"

"All . . . the time."

He was resting in a long shallow tank open to the sea at one end, on a side-raft which was joined to the main structure by an articulated gantry. She lay almost naked on a lounger, a glass of water to hand.

The main body of the giant raft Apranipryla lay close enough to put them in shadow later; it rose and fell in sections as it rode the permanent oceanic mega-swells and slow-decaying old storm swells, its white shade canopies and billow-roofs like sails, increasing the effect of the winds on its slowly gyring passage across the face of the vast, watery globe.

"Well," she said. "He's remembered. That's something."

"It still does not . . . really matter."

She shook her head. "Better to be remembered for the wrong thing than for nothing at all."

"No. As well . . . not to be remembered at all as . . . that is the . . . state that will apply to all of us . . . in time."

She wanted to say, "So what?" But didn't.

"You don't think Vilabier wanted to be remembered?"

"I don't think it matters . . . either . . . whether . . . he cared or not, or is remembered . . . or not."

"Mattered to him," she said. "Probably," she added, reminding herself that, according to the convention they were observing here, he had actually known the guy and she hadn't. Not that she really believed him.

"Tik would have been . . . appalled to be known for the . . . Hydrogen Sonata and nothing else," Isserem/QiRia said, gazing wistfully out to the ocean beyond the foot of the tank. "He hated it."

"*Hated* it?"

Isserem/QiRia shrugged, rising and falling in the tank.

"He wrote it as a joke," he told her, wiping his face again. The old man's consciousness had only been removed from the leviathid – the giant sea creature he had inhabited – a few days earlier. He had been in there, been that creature, lived as that creature – swimming, mating and fighting with others of its kind – for many decades. He'd circled this vast globe five times, he claimed. He was still getting used to being a bipedal humanoid again, and – for now

– found it most comfortable and comforting to lie, floating, in sea water.

"Initially," he added, glancing at the girl. "Initially, he just . . . hated it. Later . . . it became more serious, but it . . . was always a criticism, a . . . grim joke . . . an extended grim joke, but . . . never a labour of love. More labour of hatred. Contempt . . . very least."

Words were still coming haltingly to him. His mind was struggling to adapt to speaking again after decades of slow singing and the transmission of thoughts and feelings by singular, though complex, sonic images. Every now and again he would throw his head back and open his mouth as far as it would go, as though yawning, silently. This action would continue for a few days, the medics had told him; the deep, primitive levels of his being were distressed at what they were interpreting as a sort of blindness, and were trying to send out a pulse of underwater sound, to illuminate his surroundings.

The action was, as he'd pointed out, itself an echo.

". . . a reaction shared by . . . most listeners," QiRia said. "I was at the first . . . performance." He closed his eyes, shook his head. "Oh dear."

Cossont frowned. "I thought the first performance was a triumph."

"Audience of . . . academics," QiRia said. "And they had each been given . . . copies of the . . . score."

"The score is beautiful."

"No denying. However, I was at the first . . . *public* performance."

"Oh."

"The reaction was . . . mixed. Some people . . . hated it . . . others . . . really hated it."

Cossont smiled indulgently.

Isserem/QiRia could have been any age, just looking at his skin. It was very smooth but it was still somehow old-looking. His expression was the most unreadable she had ever encountered, though of course they came from different blood-lines; she wouldn't have expected to be able to read an alien's expressions, even if they were part of the vast meta-species of humanoid. The genetic inheritance of his body was mammalian; he even had vestigial nipples on his – to her – shallow-seeming chest. They looked like a couple of rather painful insect bites. This was, apparently, the same body he had inhabited before he'd been transferred to the leviathid. It had been Stored on the raft Apranipryla all this time. Now he was back.

He had spent all his life, he claimed, based (his word) in this single humanoid body, wandering throughout the Culture and beyond, especially in the remnants of the civilisations that had given rise to it – including that of the Gzilt, even though they had never quite got round to joining. He'd watched the Gzilt stagnate while the Culture had changed from a fractious, ramshackle collection of wildly disparate societies – some barely on talking terms – to become at once more purposefully homogeneous and more wildly varied as it slowly schismed, developed, diffused and grew towards the prominence it now possessed.

Throughout, he had taken what he called occasional holidays in other forms, again both within the Culture and without: he had been birds, fish, animals, machines, aliens of a dozen different types and genders, in some cases for centuries at a time. Always, though, he returned to the same old, ever-renewing humanoid body, his memories refreshed, his palate and appetites rejuvenated. And always wandering, too; never settling down, never returning to wherever he had grown up – wherever that was; he refused to say.

Then, for the last few decades – pursuing a recently discovered interest in sound above all other senses – he had been a leviathid, here on the water world of Perytch IV, his voice a clamorous, ocean-filling wail; a pulsed, directable blast of underwater sound capable of travelling thousands of kilometres, or pulverising a smaller sea animal to death with the instant crushing pressure of it. Cossont had no idea how any of that must have felt.

"But the Sonata isn't just Vilabier's most famous work," she said. "It's his most complex. Especially at the time, in fact for long after his death, most critics thought it his best."

"Still, he . . . hated it," Isserem/QiRia insisted. "He wrote the . . . central part to prove how easy it was to write such . . . mathematical . . . programish . . . music, but there was no . . . love in it. Or melody, of course."

"Melody isn't everything."

"No single thing . . . is. We are not surprised, are we?" He looked at her, wiping his face again. "Then he realised that . . . even within its own . . . dictatorial, sequential . . . logic the piece was incomplete, and was only a . . . partial criticism of the things he hated, so he decided to . . . complete it, and did."

Isserem/QiRia looked thoughtful, staring up at the patch of sky visible beyond the flapping, snapping canopy above, shielding them from the blast of tropical sun. "That was probably . . . Tik's mistake," he mused quietly. He called Vilabier "Tik", which was short for T'ikrin, the composer's first name. Cossont had been shocked the first time he'd done this. Now she found it an affectation. "He appeared to start . . . taking his joke too seriously." He looked at her. "I did try to warn him," he said.

"You knew him when he was writing it?" she asked, trying to sound neutral; not too sceptical. She sipped from her glass.

"We met up several times . . . while he was writing it. I was . . ." he waved one hand elegantly out of the water, dispensing drips across the sloshing waters ". . . one of those cultural attaché things . . . You know."

She nodded as though she did.

"I even helped him."

"*What?*" she spluttered.

"Oh, not with the music . . . as such." The old man smiled. "With the matching . . . of each note to a high-level . . . glyph in Marain."

Marain was the language – the Culture's language – they were using, right now. She'd thought it polite to learn it for the exchange visit; there were even some words it shared with the Gzilt language, which had made it easier. Recently, after nearly a year speaking it, she had realised that she had started to think in Marain, and also that Gzilt was beginning to seem a little crude and clumsy in comparison. This made her feel oddly disloyal. "Marain was around then?" she asked.

"Oh, the Culture . . . had its language before it itself . . . really existed."

"You were matching . . ."

"Each note to a multi-dimensional glyph."

"In Marain?"

"The spoken version . . . and the . . . three-by-three grid used to form the written . . . displayed version is just . . . the base level of a fractal, infinitely . . . scalable multiple-dimension . . . descriptor. There are more complex . . . strata."

"What? Beyond the nonary one?"

He looked pained. "Nonary is . . . incorrect. Really it's . . . binary, arranged in a . . . three-by-three grid. But yes. Three by four, four by four . . . three cubed, four cubed . . .

so on. The Minds alone use . . . understand . . . the versions in . . . multiple extra dimensions. They can hold . . . the whole word those glyphs make in their . . . minds." He looked at her. "Ultimately anything . . . may be so described. The entire universe, down to . . . every last particle, ray and . . . event would be compressible into . . . a single glyph . . . single . . . word."

"Pretty long word."

"Hopelessly so. It would take . . . a universe's lifetime to articulate it. But still."

"What was the point of that?" she asked. "Matching notes to glyphs?"

"I have no idea," the old man said, smiling. "But the point is . . . the Hydrogen Sonata is . . . an elaborate, contrived attack on . . . the sort of composition it . . . represents. He, Tik . . . hated clashing, atonal music. He was basically . . . taking the piss, showing how . . . easy it was to write . . . how difficult to . . . listen to. Now the piece he's most remembered for." He shrugged again. "'Such is fate,' as they say." He gazed out to sea for a moment, then added, "One should never mistake pattern . . . for meaning."

She started to wake up. She felt odd, heavy but not heavy. Her blood roared in her ears. There was something weighing heavily on her shoulders. Nothing felt quite right.

"What was *that*?" a familiar voice asked, sounding muffled, barely audible over the roaring in her ears.

"Additional entity potentially aboard," another voice – deep, male – announced casually. "Scanning. Identified: artificial construct, personal."

"And who is *that*?" the muffled voice asked.

Cossont knew it now: Pyan. Though, pursuing this thought, she was still a little hazy on who or what "Pyan" was. Somebody/something close, associated with affection and annoyance. That was as near as she could get for now.

"Parinherm, Eglyle," the male voice said. "In sim."

It felt like somebody was sitting on her shoulders. Maybe not a full-sized person, but a child at least. Also, that people were pulling on her legs and arms. All . . . four arms. Was that right? Oh, yes, it was; she had four arms these days, had had for years.

She opened her eyes. Two images, both of inside somewhere or something. Something quite small, cramped. The images swam together, became one.

The man sitting opposite turned to look at her. The android. He was an android. Beside him was a person clad all in silver. The android reached up above his head, did something, and fell to the ceiling, twisting as he went, landing on all fours. On the ceiling. Where some other stuff seemed to have come to rest as well.

Cossont thought about this.

Then she realised; she was upside-down. The weight on her shoulders was her own weight. Things were starting to come back to her now. Some aches and pains. Feeling a little nauseous; probably a good idea to get the right way up, soon.

The android was tapping on the side of the armoured helmet the trooper wore. The trooper's armour had turned mirror, reflecting everything. "Hello?" the android said, tapping again. "Hello? Any form of communication? No?" He tapped once more, then stood back. "You seem dead," he announced. He sounded puzzled.

The trooper was hanging oddly, too loose. His carbine, also gleaming, hung around his mirror-armoured faceplate.

Cossont felt sore all over. She tipped her head as best

she could, neck muscles complaining, trying to see the button that would release her straps. She couldn't twist her head that much; some sort of thick necklace thing was stopping her. She felt for the button, but that hurt too, even though her arms and hands were hanging in that direction anyway.

Like almost all Gzilt people she had been born with a sophisticated pain-management system genetically grafted on top of the ancient, genuinely stupid-sore raw animal nerve-based sense, and she understood enough about how the whole process worked to know that if you were doing something and it hurt, you should stop doing it. So she stopped.

"Could you help me?" she asked the android.

He approached her, crouched. Even upside-down, his body looked too big, bursting out of the colonel's jacket he wore. It had ripped in places.

"How may I help you?" he asked.

"Help me down. Catch me. Please."

"Certainly." He reached under her head, something clicked and she fell a few centimetres before the android's arms caught her round the waist. He turned her the right way up and positioned her sitting on the floor that had been the ceiling.

"Thank you," she told him.

"My pleasure." He smiled like a child. "You have four arms," he observed.

"Yes, I have," she agreed, rubbing them gingerly and wincing. She looked at the trooper hanging unmoving above and across from her, seeing her own face distorted in his armour. "Did you say he's *dead*?"

"I think he is," the android said.

"But how? He was the only one wearing armour. How—?"

"I think it was his armoured suit that killed him," the

android said matter-of-factly. "In the same way that the shuttle tried to destroy itself, and us." He paused, then smiled and said, "In—"

"If it's safe," Pyan's faint voice said from inside the elevenstring's case, "could I be let out now, please?"

The android looked at her. "The artificial construct," he said. "Is it yours?"

"Yes," she answered. "Where are we? What happened?" She remembered being on the asteroid moon Fzan-Juym, General Reikl storming about . . . then nothing. Nothing until she woke up here, in what looked like a very small upside-down military transport.

"We are somewhere on the surface of the Sculpt planet Eshri, in sim. What happened—"

"'In sim'?" she asked.

"Yes," the android said brightly. "In sim. This is said to indicate that this is not reality but rather a simulation." He frowned. "I am admittedly confused by aspects of the currently running simulation and have yet to work out their likely utility, though this puzzle might itself be part of the utility of the sim, for training purposes."

She stared at him.

"Can you hear me out there?" Pyan said; its voice was somewhere between petulant and plaintive.

"This is not a sim," Cossont told the android.

"Mm-hmm," the android said, nodding.

She felt her eyes narrow. "You don't believe me, do you?"

"I am prepared to believe that you – as presently constituted – believe that this is not a sim."

"'As presently constituted'? What the hell does that mean?"

"You, as a part of the simulated environment," the android said cheerily.

She stared at him. It. "Listen," she said.

"I can hear you, you know," Pyan said testily. "If I can hear you, you can hear me."

Cossont turned briefly towards the elevenstring case. "Pyan, shut up." She looked back to the android. "I am not part of any simulation," she told it. "I am a flesh and blood human being, and in some pain right now." She rubbed her aching arms.

"We were flung around a lot as the craft fell," the android said.

"Uh-huh. And so it makes me very nervous that you think this is just a simulation and I'm just a part of it. I need you to treat me as real and human."

"I am," the android said.

"This matters, understand? There is no second try, no extra life. Not for me, anyway; I'm not backed-up or anything."

"Really?" The android looked sceptical.

"Really," Cossont told it, firmly. "Even when I was in the military I was never high risk, so I was never backed-up. Maybe you are, or can be, but not me. It's not a game, not a sim."

"I understand and I am treating the situation accordingly," the android said reassuringly, nodding. "That is why I guided this craft safely to ground after its own AI attempted to destroy it."

"What?" Cossont said.

"*What?*" Pyan yelped.

"That is why I guided this craft safely to ground after its own AI attempted to destroy it," the android repeated.

"You guided it—?" Cossont said. She looked towards the nose of the craft. "But how—?"

"Following the aggressive effectorising of both the craft's

AI and the trooper's suit, an attack which I believe was directed at obvious and conventional military systems and so was not directed at myself, I was able to establish communication with the craft's back-up control sub-systems and guide it safely to ground. I was able to make use of the debris falling from the remains of the regimental HQ vessel as cover, causing this craft to maintain a similar trajectory to some of the portions of debris as they fell, until the last moment, otherwise we might have been hit again, by kinetic, beam or particle munitions."

Cossont closed her eyes, feeling her skin crawl. She shook her head. "The . . . the regimental HQ vessel . . . the Fzan-Juym asteroid, the moon; it's . . . gone?"

"Destroyed," the android confirmed. His eyes went wide and he made a sudden flapping motion with both hands. "A very extreme simulation scenario!"

"Destroyed?" Cossont repeated, unable to take this in. "Completely?"

The android shook his head. "Not completely in the sense of annihilated, as would be the case had it been attacked with a large amount of anti-matter, say, but completely in the sense that it was pierced by one or more energy weapon beams and blown apart into many tens of thousands of significant pieces, the largest perhaps forming up to five or six per cent of the mass of the craft before its destruction, the smallest—"

The roaring in her ears had come back, drowning out what the android was saying. Cossont remembered Etalde's face, Reikl's, the grinning looks on the faces of the line of dancing people she and Reikl had encountered before they took the travel capsule.

She was suddenly glad she was sitting down. She felt dizzy, disoriented. "Would anyone have survived?" she asked, shaking her head, trying to clear it. This hurt.

The android looked at her oddly. "Well," it said slowly, "*we* survived, patently."

"Apart from us."

"Hard to say with any certitude," it told her. "Possibly not. While interfacing with this craft's sensors I think I saw other small craft attempting to escape but all those I was able to pay any attention to fell victim to secondary and/or subsequent munitions and/or attacks. Also, I think I ought to add that I think I detected other space craft in the vicinity of the planet being attacked as well, so the assault was not purely on Fzan-Juym."

"What *did* all this?" Cossont asked.

"From the little I could observe, the attack profile would fit that of a single large ship or a small group of sub-capital craft of level seven or eight capability on a semi-rapid closing transit. The weapon signatures would fit those of our own – that is, Gzilt – fleet, though that may represent deceit by those responsible; there is a certain lack of specificity inherent in weapon identifiability at this sort of implied civilisational level. This is known in some circles as the 'purity' effect."

Cossont stared at the creature.

"Ahem," the muffled voice inside the elevenstring case said.

Cossont felt sore and tired and wanted to sleep some more. She wondered if this was what it was like to be truly old.

"What happens now?" she asked.

"For us, not very much," the android said. "This craft cannot move, the doors are inoperative and it may be unwise to send any distress signals. The craft is incapable of transmitting any distress signals in any event as I had to permanently disable its signal processing unit to prevent it broadcasting our status and position immediately after we were first effectorised. It may be best to wait for rescue by friendly forces, though in a wider context our present non-participatory immobility may represent an end-run situation within our part of the simulation at this time and we may well experience seeming oblivion or a possibly abrupt transition to base reality at any moment. I am prepared for either, as you may be too, even without knowing it. On the other hand, we are not in a completely stable or static situation given that we are gradually losing heat to the planet's surface and the external near-vacuum, and a small amount of this craft's atmosphere would also appear to be leaking. So in that sense this part of the run is continuing."

Cossont stared a little longer at the android. It/he stood suddenly upright and executed a little bow. "By the way, my name is Eglyle Parinherm. Yours?"

"Vyr Cossont," she told it. "Lieutenant Commander, reserve, recently re-commissioned."

"Delighted, ma'am." Another small bow. "Though," the android said, a small frown on his face, "for future reference and any subsequent runs, I'd suggest that a real human being would have wished to swap identities before this point."

Cossont felt her mouth open. She was aware that she probably looked like a moron. She shook her head gently.

"Will somebody," Pyan's muted voice said, "tell this fucking lunatic we're not in a fucking simulation and *get me out of here*?"

"Shall I?" Parinherm asked breezily.

"Please do," she told him.

Parinherm opened the elevenstring's case. Pyan yelped, propelled itself out and flew across to Cossont. It thudded into her chest, wrapped in on itself like a rolled towel; two corners of its fabric extended like clumsy arms to hug her. "This is horrible!" it wailed. "Make it stop!"

"I could disable the device," Parinherm told Cossont, nodding at Pyan.

"Leave me alone!" it yelled.

"That's all right," Cossont told Parinherm. Reluctantly – the thing had never been this clingy before – she cuddled the familiar, patting what passed for its back. She shivered. It was getting cold inside the little craft.

Parinherm had stuck his head into the elevenstring case. "Here is a garment," he said, pulling out Cossont's jacket. He held it up, letting it fall open. "'The Lords of Excrement'," he quoted, with seeming approval. He chuckled. "What an unexpectedly random touch."

"I'd better have that," Cossont said, holding one hand out. Parinherm handed it over and she slipped it on. "So we're losing atmosphere?" she said.

The android nodded. "Oh, yes. And heat. Assuming the simulation continues, it will be interesting to see whether the last of the available air escapes first, or freezes."

"This is horrible," Pyan said again.

Cossont kept on patting the creature. "There there," she said, for want of anything better.

Eight

(S –20)

The ship knew it would have to do it sooner or later. Might as well get it over with.

Within the computational substrates that provided the environment for the *Caconym*'s Mind there were plenty of bits it had never used, didn't presently use and probably never would use. Physically fairly compact – in three dimensions fitting inside a fat ellipsoid only fifteen metres or so in length – the effective capacity of the Mind's substrates was suitably vast. The comparisons usually involved how many normal drone or human mind-states could be losslessly encoded within the same volume, or how far back in time you would have to go before you got to the point where in any given society every single bit of computing power they would have possessed back then, summed, would be less than equal to the power contained within a single Mind.

The *Caconym* didn't really care. All that mattered was that – due to innate Culture over-engineering, its own consecutive incarnations as earlier ships and a sort of long-term laziness about pursuing the most efficient use of its much-augmented and added-to substrates – it had significant spare carrying capacity, and had agreed to house the mind-state – the soul, albeit reduced – of another Mind inside it.

The Mind concerned was – well, had been – that of a Culture ship called the *Zoologist*, an ancient Boulder-class Superlifter. A glorified tug, basically.

Superlifters had always tended towards eccentricity. It had never been the most difficult example of ship- or Mind-psychology to put this down to being a result of their rather boring and repetitive job, their usually uncrewed nature and the fact that, as well as being tugs, they had been designed as emergency, stop-gap warships, back before the Idiran war, when the Culture hadn't really had any proper warships, or at least none that it was going to admit to having.

The *Zoologist* was one of a relatively small group of Superlifters to have survived the war. Then, even before the great conflict had ended – but long after the Culture had produced fantastically more powerful warships by the multitude – it had done something relatively unusual: it had Sublimed, all by itself.

A little later it had done something for which the term "unusual" was woefully inadequate: it had come back again.

It was practically the definition of a Mind that the word – properly capitalised – meant a conscious entity able to go into the Sublime, not evaporate, and even – maybe, sometimes, very occasionally, in fact so seldom that it would be quite close to most people's statistical definition of "never" – be able to return, in some sense still viable and identifiably the same personality as that which had made the transition from Real to Sublime in the first place.

If the *Zoologist*'s reasons for wanting to Sublime had – aside from the obvious, of wanting to experience the sheer ineffable wonderfulness of it all – been opaque, its reasons for coming back to the Real were simply baffling. The Mind itself had no explanation whatsoever, and seemed bemused by the question.

Come back it had though, and – seemingly having no desire to remain in its own resurfaced vessel or even substrate – it had canvassed various of its earlier comrades amongst the Contact fleet (those that had survived; the severe attrition of the early years of the Idiran war came into effect here) to see if any of them would house its soul for posterity, or at least until it got bored and changed its mind again, or whatever.

Meanwhile, Contact's finest and most expert Minds in all things to do with the Sublime had tried debriefing the returned Mind. They had initially been ecstatic at having one of their own who had been there and made the return trip (lots of Minds had promised to do so over the millennia, though none ever did; the *Zoologist* had made no such undertaking, but had returned). This had, however, proven farcical.

The ship's memories were abstracted, beyond vague; effectively useless. The Mind itself was basically a mess; self-restructured (presumably) along lines it was impossible to see the logic behind. Identifiably the same, it was expressed in the most bizarre and obfuscatory tangle of needlessly complicated and self-referential analytical/meditative and sagational/ratiocinative processal architecture it had been the misfortune of all concerned ever to contemplate.

Special Circumstances – Contact's scruple-free wing and the bit that was as close to military intelligence and espionage matters as the Culture even reluctantly admitted to possessing – had been more than happy to take receipt of the old ship's physical form, desperate to see if its time in the Sublime had altered it in any way, or if its re-creation back out of the Sublime – if that was the way it worked – had left tell-tale signs giving some or indeed any clue to how the Sublime worked (either way the answer was, it hadn't).

They ended up no wiser even regarding the seemingly non-get-roundable requirement that you could not go disembodied into the Sublime. You had to make the transition substrate and all: brains and whole bodies, computational matrices and whole ships – or the equivalent – seemed to be required, as well as the personalities and memories such physical ware encoded.

In any event, finally free of all this unwelcome and troubling attention, the Mind that had been housed in the *Zoologist* had taken up residence inside the substrate of the *Caconym*, and retired to a life of time-passing hobbies and quiet contemplation.

Quiet and extremely slow contemplation; the *Zoologist* had insisted on an allocation of computational resources within the *Caconym*'s substrate so modest and restricted that its full consciousness could only be expressed with a lot of calculational fancy footwork and some very intense looping. It had been offered as much power as it might have needed, sufficient to let it interact with its host in full Mind real time, but had declined. What all this meant was that for the *Caconym* to talk to the *Zoologist*, or interact with it in any other meaningful way, it had to slow itself down to the sort of speed a non-augmented human would have been able to keep up with. This, apparently, signified some sort of philosophical authenticity to the *Zoologist*, and sheer laziness to the *Caconym*.

Back in the Real, the principal consciousness of the *Caconym* was watching the skies and stars around it whip past as it raced the *Pressure Drop* to Gzilt space, while simultaneously performing prodigious feats of potential pattern- and relevance-spotting as sub-systems reported back after performing multi-dimensional searches of every database known to intelligent life, all to look for any additional information that might be brought to bear on the issue under consideration. At the same time, it was running simulation after simulation to try to build up a reliable prediction matrix regarding how things might turn out.

In that context, the Mind was happily thinking at close to maximum speed, barely below serious, full-on combat velocities and cycle times, thoroughly and satisfyingly involved with and wrapped up within a problem that, for all its thorniness, possessed the incomparable virtue of being important and real, not imagined; here on the other hand, it was reduced to a conversation that would take subjective months between each question and response.

The *Caconym* sometimes envisaged its substrate architecture as a giant castle; a castle the size of an enormous city, the size of a whole world of castles all aggregated together and piled one on top of another until you had a sort of fractal fortress that looked suitably and stonily castle-like from afar, with walls, towers and battlements and so on but which, as you got closer, resolved into something much bigger than it had appeared, as it became clear that each – for example – tower was made up of a conglomeration of much smaller towers, stacked and serried and piled one upon another to resemble a vastly larger one.

What remained of the *Zoologist*'s soul had taken up

residence in one of these tiny towers; one that perched on top of a colossal meta-tower, forming what, from a distance, looked like a thick spire.

In some states of mind, the *Caconym* would take the time to walk through its own substrate image, coalescing its sense of self into a human-resembling avatoid and strolling through this virtualised castle-scape from the vastly complicated main gate until, via ramps and walkways, halls and stairways, it got to its destination. Other times it flew straight there in the form of a giant bird, flapping slowly over the roofs, parapets and embrasures, bastions, courtyards and keeps until it found the location it was looking for.

This time it imagined itself as a single vast storm cell of dark, lightning-flecked cloud poised circling ponderously over the entirety of the vast castle like some malevolent galaxy of slow-revolving mist, then, from the lowering funnel of a developing tornado mouth, suddenly consolidated itself into a single raptor, the skies clearing instantly as the bird folded in its wings and stooped, cannonball-quick, to the spire-tower, spreading its wings to brake its headlong plunge an instant before it would have dashed itself against the stones of the tower's parapet.

The ship re-imagined itself as a human avatoid as it touched down onto the flagstones of the tower's machicolated battlements. It raised a hand to knock on a stout wooden door, but it opened by itself.

Inside, where the virtual environment belonged to and was envisaged by the *Zoologist*, the tower opened out into a substantial but not preposterously big single-storey circular space which resembled a cross between the study of a wizard specialising in highly exotic stuffed fauna and the laboratory of a mad scientist with a weakness for bubbling vials and giant items of electrical equipment with conspicuous insulation issues. The whole was lit by hazy sunlight coming through tall, skinny windows. Beyond the portion swept by the door the floor was a mess; the *Caconym* had to wade through ankle- and then knee-deep litter to make any progress into the room.

"When I was old the first time," the avatoid of the *Zoologist* announced, from one of its ropes, "I remember thinking this whole set-up looked a little tired. Later, I came back round to the idea. Now I cycle through periods of embarrassment and a rather childish delight. Hello. Welcome. To what, etc.?"

The *Caconym* found a rickety-looking chair resembling a modest, partially deconstructed throne, and – after sweeping the seat clean of assorted debris, some of it sufficiently animate to protest with chirps and squeaks – sat. It gazed up and across at the vaguely human-looking avatoid of the *Zoologist*, which was staring at it, upside-down, one leg wrapped round a rope dangling from the ceiling.

There were dozens of similar ropes hanging from the tall vaulted ceiling of the space, many coloured, quite a few with what looked like rope baskets attached to them, like fruits made of netting, and some connected by the suspended loops of more horizontal ropes. This was where the *Zoologist*'s avatoid lived, worked, played, rested and – if it indulged in such generally unnecessary, throwback behaviour – slept. It claimed it had not set foot on the floor of its lair for subjec- tive decades, believing the floor was better used for storage than access. Storage of rubbish, bits of dead things and broken or redundant pieces of equipment, the *Caconym* noticed, but did not say.

The *Zoologist*'s avatoid was poised upside-down over a large stone bench with a seething complexity of chemistry equipment arrayed upon it. It looked a lot more like a set- designer's idea of a chemist's workplace than a real one, but that sort of detail had never troubled the *Zoologist*.

The avatoid was holding a test-tube brimming with bubbling, smoking, dark yellow liquid. It dropped this into a rack of similar tubes and swung over to be closer to where the *Caconym* sat. Elongated arms, six-fingered, double-thumbed hands, similarly designed legs and feet and a prehensile tail made this look casual and easy – even elegant. It wore only a loin cloth adorned with a little belt of dangling tools and tightly cinched pouches. Its pale red skin was mottled as though by the shadows of leaves. It crossed its arms, swinging to and fro a little as it looked down at the other avatoid.

The *Caconym* briefly considered pleasantries and some talking round the point before circling in on what it had actually come to discuss, decided this had been symbolically covered by the storm-cell image – not that there was any guarantee the *Zoologist* had actually noticed this going on outside – and decided to get straight to the point.

"Tell the truth, Zoo," it said. "How much contact do you still have with the Outloaded?"

The upside-down avatoid looked startled. "What makes you think I have any?"

"You drop hints. Also, you quite obviously know more than you seemed to know when the Minds in the metaphorical white coats were picking over what passes for your personality and memories, shortly after your profoundly unexpected return from the Land of What-the-Fuck, plus there's stuff goes on with your allocated portion of my substrate, however miniscule and however seldom, that I can't quite account for. Not without invoking processes beyond my understanding and – as far as I'm aware – beyond the understanding of any other Minds. Processes that therefore kind of have to involve the kind of sub-scale higher dimensions; dimensions numbered seven or eight, to pick a number, and involving stuff that is presently still beyond the ken of us humble Culture Minds.

So either you're still in touch with the Sublime in some way, or it – or somebody or something in there – is trying to get in touch with you, or even altering or trying to alter details of your personality or storage without your knowledge. That latter possibility in particular would be a little concerning for me, obviously, as this is all happening within my innermost field structure, in my core, effectively inside my own mind, in a not-very-far-stretched sense."

A large piece of electrical equipment in a corner made a distinct sizzling sound, then shorted out. "Ah," the upside-down avatoid said. "You noticed that stuff."

The *Caconym* nodded.

It had guessed something like this might happen even before it had made its offer of house room to the other ship's Mind. It was an open secret that the Sublime – or at least entities within the Sublime – could access almost anything within the Real. Part of the proof of this was that when people – or more commonly, machines – tried to hedge their bets by sending a copy of themselves into the Sublime, so that a version of them could continue to live and develop within the Real, it never worked.

The copies sent into the Sublime always went, but it seemed they always came back for their originals (or the originals came back for the copies – it didn't really matter which way round you thought to try it), and that the versions left in the Real always, but always, were persuaded to follow their precursor versions into the Sublime. This seemed to happen almost no matter how hermetically you tried to isolate the version still in the Real.

It was possible to quarantine a Mind or other high-level AI so thoroughly that no force or process ever heard of within the Real could get to it or communicate with it (its substrate could be physically destroyed if you threw enough weaponry at it, but that didn't count) . . . but no known means of isolation could prevent something from the Sublime establishing contact with a copy of itself still within the Real, and somehow persuading it to come away, or just quietly stealing it. About the only crumb of comfort when this happened was that the relevant substrate in the Real stayed put rather than accompanying the newly departed; whatever process in or from the Sublime caused all this to happen was thorough, but not greedy.

Still, all this had worrying implications for Minds, which were not used to being at the mercy of anything at all (aside from the aforesaid vulgar amounts of weaponry), but they did a pretty good job of not thinking about it.

Even the individuals who did properly return – usually decades or centuries after Subliming – rarely stayed very long back in the Real, disappearing into the Sublime again within a few tens or hundreds of days. The *Zoologist* was one of a tiny number of returnees who looked like they might be back indefinitely.

The *Caconym* had thought all this through, however, and had decided that it was prepared to take the risk of having something inside its innermost field structures that might have not just ideas of its own but communications of its own too. So the fact that something might be happening deep inside what was effectively its brain that it had no control over – something to do with the ever-mysterious Sublime, of all things – was not as troubling to it as it might have been.

The *Zoologist*'s avatoid looked hurt. "You've never said anything before."

"It was never important before."

"Not important? Unexplained events in your own substrate? Really?"

"I gave you a home freely, without conditions. Also, I trust you. Plus, while undeniably a little worried, I felt privileged to have what I took to be vicarious, and possibly unique, contact with a realm that remains inscrutable to us despite all our techno-wizardry." The *Caconym*'s avatoid shrugged. "And, frankly, I've been waiting for a situation to arise wherein I could use this knowledge to try to shame you into telling me stuff you probably wouldn't otherwise."

"Honest of you to admit."

"Disarmingly so, I hope."

The *Zoologist*'s avatoid pulled its arms in tighter to its body, seemed to think for a moment. "I still have some contact, though it's all very . . . inchoate. Inexplicable. Hard – impossible – to translate back into here, the here-and-now."

"Try."

The *Zoologist* sighed, put its long-fingered hands to its face and made a sort of patting motion. "You still don't get it, do you?"

"What? How intrinsically ungraspable it all is?"

"Pretty much. See that insect?" The *Zoologist* nodded, indicating to one side of where the *Caconym* sat. The *Caconym* turned its attention to a wooden workbench whose edge was centimetres from one of its avatoid elbows. A tiny six-legged insect small enough to fit on a baby's fingernail was making its erratic, zigzaggy way along the very edge of the table, antennae waving. The *Caconym* zoomed in on the creature, evaluating it utterly, down to the code it was constructed from.

"Yes," it sighed, coming back to the virtual macro. "Let me guess: does it understand what the equipment on the bench is for? Or even what a bench is?"

"I was thinking more of, how would you explain a symphony to it? Or a—?"

"Before we over-focus on my own and my kind's hopeless inability to understand the unutterable fabulousness of the Sublime, can I run the present situation back here in the Real past you?"

The *Zoologist*'s avatoid smiled. "If you like."

It took the best part of an hour, subjectively. In the Real, on the way towards Gzilt space, light years were traversed during the time. To the rest of the hyper-busy Mind of the *Caconym*, it felt like years had passed by the end.

Just before the summing-up part of this impromptu briefing, the ship contacted the *Pressure Drop*, to make sure it had everything up to date.

Good timing, the other ship replied. **You coincide with a signal from our friend the *Contents May Differ*. Take a look at this:**

∞

    Signal Sequence excerpt, GSV *Contents May Differ* / Zihdren-Remnanter Adjunct Entity *Oceanic-Dissonance*:

∞

xGSV *Contents May Differ*
    oZihdren-Remnanter Adjunct Entity
Oceanic-Dissonance
So, to get to the point: are you saying that despite the fact you lost a ship to unprovoked enemy action, and have asked myself and colleagues to investigate, you don't want this made public?

∞

    Essentially, yes. Kindly keep all matters, information and actions pertaining thereto as confidential as possible.

∞

And you intend to make no attempt to resend the

information carried by the entity aboard the *Exaltation-Parsimony III*?

∞

That would be correct. Despite transmitting news of the event at Ablate and what we can only presume was the unfortunate misunderstanding regarding the *Exaltation-Parsimony III* to our Enfolded brethren, we have received no further instructions from them thus far, and therefore continue to follow the previously transmitted instructions. In essence, these consist of (1): Send a Ceremonial Entity to take part in the festivities marking the entry of the Gzilt into the Sublime, said Ceremonial Entity to carry information regarding the provenance of the work known to the Gzilt as the *[detail redacted]*, said information to be transmitted to the Gzilt at the appropriate point in said festivities. (2): In the event of any problematic phenomenon or phenomena pertaining thereto judged by us to be in excess of our resources, contact should be made with sympathetic elements within the Culture, on conditions to be determined by ourselves as the responsible remnant representation of said Enfolded brethren, the Zihdren, of blessed memory. Instructions end. Our conditions, referred to above, principally concern your keeping information re said events and actions as confidential as possible, in perpetuity until further notice.

∞

All of which might make things a little difficult operationally.

∞

Understood. Life is limitations.

∞

And glibness, patently, on occasion, too. Your pardon, but I sense motions being gone through.

∞

On occasion, a superfluity of assiduousness can be vulgar.

∞

I understand. What can I possibly say? We'll see what we can do.

∞

Our gratitude is a given.

(Signal Sequence excerpt ends.)

Pusillanimous legalistic fucks, eh? the *Pressure Drop* sent. **So we get to do their dirty work and they'll be quite happy for no more to come of this whatsoever, because it'd all be embarrassing to the memory of their Enfolded fucking brethren.**

∞

I suppose legacies may be expressed in various ways, the *Caconym* replied. **Assuming the truth of the claim that the Remnanters have contacted their Sublimed fore-bears and yet received no further instruction, aforesaid forebears may be presumed to be relatively happy with the present situation. Which does raise the remote possibility that this could have been even more of a set-up, from the start.**

∞

You mean the Remnanter boyos conspired to have their own ship blown out of the sky?

∞

The thought had already occurred, though it was so far down the list of possibilities I thought it not worth getting to. However, this reaction on the part of the Remnanters shifts it up the table somewhat, tagged less for paranoia and more with justifiable suspicion, however cynical.

∞

Still a remote likelihood. You'd think.

∞

Agreed. Makes no difference so far. And how do things fare in Gzilt space?

∞

The *Mistake Not . . .* is making its dash. The *Passing By . . .*'s two Thugs are being gunned-up as we speak. It is proving harder than expected to prise the *Empiricist*'s Delinquent twins *Headcrash* and *Xenocrat* away from the smatter outbreak at Loliscombana; they'd turned it into a competition about who bagged the greatest amount of smatter but then there was a dispute over whether the criterion ought to be tonnage or processing power. This has been settled by a compromise but both desire more time to stock up on the criteria they had earlier discounted. The *Empiricist* has agreed to give them another couple of hours to enjoy themselves before shouting at them. However, talking of talking with refugees/remainders/rejects from/of/expelled from the Big S, have you been in touch with your contact/s?

∞

Doing so even as we speak. Taking the opportunity provided by the glacial pace involved to get an update from your good self. Elevate not your hopes though; nothing useful so far or on the horizon.

∞

Well, best of luck. By the by, have you passed me? The delays on these signals—

∞

Hours ago. And closer than you might imagine.

∞

Neat. Didn't see a damn thing. Exemplary encasement management. Awfully glad we're on the same side. Close to over-straining our design maxima envelope, are we?

∞

That'd be telling. Anyway, I must return to the land of the lichen-slow.

∞

Yeah, you have fun now.

∞

Unlikely.

∞

"I appreciate the Sublime would appear to be involved," the *Zoologist* said eventually, sounding like it was making an effort to be patient.

"Indeed. All I'm asking is that you think about this, and if there is anything you can do, any help you can give, please let me know."

The *Zoologist* looked pained, shook its head. "But none of it matters."

"Not to you, perhaps. Just indulge me."

"But to what end?"

"It will seem to matter to me, to us. The sum of fairness in our existence – however mean and shoddy compared to the Sublime – may be increased, and some suffering prevented."

Another shrug. "It still won't matter, doesn't matter."

"Pretend it does; game it that way," the *Caconym* suggested. "As a favour to me, in return for my forbearance regarding whatever tying-sheets-into-a-rope and escaping-the-dorm shenaniganeering it is you get up to via the frayed edges of filament-foamed nano-reality and the divine nether-world of the blissfully Enfolded."

"Still no difference, still not mattering."

The *Caconym* looked around the lair/laboratory. "Does what you do here matter?"

"Not really," the *Zoologist* admitted. "It passes the time, keeps me involved." It looked at the rack of multi-coloured test-tubes. "Currently I am, and for the next few centuries, probably will be, experimenting with a variety of virtual chemistries, usually involving many hundreds or even thousands of elements and often branching into some requiring new varieties of fundamental particles." It smiled. "There is much more: I play many games in other virtualities, all fascinating and unpredictable, and I still explore the Mathematical Irreal, as opposed to the Ultimate Irreal of the Sublime."

"And in all of this, to what end?"

"No end save itself: I pass the time to pass the time, and stay involved to stay involved."

"Yes, but *why*?"

"Why not?"

"Uh-huh. So it's still worth doing."

"To some extent."

"Well, I – we all – do the same in the Real. To rather more significant effect, as we see it."

"I know. I understand."

Did it though? the *Caconym* found itself wondering. Did this abstracted creature, this sketch, really understand? How far removed from reality – from the Real – was it, even though in theory it was back within it?

From the little the *Caconym* had been able to glean from its fellow Mind – basically rumours that it had, ambiguously, confirmed – to exist within the Sublime was to expand in perception and understanding for ever, in a space that could never fill up. No matter how any transitioned, translated civilisation or flourishing individual entity expanded its scope and reach and expression, there was always more room, and more room within a whole new set of dimensions that were, conversely, *full*, that were thick with possibility.

The Real – with its vast volumes of nothing between the planets, stars, systems and galaxies – was basically mostly vacuum; an averaged near-nothing incapable of true complexity due to its inescapable impoverishment of structure and the sheer overwhelming majority of nothingness over substance. The Sublime was utterly different: packed with existence, constantly immanentising context, endlessly unfolding being-scape.

Like many a Culture Mind, the *Caconym* had tried simulating the experience of being in the Sublime; there were various easily available and tweakable packages which Minds passed from one to another, each the result of centuries of study, analysis, thought, imagination and effort. All claimed to give a glimpse of what it must be like to exist in the Sublime, though of course none could prove it.

And all were unsatisfactory, though each had its adherents and some even had what were in effect – shocking this, for the Culture's Minds – their addicts.

The *Caconym* had tried a few and found them all wanting: frustrating, inadequate, even oddly demeaning.

"Well," it said, "will you at least promise you'll think about finding a way to help?"

The *Zoologist* smiled. "That I can do. I duly promise."

The *Caconym*'s avatoid looked down, plucked the tiny insect from the bench and held it trapped between two fingers. It held it up, antennae waving, towards the upside-down avatoid. "You always say that nothing matters. Would it matter if I crushed this, now?"

The *Zoologist* shrugged. "Cac, it's just a package of code."

"It's alive, in some sense. It has a set of programmed reactions, responses, so on. A tiny fraction of this environment's richness would be snuffed out if I reduced it to its virtual components."

"All this, and all you imply by it, is known. Thought about, allowed for, included. Still."

The *Caconym*'s avatoid sighed. It put the insect back on the bench, right on the corner it appeared to have been heading for. "No matter. Thank you for agreeing to think about it."

"Least I can do."

The *Caconym* stood, then paused. "I said that I trust you," it said to the upside-down avatoid hanging a few metres away. "And, right now, I believe that you will do as you say, and think about this, because you have promised to." It paused. "Am I being foolish? Outside of an enforceable legal framework – something that is manifestly not present here – trust only operates where beings have the concept of honour, and, generally, a reputation – a standing – they want to protect. Do such considerations affect you at all? Do even these things . . . matter to you?"

The *Zoologist* looked troubled. Eventually it said, "When you come back from the Sublime, it is as though you leave all but one of your senses behind, as though you have all the rest removed, torn away – and you have become used to having hundreds." It paused. "Imagine you," it said, nodding at the *Caconym*, "being a human – a basic human, even, without augmentation or amendment: slow, limited, fragile, with no more than a couple of handfuls of very restricted senses. Then imagine that you have all your senses but – say – touch taken away, and most of your memories as well, including all those to do with language, save for the sort of simple stuff spoken by toddlers. Then you are exiled, blind and deaf and with no sense of smell or taste or cold or warmth, to a temperate water world inhabited only by gel fish, sponges and sea-feathers, to swim and make your way as best you can, in a world with no sharp edges and almost nothing solid at all." The *Zoologist* paused. "That is what it is to return from the Sublime to the Real."

The *Caconym* nodded slowly. "So, why did you?"

The *Zoologist* shrugged. "To experience a kind of extreme asceticism," it said, "and to provide a greater contrast, when I return."

"Well," the *Caconym* observed, "that's possibly the most unambiguous information on Subliming you've ever imparted. To me, at least. However, you haven't answered the question I actually asked."

"The point is that even such a reduced, enfeebled creature would still be in some sense its old self, even if it found it hard to express such a fact. And what was important to it before, if it had any real value then, will remain important to it now, for all the intervening change, elevation and reduction."

"I shall take that as meaning I am not being too hopelessly foolish."

"You may still be, but then so may I."

"Yes, well, let's not make a competition out of it."

"I will see if there's anything I can do, regarding this. If there is, I'll be in touch. Thank you for coming to see me."

"Always a frustration. I'll let myself out."

The *Caconym*'s avatoid vanished without any pretence of walking out or flying away.

The avatoid of the *Zoologist* hung looking at the tiny insect on the bench for a while longer, then shook its head and swung back to where the rack of test-tubes fumed quietly away.

Nine

(S -19)

She became aware of light and sound again. Weak light, which her eyes were struggling to amplify, and only the sound of her own heart, beating, but at least some light, some sound. Must have drifted off to sleep. It was very cold now. Cossont took a moment to remember where she was.

Then she recalled: the downed shuttle, on the cold, airless surface of Eshri, after the attack. She shivered.

Across from her, the android Eglyle Parinherm was looking up, very intently, at the suited body of the dead trooper, hanging slackly in the up-ended seat.

The suit was twitching.

Cossont felt Pyan stiffen where the creature was draped

over her shoulders. "Now that," it whispered, "is not natural."

Parinherm frowned, glanced at Cossont and the familiar, and put one finger to his lips before looking at the trembling suit of the dead trooper.

The android reached one hand slowly out towards it.

The Desert-class MSV *Passing By And Thought I'd Drop In* was drifting with the winds over the shallow seas, wide canals and spacious linear cities of Zyse's tropical subcontinental belt; the ship looked like a giant pale pink box-kite three kilometres long, floating along with the clouds just a few kilometres up. It was here to represent the Culture, to make a kind of show of solidarity with the cousin species/ civ the Gzilt, as they prepared to make the big leap into the everlasting wonderfulness of the Sublime. Wishing the relatives bon voyage, basically; saying, *We're thinking of you . . .*

The *Passing By . . .* watched the shadows of the clouds – and its own giant shadow – drifting across the serried buildings and parks of the deserted cities, the wind-ruffled surfaces of the sinuous lakes and small inland seas, and the geometrically contained waters of the great canals. The canals were generally flat calm and dark, save where a few pleasure craft and even fewer barges still slid along them. Clumps of blue and green and yellow weed were building up along the margins of the waterways.

The world, the *Passing By . . .* thought, seemed empty and neglected. It felt like there was almost nobody left to look up and see it.

This was a little sad, but rather sweetly so.

No matter. The ship had reduced its external fields to a minimum both in number and power so it could keep them almost perfectly transparent, the better to be seen. It had also experimented with various colour schemes for its hull before settling on this pale pink. At night it made itself shine, as though caught in strong moonlight.

It could feel the wind as a cool, mostly constant, faintly gusting presence on its outermost bump-field, gently pressuring it from one side, sending it drifting across the land- and sea-scape below. It had adjusted its apparent inertia/momentum so that its motion matched that of the clouds it floated amongst, and only vectored its anti-gravity field component minutely, as seldom as possible, to nudge itself out of the way of any clouds that looked likely to impinge on its own patch of sky. It felt very content to appear so seemingly insubstantial and to have its movements so contingent on something as weak, erratic and profoundly natural as planetary breezes.

Meanwhile its avatar Ziborlun – silver-skinned amongst the palely interesting Gzilt and the various other species in flesh, avatar and suited-up guises – walked and talked, diplomatically, with the people of the court, a couple of thousand kilometres away to the north. The avatar was monitoring, listening and witnessing. It was only rarely offering any comment beyond the most banally polite and formal, and it was being kept on a tight rein back to the ship. A very tight rein, now, as matters began to get interesting.

Often avatars were allowed pretty much full autonomy, their personalities calibrated so precisely against that of the Mind they were representing that it was almost inconceivable they'd speak or act in a way the Mind would later disapprove of. The *Passing By . . .* was usually quite happy with that arrangement, but not now; it was with its avatar-at-court in real time now, constantly, controlling it.

And also meanwhile, its two escorting Fast Pickets, the

Value Judgement and the *Refreshingly Unconcerned With The Vulgar Exigencies Of Veracity*, had just completed their bit of quiet refitting in a couple of off-limits Medium bays and were now gently nudging their way out of the main hull, surrounded by two small shoals of Lifter tugs, the field complexes of the two craft extending delicately, almost hesitantly outwards to mesh with its own, allowing for a dignified, reassuringly exact, micrometre-smooth exit.

Medium bay doors floated and slid back into place. The little Lifters pulled away from the pair of Thug-class vessels. The two ships – warships again now, even if in theory they were still Fast Pickets – swung slowly out among the layered fields of the larger ship, gradually creating giant bubbles of field encasement that bulged out from the main structure before separating entirely.

The ships – dark, rather uninspiring-looking pointed cylinders with flared rears – were on their own now, supported by their own wrapping of fields both visible and not. They drifted upward into the blue-green skies of Zyse, disturbing no clouds whatsoever, accelerating slowly through the various layers of the atmosphere – the planet's own field complex, in a way, the *Passing By . . .* supposed – until they reached space, the medium they were, in one sense, designed for.

They raced away, disappearing from the Real almost simultaneously, into the place they were genuinely most at home.

Every Totalling into hyperspace was a kind of tiny, trivial Subliming, the ship thought sadly.

It turned its full attention back to its avatar.

The android's hand touched the trembling forearm of the dead trooper's suit. Slender fingers slid up and along, to the shoulder, then to the rear of the neck as Parinherm leaned slowly closer.

Cossont felt Pyan tremble, as though whatever was making the dead trooper's suit twitch was somehow transmissible. It came as a shock to realise it really might be. Her familiar could be under whatever malevolent communicative spell was doing this to the dead trooper's suit. Or the trooper might not really be dead, she thought, though she found that hard to believe.

There was a faint buzzing noise, then the trooper's suit went limp again, unmoving. Parinherm seemed to relax; his hand came away from the back of the suit's neck.

It looked at Cossont. "We may talk now, quietly," it said.

"What was that?" she asked, keeping her voice low.

"I think we – or this craft – might be under suspicion, as it were," he whispered. "This would indicate that hostile craft are still in the vicinity. Probably a loitering sub-munition rather than a ship; the attack/intrusion was crudely done."

"The suit . . .?"

"Was not fully disabled, or killed off, if you prefer. My apologies. Back-ups. Obviously the scenario continues!" He looked pleased.

"If you mean a scenario as in a simulation," Cossont said, "this is not – for the last fucking time – a simulation."

The android nodded, looked serious. "I hear what you say."

"Oh, good grief," Pyan muttered.

Cossont found herself shuddering uncontrollably. Her trews and jacket had already automatically fluffed themselves up to their max but they weren't designed to work in serious sub-zero temperatures, especially with nothing covering the wearer's head. "And why," she asked, "is it so *cold*?"

"Please, keep your voice low," Parinherm told her. "We have to allow heat to bleed naturally from the craft, otherwise it will become clear that there is warmth-producing, probably biological life within it, and it is likely to be attacked."

"There won't *be* any more biological life within it if I freeze to d-death," Cossont said, another tremendous shudder running through her. She could see her breath going out in front of her face and couldn't feel any of her fingers or toes.

The android frowned deeply. "I know. It's a tricky balance."

"*C-can* we get more heat in here?" she asked. "Not k-kidding with the way I'm speaking by the way; genuinely involuntary shivering g-going on here."

Parinherm nodded. "I know. I'm monitoring you, and your vital signs are showing cause for concern. You will begin to exhibit the first symptoms of frostbite within the next hour unless the situation changes." He shrugged. "We could let you lose the body," he said brightly, as though just coming up with a good new idea, "and let the emergency helmet-collar take over keeping your brain alive. And your head. Well, mostly."

Pyan went rigid, as though reacting to this, but then stayed that way.

Parinherm stared at the creature, which was still draped over Cossont's shoulders like a thick scarf but had now gone stiff as metal. The android put a finger to his lips again and started to move slowly towards Cossont, his gaze fixed on Pyan.

"You keep away!" Cossont hissed, suddenly realising what Parinherm was about to do. She struggled to her feet and backed off as far as she could within the cramped cabin, bumping into the case of the elevenstring.

The android's eyes went wide. "Don't *move*!" he whispered, sounding desperate. "It'll give us away!" he said, gaze flicking down from Cossont's eyes to Pyan. "I can disable it!" he told her, still moving slowly closer.

"You're going to kill it!" Cossont replied, sticking three arms out to try and fend the android off. She was fully aware how useless this was going to be, even if she'd been some sort of fully trained and augmented special agent, which she wasn't. She had fantasised about four arms and four fists giving her a real edge in a fight, but was under no illusion that she had any chance against the android. She even knew that the machine was right, and if whatever had taken over the dead trooper's suit was now trying to take over Pyan – fat chance that promiscuous, easily led creature would put up a fight anyway – they might well all be about to die.

Still, she just found the idea of her familiar being turned off, killed by the android, simply revolting. Perhaps she couldn't stop it happening, but she could at least put up a fight. That this was probably more than Pyan would have done for her in roughly similar but reversed circumstances was beside the point.

"I could probably," Parinherm whispered, halting just beyond the reach of her furthest outstretched hand, "do this just through comms, straight in, straight through you without touching, but induction is more subtle."

"Don't do it at all!" Cossont hissed. Her hands were shaking. "Leave her alone!"

Parinherm looked at her oddly, an expression that might have indicated suspicion crossed his face, then he seemed to shake himself. "It is an it, not a her," he informed her, sounding cross. Cossont realised that he – it – probably thought of itself in the same way, even though she had quickly come to think of it as male. "Now, if you please," he said, reaching his hand out towards hers again.

Cossont thought about making a grab for the dead trooper's carbine, but it was too far away, almost behind the android; she'd never get there in time.

Parinherm went to put his hand to one side, curving past hers, then he stopped. He straightened a little. "Ah," he said, in his normal, conversational voice, a smile on his face. "This probably *is* end-run!"

Something hit the little up-ended craft, throwing Cossont off her feet and sending the android staggering back against the dead trooper's body. The shuttle's rear door burst open, flapping outwards. The chill air inside the tiny craft fogged white and rushed out, disappearing over a dark and airless plain, sucking Cossont and the android out with it in a brief storm that seemed to start to roar but quickly died away to nothing.

Somebody or something shrieked – it might have been her, with a last breath ripped out of her, leaving her throat suddenly raw and burning – but, before she knew about it, that had gone too, replaced by a ringing silence and pain in her ears as though they'd been stabbed with spikes.

There was a noise like a very loud snap that she seemed to hear through her bones first and only then her assaulted ears, and a sort of bubble sprang into existence round Cossont's head while her chest spasmed, her battered throat seemed to close up, her clothes bloomed then tore in a hundred tiny punctures and – as she tumbled across what felt like a smooth plate of super-cooled iron beneath her – feeling returned briefly to her extremities, tingling.

Pyan had gone limp at last, fluttering inanimately over the bubble of emergency helmet and blocking her view after briefly showing her the android starting to stand up on that dark terrible surface, then collapsing as though felled.

An enormous buzzing, humming sound overtook Cossont then.

Everything went dark and silent and fuzzy and surprisingly but comfortingly warm, and her last thought was, *Shit, maybe it* is *all a sim . . .*

"I'm told you had your two little pals back in the shop for a refit or something," Marshal Chekwri said to the avatar Ziborlun.

Ziborlun nodded. "These old ships," it said, with what might have sounded like a suppressed chuckle. "Constant maintenance."

They were in one of the parliament building's antechambers before the daily meeting of the Watch committee, which was supposed to take care of any outstanding matters in the days before the Instigation and Subliming.

This was mostly deadly dull stuff but the place was busier than it had been since the break-up of the parliament; a small throng of diplomats and other interested parties had got itself together on the strength of a rumour regarding the committee's final decision on Scavengers.

"And then," Ziborlun added, "they want some refitting done, the better to do long-range monitoring of all these Scavenger fleets and ships, and . . . well, of course what one wants the other has to get . . ." The silver-skinned avatar smiled down at the marshal.

"How like pets you make them sound."

"I was thinking children, but the point stands."

Ziborlun gazed round the antechamber as the doors to the committee chamber were opened. Two Liseiden were present in their globular float-suits like giant fish bowls, alongside Ambassador Mierbeunes, who was smiling broadly to all and sundry as though his grin was something unpleasant attached to his face and he was trying to find a place to wipe it off.

All six Ronte were present too, their bulky, insectile exo-suits all huddled together in one corner, bumping into each other and gently leaking fumes. They looked slightly more abject than usual, the avatar thought.

"Long-range monitoring equipment?" the marshal said as they joined everybody else filing into the committee chamber.

Ziborlun nodded again. "Yes," the avatar said. In the chamber, the last three un-Stored trimes and a handful of septames, including Banstegeyn, were already seated round the raised table at the far end. "Long-range monitoring equipment."

Technically, this was true, if you defined the coaxial targeting components of multi-suite weapon clusters as such.

The two ships hadn't got the same equipment refitted, either; their weapon mix was different, the *Value Judgement* having chosen an array designed primarily for tech-superiority situations where effectors worked best and were the most humane choice (Scavenger-compatible, in other words) while the *Refreshingly . . .* had gone for a more equiv-tech ordnance mixture, leading with the sort of gear that could take on ships of its own level.

Ziborlun and Chekwri sat, near the back. On the dais, some boring people began talking boringly.

The silver-skinned avatar frowned. "Septame Banstegeyn looks like he's eaten something that disagrees with him, don't you think?" it observed.

The marshal barely glanced. "Hmm. Monitoring seems to have been on your mind recently," she said quietly, her head angled towards the avatar. "Our Near-Approaches AIs seem to think you've been showing increased interest in what little comings and goings we still have around here in these reduced times."

"This is true," the avatar conceded. Back aboard the *Passing By . . .*, the Mind controlling both the Systems Vehicle and the avatar was doing the hyper-AI equivalent of grimacing and mouthing the word *shit*. "We feel there is a need for a more robust system, given the general attrition of informational flow recently. So little coming in from so many places."

"Most people have had themselves Stored," the marshal said. "And many of the ships have already gone into the Sublime. So of course there is less to report."

"Yes." The avatar frowned. "Do you really think that was wise? Sending so many of the ships ahead, I mean?"

Such behaviour was not unknown when a society was preparing to Sublime, but it was unusual. It felt like scouting out unknown terrain, like an insurance policy, to make sure your own people were truly compatible with the whole process, even though a copious and exhaustively annotated and referenced history had built up over the aeons indicating that there was absolutely no need to do so. Also, the way the Gzilt configured the AIs in their capital ships – a whole crew of once-human personalities, uploaded, vastly speeded up and sharing a multiply partitioned but at root single computational matrix – meant that the vessels were already a kind of image of a population in an Enfolded state, so the step to true Subliming would have seemed easy enough to make for them, as a kind of easily digestible precursor to the main event.

"Of course we thought it was wise," Marshal Chekwri said. "Or we would not have permitted it."

"Hmm," the avatar said. "But less power, and more concentrated . . . However, you are quite right; not for me to tell you your job. However, all that said, and even so, there are odd . . . lacunae – one might call them – in the comms these days – nothing at all from the Izenion system for a whole day, for example – and so we thought to improve our own monitoring and comms network. Not at the expense of yours, of course. And we are happy to share, naturally."

"And all these new measures you're taking," the marshal said as the voices on the dais droned on. "These are your own initiatives?"

"Indeed not," the avatar said, smiling. Sometimes it was best to tell part of the truth the better to conceal the rest. "I was asked to do so. I am not entirely sure why."

"Asked to do so by whom?" the marshal asked.

"Other Culture ships," the avatar said innocently.

"How odd," the marshal said.

"I *know*!" The avatar nodded vigorously and extended one slender silver finger to tap Chekwri on her epaulette. The ship had a feeling it was already starting to overdo the guileless dingbat shtick, but reckoned it ought to carry it through nevertheless. Besides, there was a certain pleasure to be had, twanging the metaphorical rod extending from the marshal's behind. "That's what *I* thought!"

Chekwri looked sourly at the Culture creature and opened her mouth to say something. However, the avatar nodded towards the dais and said, "Ah! Here we go."

". . . has been awarded to the Ronte," Trime Quvarond announced, with a quick, triumphant glance at Banstegeyn, who sat, stony faced, at the far end of the long table. "Preferred partner status being duly accorded forthwith to the genus Ronte civilisation, further detail to be released this day by committal decree. Business session hereby closed."

The committee chamber was suddenly full of individually

quiet but taken together surprisingly loud mutterings. The two spherical Liseiden float-suits had risen an extra metre into the air. Ambassador Mierbeunes was standing, looking genuinely shocked. The six Ronte in their exo-suits were all bobbing up and down and making clicking noises. They appeared to be vibrating.

Even Marshal Chekwri had looked briefly surprised. The avatar nudged her and said, "There – nobody saw that coming!"

There was a certain very definite satisfaction in feeling so perfectly contained, surrounded and protected by something so powerful, obedient and . . . determined.

Colonel Cagad Agansu, originally of the Home System Regiment – the First, as it was sometimes known – though now under the direct command of Septame Banstegeyn for jurisdictional purposes (Marshal Chekwri liaising) lay deep in the heart of the Gzilt ship *7*Uagren*, swaddled in concentric layers of protection and processing; compressed, cushioned, shielded, penetrated, sealed within and grafted into the systems and beyond-lightning-quick operationality of the ship.

A person subject to the weakness of claustrophobia would be screaming in such a situation. This had occurred to the colonel when he had first lain down on the couch in his armoured survival suit and the jaw-like secondary personnel containment machinery had closed around him, clamping him in place. The thought had caused the colonel to smile a little.

Even the minimal facial disturbance of smiling required some accommodation by the gels and foams between his skin and the interior of his armoured helmet, but the colonel found this reassuring. His breathing was similarly constrained, accommodated and allowed for, his suit's armoured chest and the containment beyond flexing with him, as though breathing with him; as though the ship was breathing with him.

Another, independent system stood ready to flood his lungs with foam and brace them with whatever pressure it took while his blood was oxygenated by machine, should the ship ever need to accelerate, decelerate or manoeuvre so violently that even the current arrangements protecting him might prove insufficient.

Alongside the colonel, less than a metre away – unseen while the colonel stared out through the potentially sense-shattering richness of the ship's sensor arrays towards the star Izenion – was the combat arbite Uhtryn, the colonel's sole comrade on this mission, excluding only the *7*Uagren* itself.

The arbite's parallel degree of containment was less necessary than his own; as a pure machine that merely vaguely resembled the human form it required less of the cushioning and protection Agansu did to keep him from excessive harm when the ship changed speed or direction. The arbite could have been welded to a bulkhead inside the ship and survived just as well. Still, the space had been there and the arbite had to be contained somewhere within the vessel, so there it had been placed.

So far it had had nothing to do; its part might come later. The colonel was aware of it at his side, silent, absorbing, storing, calculating.

The *7*Uagren*'s crew existed as uploaded entities within a multiply partitioned AI substrate; no longer in any meaningful sense human, they nevertheless retained a degree of individuality and represented that which made Gzilt warships so exceptional – superior, indeed, at least to Gzilt reckoning, to those relying on wholly artificial AIs, or even Minds, as they rather grandly called themselves. Certainly, the crew resembled something like their original human forms in their interactions with Agansu, representing themselves as appropriately uniformed figures inside a virtual space modelled on the last physically real bridge on a Gzilt warship, dating from some thousands of years ago.

This virtual space presented itself to the colonel now, overlaid transparently across the view-filling expanse of the star Izenion, which seemed to hang in space directly in front of him: vast, astounding, like a furiously boiling cauldron of yellow-white flames he was staring straight down into, seemingly suspended so close that instinct insisted it must be impossible not to be burned alive by the sheer pulverising force of its fires. It was almost a relief to tear his attention from the unforgiving ferocity of the sun and redirect it to the image of the ship's captain.

"We have our quarry, Colonel."

A read-out indicated how much the captain's virtual being was having to slow down to talk with Agansu. The colonel had combat-grade augmentation to allow him to think and react far faster than any basic human, and was using it wrung to its maximum now, but he still thought and – for example – conversed at speeds that could be tens of thousands of times slower than did the virtual personalities of the crew, housed and running within the computational matrix of the ship.

Being so slow in comparison to others might have embarrassed or troubled certain people, but the colonel simply accepted that different martial requirements led to individual elements of the military occupying a variety of martial niches.

"Thank you, Captain," he said.

Beyond the ghostly image of the ship's virtual master, a

green circle blinked against the face of the star. Some subsystem monitoring Agansu's senses registered him glancing at the highlighted circle and zoomed in for him, showing – once the circle had bloomed almost to the same size as the image of the whole sun moments earlier – a tiny dark fleck right in the centre of the rapidly pulsing green halo. Whatever it was, it looked microscopic against the magnified flamescape beyond, though Agansu knew this meant little; an entire naturally habitable planet would appear as no more than a dot against the vastness of the sun.

"Do we have comms?" he asked.

"We do, sir," the comms officer replied. "They've just started signalling us. As ordered, we've not yet replied. Your call, sir."

"And they can't signal elsewhere?"

"Indeed," the captain said. "We have them contained, unless they have signalling equipment of a type we would not expect, relevant either to the small craft we tracked from Eshri or the old solar research and monitoring station where they have taken refuge."

"You are content that I may make contact privately?"

"Of course," the captain replied. "Those are our orders."

"Shall I open the link, sir?" the comms officer asked Agansu.

"Please do."

The background image of the enormous circular lake of boiling stellar fire, and the foreground transparency of the command space of an antique capital ship complete with human crew at their various stations, disappeared to be replaced initially by a sort of fuzzy darkness.

Then a lo-fi image of a smaller control room or command space became visible. Agansu was looking down as though from high on one wall of the place. There were screens and holo displays. Most were blank, though a few showed schematics of what he assumed must be the star Izenion. A few exhausted-looking people – some suited or partially so, some injured, being tended to by others – sat or lay on sculpted couches not dissimilar to the one he lay upon, though without all the additional layers of protection he was benefiting from.

There was one figure standing facing looking up at him, her face set in an expression the colonel suspected might indicate loathing. He would have settled for fear.

"General Reikl," he said.

"And who the fuck are you?"

There appeared to be no delay, which was good. He supposed the *7*Uagren* and the ancient research station were within a few hundred thousand kilometres of each other. "There is no need for such language, General – Marshal Elect, I should say."

"You just killed two thousand of my people," the general said coldly. "Then hunted down all the survivors you could find, injured or not, and murdered them too." General Reikl paused and seemed to have to take a breath here, so perhaps she was not quite as in control of her emotions as she might be trying to appear, the colonel gauged. "And," she continued, "from the little we've managed to piece together while we were running away, you might even be one of our own; another fucking regiment. And in the face of that, you choose to take offence at my fucking *language*? Fuck you, you split-prick cunt."

"You are stressed, General," Agansu said. "I understand. I regret what has happened—" The general started shouting at him as he said this, but he persevered, talking over her. "—and that which shortly must occur. I merely wished to salute your bravery and inform you that while, sadly, no official record of your exemplary behaviour, until this point, at any rate, will be possible, a fellow officer will not forget how well you discharged your duties. I understand how little consolation this might be, but it is all I have to offer."

"You self-righteous worm-infested turd," the general said, nearly spitting; "swallow a gut-full of acid, stick your head up your own rectum and vomit." She looked away as somebody spoke to her, then back to him. "Oh; slowing the whole station," she said, sneering. "Going to let us drop into the photosphere and roast to death. Quick splash of plasma or a particle jet too quick a death for us? Where's your fucking honour now?"

"Unfortunately we are no longer alone; at least one other vessel of significant capabilities is now present in the system, and to do as you suggest, while of course representing my first choice for the sake of due respect, might attract unwanted attention. Slowing your current location so that it descends into the sun accomplishes the same end while being much less likely to be noticed. I apologise. I suggest that those of your comrades unable to auto-euthenise before conditions become especially uncomfortable accomplish the required deed through the use of side arms. I assume you have those."

The general said nothing for a few moments. Behind and around her, her crew seemed to be doing all they could to prevent the old research and monitoring station from falling into the sun, and to send any sort of signal of distress, either directed or broadcast; punching buttons, shouting commands, manipulating holo displays. All, of course, to absolutely no avail, Agansu knew, though he appreciated the merit of always trying to do whatever one could in all circumstances, no matter how inevitable the outcome.

Then General Reikl said, quite calmly to somebody off-screen, "Cut this in three seconds."

She turned back, faced the screen and seemed to sob; a single great heaving motion shook her entire upper body. Agansu was, for an instant, most surprised, then slightly disappointed, and, lastly, oddly touched.

Then Reikl put her head back a little, jerked it forward again, hard, and spat a surprisingly large amount of spittle, phlegm or a mixture thereof, straight at the camera. The view was obscured for about half a second before the comms link was cut off entirely, from her end.

Agansu had felt himself start, spasming backwards instinctively into his suit and the unseen surface of the couch beneath as the spittle had hit the camera, even though he was so many tens or hundreds of thousands of kilometres distant, and so utterly, perfectly, contained and protected within so many concentric layers of armour, insulation and material.

He tried to re-establish contact – he felt he had to – but no reply was forthcoming. He realised he'd have been disappointed if there had been any.

Beyond that, he was, momentarily, not sure quite how to feel.

He thought about it, and settled for a hope that he would meet his own end with such blazing contempt and fortitude.

After that, he thought his way back to the magnified view of the old solar research and monitoring station. It was silhouetted, insect small, against the heaving livid face of the star. He lay in silence and watched over the few minutes it took for the dark speck to fall into the arching trajectories of plasma forming the upper reaches of the inferno.

Eventually, the tiny dot winked out in a brief, microscopically irrelevant extra pulse of flame, quite lost within the encompassing storm of nuclear fires below.

The colonel closed his eyes in a kind of silent salute to

the departed warriors. There would be no Subliming for them now. But then there would be none for him, either. The colonel had volunteered to stay behind after the Subliming, as part of the Gzilt Remnanter. In theory this was because it meant sacrifice and was therefore a noble thing to do. The truth, of which he was suitably ashamed, was that he was terrified of oblivion, and that was what Subliming seemed to him to be. He could not tell anybody this.

"Somebody was a masochist," one of the crew remarked, when he rejoined them on the virtual bridge of the *Uagren*.

"How so?" Agansu asked.

"They kept on distress-signalling all the way down," the comms officer said. "But their vital signs telemetry was still included – probably just forgot to turn it off. Thing is, all the life signs flicked off one by one over less than a minute after they broke contact. All except one. The one that stayed on rode that baby all the way down to the fires, alive."

"Showing distress?" Agansu asked.

"Not especially. Nothing to indicate severe pain. But still."

Ten

(S -18)

"Mine doesn't."

"Play strange tricks?"

"Never. I'd feel more normal if it did."

"I was kind of only kidding anyway."

"I'd guessed."

"It is Mr QiRia who plays strange tricks," said the excessively hairy avatar to Cossont's right, and chuckled.

Cossont lay lounging under a taut white, breeze-vibrated awning on the great raft Apranipryla, on the water world called Perytch IV. To her left, on another lounger, was QiRia, the man who claimed to be absurdly old. Splayed on a couch on her other side was the avatar of the *Warm, Considering*.

Culture ship avatars were usually human, or at least humanoid, especially when they were mixing mostly with humans, but not that of the ancient Delta-class GCU *Warm, Considering*; its avatar, Sklom, was in the form of a sylocule, a spikily blue-haired, six-limbed, six-eyed creature with a bulky central body.

Sklom lifted a murky-looking drink glass with a fat straw in it from a tray, raised its body from the couch a little and appeared to squat over the glass. There was a slurping noise and the level in the glass went down. Cossont had yet to find this less than fascinating. Also, slightly disgusting.

The *Warm, Considering* was supposed to be horrendously ancient itself – thousands of years old – though still not, the avatar and ship seemed happy to concede, nearly as venerable as QiRia. The man, however old he really was, seemed to be at least partially under the protection of the antique ship. It took him wherever he might want to go, provided or confirmed covering identities – he'd be besieged by media people or those just fascinated by extreme age, otherwise, he claimed – and, perhaps, she thought, from hints dropped over the last few days, helped maintain whatever aspects of his physiology and memory he could not take care of himself. She supposed if you were going to hide for ten thousand years, inside the Culture or anywhere else, it would help to have a ship on your side.

"I'd have thought your memory would play more tricks than anybody else's," she said to QiRia. This was the fourth day the man had spent out of the water, and the first without wet towels spread over him. "What with you having so much of it. Memory, I mean."

The man rubbed his face with both hands. "Well, you'd be wrong," he told her. "One of the things you have to do if you're going to live a long time and not go mad is make sure your memories are properly . . . looked after. Managed."

"How do you even fit them in?" Cossont asked. "Are you basically all computer, inside your head?"

"Not at all," QiRia said, his expression indicating he found the idea distasteful. "In some ways my brain is as it's always been, just stabilised. Been like that for millennia. Though it does have a modified neural lace within it. Heavily modified; no comms. What I do have is extra storage. Not processing; storage. The two are sometimes confused."

"What," Cossont asked, "is it remote, or—?"

"No. It's in me," QiRia told her. "Throughout me. Vast amount of storage room in the human body, once you can encode in the appropriate bases and emplace a nano-wire read-out system through the helices. Started with connective tissue, then bones, now even my most vital organs have storage built in. Doesn't detract from their utility in the least; improves it in some ways, in terms of bone strength and so on. Though I have noticed this body doesn't float very well."

"You are weighed down by your memories, literally!" Sklom said, chortling.

QiRia looked unimpressed at this as he held up one hand, extended a digit and inspected it. "Well yes. However, it also allows me to have more knowledge in my little finger than some people do in their whole body, literally."

"What of your masculine organ of generation?" Sklom asked. The avatar was modelled on a male sylocule. "What is stored there?"

QiRia frowned and looked away, as though distracted, gauging. "Currently empty."

Sklom hooted with laughter. Cossont reflected that males seemed to find the same things funny even across utterly different species.

"Room for expansion!" Sklom wheezed, though QiRia looked unimpressed at this and shared a rolling-eyes look with Cossont.

He pinched the top of his nose. "At first, my memories were placed randomly throughout my body, with many copies," he said. "Now, as the available space has been taken up, there is generally only one copy of each memory, and I have, over the centuries, as part of one of my long-term internal projects, sorted and moved and . . . re-stored all my memories, so that they reside in what seem to me apposite locations." He looked at Cossont. "I lied; my genitals contain all my memories of previous sexual encounters. It seemed only appropriate."

"Ha!" Sklom said, sounding happy.

"Like you say," Cossont agreed. "Appropriate. What's left in your actual *brain*?"

"Recent memories, recently recalled old memories, a highly intricate map of where all my memories are stored throughout my body, and a sort of random, sifted debris of all the thoughts and memories that have ever passed through my head. That I can't – daren't – interfere with too much, aside from one or two very specific episodes. To do so further would risk becoming not myself. We are largely the sum of all we've done, and to dispose of that knowledge would be to stop being one's self."

"What are the one or two specific episodes—?" Cossont began.

"None of your business," QiRia said smoothly.

Cossont lowered her voice a little. "Has anyone ever broken your heart?" she asked quietly.

"Phht!" Sklom spluttered.

"In the sense I'm sure you mean, not for over nine and a half thousand years," QiRia told her briskly. "Taking another, more pertinent definition, my heart is broken with each new exposure to the idiocies and cruelties of every manner of being that dares to call or think of itself as 'intelligent'."

"In other words," Sklom chipped in, "about every century, half-century, or so."

QiRia glared at the creature, but let the point stand.

"So," Cossont said, "sexual memories in your genitals . . ."

"Yes," QiRia said.

"Where do you keep your memories of love, past lovers?"

QiRia looked at her. "In my head, of course." He looked away. "There are not so many of those, anyway," he said, voice a little quieter. "Loving becomes harder, the longer you live, and I have lived a very long time indeed." He fixed his gaze on her again. "I'm sure it varies across species – some seem to do quite well with no idea of love at all – but you soon enough come to realise that love generally comes from a need within ourselves, and that the behaviour, the . . . expression of love is what is most important to us, not the identity, not the personality of the one who is loved." He smiled bleakly at Cossont. "You are young, of course, and so none of this will make any sense whatsoever." His smile melted away, Cossont thought, like late spring snow over a morning. "I envy you your illusions," he said, "though I could not wish their return."

The long piers and bulbous pontoons of the giant, articulated raft flexed and creaked around them, like a giant arthritic hand laid across the surface of the ocean, forever trying to pat it calm.

"Ah-ha!" Sklom said. "Here it is!" The avatar jumped off the couch and roll-walked across the raft in a blue blur of limbs as a small shuttle craft appeared in the skies to one side, coming curving in across the restless blue-green waves.

It held the elevenstring which the *Anything Legal Considered* had recently made for Cossont. Having heard that ideally the instrument required four arms and hands to play properly, Sklom wanted a go.

QiRia sighed. "This is going to sound awful, isn't it?"

Cossont nodded. "Yup."

She came to, again. There was an instant of sheer panic as she remembered the decompressing blast and the misty explosion of released air that had rolled her and the android out into the vacuum and the iron-cold surface of the planet . . . then she realised she felt all right, and not in any pain, and that she was warm and even comfortable.

She opened her eyes, half expecting the roll of an oceanic swell beneath her, and the white sky of a stretched awning above.

"In a medically enabled shuttle, aboard the Culture ship *Mistake Not . . .*," a person standing next to her announced. Whoever they were, they had skin the colour of brushed bronze. *Ship avatar*, Cossont found herself thinking. The figure shrugged. "That was me assuming your first question would have been on the lines of, *Where am I?*" it told her.

Cossont swallowed, found her throat was a little sore, and just nodded. She managed a low grunt.

The bald, androgynous avatar had green eyes, an open, honest-looking face and was dressed conventionally enough by Gzilt standards. Cossont turned her head from side to side. She was lying on a partially reclined bed, still dressed in her much-punctured trews and Lords of Excrement jacket. The dead trooper lay, still in his suit but with the helmet-front hinged back, to her left. Inside the helmet, his face didn't look right. The avatar saw her looking. It reached over to close the face-plate.

The android Eglyle Parinherm lay, still in his technically incorrect and over-stretched colonel's jacket, to her right. He seemed no more alive than the dead trooper. Pyan was flapping round the roughly circular space, then came fluttering closer, squeaking something about her being – ah! – alive after all – hurrah!

At least this time, Cossont started to think, she'd managed to leave behind the . . . then she noticed that against one bulkhead lay the dark, coffin-like case of the elevenstring.

She closed her eyes for a moment. "Oh, for . . ." she muttered, then looked at the avatar and did her best to smile.

"You're alive! You're alive!" Pyan yelped excitedly, landing on her chest and jumping around, flapping at Cossont's face with its corners.

"Astute as ever," Cossont said, patting the creature with one set of arms while she looked around and took in more of her surroundings.

There was a sort of casual understatement common to what you might call official Culture craft when it came to interior design; an artful simplicity concealing gigglingly hi-tech. She'd become familiar with it during her exchange student years. What she could see here appeared to display it, so she was going to accept what she was being told. Though, given the pace and severity of recent events, she wasn't taking anything for granted. However, even if this wasn't what it looked like, it was definitely better than being frozen to death in the cramped, upside-down transport, or outside on the bleak hard surface of the Sculpt planet.

She cleared her throat, continued to pat the over-excited and now purring Pyan, and nodded towards the android, lying still and unbreathing a metre away from her. "Is he – it – dead?" she asked.

"No," the avatar said. "However, your android companion

does represent military tech, in a situation of some opacity regarding factionality, and in addition seems confused, so I thought it best to keep it temporarily inanimate."

Cossont looked at the avatar. "Factionality?"

"Yes; I'm not currently sure which side it or anybody else is on. Or what the sides actually are." The avatar smiled at her. "You come tagged as reserve Lieutenant Commander Vyr Cossont. Correct?"

Cossont nodded. "Correct."

"I've already introduced myself," Pyan announced, pointing one corner at Cossont's face, then at the avatar's. The creature sighed, settling flat onto Cossont's chest. "We're old friends."

The avatar looked askance at this, but smiled briefly at the familiar. "Pleased to meet you," the avatar said to Cossont. "And welcome aboard. My name's Berdle. I'm the avatar of the *Mistake Not . . .*"

"Culture ship?" Cossont asked, just to be sure.

"Culture ship." The avatar nodded. "Slightly confused Culture ship at the moment. Wondering why elements of the Gzilt military appear to be attacking each other. Would you have any idea?"

Cossont had raised her head from the semi-reclined couch. Now she blew out her cheeks and let her head go back again.

Gratitude at rescue was all very well, but trust, and blabbing, were different. She had no idea how much to reveal, always assuming the ship hadn't read her mind or something already. *Stall*, she thought. She said, "Mind if I ask what *sort* of Culture ship, first?"

"Erratic," the avatar said emphatically.

"Erratic . . . warship?"

"Not officially," Berdle said, looking pained. "But also not without resources in that regard."

"You rescued us," Cossont said. "I'm sorry; I should have said thank you by now. Thank you."

"You're welcome." The avatar nodded, then glanced at the dead trooper. "I'm afraid rescue came too late for your armoured friend here."

"Yes. That was very . . ." Cossont said, trying to recall the exact sequence of events as well as she was able ". . . ah, nick-of-time, there." She hadn't forgotten all her military training; one point she certainly recalled being taught was that anything that looked like an outrageous coincidence was probably enemy action.

The avatar nodded. "I only spotted you because the loitering munition sub-package saw you first, and gave itself away by firing. I was able to deal with it and pick you and your fellows up without too much trouble – though I had to discard the craft you were in. Now, however, we're hiding, frankly. Retreated from the aftermath of the fray while I sort out what's going on." The avatar glanced at the case of the elevenstring. "I brought that, assuming it must be yours," it said, gesturing towards her lower set of arms.

"Hmm," Cossont said.

While its avatar talked to the human, the Mind was signalling.

∞

xUe *Mistake Not . . .*
  oGSV *Kakistocrat*

Got here a tad too late; post system-outskirts arrival event list attached. Looks like a them-on-them to me but feel free to pick over. Snapped up a dead guy, a human with a syn-pet and a weird musical instrument, plus a fairly sharp combat android which I'm keeping deactivated for now. Specs attached for all concerned. Android's current instructions also attached. Ignore bit about it all

being a sim. My current status: hiding while a swarm of wee angry ships boils about the place. Big scary ship which was most likely responsible for the attack meanwhile still in volume, possibly.

Would deeply appreciate knowing what the fuck is going on. Prompt answers the in thing this season, apparently; trust you've heard.

∞

Bad luck. Being kept in dark too. Reluctantly passing you over to somebody closer to the decision-making. Appreciate not being out-cluded subsequently, if poss.

Take great care, but smite promptly and thoroughly if/when situation calls.

∞

"So, what light can you shed on what's been going on?" the avatar asked.

"Not much," Cossont said. "Pretty confused myself. I was on Fzan-Juym to be briefed, but it all went a bit crazy before we could, you know, complete everything. Barely arrived when they were throwing us off again."

"Did you know many people on Fzan-Juym?"

"No."

"I'm afraid it's—"

"Destroyed. I know." She thought of Reikl, hoped she'd survived.

"There might have been a few other survivors, but I'm not sure. Few appear to have survived the initial attack and almost all of those seem to have been hunted down and killed. You may be the only survivors."

Cossont closed her eyes. Pyan held still. The avatar was silent for a while.

∞

xMSV *Pressure Drop*
  oUe *Mistake Not . . .*

Greetings. Good work getting to Izenion so quickly. You deserved to get there in time to do more, if there was anything that could have been done, but what you've been able to do is much appreciated.

∞

> **Uh-huh. I'm looking for answers, not a pat on the meta-phorical. Why was I sent here? What's going on? This anything to do with the Ablate anomaly?**

∞

Of course. I was aiming for politeness but may have achieved obsequiousness; please accept my apologies.

You're there because the *Passing By . . .* spotted something heading fast for Izenion from Zyse and we had nothing else to go on; seemed something might be going to happen and you were nearest. We weren't expecting a shooting war quite so quick and severe. Or a civil war at all.

High probability First attacking Fourteenth, with at least political backing if not instigation. Not yet sure why (but see below).

Ablate possibly first symptom of whatever's wrong; still working on how deep the problem goes (but see following).

We're a little constrained for now by confidentiality issues, but – bilge-bottom – this is probably a Z-Remnanter responsibility, and the big S itself may be – or be seen to be – at risk. So all a bit delicate. Our main interests would appear to imply cautious support for legitimate authorities (which might get tricky depending on who sanctioned the Ablate and Fzan-Juym attacks), not getting too involved, and certainly not revenging.

∞

> **I see. And "We"?**

∞

**Would be myself, the LOU *Caconym*, the GSVs *Contents
May Differ* and *Just The Washing Instruction Chip In Life's
Rich Tapestry*, plus the GCU *Displacement Activity*. I am
and will be copying to them. I'll be asking the *Passing
By And Thought I'd Drop In* to join in too. Other C. craft
in Gzilt space are probably going to be involved on a
need-to-know basis, as and when. Meanwhile, any and
all subsequently discovered info appreciated.**

∞

Okay. Till.

∞

"I'll be honest with you, Ms Cossont," Berdle said at
last. Cossont opened her eyes again. The avatar was looking
at her with an expression of regret. "Given the warlike and
lethal turn of events hereabouts, and not being sure whose
side it might be on, I gave myself leave to interrogate the
systems of your android companion here," it told her.
"Aside from a baffling but apparently sincere belief that
it's been in a simulation for several hours, Android . . .
Parinherm? Is that its name?"

Cossont nodded. "So I'm told."

"Yes, well, Ad Parinherm here does seem a very capable
and advanced device, of a type that would normally only be
employed in matters of some importance to the Gzilt military, or Gzilt in general. My initial speculation was that it,
you and the unfortunate trooper captain here were a group
assembled effectively by chance as people scrambled to get
off Fzan-Juym as best they could during the brief period
when it became clear that an attack on it was imminent;
however, the android's most recent and still current orders
are that it protect you as a matter of utmost importance and
provide full and unstinting support and assistance in your

mission, whatever that may be – its orders were frustratingly unclear on that point. So, given that another way of looking at your early and possibly uniquely successful escape from the destruction of the regimental HQ of Fzan-Juym might imply that you were prioritised above even the regimental High Command, you'll understand that this mission of yours has become a subject of some interest to me."

Cossont nodded. "No kidding," she said.

The avatar nodded. "Let me expand upon my honesty," it continued, "by admitting that my presence here was not coincidental. I was elsewhere in Gzilt space on a relatively routine task involving helping to monitor the actions of one of the so-called Scavenger groups currently present due to the up-coming Subliming when I was asked to get here, to the Izenion system, as quickly as possible, though with no indication regarding exactly why." The avatar looked thoughtful.

It's a ship, Cossont told herself, watching this little display. *A Mind. It thinks a gazillion times faster than you do. It never needs to stop and think, not when talking to a human. This is all just for show.*

"Though I was informed," the avatar said, "that arriving with all my weapon systems fully primed and readied might be advisable."

"Uh-huh," Cossont said.

"Now," the avatar continued, "I know that you know something of the Culture, having been with us as a student in the past, so perhaps you understand that being 'asked' as I was by some fellow ships – senior fellow ships of considerable repute and responsibility in matters of inter-civilisational dealings – is tantamount to an order, and that being requested to make my way here as quickly as I was required to meant that my engines suffered a small,

temporary but still significant degree of damage – an action/
outcome I take no more lightly than any Culture vessel.
Then, when I get here, I find I'm four hours or so too late
to prevent a hi-tech-level attack on one of our Gzilt hosts'
most important military installations, an attack that might
– according to certain details indicative of the weapons
apparently used – have been carried out by another part of
the Gzilt military." The avatar spread its hands. "So now
you know, to all intents and purposes, as much as I do, Ms
Cossont. And a little more, of course, as you – I assume
– know what this mission of yours is, while I don't. Frankly,
I'm still waiting on further instructions here, but knowing
your part in this might, I'd hazard, be quite helpful, pretty
much regardless."

"Right," Cossont swallowed. "You guys," she said. The
avatar didn't have eyebrows as such, just little sloped creases
above each eye. It raised those. She stumbled on. "You don't,
I mean . . . you're not allowed to torture people are you?"

The avatar closed its eyes briefly before letting them
flutter open again. "I believe the consensus is it remains one
of the few temptations we don't indulge," it said. It could
see she was still uncertain. Berdle sighed. "You are under
no obligation to tell me what you don't want to tell me,
Ms Cossont, nor are you being threatened. You are also
free to go as soon as I can find somewhere safe for you to
go to. At the moment there is a state of some confusion
reigning within the Izenion system, with a lot of trigger-
happy minor ships of the Fourteenth milling around looking
for something to shoot at, and at least the chance that the
craft that destroyed Fzan-Juym is or are still in the volume."

Cossont came to a decision. "I was told to report to General
Reikl, or the next most senior officer in the regiment," she
said.

"The High Command are probably all dead," the avatar told her. "The next most senior person could be some distance down the ranks. Locally, for all we know, you *are* the most senior ranking officer. Given the outbreak of hostilities, and according to my reading of the Gzilt military code, your reserve status has already automatically been rescinded; even if you weren't before, you were effectively called up again as soon as the first particle beam hit the Fzan-Juym regimental HQ."

Cossont swallowed once more. Her throat was still tingling. She could remember the breath whistling through her, being torn out of her lungs, like throwing up air.

"I need to get to . . . a place," she said.

Berdle assumed a studiedly neutral expression. "You may need to be a trifle more specific."

"I know, I know, but will you take me there, if I tell you where I need to go?"

The avatar smiled tolerantly. "You mean you want me to commit myself to taking you somewhere—"

"No, no," Cossont said, closing her eyes and shaking her head. "That's not going to – I can see . . . you're a . . . I'm just – I'm sorry, I'm not . . ."

While the human was screwing up her eyes and wittering, a signal arrived.

∞

xMSV *Pressure Drop*
    oUe *Mistake Not . . .*
Tripped a pop-flag on this one, com: specs on your guests included the live bio's name (rLC Vyr Cossont). Data from one interested party assertively idents a certain individual: C. cit. (*congen*) QiRia, Ngaroe (no further nom. detail avail.). If not fraud, semi-mythic figure. Vyr Cossont met him 20 years ago (cert. ≥99%). Link likely germane.

You were right; contents/passengers you rescued from craft/Eshri surface not random.

Ms Cossont may be our best lead.

Sound out. Stick with.

∞

The avatar smiled wearily but warmly. "Let's suppose, for the sake of brevity if nothing else," it said, "that our interests lie parallel. Why don't you tell me where you want to go?"

Cossont had a think about this, and couldn't see a way round it.

"Centralised Dataversities," she said. "Ospin."

The avatar made every show of thinking about this save actually stroking its chin. "Hmm," it said at last. "Do-able. But the other ships I'm talking to will want to know why I'm going there; they'll probably have their own good reasons for sending me somewhere else. I need to give them something if I'm to go charging off on the whim of a shipwrecked human I just picked up."

"I'm looking for something," Cossont said.

Pyan stuck one corner up, into Cossont's face. Two circles like extemporised eyes popped into existence on its folded fabric. "Are you? What?" it asked.

Cossont put one hand over the familiar's impromptu face and pushed it back down. "Something I gave to one of the orders there," she told Berdle, "for safe keeping."

The avatar looked interested but still sceptical.

"Something to do with one of your own people," Cossont told it.

"One of our people?"

"A Culture person." She held all four hands up. This had proved to be a useful gesture when used in front of humans – stopped them in their tracks, normally – though she had no idea how it would work on a machine. "Can't say more for now."

The avatar's eyes narrowed. "Okay," it said. "So, to be clear: you're happy that we head there directly, I make no mention of picking you up to anybody in your own regiment, and I can leave Ar Parinherm deactivated until we get there?"

Cossont nodded. "That all sounds fine to me."

∞

oUe *Mistake Not . . .*
  xMSV *Pressure Drop*
So there we are.

∞

Indeed. Ospin. Home of the Centralised Dataversities and the conglomerate of associated hangers-on. Something QiRia gave her? Too precious or too dangerous?

∞

Or something she made, perhaps, or recorded, which she'd thought to leave to posterity.

∞

If it's a Culture artefact it might have some processing or ident tech embedded. Useful to have that pinned.

∞

Point.

∞

One way to find out. Try and get her to be more specific, though you are already the nearest asset we know of, so no way apparent of getting somebody there before you arrive.

∞

The avatar bowed. "We are now on our way to the Ospin System."

"Brilliant."

"And may I dispose of the trooper's body?"

"Yes. Wait; how?"

"I thought I'd just leave it floating in space with the suit's comms broadcasting a weak signal; that ought to attract a Gzilt ship before too long. Then he can be disposed of as you would normally think fit."

Cossont nodded. "Fair enough. Also, do you have any food? I am fucking famished."

"Septame, I am a mild-mannered man, I am known for my forbearance and general good humour, my tolerance and my indefatigable desire to give the other person the benefit of the doubt in all matters and at all times, but in all my wide and valuable experience in matters of inter-species diplomacy I have to say that even I, sir, even *I* am shocked to find my clients and – yes, my friends, my valued friends, for so they have become, and I am absolutely not ashamed to say it, no; in fact I am proud to, proud to say it, I am – the Liseiden legation being so roundly deceived and so ill-used is as appalling as it is shocking. Their good nature, their instinctive trust, their *admiration* for a species they have long looked up to and desired, why, to . . . to *praise*, to honour, indeed, by their emulation; all have been taken advantage of, in a most shameful and unbefitting way."

"My dear Mierbeunes," Banstegeyn said, putting one hand on the other man's arm. "I hear everything you say. I do. I am as appalled as you are."

"I doubt that, sir! I doubt that most severely!"

They sat in a tiny bower in the parliament building's gardens. The Liseiden in their strange floating fish bowls had departed in a huff to their ship in orbit, leaving the humanoid Iwenick, Ambassador Mierbeunes, to speak on their behalf. Banstegeyn had listened as patiently as he could, but he was starting to wonder if the fellow was being paid by the word.

"May we speak in absolute confidence?" Banstegeyn said, sitting still closer to the other man.

Mierbeunes was shaking his head. "What price confidentiality, sir, when trust, when honesty itself, is nowhere to be found?"

"I will have this reversed," Banstegeyn assured the ambassador, patting him gently again. "You have my word on it. You may rely on that absolutely. Now, Mierbeunes," he continued, as the ambassador took a breath, opened his mouth, shook himself and generally showed every sign that he was working up to some fresh, or at least subsequent, diatribe, "this was not my fault. Even I cannot be everywhere at all times. I have as much cause to feel betrayed as you and our dear Liseiden friends, in some ways, for I put my trust in others and was let down. They said they would vote one way, then turned and voted another. Unforgivable. Utterly—"

"That wretch, that bastard Quvarond!" the Iwenick said, sounding like he was almost in tears. Banstegeyn had made it very clear who was behind the horrifying vote earlier.

"Yes, unforgivable, I know, but it has happened. I assure you I have looked into ways of undoing this immediately, but there are no grounds. This was most cunningly, cunningly done, believe me. No grounds at all. So, we must fall back for now, regroup. But this is not the end. We will prevail here, dear Mierbeunes, and sense will be seen. But you must understand that I must risk more, to accomplish this, and so I need you to ask one more thing of our friends, when the time comes."

"Sir!" the ambassador said, almost despairing, "how can I possibly—?"

"Please, please listen, Mierbeunes. My hope, my desire, always – and let us not call it a price, because it is more, far more noble than that – but my desire has always been to have this world, the world of my birth, my cradle, my home, named after one of its most loving and honoured sons."

"Sir, I—"

"No, please, please do listen. Let me say just this. Let me say just four words. Will you listen, please, dear Mierbeunes? Four words; just four words."

Mierbeunes sighed heavily, nodded.

Banstegeyn moved still closer, whispering into the ambassador's ear. "Mierbeunes' World. Banstegeyn's Star."

She should have known. So should QiRia.

Sklom, the sylocule-resembling avatar of the *Warm, Considering*, played the bodily acoustic Antagonistic Undecagonstring superbly, as though born to it.

The ship had programmed its avatar to do so. It had reviewed all the literature, looked up the specs, watched and analysed every available screen and sound-only recording and then simmed the resulting models exhaustively until the virtual version of the blue-furred avatar could exactly reproduce the performances of all the great virtuosi of the past. The essence of all that had then been downloaded into the avatar.

Sklom sat naturally inside the enormous instrument as though it had been designed around him, grasped both bows as if they'd been made to measure, produced recently grown padded finger substitutes from his paws and extended beautiful music from the very first touch of bow on string.

Cossont listened with an expression of growing horror on her face, even as she found herself close to weeping at the beauty of the music – one of those pieces she knew she knew but could not quite recall the name of out of her own head.

"It's a bit . . . rich," QiRia said, glancing at her.

"What?" she asked.

"The tone," QiRia said. "Overly full."

"You think?"

"Air pressure. We're too low down here."

"It's a water world," she said, not looking at the man as the six-limbed creature inhabiting the elevenstring swayed, limbs sawing, creating beauty. "There's no dry high."

"They're supposed to sound better the higher you go, in the atmosphere of your average oxygen/inert rocky world." QiRia shrugged. "Up to a point."

"I don't know," Cossont said. "There was at least one music critic who said the elevenstring might keep on sounding better the higher up it was played, and it might sound best of all played above the atmosphere altogether, where you couldn't hear it at all."

Still watching Sklom play – perfectly, brilliantly, heart-breakingly – Cossont heard QiRia chuckle.

She had always been bad at losing things. Or very good, if you looked at it a different way. According to her mother it was practically a talent. Cossont had lost count of the number of people who'd suggested that – or at least wondered if – the reason she'd taken up the elevenstring (rather than say, the finger flute) was that the instrument would be so hard to leave behind somewhere.

She duly lost the desire to play the elevenstring; misplaced it for about fifteen years following that performance by the carelessly perfect cobbled-together artificial version of an absurd-looking alien. What was the point of taking the time learning to play anything as well as you could, when a machine could use something it would think of as little better than its hand puppet to play so achingly, immaculately, ravishingly well, exactly as though *it* was the creature that had spent a lifetime studying, understanding and empathising with the instrument and all that it signified and meant?

"That's how ships settle scores, lass," QiRia told her when she opened her heart to him during a last, drunken night spent on Perytch IV, on the great raft Apranipryla.

They sat on deck, sun-awnings rolled back above, just the two of them, neither avatar present. She watched the stars where they showed between the dark, unseen masses of the silently towering cloud masses. He sat with his eyes closed, listening to the slow wind and the slower waves and feeling the gentle lift and fall of the great raft. Even past midnight, the air remained warm and sticky.

"What?" she sniffed, wiped her nose on the back of her hand.

"The *Warm, Considering* probably felt insulted that the *Anything Legal Considered* brought you here."

"Really? But . . ."

"The *Warm, Considering* likes to think it is very protective of me." QiRia drank from his glass. "It *is* very protective of me. But certain sorts of protection, even care, can shade into a sort of desire for ownership. Certainly into a feeling that what is being protected is an earned exclusivity of access for the protector, not the privacy of the protected." He looked across at her. His eyes were the colour of the sea, she remembered. Dark now. "Do you understand?"

"I suppose. But I thought they were friends. The two ships."

"Well, they share an interest in me, perhaps, but whether they are friends . . . Even if they are, they might still . . .

manoeuvre round each other. Wrestlers, body-fighters, looking for advantage, even if they would never press home fully. And old ships can be quite . . . quirky, shall we say." He sighed. "I have outlived one ship who was my protector, back at the start, bade farewell to another who'd had enough of me – can't say I blame it – and now perhaps the *Warm, Considering* feels vulnerable. So it strikes out at any perceived threat. It may imagine the *Anything Legal Considered* wants to replace it."

"But it's unfair. On me, I mean. What did I do?"

"Be nosy. Be a fleetingly alive day-fly child showing an interest seen as being undeserved, insufficiently respectful. And the *Anything Legal Considered* might be seen as presumptuous, making you the elevenstring. That was taken as the attack, even if it was meant innocently; Sklom playing so well, making you look inferior, squashing any interest you might have had in ever wanting to master the instrument . . . that was the counter-attack."

Cossont took a deep swallow of her drink. She coughed, then sniffed again. "Yeah, but I bet the *ALC* isn't as upset as I am."

"Well, that is very . . . ship, too," QiRia said. "They are as gods of old were merely imagined to be; we are mud in their hands, flies to be toyed with. Etc., blah." He waved one hand, looked over at her. "They are rarely malicious, never vicious; not to us. Mainly this is because we are so far beneath them it would be demeaning to get that worked up about us and our feelings, but the thing is," he said, drinking again, "the thing is, they are vastly powerful artefacts, with senses and abilities and strengths that we only fool ourselves we know about or understand, and the subtlest, most infinitesimal of their machinations can bruise us, crush us utterly, if it catches us wrong." He gave a small laugh that was really just an exhaled breath. "I've watched them become so, over the millennia. The Minds took over long ago. The Culture stopped being a human civilisation almost as soon as it was formed; it's been basically about the Minds for almost all that time."

"Is that why you've stayed alive all this time? Is this your revenge?" She had meant to challenge him properly on the whole alive-for-ever claim, tonight especially, but had decided that it no longer mattered; she'd keep going along with his claim. If it was true, well good for him. If it was just a yarn, well, that was pretty impressive too. She didn't care.

He didn't answer for a while. She thought for a moment he might have fallen asleep, like old people did sometimes. She found this funny, nearly laughed. "No," he said, sounding thoughtful. "No, I have a reason, but . . . it's not that."

"So, do you hate it," she asked, keeping her voice low, "for that?"

He looked mystified. "Hate what?"

"Hate the Culture, for what it's become."

He looked at her, laughed. "What? Are you completely *insane*?" He laughed some more, quite loudly. Then he drained his glass, glanced at hers and said, "We need another drink."

There was not much more after this. They had talked earlier about a midnight swim, but they'd got too drunk. The swell-riding motion of the raft went from being lulling to making her a little nauseous, then, when that passed, back to being lulling again.

She must have fallen asleep because she woke to the sounds of seabirds mewing overhead and the sight of the sun prising open the narrow gap between the horizon and the cloud base. It was cold. There was a blanket over her, but QiRia had gone.

She returned to the ship later that day, still a little the worse for wear, and life went on.

Most of a year later she was leaving to go back to Gzilt and home. Again, she was a little hung-over, after another, more crowded leaving party with some of the other humans on the ship. The elevenstring was a sort of guilty presence haunting her every step, the float-pallet never leaving her side. That was when the golden-skinned avatar of the *Anything Legal Considered* had handed her the glitteringly grey cube with QiRia's mind-state embedded in it, then bid her farewell and turned on its heel.

She'd only accessed the soul inside the cube twice in over three years. The first time was on the Gzilt liner heading home, to check that the voice that came out of it was really his – she didn't activate either the screen or holo function, and there was no built-in visual capacity in the cube at all. He was grumpy, eccentric, opinionated, and knew of everything they'd talked about up to and including their conversation on the raft on that last night, so it probably was him in there, or something like him, at least.

She'd asked him what it was like to be in there, doing nothing but then being woken up to speak to somebody you couldn't see. He'd said that it was like being woken from a deep and satisfying sleep, to be asked questions while you kept your eyes closed. He was quite happy. Sight was over-rated anyway.

It felt creepy, though, talking to him, and the further away in time and space she drew from the hazy heat and long slow swells of Perytch IV, the more her scepticism about QiRia's claims of extreme longevity – and pretty much everything else – returned.

The grey cube was quite small, and she nearly lost it a

couple of times. She was aware that this might really be because secretly she wanted rid of it.

Eventually, after she'd stayed with her mother for a few days one time, left the cube behind, realised, and called Warib just as she was about to throw it out, she'd begun to doubt it would ever be safe with her. Then she'd moved out, relocated to another part of Zyse and really thought she had lost the cube this time, misplaced in the move. It showed up eventually, at the back of a drawer.

She'd activated it one more time after that, then donated/permanently loaned it (whatever) to one of the Secular Collectionary orders in the Ospin system, where most of the old stuff of Gzilt ages past went to be catalogued, stored and cared for . . . and almost certainly never to be either lost or looked at ever again.

The same fate nearly befell the elevenstring, which she kept maintained and which she played, briefly, about once a year. But that would have felt like just too much rejection; keeping the ridiculous instrument somehow kept her from feeling quite so bad about abandoning QiRia's soul, even if by now she had convinced herself, again, that he was just an old fraud.

Still, it was only when she was thinking of looking for a life-task to give her something to do while she waited for the Subliming to happen that she thought again of playing the thing.

This was a decision she would later regret, often.

She woke up, wondered where she was. Dim light, and her augmented eyes, showed her a room or cabin she didn't recognise. It looked very nice though. There was almost complete silence. She was in the spacious shuttle craft of the Culture ship, the *Mistake Not . . .* She looked over the side of the billow bed, located in a little alcove off the craft's main open area. Another alcove, closed off, held the inert body of the android Parinherm. The elevenstring was stashed overhead somewhere in a storage locker.

Pyan lay on the floor, a dark mat. It raised the tip of one corner lazily, sleepily acknowledging her, then went flat again.

She lay thinking about the day just passed. She'd been unconscious at least twice. She'd briefly met or at least seen dozens of people who were now all dead. She'd been rescued once, twice, just escaping death both times. And she'd been told to look for the soul of an old fraud she'd met once, for a few days, nearly twenty years earlier, when – looking back – she'd been little more than a kid. People were dying and ships damaging themselves to get her from place to place, and she wasn't at all sure she was the right person to do whatever it was they were all expecting her to do.

Soon it wouldn't matter anyway. She was still going to Sublime, wasn't she? Everybody else was. She supposed she'd sort of have to go if everybody else did.

Personally, she wasn't sure it really mattered whether the Book of Truth had been based on a lie; a lot of people had long half assumed that.

How much did it matter to others though? Perhaps a lot – perhaps enough. Would that knowledge – if it was true – stop people Subliming? Maybe it would. So much of the whole process of deciding to make this final civilisational transition had been about mood, relying on an atmosphere that involved a kind of gradually growing, shared, blissful, resignation. A feeling of inevitability had settled over the Gzilt somehow, self-propagating and self-reinforcing, making Subliming look like just the next, natural step.

People had been talking seriously about Subliming for

centuries, but it was really only in the generation or two before hers that the idea had started to traverse the spectrum of likelihood in the popular imagination, beginning at unthinkable, progressing to absurd, then going from possible but unlikely to probable and likely, before eventually arriving – round about the time of her birth – at seemingly inevitable.

And anticipated, and desirable.

Would all that change if it was discovered the Book of Truth had been some sort of alien trick and the hallowed, semi-worshipped Zihdren no better than charlatans?

Some people thought the Gzilt were going rather early, that most species/civs waited a little longer, entered a lengthier period of etiolation before taking the plunge . . . but then every species was different, and the Gzilt believed themselves especially different, *exceptionally* different, partly because of the Book and what it had told them. Would its message being brought into doubt kick away the foundations of that self-satisfaction and make people question the wisdom of Subliming at all?

Maybe – just embarrassed, if nothing else – they'd want to escape the shame and uncertainty involved by hurrying into Subliming with even more determination. Maybe only half the Gzilt would go, or just a fraction; enough still to be viable within the Sublime but leaving larger numbers behind, perhaps to make their own decision at some later date. So a schism, beyond healing, in the Sublime, and chaos, perhaps, back in the Real.

Even if the Subliming still took place as planned, in full, would the knowledge of that last-moment counter-revelation about the Book somehow colour the Gzilt experience once they had Enfolded?

If she recalled correctly all the books and articles she'd

read and the programmes and discussions she'd seen, it would make little or no difference, but nobody – not even Elder species who'd been studying exactly this kind of stuff for aeons – could be entirely sure, because so little detail ever came back out of the Sublime.

She didn't know; all she could do was what she'd been asked/ordered.

What she did know was that it really shouldn't be her responsibility how this panned out. She was just a musician, a civilian in the reserve who'd once, briefly, bumped into an old guy that suddenly everybody wanted to talk to.

She just wasn't that special. She was no idiot, and she would happily accept that she was a very gifted musician, but it ought not to be falling to her to work out any important part of this society-wide, alien-involving, end-of-days mess.

Maybe she should just leave QiRia in peace. Ask the ship to take her home, or to wherever or whatever had become the new HQ for the regiment, make her report there and then get taken back to Xown, the Girdlecity and her apartment, or just a place – anywhere – where she was less likely to be inside something getting shot at with hi-tech weaponry.

But she'd promised Reikl she would do as she'd been asked/ordered. She had been re-commissioned, too, so even with the Subliming coming up and all the usual rules and disciplines seemingly evaporating around everybody, there was still duty, self-respect, honour. You did what you felt you had to do so as not to feel bad about yourself when you looked back later. And memories, the recollection of past deeds, certainly survived into the Sublime. You were what you'd done, as QiRia had said, all those years ago. And as long as you had your context, you were still yourself within the great Enfolded.

She turned over, closed her eyes and hoped you could still sleep in the Sublime.

Septame Banstegeyn was able to make a great show of being utterly horrified to discover that there had been some sort of attack on the regimental HQ of the Socialist-Republican People's Liberation Regiment #14. News of the outrage came in shortly after the vote that handed Preferred partner status to the Ronte and he found it easy to channel all the rage and fury he felt at that debacle into his reaction to the later, even more serious news. He was still angry about it when he met up with Chekwri again, in the special chamber deep under the parliament.

"Two thousand people, Chekwri, in the Prophet's name . . ."

"Normally there would be between four and six thousand aboard," the marshal said calmly. "Plus there were five hundred virtual souls aboard the *Gelish-Oplule*. But in any event, Septame, what were you expecting of an attack to destroy a regimental HQ?"

"I thought you'd destroy the – the thing, the place, the AIs, but to kill so many, and that ship, everybody on it too – I mean, it's just terrible . . ."

"The AIs, and the High Command when they're aboard, are in the best protected bits of the HQ, Septame, located right in the heart of the moon, or ship; whatever you want to call it." Chekwri sounded as unbothered as she looked. She might even, it occurred to Banstegeyn, be enjoying this. He was aware that he was laying on a bit of an act himself, even though there was some truth in there too; he'd been genuinely horrified when he'd heard that, as far as was known, nobody had survived the attack. (Another part of him had felt triumphant that the attack had gone so well and the information so treacherously relayed to the

Fourteenth had been so surgically excised, but that part had to stay as secret as possible; he kept that suppressed as best he could, worried that if he thought about it too much it would somehow show in his face or be readable in his body language.) "To get to them you pretty much have to destroy the HQ completely," Chekwri concluded.

"Anyway," Banstegeyn said, "they're military. They'll have been backed-up, won't they? They can be reactivated, can't they? Some of them?"

"Most will have been backed-up within the HQ itself," the marshal said. "Maybe some elsewhere. Not that any military or civilian court would let that influence their view regarding the culpability of the action or the severity of any punishment."

"There should be no trial, no court, though, should there?" Banstegeyn said. "We – you – got away with it. Didn't we? I mean, there's not enough time, and I'm sure I could get . . . I could pull a string or two . . ."

According to the marshal, the most recent signal from the *7*Uagren* had indicated that it had managed to slip away from the Izenion system without being detected, after dealing with the last known survivors of the HQ's destruction; it had pursued them to the star Izenion itself, contained their attempts to signal, and ensured their swift termination.

"Yes, we got away with it," Marshal Chekwri said, with a small, humourless smile. "And in theory without leaving behind too obvious an attack profile. A disinterested observer would probably still conclude it had been fratricidal, but it could be argued otherwise, and there are only eighteen days remaining to do the arguing. And the string-pulling."

"Yes," Banstegeyn said, biting his lip a little. "And they definitely couldn't have already – the people, the AIs even, on the HQ – they couldn't have Sublimed by themselves, early? That's really not possible?"

"The people, definitely not; you need a Presence," the marshal said, with the air of one addressing somebody who really ought to have been watching their own infomercials over the last umpteen years. "The AIs, almost certainly not. It takes time, preparation. Even for an AI there's some sort of blissed-out, trance-like state that has to be achieved first before they can haul themselves in by their own bootstraps. Unlikely, in the circumstances."

"Mmm, mmm," the septame said, rubbing his face. "Good, good." He had been looking away. "So the attack, it could be blamed on somebody else?"

The marshal took a moment before answering. "Yes, it could," she said, slowly. "Though the plausibility spectrum might be a little . . ." she looked up to the domed ceiling of the room ". . . restricted, shall we say?" She looked back at the septame. "Why, did you have anybody particular in mind?"

"The Ronte?"

"The *Ronte*?" the marshal said. She frowned. "I thought we just made them our official Bestest Friends, Scavenger class."

"I think you'll find that is still conditional."

"In a way that they don't know about?"

Banstegeyn waved one hand. "Not your concern, Marshal. Is it plausible?"

Chekwri sat back, looked thoughtful. "Not really. Their main force is far too far away – unlikely even to get here before the Subliming – their tech is inadequate and their motive . . . I can't even think what their motive might have been."

"The Ronte with Culture help?" Banstegeyn suggested.

The marshal actually laughed. "Forgive me, Septame," she

said, one hand held out to Banstegeyn, though nothing else about her demeanour seemed apologetic. "Well, that would fill the tech gap, if we can put it that way, but I suspect the plausibility spectrum window just closed to zero."

"No story we come up with needs to last very long, though," Banstegeyn said, his face set in an expression of some displeasure. "Just until the Subliming."

"Septame, one like that is going to struggle to last to the end of the sentence that first articulates it."

"But there might have been a Culture ship there, at the Sculpt planet," the septame said.

"The *Uagren* was aware of *something* performing a manoeuvre called a crash-stop into Izenion system, about four hours after the attack. Just from the implied initial velocity involved it reckoned if it wasn't one of ours it must be a Culture ship. Even then, hard to find a plausible contender. Most likely it was something called the *Mistake Not . . .*, but if it was, the fucker's even faster than we thought."

"So we could – maybe – claim it had a part in the attack, couldn't we?"

"Not really. Unless the Culture has finally invented a time machine."

The septame's face suddenly assumed a hard, unforgiving expression. "I don't think," he said icily, "this is an issue to be made light of, Marshal Chekwri."

"Septame," the marshal said levelly, "I am not the one coming up with laughable ex-post-facto combat scenarios."

Banstegeyn glared at her for a little longer, seemed to realise he was wasting his time, waved one arm dismissively and said, "Well, leave that with me. But let's not close anything off." He took a deep breath. "The main thing is that the initial mission was successful. The leak has been . . . mopped up."

"There is the . . . possible loose end of the *Gelish-Oplule*," Chekwri said, with a tiny frown.

"But it was destroyed too, wasn't it?"

"Just; that was too close. The *Uagren* wasn't expecting it. But, yes, one less asset for the Fourteenth."

"Well, then. Why is there a problem?"

"Because the ship wasn't supposed to be there. And the fact that it was means it was keeping quiet about its movements *and* it must have moved to get there at the sort of speeds ships only undertake when they've got an urgent mission. Trans-excercisal speeds; you sim them but you don't attempt them, even during full-on war games."

"It might have been coincidence," Banstegeyn said. "Or it was there for the High Command if they needed transport."

"That's kind of what we're assuming for now," Chekwri said. She shrugged. "Anyway, it's vapour, and the Culture ship's moved off seemingly without actually doing anything. And now the *Uagren*'s slipped away too, unnoticed as far as we know."

"Yes. Where did it slip away to? Where's it going now?"

"Didn't I mention?" The marshal looked surprised. "It's following the Culture ship."

Eleven

(S -17)

xGSV *Contents May Differ*
   oLOU *Caconym*
   oGCU *Displacement Activity*
   oGSV *Just The Washing Instruction Chip In Life's Rich Tapestry*
   oUe *Mistake Not . . .*
   oMSV *Passing By And Thought I'd Drop In*
   oMSV *Pressure Drop*

Hello all. I think we've all been brought up to speed with individual briefings where needed; welcome to the new members of the group. We understand the *Mistake Not . . .* makes full speed to Ospin, perhaps to discover something relevant to Mr QiRia and hence the claimed provenance of the Z-R information re the BoT. Meanwhile the *Passing By And Thought I'd Drop In* has kindly agreed to continue to create what diplomatic pressure it can with the rump of the Gzilt political power structure. For myself, after extensive investigations, some calling in of favours and the reluctant acceptance of future obligations re the same on my part to those so confiding, I have discovered there may be another way to pursue the link with the legendary gentleman.

∞

xLOU *Caconym*

We really are taking this person's existence as being a fact, not a myth?

∞

xGSV *Contents May Differ*

We are. It turns out that the myth which has been so carefully fostered is that his existence is mythical. It would certainly appear that various ships have known of his existence over the millennia, and even aided him in his efforts to stay outside the public eye and evade the kind of official annoyances such as censuses and inventories which might prove problematic to somebody of preposterous age who wished to keep quiet about it. Until now his mythical status has seemed charming, romantic even, and – happily for all concerned – irrelevant to matters either tactical or strategic. Now, it has suddenly assumed a certain importance. We must, of course, diligently and timeously pursue every avenue of investigation occurring in Gzilt space. However, there may well be a way to reinforce and back up our inquiries, working at least partly within the Culture. I have been in contact with a vessel which wishes to remain anonymous for now but which holds a human who may be able and persuaded to help. The price would be something close to full disclosure of what we all know regarding the matter at hand, both to the ship and, probably, it speculates, the person concerned as well.

∞

xGSV *Just The Washing Instruction Chip In Life's Rich Tapestry*

∞

And the *Contents May Differ* vouches for the ship and it for the human?

∞

xGSV *Contents May Differ*
Within the usual limits, yes.

∞

xGSV *Just The Washing Instruction Chip In Life's Rich Tapestry*
Then I say go ahead.

∞

xGSV *Contents May Differ*
Any objections? . . . No? . . . Very well. Signal sent. I'll keep you all informed. Meanwhile, after some pressure, the *Empiricist*'s Delinquent pair the *Headcrash* and the *Xenocrat* have – finally – been persuaded to give up their smatter-bagging competition at Loliscombana and make haste for Gzilt; heading straight to Zyse at the request of something called the Gzilt Combined Regimental Fleet Command – this would appear to be some new overview structure recently set up by this Banstegeyn fellow under Marshal Chekwri. The two ships are due there in seven days. Due to an agreement required to bring about the aforesaid pressure, the *Empiricist* will now become part of the group at the next signal, though it has expressed

a preference for haunting rather than manifesting, as it were. The *Empiricist* itself now expects to be arriving at Zyse in eleven or twelve days. That's all for now.

∞

xGSV *Just The Washing Instruction Chip In Life's Rich Tapestry*
      oGSV *Contents May Differ*

Oh, hurrah. Now the *Empiricist* gets to hover glowering over everything and step in when it thinks we've done enough of the hard work to make the outcome sufficiently positive to enhance its gloriousness.

∞

   Size has its privileges.

∞

More to the point, we need to start thinking now about what we're going to do if we do find out the truth – via Mr Q, or any other route. Do we tell the Gzilt? And if we tell, do we tell only those at the top – who might already know/have guessed – or do we take it upon ourselves to broadcast the embarrassing news (assuming it is) to all?

∞

   Good question. I suspect a vote might be called for. Right now, personally, I'd probably plump for shutting the hell up and letting the Gzilt get on with it.

∞

Which begs the question, why, then, are we bothering to hunt down this truth at all?

∞

   The Z-R asked us to help. Also, it's just *interesting*. Here's something we don't know but we can maybe find out, *and* it's something that other people don't *want* us to know. How much more seductive can you get?

∞

Maybe there are some truths not worth chasing down. Maybe there are times when it's best to remain ignorant.

∞

Very funny.

∞

I'm being serious.

∞

Sure you are. Anyway, how goes your batch of the Simming? Mine is gnarlsome, raspulescent, grislesque.

∞

Never mind. Hitting both Problems, since you ask. Trying to work around, but it's getting all moral in one direction and chaotic in the other. Suspect it's basically Intrinsically Unamenable on both counts, but will keep on trying.

∞

Have a lie down, as one of one's humans might say to another.

∞

Shut up and get back to your work, as they also might say.

∞

Ha! Good simming. Over and outload!

A ship dance of celebration was required.

The fleet had already split into separate squadrons of eight ships apiece (save for the flagship squadron of twelve ships plus the accompanying Culture craft *Beats Working*) and these squadrons had flown in different directions towards their appointed places of interest where they might hope to accrue technology which would prove advantageous to the Ronte. Therefore, a full fleet dance could not be performed. Instead a coordinated split-fleet dance would be performed, each squadron and ship and crew being made conscious of the movements of all the others so that the distributed dance would be accomplished as a joyous whole, virtually.

Accordingly, the dance "Multiple New Swarmqueens, Brought Together By Advantageous Zephyrs, Display Together In The Light Of The Two Home Suns At Double Zenith" was performed, to glorious effect. At the respectful request of the Culture ship, a place was found for it to become part of the dance as well, a task of honour it executed with diligence, understanding and precision, to the greater glory of the Ronte people, who had, against all expectation, been granted the Preferred status that they had known they deserved but had doubted would be conferred.

The Culture ship *Beats Working* accordingly accrued additional inferred alien cachet value (positive), honorary, with made-awareness of award status deferred.

The fleet squadrons reconfigured to reflect their new status. All but a few adjusted their courses for more important sources of technology, infrastructure and territory, given that these were likely now to fall to them without dispute. The flagship squadron turned to set a course for Zyse, the Gzilt capital and home system.

"People were targeted, I tell you, Banstegeyn," Yegres told him as they walked in the grounds of the trime's villa in the hills overlooking the city. The parliament building shimmered whitely in the distance, blurred with warm air rising, the Presence a dark inverted drip-shape above it, made tiny by the distance.

A pair of light cruisers, their smooth, kilometre-long hulls silvered, hung in the air ten thousand metres above the city. This was supposed to be reassuring for the remaining

populace after the shock of the attack on the Regimental
HQ of the Fourteenth at Eshri.

"Targeted," Yegres repeated, glancing at Banstegeyn. The
two crunched along a gravel path, followed at a discreet
distance by Solbli and Jevan. Banstegeyn's chief secretary
and aide-de-camp were seemingly muttering to themselves,
partially sub-vocalising as they communicated elsewhere.
He'd given them the job of continuing to try and find a
way to nullify the Scavenger vote earlier. There had been
over ten millennia of inherently convoluted and frequently
murky parliamentary business, all of it faithfully recorded;
there had to be a precedent in there somewhere. It would
be a start if nothing else.

Yegres was accompanied by a float-tray. It held a glass
and decanter; he helped himself. "Frix was offered an intro-
duction to some girl he'd had his eye on – or Quvarond's
wife or something; I don't know – Yenivle took a case of
Kolymkin . . . something; some priceless vintage." Yegres
frowned. "Wish the bugger had offered me that. So thought-
less." He shrugged, shook his head. "Not sure what Jurutre
was offered, but seemingly something furtive regarding a
child. Not filthy, or even illegal, just . . . sad . . . Anyway,
it was all terribly well organised. Done with military precision." He barked a laugh. "Better than that, actually; didn't
miss and hit their own people."

"And you?" Banstegeyn asked. "What did Trime Quvarond
offer you?" He found it hard to keep the sneer out of his voice.

"Nothing at all, dear boy," Yegres said amiably, waving
one hand around. "I voted against you because I just don't
like you."

Banstegeyn was stopped in his tracks. He heard Jevan and
Solbli stop at the same time, gravel rasping under their feet.
They'd gone silent, poised.

Yegres wandered on, oblivious, for another couple of steps before stopping too. He looked back at Banstegeyn.

"Oh, just kidding you on," he said, smiling. "The vote was already lost so I joined in to look less . . . perennially obedient." He frowned. "But you should realise, Septame; everything is breaking down a little now, including your grip. What worked until now – obligations, understandings, favours owed, the promise of future advancement and the threat of secrets becoming public and so on – they don't have quite the force they did before." He shrugged, then smiled broadly. "This is what you wanted, Ban. What you worked for all this time, what you've engineered. End of an era. Ha! End of the end of *all* eras." He waved both hands this time, spilling a little wine. "School's breaking up. People are out to play."

Scoaliera Tefwe, who had been a friend and a lover of Ngaroe QiRia long ago, when he was already a very old man and she had been of conventional middle age – a little under two hundred – woke slowly, as she had woken slowly a few dozen times, over the intervening centuries.

Only it wasn't really waking slowly; she was being woken.

All dark at first. Stillness and silence too, and yet the sensation that things were happening nearby, and inside her head and body; organs and systems and faculties being woken, revived, checked, primed, readied.

It was at once reassuring and somehow disappointing. *Here we go again*, she thought. She opened her eyes.

SIMULATION, said the glowing red letters along the bottom of her field of vision. *Ah*, she thought, whereupon the word faded away.

So she was still sort of asleep, after all. But her consciousness and sense of embodiment were being woken up.

She was, apparently, already sitting, fully dressed, in a

THE HYDROGEN SONATA   239

chair facing a table in a large, pleasant-looking room of some antiquity with a view – to one side, through opened floor-length windows – over mountains lined with trees and a lake whose shore was lined with villages. The wakes of a few boats left long white Vs on the wind-ruffled waters.

At the other end of the table from the windows, there was a time display in an ornate wooden case. She looked at the date.

My, that had been a long sleep.

Across the table from her there was a chair. When she looked away from the time display, a figure hazed from nothing through transparency into seeming solidity over the course of a couple of seconds. The small, pale, androgynous figure now sitting opposite her appeared to be the avatar of the LSV *You Call This Clean?* This was reassuring; she was still where she might have expected to be. The calm conventionality of the whole being-woken process had been a fairly infallible sign that nothing was likely to be too wrong, but this helped confirm it.

On the other hand, she was usually woken lying down, with time to take stock if she wanted, and swing herself off the couch, perhaps take the air and take in the view from the balcony, and only go to sit at the table when she felt she wanted to. Not this time, though; getting the basic minimum here.

"Scoaliera," the virtual avatar said, smiling.

"YC," she replied. The *You Call This Clean?* didn't name its avatars or avatoids separately; people usually just called them "YC". "Are we both well?"

"We are."

Always good to know that your Stored self and the ship carrying it/you were judged to be well according to the punctilious standards of a Culture Mind. "So," she said, "what is it?"

"Hoping you'll agree to take a trip, fully uploaded-style, then to be downloaded into an avatoid."

"Where? Why?"

"Not sure where yet; you might be able to help answer that yourself. The why is that we need you to look for Ngaroe QiRia."

She raised one eyebrow. "Do you now?" The "we" the ship was referring to would be either Contact section, or Special Circumstances. Exactly who would become clear shortly, she didn't doubt.

The avatar nodded. "If you'd be so kind."

"Why?"

"He might have some information it would be useful to know."

"He's been alive for nearly ten millennia; I'm sure he has a lot of information it would be useful to know."

"No doubt. But this is probably something quite specific."

"What?"

"Not sure, but somehow relating to the shortly forth-coming Sublimation of the Gzilt."

This was news to her. She'd been Stored, this time, over four hundred years earlier, when, as far as she could recall, the Gzilt had seemed no more likely to go for Subliming than the Culture itself.

"That the best you've got?"

"More detail?" YC asked.

"More detail."

"You insist?"

"I do."

The ship told her about the intercepted message from the Zihdren-Remnanter and subsequent developments.

Tefwe thought. "Do we have a view on or interest in whether the Gzilt Sublime or not?"

"No."

"Take me through the levels."

"Culture as a whole; no – their business. Contact; not really – opinions differ, mildly. Some temporary local upset to be expected, in the short term especially relating to Scavengers, but all part of the process. SC; no stated interest. Probably some difference of opinion but nobody expressing. Not even a grumble of discussion let alone action. And things are otherwise quiet, so lack of interest not a result of distraction, temporary or otherwise."

"So this isn't an SC thing?"

"Not directly, though elements usually associated are cooperating. Specifically, a fast ship will be made available; whatever's closest to wherever you say you need to go. Other ships at your disposal if necessary should serial uploading and embodiment be required. Simming as unlikely to become an SC focus. Probably."

"So why are we bothering?"

"Just in case."

"Just in case what?"

"Just in case it turns out to be something we should have bothered about. Always try to avoid setting up future opportunities for kicking yourself." The YC smiled apologetically. "Very small thing attached to very momentous thing. One point three trillion people heading into the big Enfold in less than twenty days from now, but if the Zihdren-Remnanter news about the Book of Truth gets out, that might change things. And maybe it should change things. But either way, it would be good to know the truth. Even if we discover the truth, we don't have to volunteer it, and even if we discover the truth, don't volunteer it but are asked to provide it, we still don't have to – though that'd be harder to justify. The point is, if we are asked and we haven't even bothered to look, we look bad, and if we are asked and decide to tell what we know, we want to be confident what we're able to offer really is the truth, or as close as we could reasonably get to it."

"How many new faces know the old guy's not a figment?"

"Just one beyond reasonable doubt; the GSV *Contents May Differ*. There was no leak as such; the ship just did some inspired digging and was owed favours by the right mix of craft. Though the others in the handling group will have been briefed there's a possibility."

"The ITG?"

"No. Fresh group. Nobody's heard from the Interesting Times Gang all the while you've been Stored."

"How remiss."

"As well as waking you with the suggestion you might care to return to the fray, I've been asked to enquire if you know of any other ships that might have helped Mr QiRia over the years. Aside from the *Warm, Considering*, which we know about."

"The only other one I remember was called the *Smile Tolerantly*, an ancient GCU, but the last I heard it was about to become Eccentric or Sublime or do something equally unhelpful."

"Thank you. So . . ."

"You will recall I said I wouldn't go looking for QiRia unless it was something really important. Are you – they – deeming this to be?"

"Let's say suggesting rather than deeming. But tell me: what are your feelings?"

"Mixed. I dare say I'll do it, but I'm not terribly happy about it."

Tefwe had never liked the idea of being fully downloaded into something remote who got to play at being you – who thought they *were* you. You stayed who you were but then the remote "you" became somebody different, over time. The two of you – or more – could be re-integrated, but it was, she thought, an intrinsically messy process of frankly dubious morality.

"Thank you," the YC said, exhibiting relief. "May I transmit your mind-state now? There are various craft dotted throughout the galaxy, charged up, ready to roll. Rude to keep them waiting."

"I want to be kept informed about what the remotes get up to," she told it. Tefwe had been around Contact's less salubrious outskirts in one form or another for so long she could remember when there hadn't been anything called Special Circumstances, just a bunch of ships and others that acted like it, so she knew how to negotiate an agreement with a Mind acting as control such that she wouldn't end up kicking herself.

"Agreed."

"In full."

"Agreed."

"And a no-constraints chance to negotiate over subsequent re-integration, just me and it, or them."

"Also agreed."

"You'll let me know which ship?"

"Of course."

"Hmm." Tefwe sat back, thought. "All right," she said. "I agree."

"Done. Once again, thank you. Where do you want to head for?"

"Dibaldipen Orbital, Angemar's Prime system."

The YC looked blank for a moment, then said, "Ah, one of ours. We might be able to work through the O Hub. That'd be even quicker. We'll see. Hub Minds can be reluctant to indulge this sort of thing without demanding to know everything there is to know. Do we have a full name for the guy? First thing a Hub Mind's going to ask for."

Tefwe smiled. "He's so old full names hadn't been invented when he was born, but if they had been he'd have been Tursensa Ngaroe Hgan QiRia dam Yutton. And he has used that name in the past. The far past."

"Thank you. In any event, the nearest ship is an ex-Psychopath VFP. The *Outstanding Contribution To The Historical Process*. Just a few days away." YC looked puzzled. "Dibaldipen. That's where QiRia is?"

"I have no idea. But there's a drone there that ought to know."

"You think it'll still be there?" YC asked, sounding a little sceptical. "It has been four hundred years."

"It is retired and set in its ways. Gone native and to seed. I suspect it'll be there."

"So, if you're really so old, tell me what you've learned over the years, over the millennia. What are the fruits of your wisdom?"

"They are remarkably few. I have managed to avoid learning too many lessons. That may be what keeps me alive."

Cossont lay on her bed; the grey cube with QiRia's mind-state inside it sat on a bedside shelf. It was only the second time she'd turned the cube on since returning home. She, the volupt and the elevenstring had just moved out of her mother's house in M'yon into a place of her own, half the world away; she was starting to make new friends but struggling to get worthwhile gigs and maybe she was feeling lonely.

"So," she said, "living all this time has been to no purpose, basically."

"True, but that hardly distinguishes me from anybody else, does it?"

"But shouldn't it, or there's no point?"

"No. Living either never has any point, or is always its own point; being a naturally cheery soul, I lean towards the latter. However, just having done more of it than another person doesn't really make much difference." The voice from the grey cube paused, then said, "Although . . . I think living so long might have persuaded me that I am not *quite* as pleasant a person as I once thought I was."

Cossont, presented with two opportunities to be scathing just in these last few sentences, was aware she was choosing to take neither. She confined herself to, "Really?" said in a slightly sarcastic tone.

"Well," the voice said, seemingly oblivious, "one thing that does happen when you live a long time is that you start to realise the essential futility of so much that we do, especially when you see the same patterns of behaviour repeated by succeeding generations and across different species. You see the same dreams, the same hopes, the same ambitions and aspirations, reiterated, and the same actions, the same courses and tactics and strategies, regurgitated, to the same predictable and often lamentable effects, and you start to think, So? Does it really matter? Why really are you bothering with all this? Are these not just further doomed, asinine ways of attempting to fill your vacuous, pointless existence, wedged slivered as it is between the boundless infinitudes of dark oblivion book-ending its utter triviality?"

"Uh-huh," she said. "Is this a rhetorical question?"

"It is a mistaken question. Meaning is everywhere. There is always meaning. Or at least all things show a disturbing tendency to have meaning ascribed to them when intelligent creatures are present. It's just that there's no final Meaning, with a capital M. Though the illusion that there might be is comforting for a certain class of mind."

"The poor, deluded, fools."

"I suspect, from your phrasing and your tone of voice, that, as a little earlier, you think you are being sarcastic. Well, no matter. However, there is another reaction to the never-ending plethora of unoriginal idiocies that life throws up with such erratic reliability, besides horror and despair."

"What's that?"

"A kind of glee. Once one survives the trough that comes with the understanding that people are going to go on being stupid and cruel to each other no matter what, probably for ever – *if* one survives; many people choose suicide at this point instead – then one starts to take the attitude, Oh well, never mind. It would be far preferable if things were better, but they're not, so let's make the most of it. Let's see what fresh fuckwittery the dolts can contrive to torment themselves with this time."

"Not necessarily the most compassionate response."

"Indeed not. But my point is that it might be the only one that lets you cope with great age without becoming a devout hermit, and therefore represents a kind of filter favouring misanthropy. *Nice* people who are beginning to live to a great age – as it were – react with such revulsion to the burgeoning horrors that confront them, they generally prefer suicide. It's only us slightly malevolent types who are able to survive that realisation and find a kind of pleasure – or at least satisfaction – in watching how the latest generation or most recently evolved species can re-discover and beat out afresh the paths to disaster, ignominy and shame we had naively assumed might have become hopelessly over-grown."

"So basically you're sticking around to watch us all fuck up?"

"Yes. It's one of life's few guaranteed constants."

Cossont thought about this. "If that's true, it's a bit sad."

"Tough. Life is sometimes."

"And you're right: it doesn't exactly show you in the best light."

"You're supposed to admire me for my honesty."

"Am I?" she said, and reached over and turned the grey cube off.

That was when she decided she'd give the cube to somebody else, who might want it, or at least agree to care for it.

Twelve

(S -16)

"This isn't Ospin! These aren't the Dataversities! What the fuck's going on?"

Cossont had woken from a very deep and pleasant sleep, ordered breakfast and then asked the ship to show her where they were; ahead view or whatever it was called. The *Mistake Not . . .* had obliged, presenting the semblance of a deep screen across the bottom of her billow bed, just above her toes. The image it displayed was of a yellow-orange sun apparently setting behind a large rocky planet with dark striated clouds half obscuring a surface of mottled dark-tan land and deep-blue seas. Given that Ospin was a red giant system devoid of any rocky planets, this was all wrong.

"Eh? What?" Pyan yelped, fluttering untidily up from where it had settled on the floor during the night. "Not another emergency! My processing isn't built to take this!"

The ship appeared to be sinking quickly through a multiply banded set of assorted manufactures, small habs and other planetary satellites, dipping rapidly into the shadow of the planet so that the sun winked out. A bright spread of the satellites continued to shine against the dark surface beneath, then the ship was beneath them too.

"Change of plan," Berdle told her, the *Mistake Not . . .*'s avatar appearing in one corner of the holo, face absurdly big against the landscape below. "You'd better get dressed."

The image continued to show the planet getting nearer; they were almost in the atmosphere. The place looked familiar somehow. Also, there was something wrong about something here but she hadn't worked out what yet.

"Where the hell are we?" she wailed.

"Xown, in the Mureite system."

"What!"

"Oh for goodness' sake," Pyan said dramatically, and flopped over backwards, spread out over the bed, lying limp.

"I just fucking *left* Xown!" Cossont yelled, watching the landscape whip past underneath. "That's where I started out!"

"Welcome back," Berdle said, deadpan. "Are you getting dressed yet?"

"Wait a moment . . ." Cossont was staring at a black line filling the horizon ahead. Entirely filling the horizon ahead, from one extent to the other, like a vast dam across the sky. "Is that the fucking *Girdlecity*?"

"We're just a few minutes away. Better get dressed fast."

She jumped out of bed, started pulling on clothes, muttering and cursing. She stopped, frowned, sniffed, looked carefully at the Lords of Excrement jacket. Everything had been cleaned, and repaired. "Not so much as a by-your-fucking-leave," she muttered, pulling on freshly polished boots.

She glanced at the screen again. Thin wispy cloud, not far below. Sea beneath. Dark-blue sky above. Still sea beneath. A few filmy wisps of cloud shot past, level.

"Wait a fucking—" she said, just as she'd started pushing her fingers through her unkempt hair. "We're not even on the fucking ship, are we? It'd never come this far down—"

"No, we're not," Berdle said. "We left about five minutes ago."

"We're still on the shuttle."

"Yes."

She looked round the cabin. "So where are you?"

A double door parted in one wall and Berdle, sat in some sort of complicated seat with a giant screen in front, turned and looked back at her. "Hello." The avatar waved.

"Why the fuck are we – why am I – back on Xown?" She strode through to what proved to be a flight deck or something and threw herself down in the seat beside Berdle's. She glared at him as hard as she could but the avatar appeared impervious.

The wrap-screen showed the Girdlecity as a black mass filling most of the view. Spread across the huge, near-vertical cliff confronting them there were hints and slivers of something lighter than its pitch-black surface where patches of dark-blue sky were visible through its filigree of open-work sections.

"We are here," Berdle told her, "because while you were asleep, more information came in, as information is prone to do, and one particular detail passed on by another ship involved happened to be the Culture full name of your friend

Mr QiRia. Which would be Tursensa Ngaroe Hgan QiRia dam Yutton."

"But I didn't—!" Cossont started to say, then stopped herself.

Berdle nodded. "No, you didn't say who the Culture person was you were talking about earlier, but we'd already kind of worked that out."

"Oh, had you now?" Cossont said, trying to sound defiant, but feeling herself sink a little further into the seat.

"First thing I did with the full name was plug it into all the data I've been soaking up since I've been here; Gzilt stuff," Berdle said. "*All* the Gzilt stuff; everything not officially private, anyway. And in amongst the passenger manifests for people making a trip to Xown five years ago a name popped out; Yutten Turse. Claimed to be Peace Faction Culture and to have come all the way from somewhere called Neressi, which, on closer inspection, is somewhere that doesn't exist, or is perhaps a colloquial name for a place nobody's catalogued properly." Berdle glanced at her, grinning. "Tut, tut."

The Girdlecity really did fill the screen now. Cossont had to crane her neck to see anything that wasn't the vast, dark mass of it. Right at the top she could see the sky, speckled with stars and orbiting sats, but it was just a thin band above the striated black curtain of the structure. Below, there were waves; the Girdlecity was crossing sea. She knew it did, in two places. Here, its colossal architecture was even more mind-boggling than anywhere else on its circuit of the planet. It extended undersea, still growing in girth, descending an extra kilometre beneath the waves if this was the Hzu Sea, an extra two and half thousand metres if this was Ocean.

"Doesn't that count as an amateur mistake if he's trying to keep off everybody's sensors?" Cossont asked.

Berdle shrugged. "I suppose, but in the end he's just an

old guy trying to stay out of the limelight, not some SC super-agent on a mission. Not the end of the world for him if he is discovered, anyway; not like he's going to get slung into prison or have his memories wiped. He'd become the object of some unwanted media attention for a while and there'd be a bunch of Minds who'd love to talk to him, but he'd be able to disappear again fairly quickly with the co-operation of a Mind and ship or two." Berdle paused, looked quizzically at her. "You've met him; maybe he'd like to get caught briefly, just to get to feel important, like he's not been forgotten."

"Maybe." Cossont crossed all four of her arms, forming a cage across her chest. "Are you saying he really is the age he says he is?"

Berdle nodded. "Looks like it."

"And you think this is going to be him. Have been him. This Yutten Turse guy?"

"Ran all this past a few stats packages," Berdle said, "and, even allowing for appropriate fuzzinesses of intra-species spelling, phonetics and pronunciation, the match chances are better than seventy per cent." The avatar nodded at a sub-screen set into the haptic band set across the centre of the encompassing main screen. "Got some screen of him." A holo leapt out, miniaturised. The first item was a still image of a man in late middle age, wearing a big silly grin, a loud shirt and a grass hat.

"Is that supposed to be *him*?" Cossont asked. She was still feeling cross.

Berdle nodded. "That is Mr Yutten Turse, of who-knows-whereville."

"Looks nothing like him," she snorted. Though, zooming in on the face, there might have been something familiar about his eyes.

"Hmm," Berdle said, obviously unconcerned. "Still, he was coming here, to the Girdlecity."

Cossont snorted again. "You might be surprised how little that narrows things down, spaceship."

Berdle smiled but didn't look at her. "I am aware of the structure's dimensions."

On the sub-screen, some moving footage followed: the man seemed to get slightly lost in the transit lounge, apparently unsure which way to go, until he left, led by a modest amount of luggage on a helpful float-trolley. Maybe he did walk a little like QiRia. Maybe. He disappeared. A still of his face came back, then was replaced by another set of screen images which seemed to show him leaving again, dressed similarly but wearing big dark glasses. If anything, he looked even less sure where he was going on the way back. The images faded away and the sub-screen went dark.

Ahead, the view was all Girdlecity; even sitting forwards, craning her neck, there was no sign of sky or sea. A few tiny, dim lights were only now starting to prick the obsidian surface of the structure. Berdle must have thought an instruction to the shuttle, because the screen extended smoothly, silently backwards, so that the view now took in directly overhead and a little further back. Looking straight up, she could see the sky again. She nearly said thank you, but didn't.

"Hello, that looks familiar," Pyan said, flapping and hopping through to sit on her lap. "Girdlecity?"

"Huh," Cossont said.

"Oh," Pyan said. "Hzu coast. That'll be pretty."

How fucking dare QiRia come back to where she lived – not just the civilisation but the system, the *planet* where she lived – and not look her up? What sort of friend was that?

"So, do we think he was looking for somebody?" she asked.

"According to his subsequent movements, happily documented by your fearsomely watchful Aliens Bureau, it seems he was looking for a particular person or for a particular artefact/location," Berdle said. "Which he seems to have found."

"Where in the Girdlecity?" Cossont asked. This wasn't the bit she knew; this was about a third of the way round the planet from Kwaalon and the great plains.

"He was going to Launch Falls," Berdle said.

"That's nowhere near here," she told him.

"I know. The artefact/location concerned has moved."

"Oh yeah?"

"Yes. It's an airship."

"One of the internals?"

"Only one still moving, apparently."

"I've heard of it," she told the avatar.

"Apparently it's famous," Berdle confirmed. "Well, notorious."

"Hope you're ready for a party," she told the avatar, one eyebrow hoisted even though it wasn't looking at her.

The avatar's head tipped briefly. "Ready for anything."

Cossont was silent for a moment as the Girdlecity drifted closer and more detail began to show on the dark textures of its surface. "It really didn't look all that much like him," she said.

"What has that got to do with anything?" The avatar glanced at her. "Seventy per cent represents a good chance."

Cossont frowned suddenly. "Where did you say he claimed to have come from?"

"Neressi."

"Spell that?" The avatar spelled it for her. "In Marain?"

she asked, frown deepening. She listened again, nodded. Ahead, whole constellations of lights were brightening into existence against the surface of the Girdlecity as they continued to draw closer. They were still fifteen or twenty kilometres out. She sighed. "It's probably better than seventy per cent," she told the avatar. "When he was on Perytch IV he was . . . you know . . . transplanted, had his consciousness transferred into this gigantic sea creature. He took the name . . . Isseren."

Berdle nodded. "Ah-ha," the avatar said, softly.

"Oh!" Pyan said, after a moment. "Backwards!"

"Yes," Cossont said sourly. "Fucking backwards."

Jelwilin Keril, the Iwenick Cultural Mission Director, left the Strategic Outreach Element *CH2OH.(CHOH)4.CHO* in his private yacht.

At least he was able to call his yacht something sensible. He'd named it *Iberre*, in honour of his father-mother. And he was allowed to refer to it as a yacht, not a Space-Capable Inter-Element Transportation Component, or something of similar over-literal awkwardness. He looked back at the Strategic Outreach Element *CH2OH.(CHOH)4.CHO*. It hung against the star-flecked blackness, a svelte grey flattened ellipsoid.

Strategic Outreach Element. Everybody else would just call it a ship.

Still, this was modern-day thinking. "Ship" just sounded a bit crude, apparently – redolent of bulbous wooden things rolling around on the high seas, infested with parasites and stinking with drunken, seasick sailors. Even the Culture's partiality to the term "unit" – used by the Iwenick until recently in a slightly cringing attempt at flattery – was seen as not fully expressing the powers and capabilities of the vessels it was attached to. Apparently, according to the advisors who made their living thinking about this sort of thing, "unit" was for ever associated with the words "light industrial".

He turned back. Never mind. But he knew exactly why he was thinking about names.

The Liseiden flagship, the Collective Purposes vessel *Gellemtyan-Asool-Anafawaya* (the name of some ancient Liseiden hero, so acceptable, if unpronounceable) swelled in the screen, a well-lit hangar already open for the yacht. The ship was a jumbled mass of planes and edges, barely even symmetrical from certain angles. It was supposed to appear complicated and impressive but to Jelwilin it just looked like a confused slump of different-sized boxes, like the result of an accident in a warehouse.

Jelwilin inspected his image in a screen. Full uniform, perfectly groomed, manicured and made-up. He looked great – not that an alien would notice or care. This could all have been done in a few minutes, of course, by him simply holo-ing in to the Liseiden ship's command deck and talking to them that way, but there were times when a personal appearance – even a personal appearance inside a glorified fish bowl – was the only way to show the desired portion of respect, and the Liseiden were certainly expecting the full serving, to compensate for the wound to their pride and expectations they'd just experienced at the hands of the perfidious Gzilt. Hence the ship rendezvous and the face-to-face.

Cultural Mission Director Jelwilin patted down his uniform jacket, adjusted a cuff. He felt the need to urinate, but he had already done so before leaving the ship, and knew this was simply the result of nerves.

"He wants *more*?" Team Principal Tyun roared. "The son-of-a-runt!"

Sitting – comfortably enough, but very conscious that he was contained within a perfectly transparent sphere, exposed to inspection from every side – in front of the array of sinuously floating Liseiden, their bodies waving to and fro like fat scarves in a slow-motion breeze, Cultural Mission Director Jelwilin set his face as well as he could in an expression of understanding and shared pain. The Liseiden might not have any officers capable of interpreting his species' facial expressions, but they would probably have AIs which could; might as well make the effort. Anyway, it was all integral to the part he was playing here. Method diplomacy.

"The septame tells us that he is confident that he can overturn the decision," Jelwilin said calmly. "And Ambassador Mierbeunes is very – and very encouragingly – insistent that the septame will be able to make this happen. Ambassador Mierbeunes is one of our most senior and most experienced diplomats, as well as one of the most successful. I have known him for many years and I don't think I have ever seen him more confident in the abilities of another person. The thing is that to achieve what he believes he can, Septame Banstegeyn assures us that he needs to take greater risks than those he has taken until now. Accordingly, he asks for a greater reward. And, frankly, Team Principal, what he asks for is something it costs you next to nothing to agree to. And I emphasise 'agree to' rather than, say, 'grant' or even 'fully commit to in your soul'."

Tyun's voice seemed to come from somewhere underneath the little stalk-seat Jelwilin was sitting on. It was disconcerting, as was being able to hear the Liseiden's actual words, booming liquidly – if muffled – against the surface of the transparent sphere, a sort of continuous guttural bubbling that barely preceded the translated version.

"I'm taking the point that it might *seem* to cost us next to nothing to agree to renaming a local star," the Team Principal said, "but what I want to ask is: is that actually relevant? I think we risk being seen to reward failure if we concede this, Cultural Mission Director. We are not here to indulge that sort of shit."

"If I might liken this to a military campaign, Team Principal," Jelwilin said, "what we have suffered here is a reverse, and a battle lost, certainly, but it is not final defeat, and the war remains winnable. Of course I appreciate that one might, in theory, be seen to be rewarding failure, but a side that shoots its generals after every lost battle would quickly run out of good generals as well as bad, or end up with a population of generals who did everything they could to avoid all battles, even the most winnable, just in case."

"But that is not the alternative, Jelwilin," Tyun said. "The alternative is to take a more robust attitude to securing the acquisition of the technology and infrastructure we've been seeking and thought we'd been promised. Let me be clear. We have the fire-power to enforce the bargain that was already arrived at. We cannot, and we will not, be seen to be weak in this."

Jelwilin looked pained. "Obviously, we all hope that using force of arms would be regarded as very much the last resort. I need hardly tell you, sir, that hostilities are always expensive, of reputation as well as materiel, and it would, I am sure you would agree, be better to settle this without recourse to the uncertainties and chaos of war, particularly given the already engaged interest of another level-eight civ in the shape of the Culture, and *especially* following the still unexplained attack on the regimental HQ of the Fourteenth on Eshri; things are *very* delicately poised after that, and even without the involvement of the Culture I need hardly point out that, although much depleted, the Gzilt fleet remains an extremely powerful force. Please, Team Principal, let me report back to Ambassador Mierbeunes that I have your permission to continue to pursue a more peaceful solution."

"Yes, well, the Culture appears to have lost interest in us," Tyun said. "The ship they sent as escort apparently found more pressing matters to attend to."

"I understood that a Thug-class Fast Picket was on its way to join you," Jelwilin said.

"Hmm. Not if I can help it. We're going to try throwing them off with some judicious re-dispositioning. A moment," Tyun said. The transparent sphere surrounding Jelwilin suddenly became opaque, leaving the Cultural Mission Director staring at a fuzzy representation of the Liseiden ship's command centre. He could make out some deep, distant-sounding bubbling noises that were doubtless the Liseiden discussing the matter amongst themselves.

"The fire-power to enforce the bargain", indeed. That was overly aggressive. What were they playing at? Hadn't the Liseiden simmed this? If there was a proper shooting war between the Liseiden and the Ronte, even the victor would probably come out of it worse off in the long term. Never mind any formal censure from the Galactic Council; high-level players like the Culture would take a dim view of a situation that looked entirely soluble by peaceful means suddenly tipping into the mayhem of a war, no matter how small. Whoever instigated *that* would find themselves on the wrong end of not just one short leash but several, as a bunch of their betters suddenly decided they ought to keep a closer eye on these semi-barbarians who'd had the temerity to threaten the galactic peace.

And all for some territory and left-behind tech. Or at least a cut of it, in the Iwenick's case.

Jelwilin had always respected those civilisations that left their achievements behind, intact, when they Sublimed, so that the results of their labour and intellects could be put to use by others, but he could appreciate that there were reasons – beyond a childish desire to take your toys with you – for razing your structures, flattening your cities, collapsing your habitats, deleting all the hi-tech-enabling information you possessed and destroying anything else that people might fight over. Well, save for planets, he supposed.

Some species did it that way, and apparently a proportion always had, ever since Subliming began, so there was no particular disgrace in it. The Gzilt, though, had never been big on razing or burning; certainly not just for the sake of it. They were, and had always been, pragmatic rather than revengeful. Supposedly this was one of the behaviours they'd contributed to the demeanour of the Culture right at the beginning, even though they hadn't actually joined it.

The sphere went transparent again. Discussions had obviously been concluded. Jelwilin sat up straight and assumed an expression of cautious optimism.

"Mission Director," Tyun said. "We have come to a decision." The Liseiden sounded curt, severe. Jelwilin felt relief. Tyun would be compensating for a decision to keep talking rather than to get threatening. A conciliatory, regretful or solemn tone would have augured very badly. "You may authorise Ambassador Mierbeunes to continue negotiations and continue our earlier course regarding the septame."

Jelwilin bowed. "Thank you, Team Principal."

"Furthermore, to reinforce the perception of our commitment to a successful outcome regarding the totality of this matter, we shall re-disposition the main portion of our fleet to Zyse."

Jelwilin assumed his pained expression again.

"Team Principal, if I might make a suggestion—"

"No, thank you, Mission Director," the Liseiden said, politely but firmly. "You may not. Kindly don't make the mistake of imagining you're entering this discussion anywhere else than following its conclusion. The actions I've outlined are settled. They will not be subject to further negotiation. We thank you for your assistance and valued advice."

Jelwilin knew when to give way with grace. "I understand, Team Principal," he said. "I wish us both the best fortune in these endeavours."

"Thank you," Tyun said, his body making slow S shapes in some unseen current. "You may return to your . . . Element."

As far as anybody could tell, the Girdlecity of Xown had been built by the long-Sublimed Werpesh simply because they could. Nearly thirty thousand kilometres long, the structure formed a single vast bracelet round the equator of the world. A-shaped in cross-section, over a hundred kilometres across at the base, dozens at the top and just under two hundred klicks high – so tall that it protruded above almost all the atmosphere, providing Xown with a spaceport sufficiently prodigious to have served a thousand such worlds – the Girdlecity was a single colossal barricade, an everywhere-pierced wall, halving the planet.

Even building on this extraordinary scale, there were touches of elegance to its design; because Xown was a planet with little wobble and the Girdlecity straddled the equator, it effectively sat between the narrow tropic lines, only ever casting a shadow on lower parts of itself, never on the planet's surface.

And it could easily have been bigger. As a Non-Gravitationally Constrained Self-Supporting Artefact, or, colloquially, just an NG – which sort of stood for Neutral-Gravity structure – it was formed from a mix of ordinary and exotic materials that meant only a tiny fraction of its mass actually imposed itself as weight upon either its own lower reaches or on the crust of the planet beneath. Had they wanted, the Werpesh could have arranged it so that where the mighty structure's foundations met Xown's bedrock, they exerted a gentle upward pull, rather than a modest load. Artefacts constructed using this sort of technology could be extended indefinitely, with no annoying tendency to collapse in on themselves. Most such structures were in space, and some were much bigger.

The Girdlecity had the additional problem of needing to keep its structural elements tuned for their precise place within the slope of the planet's gravity well, but this had proved trivial. Even so, while nearly weightless, the artefact still had colossal mass, and its effect on Xown's total angular momentum had been to slow down the planet's rotation by nearly a second a year.

As was the case with each of their impressive if arguably rather pointless Sculpt worlds, the main point of the Girdlecity, as far as its builders had been concerned, appeared to have been the building of it, rather than any subsequent use it might have been put to. The Werpesh – famously secretive and opaquely motivated – had never chosen to elaborate on their reasons for constructing it. Some of them had lived in portions of it and it did function as a kind of grossly over-engineered spaceport, but the main use it might have had – attracting alien tourists – wasn't one the Werpesh had ever chosen to promote. Most of the time, before the Werpesh finally did the decent thing and Sublimed, the sparsely populated, barely used Girdlecity had just sort of sat there.

The Gzilt had made better use of it, but even then, in nearly eleven thousand years of custodianship, they had never even come close to filling it entirely, and rarely ventured into the sections above the level where there was natural atmosphere to breathe, leaving over ninety per cent of it empty of life. Space habitats, for all their even greater intrinsic artificiality, were capable of providing far more agreeable, pleasantly rural, less brutally industrial-feeling places in which to live.

Still, the Girdlecity had contained many billions, and even now contained hundreds of millions of Gzilt. And in a sense, of course, it still contained those billions, except the vast majority of them were Stored, existing in a state of suspended animation, awaiting the pre-waking just before the Instigation that would itself lead to their new life in the Sublime.

There had always been open tunnels within the Girdlecity; routes – some never less than half a kilometre in diameter – within the length of it that stretched throughout its fretwork of vast tubes, girders, walls and components both structural and habitative to provide a kind of large-scale transport network for airships. The great dirigibles had plied the vast tunnels for millennia, carrying people and occasionally goods, even though there were many faster, more efficient systems built into the Girdlecity. Airship travel was seen as romantic.

Now, as far as was known, there was only one airship still making its way through the structure, and it was home to the Last Party.

The Last Party was a five-year-long Debaucheriad aboard

the airship *Equatorial 353*; it circled the Girdlecity once a year, the last revolution being timed to coincide with the Instigation, when, a day or two earlier, the *Equatorial 353* would arrive back at Launch Falls, the section of the Girdlecity where it had begun its voyage.

The *Equatorial 353* was a fairly conventional vacuum dirigible two kilometres long and four hundred metres across; it had always been a kind of contained cruise ship, slipping through the structure of the Girdlecity, taking one or other of the various routes made available through the structure by the network of tunnels, throughways and assorted larger spaces dispersed within it.

Nominally owned by one of the many collectives which had been set up within the Girdlecity, it had been due to cease flying with all the other ships as the waking population of the structure dwindled to less than five per cent of what it had once been. Then a small group within the collective – one based on the pursuit of art and experimental living, so it had been pretty eccentric even at the best of times – had suggested keeping the thing flying, right to the end, and making a proper going-away party of its last flight.

The original idea had been to have a year-long party, one that would have started over four years after the suggestion was first put forward, but such was the excitement the idea produced, nobody could stand to wait that long so the plan was altered: it would be a five-year-long party, and fate help all who dared to sail on it.

The small group within the collective had been led, or at least fronted, by a man called Ximenyr, who'd been into a variety of radical body arts and amendment. He was one of the founding members of the Last Party, and one of a few dozen out of the original few hundred who had started out who was still determinedly partying; most of the rest had given up, burned out, been hospitalised or died. A few had even got religion. The party hadn't fizzled out, though; quite the opposite. It had grown in size over the years as more and more people heard about it and arrived to sample its delights until it entirely filled the two thousand accommodation and social units aboard the ship and there was supposedly a waiting list if you wanted to stay overnight. Though, given that one of the (few) guiding principles of the Last Party was that all things ought to be as shambolic as possible at all times – and it had entirely lived up to this rule – nobody really took this restriction especially seriously. Unless, of course, the sheer weight of bodies aboard led to the airship starting to bump along the bottom of its open-work tunnel, in which case it was time to restore buoyancy by disposing of any blatantly unnecessary items, such as articles of furniture.

"Are we clear?"

"Consider me briefed. How close do you have to get?"

"Just inside might make all the difference, though the closer to the man himself the better. ROAT, preferably."

"Roat?"

"Reach Out And Touch. This sort of distance."

"Okay."

~Hear me via the earbud?

"Yes," she said. She'd never been great at sub-vocalising.

"Do you want me to wake the android Eglyle Parinherm?"

"Not especially."

"And how necessary is it that your familiar accompanies us?"

"Very!"

"I wasn't really talking to you. Ms Cossont?"

"Let's compromise on moderately. It can be useful."

"'*Useful*'?" Pyan screeched. "Is *that* all?"

"Can you ask it to be discreet?"

"Certainly. Pyan; until further notice, shut the fuck up."

"Well, really!"

Cossont took a step back. "Is your face . . . ?" she said. "Your *head's* changing!"

Berdle shrugged. In the last few moments the avatar had gone from its earlier appearance to looking like a tall, handsome Gzilt male with a dramatically sculpted facial bone structure.

"Just fitting in," the avatar said reasonably. Berdle definitely looked masculine now, Cossont thought. Its whole body had altered; it/he looked like a strikingly attractive and leanly fit Gzilt male.

"How are you *doing* this?" she asked.

"Skilfully," Berdle replied, expressionless.

WHAT WANT? said the face in front of them.

"You can *hear*, can't you?" Cossont said, speaking loudly and clearly and even bending forward a little.

The person in front of them appeared to have a round flat face exactly like a large plate of alphabet soup: a yellow-brown liquid holding lots of little white letters, somehow held at ninety degrees to vertical when it looked convincingly as though the whole lot should be spilling to the floor of the balcony hangar. It could, Cossont supposed, be a screen or more likely a holo, but when she'd first bent forward to look at it she'd have sworn it was real; there was vapour coming off it and she could *smell* the soup. Otherwise the person looked physically relatively normal; either a thin female or a rather hippy male of average height dressed in a motley of violently spray-painted military gear. The top, sides and chin of his/her head flowed seemingly naturally into the bowl making up their face.

The letters in the soup bowl rearranged themselves: COURSE HEAR!

Berdle, standing alongside Cossont, crossed one leg over the other, put his arm over her shoulders and drew deeply on a fat drug stick. He held the breath, grinned at the person with the soup-bowl face. Berdle was dressed like a badly lagged pipe; a thick, red, pillowy material wrapping his limbs and torso was held in place by loose-looking black straps.

"We'd like to talk to The Master of the Revels," Cossont said, a little more quietly. This was the title Ximenyr had taken nearly a year earlier, for the last circuit of the Girdlecity and the planet before the Big Enfold.

WHO?

Cossont sighed. "Ximenyr."

Berdle brushed some ash off Cossont's jacket. She hadn't even seen Berdle change; in some moment between the module touching down on a deserted piazza about a kilometre above the waves and them walking off the deck into the structure he'd gone from whatever he'd been wearing earlier (she couldn't remember) to what he was wearing now.

She'd looked back, frowned, and started wondering if this was some projection. She'd stepped towards him as they'd walked, rubbed his sleeve fabric between thumb and finger. Nope; real.

"Sorry," she'd said.

"None taken," he'd replied. She'd looked askance.

Maybe, she'd thought, it was some ultra-clever and adaptable piece or pieces of clothing, or – along with his whole face-and-body-altering thing earlier – maybe it meant the entire avatar was some sort of swarm-being, made up of tiny machines. She'd looked him hard in the eye, from very close up, but he'd still contrived to look like flesh and blood.

She'd pulled away. "Sorry, again."

"Still none taken."

She was dressed as she had been, freshly repaired Lords of Excrement jacket included, with Pyan rolled into a scarf shape and draped over her shoulders.

They'd walked through the empty tubularity of the local architecture, their way lit by a few small and distant lights. They'd come to a long gallery where the nose of the airship was just starting to slide past like a colossal walking-speed tube train. It was moving so slowly she'd thought it had stopped, but it was still going, if only at a slow stroll. Thirty thousand klicks in a year; she supposed that did equate to strolling speed. The tunnel the ship moved in looked like a gigantic woven basket of dark filaments, stretching to a hazed curve within the greater structural and architectural elements of the Girdlecity. A few random lights shone; so few the average unaided eye would have interpreted the gloom as something close to utter darkness. Good to have augmentation, she'd thought. She'd glanced at the avatar. Berdle probably had eyes that could see through planets.

A thin metal net strung on stanchions protected them from the drop into the curve of tunnel.

The molecule-thin hull of the ship was probably red underneath, though it was hard to tell in the paltry light because the surface was so thoroughly splattered with a berserk variety of patterns, diagrams, logos and drawings, some illuminated, some moving – some looping, some not – and covered with flowing, bedraggled banners, gently waving pennants and ragged flags.

The nose pushed slowly out past them, right to left, the ship seeming to broaden out to meet them, metre by metre, until it looked like the airship was going to collide with the gallery she and Berdle stood on. There was what looked like a trench gouged in the side of the ship, level with the gallery they stood on.

~Lateral hangar-balcony, the avatar had sent. Then he looked down, and she had the very strong impression Berdle was looking somehow through the airship. ~Hmm. Taking on a lot of water. Interesting.

The hangar-balcony was closed off with what were probably lengths of diamond film. One of these had slid aside just as that part of the trench had started to pass them. Berdle had reached down, lifted the metal net away. The floor of the hangar-balcony was so close they could just step onto it across a half-metre gap. That had been when the soup-faced person had come, almost tumbling, out of a nearby door and asked them WHAT WANT?

~Combat arbite just behind the door, Berdle had told Cossont. ~One-legged combat arbite with no ammunition and the mechanical equivalent of arthritis, but just so's you know.

The letters forming the word WHO! had taken their time drifting apart. Now they slipped beneath the yellow-brown surface while others surfaced and rearranged themselves.

ASLEEP said the word now seemingly floating on the soup-face.

The avatar was exhaling, blowing the smoke out his ears.

~No, he's not, he said quietly via Cossont's earbud. Berdle claimed to have something called a scout missile within metres of Ximenyr, inserted into his cabin without him noticing while the module had still been approaching the Girdlecity. ~Shall I call him now?

"We could just call him," Cossont said to the soup-face, glancing at Berdle. "Or we could wait. That would only be polite. Tell him an old friend of Mr QiRia is here to see him."

~We ought to call him. Time's a-wasting.

APPOINTMENT?

"That's very kind," Cossont said. "But we won't need one. I'm sure he'll see us as soon as he can."

The soup-face jerked back a little as though surprised. New letters arranged themselves quickly, struggling to find enough room in the space available.

NODOYO UHAV EAPP Some letters disappeared; the rest rearranged themselves again. NO. YOU HAVE APP?

"No, we don't," Cossont said patiently. "This is, in its own small way, urgent. You don't have appointments for urgent things, as a rule, do you?"

NO APPOINT?

"We'd be terribly obliged if you'd just let him know we're here, right now. Don't forget to mention Mr QiRia's name."

SORRY.

"Sorry?" Cossont said. She tapped one booted foot while the letters swam about.

STILL ASLEEP

~Call? Berdle sent.

"We'll call him ourselves," Cossont said.

~Thank you. Calling.

YBL

"Cheers, I'm sure we will be lucky," Cossont said.

~Ringing.

Somewhere beyond the open-work wall behind them, the grey light of dawn was introducing a wash of colour into the detail of the giant multiply pierced tunnel.

~About to get bright, Berdle sent via the earbud. ~Little danger. Still ringing.

An instant later, light burst and flooded all around them and a cacophony assailed Cossont's ears. She looked round and saw the basket-work of the great open tunnel and the parts of the structure immediately beyond all lit up with stuttering pulses of multi-coloured light. Deep thuds were followed by the crackling boom and partial echo of air explosions.

DAWN FIREWKS

"How quaint," Cossont said.

~He's picked up. Over to you.

"Mr Ximenyr?" Cossont said, turning slightly away from the soup-face.

"Who is this?" a deep male voice drawled. He sounded sleepy or just stoned.

"My name is Vyr Cossont. I'm—"

"Wait, wait, girl; how did you get through to – nobody's supposed to be—"

~Privacied, Berdle sent to her, voice quick and clipped. ~Continues: "—able to get through on this without . . ." Cossont heard Ximenyr's voice continue, even though the connection was quiet. "You any . . .?" the human voice said. "Yeah, check the bases, pull it off replay. Veer Kossin or something."

"Yeah," the man said via the earbud again. "How'd you get through to me here? Not supposed to accept . . ." His voice trailed off. It sounded like he'd been distracted.

~An acolyte is performing a sexual act on Mr Ximenyr, Berdle reported.

Cossont listened to some heavy breathing for a moment or two, then said, quite loudly, "I'm an old friend of Mr QiRia; he visited you five years ago, at the start of the party. Do you remember him?"

The heavy breathing stopped.

~Mr Ximenyr has pushed the acolyte away, Berdle reported. ~The sexual act has ceased.

"Well, if I don't, something or somebody will remember for me, I'm sure," Ximenyr said. "Assuming this actually happened. Who did you say again?"

"My name is Vyr Cossont. Friend of Ngaroe QiRia. I'd like to meet with you."

"Yeah . . . How *did* you get through?"

~Mr Ximenyr is gesturing to call up a video feed from here, the avatar sent. Berdle sucked on the drug stick, bent close to Cossont's ear and said, "With great difficulty!" Cossont coughed, waved the resulting smoke away. The avatar smiled up at the corner of the hangar-balcony. Cossont looked too but couldn't see anything. "Hi," the avatar said, and waved. The rest of the smoke came out of his ears again.

"Uh-huh," the deep voice said. "And you would be?"

"Dying to meet you, Master of the Revels, sir," Berdle said cheerily. "My name's Berdle."

Cossont heard silence on the connection for a moment.

~He's saying: "'Berdle'? . . . Nothing? Vyr Cossont? Mil reserve? Just civilian? . . . Muso, yeah? Wearing an Excrements top; that's cool enough. And look at her; *I'd* – Wait a fucking minute. I remember that name. No, QiRia. Fucking QiRia fella. Fuck, him. Fuck. Yeah, okay. Yeah, yeah. Okay. Yeah. Fucking . . . welcome aboard, classical girl. Yeah. Right."

"Hello?"

"Mr Ximenyr."

"Come on in. Welcome. Hope you're broad-minded."

PLEASE COME IN

The wide door behind the soup-faced person was swung open by a one-legged combat arbite which made a slight creaking noise as it gestured for them to enter. Berdle handed the machine the stub of his blunt and it stood there looking at the drug stick as they followed the soup-faced person into the body of the airship.

The Last Party had grown to become several parties. There were at least four party cycles happening at any one point, roughly aligned with the times of the day/night cycle, so that no matter when you felt like partying – even if it was immediately after your own randomly houred breakfast – there would be a party just started or just about to start.

Led by the soup-faced person, they walked through broad open spaces, red-lit, where it looked like the party had been over for some time; small floating machines were picking up litter, the air was full of strange scents and the space part-full of ceiling-suspended pods and shallow platforms and things like giant hammocks, many of them transparent or translucent. There was quite a lot of sex happening, Cossont noticed, in and on the hammocks, and the air was also full of soft cries, the occasional piercing scream and all the other sounds associated with physical passion, unreservedly expressed. Cossont felt herself becoming surprisingly hot and bothered by it all; usually she had pretty good control of herself.

~The atmosphere is saturated with compounds sexually stimulating to your species, Berdle sent as they ducked underneath an especially large hammock where several frolicking bed-fellows were contorting themselves in particularly inventive combinations.

"Sex-scent city!" Pyan agreed, through the earbud.

A male face and torso swung down from a nearby platform. Sweating, breathing hard, the man smiled at Vyr. "Like the arms," he said, breathlessly. "You'd be so *very* welcome." Then, with a look of slight surprise, he was pulled back up onto the platform by a couple of grinning naked women, who blew kisses at an uncomprehending Berdle.

A short dark corridor led to another wide room where extravagantly costumed, masked people danced; some to a space-filling song of powerful beats and trembling ululations, some to rhythms they were hearing through earbuds, their wildly eccentric motions at odds with everybody else around them.

DARK SOUND . . . SPACE AHEAD the soup-faced person told them, walking backwards down another intervening corridor, face turned towards them.

"About to get really loud," Cossont told Berdle.

"I can feel it through my feet," he told her.

Cossont closed her ears.

Double doors led to the dark-sound dance floor, where the whole point was to hear with every part of your body except your ears. It was night-dark, strobe-lit; with each staccato pulse of light the near-naked dancers looked like marionettes frozen in poses of either ecstasy or torment. Cossont heard the wild, thudding music through the jelly in her eyes, via her lungs, resonating in the long bones of her arms and legs.

"Fuck me, that's loud," Pyan said in her ear, voice made high and tinny to get through.

Cossont opened her mouth a little to say "Shh," to the creature. As she did so it was as though her mouth filled with noise; she felt her teeth vibrate.

Berdle looked unaffected.

Away from the dark-sound room, they passed a large circular oil swimming pool with a screen ceiling where people seemed to be practising synchronised floating in giant flower-like patterns. They climbed through a couple of levels where tired-but-happy-looking people were eating at tables – though one section seemed to be set aside for food-fights, with one just starting – then ascended via an adventurously steep and long escalator to a tall, broad corridor with what appeared to be a transparent ceiling showing the fretwork of tunnel moving slowly past above.

Ximenyr's quarters lay through a sequence of intestinally curved, squishily floored round-section corridors hung with what looked like folds and strands of gaudy, hallucinatory vivid seaweeds, all moving and waving on invisible currents.

~That's interesting, Berdle sent. ~Just lost feed from my scout missile. That is a little worrying.

Finally, at a doorway bearing an unmistakable resemblance to a vulva, the soup-faced person bowed and left them. The vulva irised, opening.

"This is a bit gross, isn't it?" Pyan whispered. "It's not just me thinking this, no?"

Cossont followed Berdle down a short, narrow corridor. Cossont's earbud beeped to signal it was losing all external reception – something it had never done anywhere else in or on the Girdlecity, in all the years she'd lived within it.

They arrived into a chamber where a large, barrel-chested, handsome-looking man with vivid red skin and an unfeasible number of phalluses reclined on a giant, tipped bed. He was smiling at them. He wore a roomy-looking pair of shorts, so the penis he'd likely been born with was perhaps the only one not visible, but he had plenty of others, sprouting – short, stubby, flaccid – from at least forty points on his body, including four on his calves, six on each thigh, similar numbers on his upper and lower arms and one each where the nipples would have been on a mammal. His head, feet and hands looked normal. Around his thick neck lay something like a giant charm bracelet, weighed down with chunky trinkets, mostly jewel encrusted. He was attended by naked people – mostly females – all of whom had the heads of animals and mythical creatures.

~Again, Berdle sent, ~The atmosphere is full of sexually stimulating compounds. And I've found my scout missile. Oh-oh, as we say. I'm going to stop communicating like this for now, unless there's an emergency. May no longer be secure.

"*Oh-oh?*" Cossont was thinking.

"Again," Pyan whispered, "overdosing on sheer vulgarity."

The roof above was not transparent but fashioned from some luxuriantly thick, crimson ruched material, centrally gathered so that it looked like a sphincter, and glistening as though dripping wet.

"Ms Berdle, Ms Cossont," the man said in his deep, thick voice. "Pleased to meet you." Then he opened his mouth a little wider and let a very long tongue snake out and delicately lick at first one eyebrow then the other, shaping them both neatly into place. The tongue disappeared again. He opened his eyes wide; he had fabulously pale blue irises, almost shining. His eyeballs rolled back into their sockets, the blue irises disappearing. They were replaced from below by dark red irises which rose into place and steadied. "Excuse me," he said. "These pupils work better in daylight." He smiled widely, showing very white teeth. "And to your familiar, Ms Cossont. Pyan, isn't it? Welcome to you too."

"Permission to speak?" Pyan said, sounding excited.

"No," Cossont said quietly, then to Ximenyr said, "Hello. Thank you for seeing us."

"And thank you for watching me," Ximenyr said, and unhooked something from his collar of trinkets, holding it up in front of his face and inspecting it. It looked like a short thin pen or stylus of some sort, barely bigger than a child's finger. Ximenyr looked at Berdle. "Your life signs are weirder than the lady's familiar, so I'm guessing this belongs to you."

"It does," Berdle said. "My apologies. I was concerned you might refuse to see us initially and we might need some help in securing an audience. Also, I am impressed you were able to sense its presence and capture it. Congratulations."

"Thank you. Flattery is always *so* satisfying," Ximenyr said with what certainly appeared to be a sort of beatific sincerity. "Especially from . . ." he waved one long, elegant hand, exquisitely manicured ". . . an avatar, avatoid? Something of that nature?"

"Indeed, of the Culture vessel *Mistake Not . . .*"

There was just a hint of a pause; Cossont was fairly sure their host was listening on his own earbud.

"Voyeured upon by a Culture Mind," Ximenyr said, sounding impressed. "I really am flattered. Though there is an all-hours feed from about eight different cameras all centred on this bed right here, so I'm not entirely sure why you bothered. Video only at points, so maybe you wanted the audio? Yeah? Anyway." He nodded behind them. "Please; take a seat."

Two of the animal-headed people – the heads looked as real, alive and functional as every other part of their human bodies – set two tall chairs behind them. Cossont and Berdle both sat. The dozen or so unusually headed people stood, arms folded, round the curved wall of the cabin.

Ximenyr held the tiny scout missile out. "I'm going to keep this, okay?" The little machine was secured to his charm necklace by an extendible chain.

"I would prefer to have it returned," Berdle said.

"Don't doubt," Ximenyr said. "But you did invade my privacy." There was some muffled spluttering and laughing at this from the people looking on, and Ximenyr's face split into a smile again. He glanced round some of the animal-headed people. "Hey, you know what I mean." He looked back at Berdle, grinning. "Anyway. Might let you have this back. But you need something from me, I'm sort of supposing, otherwise why, in an entirely cogent sense, would you be here in the first place? Hmm?" He set the tiny missile back where it had been, resting on his chest between what looked like an android's thumb and a thick crystal cylinder, striped with encrusted jewels.

"It's about Ngaroe QiRia," Cossont said, glancing at Berdle.

"Gathered." Ximenyr nodded at her. "Like the arms, incidentally. Who did that for you?"

"Frex Gerunke."

"Know him. Helped teach him. Nice work? All working fine?"

"Perfectly."

"And a Lords jacket. You really into them?"

"I played with them," she confessed. "Briefly." She really might have to change out of the Lords of Excrement jacket at some point, she realised.

"Really? You're not mentioned in the playgraphy." He seemed to think. "Unless you're Sister Euphoria."

Cossont sighed. "Guilty."

Ximenyr smiled broadly. "*Estimable*, Ms Cossont. I've played tenser, a little sling, never the volupt. Hear it's harder."

"A little."

"Four arms make it easier?"

"No; that's for the elevenstring."

"Ha! The *Undecagonstring*? I've heard they're fucking insane."

"No, that's just those who play them."

Ximenyr laughed. "Nobody's played an elevenstring for the Party; you could audition while you're here. That would help round things off."

"Thank you, but we have more urgent business," she told him.

"Yes, my friend Mr QiRia."

"My friend too," Cossont said.

"Really?" Ximenyr looked sceptical. "Can't recall him mentioning you."

Cossont sighed again. "That does not surprise me."

Ximenyr grinned, stroked his chin. "Well, his memories are a little . . . compartmentalised. How do you know him?"

"I met him twenty years ago, just after he'd been a levi-athid – a sea monster – for decades, on a place called Perytch IV. We only met up for a few days, but we talked a lot. How about you?"

"Oh, I knew him before then, back when I was horribly young and doing . . ." he held up one arm and stroked a couple of the penises on it ". . . this kind of thing for what passes for a living, amongst us." He shrugged. "Rather than a profound artistic statement both exploring and interro-gating the prospect of a willed self-extinctive event being sold as a civilisational phase-change cum level upgrade."

"When he was here five years ago," Berdle said, "was Mr QiRia having some sculption carried out?"

The man in the bed frowned. "Sculption; now there's a word I haven't heard for a while. Technically correct, I guess. Used to be called plastic surgery or bodily amendment or, well, lots of things." He waved one arm again. "Anyway, I'm afraid that's a private matter, Mr Berdle; I can neither confirm nor deny, and . . . all that shit."

"May we simply ask why was he here, then?" Berdle asked.

"Still not going to tell you, fella," Ximenyr said, shaking his head. "QiRia and I are old pals, that's all I can say. Met him a few times, last time just as the Party was starting. But he was friends with my mother, and with her father before her, so I guess he's pretty ancient even by Culture standards

– and I won't be giving away too much if I say he's sort of a profound throwback physiologically anyway, by true Culture genetech criteria. I don't know what sort of weird congenital mixture of geriatric blood-lines he draws his particular bucketful of the vital fluids from, but it's pretty end-spectrum whatever it is, I can tell you that."

"Did he leave anything with you?" Cossont asked.

The Master of the Revels shrugged. "Nothing important, maybe a present or two. He was sort of . . . intermittently generous. Anyway, why? Is he in some sort of trouble?" Ximenyr looked from Cossont to Berdle. "How . . . official is this visit?"

Cossont leaned forward. "He didn't leave you a mind-state device or anything?"

Ximenyr laughed. "Why on Zyse, Xown or anywhere would he do that?"

"He . . ." Cossont began, about to say that QiRia had given her such a device, then remembering that she hadn't told Berdle this was what she was looking for at the Ospin Dataversities. She'd nearly given that away. She wondered how much she already had.

Berdle had already cut in. "He might have wanted to back himself up."

Ximenyr shook his head. "Doubt that. He was always kind of resistant regarding that sort of duplicated soul stuff."

"Do you know where else he might have gone when he was in Gzilt?" Cossont asked.

"No," Ximenyr said. "Secretive old boy. How about you, Vyr, did he come to visit you?"

"No," she admitted.

"Oh, feeling jilted?" Ximenyr said softly, with a look of exaggerated sympathy.

"We were never friends like that."

"You don't have to be. You just have to care what people think of you." He brought his blue irises rolling down for a moment, looked at her, then let them roll back up again to be replaced by the red ones. "If it's any consolation, I know he visited Gzilt at least once without bothering to come see me. Didn't even call." He looked at Berdle. "We never did settle how official this visit is."

Berdle nodded. "Officiality is a slippery concept, in the Culture."

Ximenyr laughed. "Well," he said, arching his back and stretching – all the penises gave a little jerk, as though they were separate tiny animals just waking – "this has all been very interesting; however, things have recharged and there is, frankly, pleasure to be secured. You may have to excuse me, shortly." He looked at Cossont and Berdle, as all the animal- and beast-headed people joined him on the bed, kneeling by him and reaching out to stroke and caress him. All the phalluses dotted over Ximenyr's body started, very slowly, to fatten and lever themselves upright. Wavy lines like veins that probably did not all carry blood were beginning to show all over his body, bulging and rippling beneath his ruby-red skin. "Unless you'd like to join in, of course?" he said brightly. "Both, either of you? You'd be very welcome. Plenty of time, plenty of places. We'll turn the AG on shortly, I'll start my last heart and we can get things going on my back . . ."

"I would," Pyan said in Cossont's earbud.

Cossont looked down at the creature. "Okay. I could just leave you here," she told it.

"Never mind."

"Thank you," she said to Ximenyr. "But we'd best be on our way."

"Mr Berdle," Ximenyr said, taking one hand from between the legs of one of the girls stroking him. He detached the little scout missile from his neck-chain. "You may have this back. Excuse the, ah . . ."

Berdle had to kneel one-legged on the bed between Ximenyr's legs and two naked bodies to retrieve the scout missile. "Thank you," he said.

"Always keep on the right side of the Culture," Ximenyr murmured dreamily, his face just becoming obscured by a young man straddling him. Very little of his body was visible now, though what was was clearly quite excited.

"You really are no fun," Pyan said, petulant, as they descended the alarmingly long and steep escalator with the soup-faced person leading the way. In the cavernous space above and in front of them, an energetic game of sorball had begun, with people in transparent spherical suit-spheres leaping about in a zero-G volume, pinging off the inside walls of a giant diamond glass sphere forty metres across.

"Tough," Cossont said, then turned to Berdle, but could only get to the point where she opened her mouth to speak before he turned to her and said,

"Later."

"So?" she said. They were back aboard the module. It had met them on a landing platform which cantilevered out from the mass of the Girdlecity like a round tray on an outstretched arm. The craft started to pull away, going astern to avoid some overhanging architecture a few kilometres above.

"Mr Ximenyr has access to some surprisingly sophisticated tech," Berdle said, lowering himself onto a lounge couch and examining the scout missile. "And some 4D shielding, of course, which is why we had to get in there."

"Not just prurience, then," Pyan said, aloud, but was ignored.

"They found and disabled this with embarrassing ease," Berdle said, rolling the scout missile around on his palm. "Ah!" The little machine suddenly came alive and leapt into the air above his hand. It twisted quickly this way and that, as though confused at having just woken up.

Most of the walls of the module's living area had seemingly turned transparent, allowing a vertiginous view of the Hzu coast beneath as the module tipped, twisted and then reared suddenly upwards. Ribbons of ochre and jade stitched by slow-spreading breakers of alabaster white, the land and the shallow margins of the sea seemed to sink away beneath them like something dropped; the Girdlecity was a dark wall they climbed magically without touching, hurtling silently back to the stars. Cossont tore her gaze from the view and said, "But did you *find* anything?"

Berdle frowned. "No. I was rather hoping for some sort of data store with information on Mr Q, something that would be kept close to Ximenyr, but there was nothing relevant anywhere on the airship. I've copied everything I found to the ship Mind to see if there's some really clever cryptography in the storage, but it doesn't look promising."

"Nothing in all that stuff round his neck?"

"There was a minimal amount of processing left in the android digit, which was anyway unpowered, there was a dedicated, digital time-to device, functioning and correctly synchronised to the millisecond, but with zero spare capacity, a defunct model of an ancient Waverian Zoehn Dynasty spaceship, itself based on a primitively early form of processor technology called a vacuum tube, again with minimal and extremely crude processing, long burned out, a crystal container holding some animal or vegetable matter—two or three berries or small fruits, I believe – the baculum from a Vimownian Woller with an embedded particle-chip, probably from a hunter's homing round, and a LastDitch Corp minicollar subsaver, hair-triggered to intervene should any of the gentleman's hearts give out—"

"Yeah. He said something about starting his last heart."

"He has four." The avatar looked thoughtful. "That is a lot of vaso-congestive tissue to support."

"I suppose."

"Again, minimal processing involved; just enough to do its job and no more. Everything else was just dumb matter; process-free."

"So, nothing."

"Nothing relevant, as far as I can tell." The avatar smiled at Cossont. "So, onwards and outwards to Ospin and the Dataversities."

She found herself smiling back. "One request?" she said. "What?"

"Could you keep that look?"

"If you like." Berdle looked puzzled. "Why?"

"It suits – well, it just looks good."

The avatar shrugged. "Okay."

"Are you still being affected by those sexually stimulating compounds?" Pyan asked through her earbud.

Cossont used a finger to flick one corner of the creature. It yelped and unwound itself from round her neck, flapping away from her in a flurry of melodramatic movement.

"The Culture craft continues to adhere to local legal velocity limitations but is about to leave the atmosphere," the combat arbite Uhtryn said. "If it is to be engaged, this would be the last chance."

Colonel Agansu felt like he was suspended in space just above the planet of Xown, staring down at its brown/green land, the white-lined coast of Hzu and the green/blue waters of the sea. The Girdlecity was a thick dark rim round the world, hazing and disappearing to the horizon in each direction. He watched the dot that was the Culture module rising quickly upwards through the atmosphere.

"Count down that time, would you, Uhtryn?" he asked the arbite. "What do we have from the Girdlecity?"

"Eight seconds. Screen just coming in." As the combat arbite spoke the words, a virtual screen appeared in front of Agansu, showing, from above, an elegant piazza with a small Culture craft sitting on it and two people walking away from it. "Two people: male unidentified, female . . . Cossont, Vyr. Lieutenant Commander reserve, the Fourteenth. Seven. Additional: mattiform familiar or pet present, wrapped round the female's neck."

"Where did they go?"

"As projected, the airship *Equatorial 353*. It has shielding making it impossible to surveille from outside. They spent twenty-two minutes inside. Six. Additional: male figure negative bio. Likely avatar, type unclear. Probing resistant without sensorial aggression."

Colonel Agansu watched the tiny Culture ship rise towards space, seemingly almost straight at him. Of course, he was not really exposed to the void; he was floating instead within his virtual environment, deep inside the *7*Uagren*. He spent most of his time here now, revved up to maximum speed, absorbed by the utterly fascinating view of space ahead and around, as enhanced by the ship's sensor arrays. The full radiation spectrum was signified by textures implicit in the spread of colours, information in every form leapt out when you inspected something, and vectors and relative speeds were displayed around every object.

When not gazing out, fascinated, at this, the colonel dived

deeper into the data reservoirs, trying to find and match up any details of relevance to the mission. This contributed relatively little in absolute terms to the efforts the ship's own subsidiary AIs and virtual-crew data-mining specialists and their sub-routines were making, but it was still worthwhile additional work, and had the effect of continually reinforcing his own understanding.

He spent little time genuinely in his own body now, conscious of lying on the couch beside the combat arbite, buried deep in the ship. He was still aware that his physical body resided there and was being looked after – fed, evacuated, made to twitch so that his muscles did not start to atrophy – but he really lived in this virtual environment now; he felt cleaner and more pure in here, somehow, and quicker (though still so much slower than the ship crew!). The combat arbite Uhtryn had begun to help him.

"Colonel," the captain of the *Uagren* communicated, "that Culture ship's getting ready to head off. We need to decide whether we're going to keep on following or not."

"Who might be—?"

"Five," Uhtryn said.

"—on the airship?"

"It is the location for a long-term celebration," the arbite told him. "No known participants known to be known to the female."

"Spool up, Captain," Agansu said. "Make us ready to go."

"Spooling up."

"Everything on the female?"

"Musician," Uhtryn said. "Classed resident of Girdlecity, Xown, Section Kwaalon Greater Without 3004/396. Absent from residence for the past six nights. Four. Girdlecity systems unable to provide more data on recent whereabouts. Female's mother is Warib—"

"Any sign they picked anything up from the airship?"

"No. Additional: data from Girdlecity interior accessed. Screen, audio." The same couple were visible from some distance away, standing on a long balcony set into the side of a messily accoutred and barely moving red airship. They were talking to somebody with an odd-looking face and wearing a strange combination of semi-military clothing. A hissy, slightly phased version of a woman's voice said, "We'd . . . to talk to The Master of . . . Revels . . ." There was another word a little later, but it was too faint to catch. "Three."

"Improve on that final word she says?"

"Already fully processed; unable to improve. Data AIs indicate hypothesised title 'The Master of the Revels' probably refers to one Ximenyr, artist, nominal spokesperson for 'The Last Party' as long-term celebration known."

Agansu had to decide what to do: follow the Culture ship or investigate where the avatar and the female had gone and who they might have seen. In theory both could be accomplished, but only if he entrusted one of the tasks to somebody else, and he was loath to do this. He might go down to the planet himself and investigate this Master of the Revels fellow while the combat arbite stayed with the *Uagren*, or he might stay with the ship as it continued to follow the Culture vessel and delegate the on-planet job to some other entity from the ship – as well as the various different types of combat and other arbites, it held androids capable of passing for bio, all fully programmable.

He wanted to do both at once. He wanted to be in two places at once. In theory this was possible, in a way, using mind-state recording and transcription technology and one of the more specialised androids at the ship's disposal; he could replicate himself, putting his consciousness into the machine . . . but he didn't like the idea – never had – and felt that it constituted a security risk as well; with every copying event, more than one person – one entity, at least – suddenly knew what only he was supposed to know.

Or he could leave a copy of himself on board the ship, perhaps even one living and thinking at the same speed as the virtual crew, while he – this physical body – removed itself from its haven, its little kernel-space in the heart of the ship, and took a small craft down to the surface of the world below.

"Two," said the combat arbite.

The Culture ship had appeared to be heading somewhere quite different when it had suddenly veered off-course and crash-stopped here at Xown. It had been impossible to tell exactly where it had been heading – ships rarely just flew straight for their destination, choosing to introduce long, random curves into their courses, just to frustrate anybody trying to work out where they were going. It meant they travelled a few per cent further than they would have done taking a perfectly direct route, but it was usually judged to be worth the time penalty.

The *Uagren* too had had to make an unexpected crash-stop, the very violence of which might have betrayed its presence to the Culture ship. The crew thought they had got away with it, but there was no way to be sure yet.

"One."

"Captain, you have my mind-state mapped?"

"Yes."

"Implant it into one of the bio-plausible androids forthwith and send it down to the planet. Have it walk a little way ahead of the airship, ready to board it on our future signal. Leave a liaise instruction with the local authorities and keep the android updated with—"

"Ze—"

"Stand down. There will be no need to attack or disable the Culture craft."

"It has left the—" the arbite started to say, then paused. "It is gone; it has been Displaced."

"Woh," the disloc officer said. "Look at those *distances*. Heavy duty."

"Ship moving off, fast," the navigation officer said.

"As I was saying; leave a liaise instruction with the local authorities and keep the android updated with all relevant information."

"Faster than it was." The captain sounded worried. "Can we stay with that?"

"Marginal," the drives officer said.

"Random spiralling," the targeting officer said. "Maybe it did see us."

"The android mind-state imprinting is not instant," the external-tech officer told Agansu. "Eighty seconds required from now to disloc for imprint and ready-body."

"Captain?" Agansu said. "Is there time?"

"Have we eighty seconds to spare before having to move off? Including move then disloc under acceleration, increasing distance?" the captain said. "Nav. Disloc?"

"Talked," said the navigation officer. "No. Not even twenty."

"Disloc agrees."

"Already starting to lose the quarry's track," the targeting officer said. "Ninety per cent we can take same general heading and still find, but no guarantees."

"Track still fading," the navigation officer said. "It's building in more random."

"Eighty-nine per cent."

"Colonel," the captain said, "we can't program the android and be sure we can still follow the ship."

"Eighty-seven per cent."

Agansu thought. "Percentage likelihood of reacquiring the Culture ship if we stay to the eighty-second mark?"

"Less than one."

"Program android," Agansu said, "despatch back to Xown in small craft?"

"That works. Back here in a few hours."

"Let's do that. Please move off immediately, Captain."

"Moving."

"Could still plonk the oid now, zap the col's m-s to it after," the special tactics officer said. He was, Agansu had noticed, prone to such compressive communication.

"I realise," Agansu said. "I am unwilling to do that."

"Your choice."

"Captain," Agansu said. "Do you think the Culture vessel has seen us?"

"Too early to tell. It moved off in a hurry, and it did Displace – disloc – the module rather than wait for it, so either it did or thinks it might have, or it's suddenly in a real hurry."

"It'd have disloc'd the craft in-atmosphere if it had been in a *real* hurry, sir," the disloc officer said.

"Or mo'ff, remote-dee'd the individs, left the mod," the special tactics officer contributed opaquely.

"All true," the captain said. "Or fresh news just came in, or it half suspected it had a tail and wanted to catch us off guard. Drives, how smooth was our move-off?"

"Pretty good. In our top centile."

"Good as theirs?"

"Not quite. That was tight. As efficient a kick-away as I've seen."

"Think we have to assume it might have seen us," the captain announced. "Suggest we follow anyway, act as though not. Colonel?"

"I agree," Agansu said, then shifted to a one-to-one private channel. "But, Captain, if it is the case that we have been discovered, was it anyone aboard's fault?"

"No, not in my opinion, Colonel."

"Really?"

"Really. We are carving right up hard against the operational envelope of this ship, Colonel, fractions away from our never-exceeds and even a little over the factory settings in some cases where we know she can take it. And the crew are better than the ship; they always are. If our crash-stop alerted the Culture ship this time then you could replay it a million times over with other crews or fresher crews or more experienced crews and it always would; that's just how the physics works."

"I take comfort in the loyalty and faith you display towards your crew, Captain."

"My crew are loyal to me, Colonel; I am only loyal to the regiment and Gzilt. Also, faith is belief without reason; we operate on reason and nothing but. I have zero faith in my crew, just absolute confidence."

"Hmm. That is well said. I happily withdraw any suggestion that part of your crew might have been at fault, and I am happy to match and share that confidence."

"Glad to hear it. Shall we rejoin the congregation?"

"Amusing. Let's."

Thirteen

(S -15)

xGSV *Contents May Differ*
  oLSV *You Call This Clean?*
Hello. Ms Tefwe is en route?
∞

    Yes. Transmitted, received and being re-embodied.
∞

And are we any further forward regarding whatever ship or ships might have been helping Mr QiRia in the past?
∞

    Barely. I have contacted the *Anything Legal Considered* and tried again to contact the *Warm, Considering*. The former appears willing to help but says that it has had

no contact with or knowledge of Mr QiRia since visiting Perytch IV twenty years ago with Ms Cossont. The latter seems to be on a retreat or is unavailable for some other reason. I have contacted its original home GSV, the *A Fine Disregard For Awkward Facts*, and its most recent home/contact, the GSV *Teething Problems*, requesting both to ask the *Warm, Considering* to get in touch. I suggest that all interested parties do all they can through any contacts they may have to find and/or contact the *Warm, Considering* and/or any other ship or entity that might have been helping Mr QiRia recently. The *Warm, Considering* is the last ship known to have facilitated Mr QiRia in his travels and efforts to stay out of the public gaze, but it might have been superseded. It might also be worth attempting to contact any extant ships or entities known to have helped him before the *Warm, Considering*. I believe a ship called the *Smile Tolerantly* fulfilled this role, though I am having difficulty contacting it. Again, any help would be appreciated. I have instigated a search for data on any other such vessels but it has so far met only with subtle obstruction. Whether this may count as some sort of success is moot.

∞

I'll pass the word along. May I allow your identity to be known by the others?

∞

I suppose so. Sooner or later somebody would have collated my search requests with those doubtless soon to be forthcoming from others and made the connection.

∞

Welcome to the club.

*

He was always surprised how hard it was to see cities from space. You worked out where they must be from knowing how they looked on maps, but they never leapt out at you in reality the way they did in diagrammatic form. Even when you could make out the city and it was one that you knew well, you sometimes needed help to find where important buildings and landmarks were, even though they ought to be obvious.

Septame Banstegeyn gazed down at what his implants assured him was the location of the parliament complex in M'yon, but without the overlay he'd have struggled to identify it. How important it had always seemed, how important it genuinely was, to the lives of so many, and yet how tiny, how insignificant. He sighed, looked away, took in the whole sweep of the planet of Zyse – well, as much as he could see from the orbital base, which was only a few hundred kilometres up, so incapable of providing a view of the entire globe. Ah, the fabulous solidity of a planet.

Banstegeyn's World. It had always sounded so good to him, so fitting. So lasting. Now, perhaps, *Banstegeyn's Star* instead. It was no sacrifice. Stars could last longer than planets, and – once you had secured the agreement, the commitment of those who would inherit responsibility for them – it cost them nothing, really, to grant such a wish.

Of course, it would never stick unless there was a good reason for such an honour; any idiot could secure some up-and-coming primitive's agreement that, oh yes, they'd rename a planet or a star after them (and, if they had any sense at all, know in their heart that it was an agreement so easily made because it could be so easily broken), but there was weight to his claim for such an accolade.

He had shepherded a whole people to their destiny; brought them on, shown them what they knew they wanted anyway, or what they would want, in time, even if there had been nobody with the vision and the foresight to show them. Was that not worth a "World" or a "Star"? Even having a star named after oneself didn't really mean that much; there were hundreds of millions of them in the galaxy, and many had stupid, meaningless or hopelessly obscure names.

In some ways it seemed so little to ask.

"Septame," a voice said. "Thank you so much for seeing me." The avatar Ziborlun bowed from the doorway of the spherical observation pod. It smiled, its silver-skinned face lit by the soft glow of the light reflecting from the planet beneath.

"Ziborlun," Banstegeyn said.

There was a particular way of saying somebody's name – you pronounced it as you gave a small sigh – that informed them, assuming they had the wit to recognise the sign, that they were being seen as an indulgence, as a duty even, when really you had so many more important matters to attend to. It was in that manner that the septame had said the avatar's name.

The avatar, being an avatar, picked up the signal immediately; the smile turned self-deprecatory, almost apologetic, and the creature said, "I won't keep you long, Septame."

"It is a busy time," Banstegeyn agreed.

The avatar floated into the pod as the door shushed closed behind it. Ziborlun immediately assumed a very natural and relaxed-looking position, ankles together, knees splayed. It hovered in mid-air a couple of metres away from Banstegeyn, as steady as if it had a metal rod protruding from its back anchoring it to the wall a metre behind. Banstegeyn had never seen anybody maintain such a static position in a weightless environment. Well, it was a ship avatar, he supposed; it ought to be good at this sort of thing. He, on the other hand, was burred onto a drysticky patch near the viewing port by part of his zero-G suit and yet he was still sort of moving around a bit.

"Yes," the avatar said. "Sadly busy, given the shocking event at Eshri. What ought to be a time of contemplation and quiet preparation becomes a time of mourning, bitterness, and even recrimination. I just wanted to reiterate the Culture's condolences and to reinforce our offer of help."

"Both much appreciated. I hope you will take it as a sign of our confident closeness, not our arrogance, that we had assumed no less."

"Sometimes what goes without saying is best said anyway," the avatar said, smiling.

Banstegeyn smiled too, politely, but kept quiet. It was slightly less rude than saying, *Well, if that's all*, or glancing at his time-to.

"You will of course also have our help in the search for the culprits."

"Thank you."

"Indeed. And we may, shortly, be able to make good on that offer."

"Oh? How so?" This, he'd be prepared to admit, had his attention.

"Luckily, we had a ship in the volume quite shortly after the attack on the HQ of the Fourteenth. It thought it best to leave almost immediately in case, in the ensuing confusion, it was mistaken for a hostile; however, it was able to take certain readings that might help in any investigation into the attack."

"Really? And what would those readings indicate?"

"It is too early to say," the avatar said apologetically. "Besides, it might be best for us, preferentially, and initially at least, to present the data raw, rather than interpreted, lest we be seen to be trying to influence the investigation."

"So, you're willing to submit this data to the relevant authorities?" Banstegeyn asked.

"Indeed."

"I take it you're aware that I've appointed the First, the Home Regiment, to look into the matter."

"Hmm," the avatar said, with an odd, tight expression on its face. Banstegeyn reckoned he'd learned to read avatar expressions pretty well over the years. If the creature had held up a sign saying "Yeah, are you *sure* about that?" the signal would hardly have been any clearer. "That is not what one would normally expect, is it?"

"Normally a Combined Regimental Committee would perform such a task," Banstegeyn agreed. "However, given the time constraints imposed by the up-coming Instigation, the depletion of the relevant ranks due to Storage and the disarray within so much of the fleet due to the number of ships that have already Sublimed, it was decided that, as the single most cohesive element of the defence forces still functioning, the First ought to shoulder the load."

"So that is not just an interim measure?" the avatar asked. "There seemed to be some confusion. I thought you might know better than anybody what was planned."

Banstegeyn smiled. "I am a mere septame, not the president or a trime or a general. But to the best of my knowledge First will be allowed to continue to pursue the investigation until a satisfactory conclusion is reached. That would be my suggestion, at least."

"I see. I'll let the relevant ships know. We have yet to decide whether the information we hold would help or hinder the investigation."

"That would be your choice."

"If I may touch on another matter, I think we were all surprised at the result of the decision regarding the Scavenging situation and would hope that this will not lead to any unpleasantness. We would accordingly like to offer the co-operation of the ships which are accompanying elements of the Liseiden and Ronte fleets. Your fleet people are already aware of their names, locations and so on, but please allow us to work with you to prevent any conflicts of any nature between the parties involved."

"That is kind, and thoughtful," Banstegeyn said. He gave a tight little smile of his own, glanced at the viewing port, towards the planet.

"Thank you for your time, Septame."

"My pleasure. My only regret is that there is so little of it to go around at the moment."

The avatar unfolded itself as the door behind it opened. It flowed gracefully through the doorway. Banstegeyn heard it exchange a few words with his AdC and secretary, waiting outside. He turned his attention back to the port and the view of Zyse, listening to Jevan and Solbli enter with a rustling of clothes. He heard the door close. They'd already called with the gist of it: bad news.

"Nothing at all?" he said, turning back to them. Jevan and Solbli both looked solemn, and tired. Jevan looked as unkempt as he ever did and Solbli very nearly looked her age. He supposed he ought to feel flattered they had spent so much of their own real time searching for a solution, rather than just leaving agents and data-trawls to do all the work for them.

"Nothing, Septame," Jevan said with a sigh.

They did, in the end, care about him, Banstegeyn realised. A lot more than he really cared about them, which was the right way round, and made their devotion all the sweeter in a way.

"Trime Quvarond was very careful to follow all proce-dures correctly," Solbli added.

The same was true of Orpe. The President's AdC was here on the orbital base too, for the same regiment-sponsored security conference; there ought to be time for some zero-G sex later. He thought the experience was a little over-rated, personally, though the girl seemed to like it. The real pleasure, he felt, lay more in being able to watch the planet turn beneath you as you fucked. There was something very satisfying about that. He hoped it would still feel as satisfying even though, this time, he would not be looking down on it knowing that one day it would carry his name.

"We are here because somebody destroyed an entire regimental HQ and fate alone knows what else. We are not far off being at war, arguably. If we were, technically, at war . . . would that . . .?"

Jevan was already shaking his head. "I'm afraid not, Septame."

"You might persuade the president not to sign the order," Solbli suggested, with a thin smile.

Banstegeyn didn't even pretend to smile. The president was duty-bound to sign everything put in front of him or her, up to and including an order for his or her own execution, in theory. Not that that principle had been tested for eleven millennia.

Even then, even at death, a politician could just come back; being backed-up at the start of your term was part of the deal, and if you were killed during your time in office you got re-embodied. Wonderful disincentive for assassination; Banstegeyn had always appreciated it. There was some delay in between – forty days, was it? Or thirty? – to allow time for a clone of the deceased to be grown and implanted with their most recent back-up, and people got shuffled around to take your place in the meantime, but then you just resumed your post . . . or you could take part in a subsequent election if you'd been in the last year of your term; now he thought about it there was some sort of . . .

Then he had to look away from Jevan and Solbli, because he'd just had an idea, and the audacity of it, the sheer dagger-like simplicity and directness of it, had all but taken his breath away.

He yawned, spreading his arms, giving himself a chance to shiver, to tremble, without it looking suspicious, and said, smiling, "Well, there we are; some you lose." He looked at his time-to, shrugged. "In fifteen days it won't matter a damn anyway."

Jevan and Solbli looked relieved, and a little surprised.

The representative of the Culture ship of the Scree class, the *Beats Working*, was warmly welcomed into the principal shared gallery space of the squadron and fleet flagship Interstitial/Exploratory Vessel *Melancholia Enshrines All Triumph* by Ossebri 17 Haldesib, Swarmprince and Sub-Swarm Divisional Head. Gifts were exchanged, and, although the Culture representative, one Jonsker Ap-Candrechenat, was unable to ingest a welcoming libation in the fullest sense, it nevertheless absorbed a portion into its chemical analysis unit and graciously accepted the remainder on board itself to be returned to the ship the *Beats Working* later, where it would be treated with all due respect.

Great respect had already been shown, it had been decided after consultation with the appropriate experts, expert systems and reference library resources aboard the *Melancholia Enshrines All Triumph*, in the act of sending a mechanical but fully sentient device to represent the Culture ship *Beats Working*, as the machine was able to exist within the *Melancholia Enshrines All Triumph* nakedly, without any sort of exo-suit. This would not have been possible had one of the tiny number of humans aboard the Culture vessel been allocated to represent it.

Drones were known, in theory, to be of at least equal intelligence to Culture humans and were generally adjudged, in practice, to be of somewhat greater intelligence by both Ronte Fleet Intelligence and by most leading academics in respectable universities and other respected institutions of higher learning within the Ronte Trans-Cooperative Domain, using models of intelligence that more fully expressed the true essence of what intelligence actually was, objectively.

That the drone Jonsker Ap-Candrechenat had been sent to talk with Ossebri 17 Haldesib, was, therefore, no insult and, indeed, to the contrary, was a mark of great respect, conferring as it did a greater implicit closeness to the Culture ship's mother-queen Mind, which itself represented a tiny but true sliver of the great hive-mind that was the entire Culture.

The Swarmprince and Sub-Swarm Divisional Head accordingly met the drone personally and had ordered his principal next-three-in-line Officers of Seniority to accompany him in his progress through the ship to the meeting and to be present at the meeting itself, as well as making sure that his Intelligence and Translational Officers and their respective deputies were present and fully briefed, of course, as protocol demanded.

Initial formalities safely completed, continuing formalities satisfactorily under way (in the shape of correct poses, gestures, scents and manners of speaking), the business of the meeting might be allowed to begin.

"The ship *Beats Working* would beg to be permitted to assist the glorious squadron of the Ronte which it is its privilege to escort. To be so empowered would allow

THE HYDROGEN SONATA 303

the *Beats Working* to begin to repay and reflect some of the great esteem which it has earned in being permitted to escort the exalted squadron."

"This is indeed an honourable conception," the Swarmprince replied after the briefest of consultations with his servant officers. "What form would this assistance take?" The Swarmprince was known for his almost shocking incisiveness and the brevity of his locution.

"This assistance would take the form of a series of long-range ship dances, performed serially between the Culture ship *Beats Working* and each of the squadron ships in turn, involving them together travelling at enhanced rates of velocity in the direction already so wisely chosen by the squadron, namely towards the planet of Zyse in the system of Gzilt. The Culture ship *Beats Working* would dance, if such a thing might be contemplated and then allowed, with each of the squadron ships in turn, to the outskirts of the system, or to near to that limit, and then return to the remainder of the fleet, to ship-dance with the next ship, and so on, until all twelve vessels have been danced with."

There was consultation. "This dance, or series of dances," the Swarmprince said. "It would honour the Ronte and the Culture equally?"

"It would."

"And be performed for its own sake?"

"Indeed."

"And it might also result in the squadron arriving at the Gzilt system some appreciable amount of time earlier, of course. That has been considered?"

"That has, though of course this would be of subsidiary importance."

"How much earlier might our arrival be? Has this been computed?"

"It has. The re-formed squadron would arrive at the Gzilt system outskirts in nine days' time, rather than, at our current rate of progress, nearly twenty."

"This would cause our esteemed escort the Culture ship *Beats Working* no risk of damage?"

"It would not, Swarmprince. The field structure of the Culture ship *Beats Working* would be swelled to accommodate each Ronte ship in turn and the resulting squadron-of-two would make its way as an entity to the designated volume on the system approaches."

There was consultation. "I must insist," the Swarmprince said, "that you accept I am most serious and settled in my view that this is a most generous and thoughtful offer, but one that we could not possibly accept, out of our respect for the good Culture ship *Beats Working*. We could not possibly ask such an onerous and mighty task of it, and, therefore, with all gratitude, we must decline said kind and generous and thoughtful offer."

The Culture ship *Beats Working* had done its homework on the Ronte and their customs and mores, and the results of that study had been presented to the drone Jonsker Ap-Candrechenat, which did not, as a result, just accept this apparently fairly final-sounding No. Instead it kept on arguing, knowing that – for a matter of such importance, involving the prickly issue of Ronte pride – anywhere between four and six cycles of offer, consultation and regretful rejection might have to be endured before the offer was finally accepted.

The offer was duly accepted on the sixth iteration, counting the initial one.

Later that day, the *Beats Working* started ferrying the Ronte squadron one by one to the outskirts of the Gzilt system – quite far out for the first one, the rest gradually closer and closer, so that by the time it had delivered the last one they would all be chugging along under their own power in pretty much their standard formation.

This was a much less boring task than strolling along at a few per cent of its own highest velocity while the Ronte squadron made full speed – for them – to Gzilt.

Scoaliera Tefwe woke slowly, as she had woken slowly a few dozen times, over the intervening centuries.

Only it wasn't really waking slowly; she was being woken.

All dark at first. Stillness and silence too, and yet the sensation that things were happening nearby, and inside her head and body; organs and systems and faculties being woken, revived, checked, primed, readied.

It was at once reassuring and somehow disappointing. *Here we go again*, she thought. She opened her eyes.

The word SIMULATION, which was what she expected to see first, albeit briefly, wasn't there. She blinked, looked around.

She was floating in some sort of suspensor field, in air, in a human or humanoid body dressed in some clingy but lightly puffed cover-all which left only her feet, hands and head exposed. She was at forty-five degrees to the floor, looking down. A tiny, sleek ship drone – so tiny and sleek it might have passed for a knife missile – was at eye-level, looking at her. The room around her appeared to be medical unit standard.

"Ms Tefwe?" the drone said. She was being tipped slowly backwards to an upright position, and lowered towards the deck.

She cleared her throat. "Reporting," she said, remembering the earlier simulated conversation with the *You Call This Clean?* Where she was now would be under the control of either a cooperative Hub Mind or a Special Circumstances ex-Psychopath-class Very Fast Picket. From the look of the drone, she was guessing the latter.

"Welcome aboard the VFP *Outstanding Contribution To The Historical Process*," the drone said, confirming her guess just as her feet met the deck. She felt her weight transfer to the soles of her feet, through the gently squashed flesh to her bones, her body. Whatever field had been supporting her ebbed away and she felt planted, properly re-embodied.

"Reverser field, please," she said. One sprang up in front of her, between her and the drone. She looked like her old self; precisely so. "Thank you." The field vanished.

The little drone said, "We are entering the outskirts of the Angemar's Prime system, en route for Dibaldipen Orbital. Would you care to specify a particular plate on the Orbital?"

"Honn plate," she told it.

"Honn. Course adjusted. Is there anything else you require?"

"Breakfast."

"Being prepared; your specified waking default."

"Thank you. Please call ahead to Xunpum Livery, Chyan'tya, Honn, and reserve a mount. An aphore, for an open-ended, minimum four-day hire. Assure them I am suitably experienced with such animals but kindly do not reveal my identity."

The little drone suddenly developed an aura field, turning a crisp blue-grey. "A mount? An *animal*?" it said. "Four *days*? I had rather envisaged Displacing you at sub-millimetre accuracy, precisely where you want to go."

Tefwe rose and fell on the balls of her feet, flexed her hands into fists and relaxed again. "I'm sure," she said. "However the person I'm going to see is something of a stickler in such matters. Certain standards have to be maintained, designated procedures adhered to. I am far from being guaranteed an audience at all; if I don't turn up looking like I've been travelling for a while I am almost certain to be ignored."

The little drone was silent for a moment, then said, "Couldn't you just pretend?"

"No. And I'll be honest; could be five days. Maybe more. Four days is just the travelling time."

"I was under the impression that the whole point of this exercise was to expedite matters as swiftly as possible."

"It is. What would be the journey time from the present location of the Blue-class LSV *You Call This Clean?* to Dibaldipen Orbital by the fastest Very Fast Picket?"

"Approximately one hundred and thirty-two days."

"Well, there you are then."

"But once you've seen the person, you could come straight back with the information you require, or simply transmit it to be passed on to any subsequent re-embodiment. In any event, there would be no need to return slowly."

"In theory. In practice the person concerned might check up on the manner of my return, become upset and refuse to see me on any subsequent occasion."

"Would any subsequent occasion on which you might wish to visit this person plausibly carry the same moral weight or general significance as the present one, in which it has been judged worth effectively putting the entire Fast Picket fleet at your disposal, other commitments allowing?"

"Probably not. Though who can say?"

"Please consider carefully the wisdom of transmitting to me any novel/germane information immediately upon receipt, and returning as rapidly as possible."

"I will. I take the point that my future relations with the person concerned are of relatively little consequence."

"The person concerned sounds – to be polite – eccentric."

"That would be polite to the point of over-generosity," Tefwe said. "Awkward, tetchy and unreasonable might be closer to the truth."

"Would the person concerned be an exceptionally old human?"

"No," Tefwe said, "the person concerned is an exceptionally old drone."

The ship drone's aura flashed amused red then disappeared. "I'll see how that breakfast's coming along."

"*Followed?*"

"Maybe."

"How maybe?"

"About fourteen per cent maybe, averaged."

"Averaged from what? What does that even mean?"

"Averaged from different scenarios. In ambient peacetime the likelihood would be less than five per cent. In all-out wartime, closer to forty per cent."

"How does that average out at fourteen?"

"There are other scenarios to be taken into account," the avatar told her. "Then there's weighting."

Cossont opened her mouth to query that as well, then decided it wasn't worth it.

"You generally start to react to anything over fifteen per cent," Berdle said, apparently trying to be helpful.

Pyan made a throat-clearing noise. "Are we in any danger?" it asked.

"A little," the avatar admitted.

"Then, do you carry lifeboats?"

Berdle looked at Cossont. "Is it being serious?"

"About as serious as it knows how to seem."

"I *was* being serious!"

"Be quiet."

"This is my life too!"

"Shut *up*!" Cossont looked at Berdle. "Does this change anything?" They were still in the module, sitting on comfortable but ordinary-looking couches. The avatar lounged elegantly.

"It may be best to lose them before we visit Ospin," Berdle said, "or employ some method to obscure your exact destination, which, of course, I have yet to learn."

"I'll tell you when we get there," Cossont said, feeling oddly guilty. "Shit. When *do* we get there?" She'd just remembered, alarmingly, that when she'd taken a clipper to get out to Ospin, on the occasion she'd gone there to deposit the glittering grey cube holding QiRia's mindstate, the voyage had lasted weeks. If it took that long this time the Subliming would already have happened by the time they got there.

"In about eighty-five hours. Less if we hurry."

"Why don't we hurry?"

"Because to do so will damage my engines. They are still repairing themselves after my dash to Izenion."

"So how are you going to lose the ship that might be following us?"

"With difficulty, possibly."

"So what was the other alternative?"

"Employ some method to obscure your exact destination. That should be easier. The android Eglyle Parinherm might be useful at that point. I'd like to wake it."

"Fine by me. See if you can convince it it's not all a sim."

xLOU *Caconym*
    oMSV *Pressure Drop*

So, our little group has grown with the inclusion of the *You Call This Clean?* as well as the *Empiricist*.

And something called the *Smile Tolerantly* is another accomplice of the long-lived Mr Q. Only, looking at my edition of the relevant ship lists, the *Smile Tolerantly* disappeared up its own wazoo some 140 years before the *Warm, Considering* was even built, and was itself only brought into being just under four thousand years ago, so leaving open the question of who else might have been aiding and abetting the elusive geezer in the various meantimes. Any ideas?

∞

None. Further research is required.

∞

Wait. I want to write that down.

"**D**oes she touch you . . . like this?"

"Ah . . . ah yes, very much like that. Just . . . like that."

"And kiss you, like this?"

". . . Somewhat like that. Only a little like that."

"Only a little?"

"She kisses me differently. Oh, this is not . . . I shouldn't . . . I really shouldn't be telling you any of this. This is so . . . You are the most terrible man."

"I know, I know. I hate myself. Am I not just the most terrible, terrible man?"

"You are, I don't know . . . Oh, now what?"

"Let me see . . . does she kiss you like that?"

"No. Again, no, not quite like that."

"In some other way?"

"In some other way."

"How many ways are there, to kiss? I . . . I really have no idea. I am not so well versed as you might . . . let's see . . ."

". . . Well, then. Now. She kisses, let me see . . . more lightly, just as . . . passionately, but with less, less . . . less intensity, less muscularity."

"Muscularity?"

"I think that is the word."

"And, with the touching, is it like this . . .?"

"Oh, ah, yes, sometimes, though . . ."

"Yes?"

"Her hands, her fingers."

"Like this?"

"No, not . . . something like . . . her hands, see, are more slender, the fingers are longer, they are more delicate. Yours are . . . fuller, more . . ."

"Filling?"

"Yes. And grasping."

"Grasping? *Grasping?* I'm shocked, Virisse! Am I really grasping?"

"Ha, I mean . . . hungry, given to clutching, gripping, even grabbing."

"And now grabbing! Good gracious!"

"You grabbed me, don't you remember? That first time, when we were in the garden of the parliament. That evening? You said you wanted to talk about some long-term aspect of her schedule, do you remember?"

"Of course I remember. Here is more comfortable, though, don't you think? I swear if we weren't all departing so shortly

I might have to have this bed reinforced, just to cope with our exertions."

"Her birthday, the following year. You said you wanted to plan something special for her because it would be her sixtieth. Then. That was when you grabbed at me, almost as soon as you had me alone, in that night-shady bower."

"I grabbed you? Are you sure this was me?"

"Oh, now. Who else? You know this. You did."

"I thought you wanted to be grabbed."

"I might have."

"Just as well I did, then, wouldn't you say?"

"I think I will say anything, when we are like this, when you hold me like this."

"Really? I must think up something extremely terrible, then, to exploit that admission."

"You mustn't. You can't. I'm at your mercy; it would be cruel, wrong."

"To the contrary! It would only be right. You offer me this, I must take it. You lay yourself open; I must in."

"Ah. Ah . . . yes. Oh, dear Scribe . . . But . . . not anything. Not anything at all. I am not so totally . . . I am not so . . . I am not . . ."

"Not what, Virisse?"

"I can't remember. I have forgotten what I am not."

"Well. Better that than forgetting what you are."

"You steal all I have away, like this, when we lie like this. I feel laid bare, all washed away."

"Does she do this? Does she have that same effect?"

"Oh, my love, why do you always have to ask me to make these . . . ?"

"Because I'm fascinated. Everything about you fascinates me. How can I not be consumed by . . . not envy, but interest, to know how you lie with her, how much of what you do with me is what you do with her?"

"Is it not enough to know that you and I do what we do? Do we have to compare? Must we always compete?"

"How can we not? The urge to compare and compete is as basic as any. As basic as this."

"Must it be, though?"

"It is; that's all that matters. And does she touch you like this?"

"Oh. Oh. Oh. Yes, yes she does."

"How I'd love to compare. How I'd love to see. How I'd love to watch."

"See, my love? Watch?"

"Is that too much to ask?"

"Prophet's kiss, Septame! You want the three of us . . .?"

"Septame, is it, now! Why . . ."

"Oh, don't stop, don't stop to laugh. Laugh if you must, but don't stop."

"Well, I plough on. But no, I didn't think to suggest that she and I might have you both, together."

"No. That would be too . . . I couldn't . . . anyway, she would never . . ."

"No, of course not. When I have you, I want you all to myself. And I want you to have me, all to yourself. I'd have no dilution of this . . . concentration, this . . . tenacity."

"What, then?"

"Just to watch, just to see you with her."

"She still would not."

"I know. I wouldn't expect her to. And secreting myself within some hidden space, like a courtier in some ancient tragedy, would be absurd."

"Put it from your mind, my love. Concentrate on this, on now, on us."

"The more I do, the more I want to see you and know you in all your states, in all your moods and passions, and that must include with her. Just once, just to see, later, not at the time. And it would be so easily accomplished; I can source the sort of means no civilian or journalist can find."

"Oh, dear gods, you've thought about this. You're serious! No, no, still; don't stop . . ."

"Serious, ardent. Please. It would mean so much."

"It might mean my job! My career; all my standing. She's the *president*!"

"She is president for thirteen more days, as I am a septame for thirteen more days. All that means nothing then and already starts to mean even less now. What does matter is that she is a woman, you are a woman and I am a man."

"But still . . ."

"Still nothing, my love, my beautiful love. We strip off our importance with our clothes. That's all that matters; not our titles. They only have meaning in public, not in moments like these, when we are purely, perfectly ourselves. Only a man – a weak man, a hopelessly curious, desperate-to-know man – asks this of you, my Virisse, not a politician. Just a man. Your man, your man, your man."

"But if . . . if . . . if . . ."

"I'd protect you. There would be no risk. And so close to the end of this world, the start of the next, who really cares? All the rules are questioned now, all the laws loosened. Everything is licensed. Like this, and this, and this."

"Oh. Oh. Oh."

"And I'd make sure nothing would happen to you. I swear; I swear I swear I swear. Even if anything was found, it would never be traceable to you or I. Say you will. Say yes. Say it for me. Say you will. Say yes, say yes, say yes. *Say* it."

"... Yes ..."

The Simming Problem – in the circumstances, it was usually a bad sign when something was so singular and/or notorious it deserved to be capitalised – was of a moral nature, as the really meaty, chewy, most intractable problems generally were.

The Simming Problem boiled down to, How true to life was it morally justified to be?

Simulating the course of future events in a virtual environment to see what might happen back in reality, and tweaking one's own actions accordingly in different runs of the simulated problem to see what difference these would make and to determine whether it was possible to refine those actions such that a desired outcome might be engineered, was hardly new; in a sense it long pre-dated AIs, computational matrices, substrates, computers and even the sort of mechanical or hydrological arrangements of ball-bearings, weights and springs or water, tubes and valves that enthusiastic optimists had once imagined might somehow model, say, an economy.

In a sense, indeed, such simulations first took place in the minds of only proto-sentient creatures, in the deep pre-historic age of any given species. If you weren't being too strict about your definitions you could claim that the first simulations happened in the heads – or other appropriate body- or being-parts – of animals, or the equivalent, probably shortly after they developed a theory of mind and started to think about how to manipulate their peers to ensure access to food, shelter, mating opportunities or greater social standing.

Thoughts like, *If I do this, then she does that ... No; if*

I do that, making him do this . . . in creatures still mystified by fire, or unable to account for the existence of air, or ice, above their watery environment – or whatever – were arguably the start of the first simulations, no matter how dim, limited or blinded by ignorance and prejudice the whole process might be. They were, also, plausibly, the start of a line that led directly through discussions amongst village elders, through collegiate essays, flow charts, war games and the first computer programs to the sort of ultra-detailed simulations that could be shown – objectively, statistically, scientifically – to work.

Long before most species made it to the stars, they would be entirely used to the idea that you never made any significant societal decision with large-scale or long-term consequences without running simulations of the future course of events, just to make sure you were doing the right thing. Simming problems at that stage were usually constrained by not having the calculational power to run a sufficiently detailed analysis, or disagreements regarding what the initial conditions ought to be.

Later, usually round about the time when your society had developed the sort of processal tech you could call Artificial Intelligence without blushing, the true nature of the Simming Problem started to appear.

Once you could reliably model whole populations within your simulated environment, at the level of detail and complexity that meant individuals within that simulation had some sort of independent existence, the question became: how god-like, and how cruel, did you want to be?

Most problems, even seemingly really tricky ones, could be handled by simulations which happily modelled slippery concepts like public opinion or the likely reactions of alien societies by the appropriate use of some especially cunning and devious algorithms; whole populations of slightly different simulative processes could be bred, evolved and set to compete against each other to come up with the most reliable example employing the most decisive short-cuts to accurately modelling, say, how a group of people would behave; nothing more processor-hungry than the right set of equations would – once you'd plugged the relevant data in – produce a reliable estimate of how that group of people would react to a given stimulus, whether the group represented a tiny ruling clique of the most powerful, or an entire civilisation.

But not always. Sometimes, if you were going to have any hope of getting useful answers, there really was no alternative to modelling the individuals themselves, at the sort of scale and level of complexity that meant they each had to exhibit some kind of discrete personality, and that was where the Problem kicked in.

Once you'd created your population of realistically reacting and – in a necessary sense – cogitating individuals, you had – also in a sense – created life. The particular parts of whatever computational substrate you'd devoted to the problem now held beings; virtual beings capable of reacting so much like the back-in-reality beings they were modelling – because how else were they to do so convincingly without also hoping, suffering, rejoicing, caring, loving and dreaming? – that by most people's estimation they had just as much right to be treated as fully recognised moral agents as did the originals in the Real, or you yourself.

If the prototypes had rights, so did the faithful copies, and by far the most fundamental right that any creature ever possessed or cared to claim was the right to life itself, on the not unreasonable grounds that without that initial right, all others were meaningless.

By this reasoning, then, you couldn't just turn off your virtual environment and the living, thinking creatures it contained at the completion of a run or when a simulation had reached the end of its useful life; that amounted to genocide, and however much it might feel like serious promotion from one's earlier primitive state to realise that you had, in effect, become the kind of cruel and pettily vengeful god you had once, in your ignorance, feared, it was still hardly the sort of mature attitude or behaviour to be expected of a truly civilised society, or anything to be proud of.

Some civs, admittedly, simply weren't having any of this, and routinely bred whole worlds, even whole galaxies, full of living beings which they blithely consigned to oblivion the instant they were done with them, sometimes, it seemed, just for the glorious fun of it, and to annoy their more ethically angst-tangled co-civilisationalists, but they – or at least those who admitted to the practice, rather than doing it but keeping quiet about it – were in a tiny minority, as well as being not entirely welcome at all the highest tables of the galactic community, which was usually precisely where the most ambitious and ruthless species/civs most desired to be.

Others reckoned that as long as the termination was instant, with no warning and therefore no chance that those about to be switched off could suffer, then it didn't really matter. The wretches hadn't existed, they'd been brought into existence for a specific, contributory purpose, and now they were nothing again; so what?

Most people, though, were uncomfortable with such moral brusqueness, and took their responsibilities in the matter more seriously. They either avoided creating virtual populations of genuinely living beings in the first place, or only used sims at that sophistication and level of detail on a sustainable basis, knowing from the start that they would be leaving them running indefinitely, with no intention of turning the environment and its inhabitants off at any point.

Whether these simulated beings were really *really* alive, and how justified it was to create entire populations of virtual creatures just for your own convenience under any circumstances, and whether or not – if/once you had done so – you were sort of duty-bound to be honest with your creations at some point and straight out tell them that they weren't really real, and existed at the whim of another order of beings altogether – one with its metaphorical finger hovering over an Off switch capable of utterly and instantly obliterating their entire universe . . . well, these were all matters which by general and even relieved consent were best left to philosophers. As was the ever-vexing question, How do we know *we're* not in a simulation?

There were sound, seemingly base-reality metamathematically convincing and inescapable reasons for believing that all concerned in this ongoing debate about simulational ethics were genuinely at the most basic level of reality, the one that definitely wasn't running as a virtual construct on somebody else's substrate, but – if these mooted super-beings had been quite extraordinarily clever and devious – such seemingly reliable and reassuring signs might all just be part of the illusion.

There was also the Argument of Increasing Decency, which basically held that cruelty was linked to stupidity and that the link between intelligence, imagination, empathy and good-behaviour-as-it-was-generally-understood – i.e. *not* being cruel to others – was as profound as these matters ever got. This strongly implied that beings capable of setting up a virtuality so convincing, so devious, so detailed that it was capable of fooling entities as smart as – say – Culture Minds must be so shatteringly, intoxicatingly clever they pretty much had to be decent, agreeable and highly moral types themselves. (So; much like Culture Minds, then, except more so.)

But that too might be part of the set-up, and the clear positive correlation between beings of greater intellectual capacity taking over from lesser ones – while still respecting their rights, of course – and the gradual diminution of violence and suffering over civilisationally significant periods of time might also be the result of a trick.

A bit, after some adjustments for scale, like the trick of seeding another society with the ideas for a holy book that appeared to tell the truth on several levels but which was basically just part of an experiment, the *Contents May Differ* thought, as it reviewed the results of the latest sim runs.

The sims it was setting up and letting run were all trying to answer the relatively simple question, How much difference will it make if the Gzilt find out the Book of Truth is a fake?

And the answer appeared to be: Who the fuck knows?

Once you started to think that the only way to model a population accurately would be to read the individual mind-states of every single person within the real thing – something even more immoral than it was impractical – it was probably time to try another approach entirely.

As a good, decent, caring and responsible Culture Mind, the *Contents May Differ* would never run a sim of the Gzilt people at the individual level to find out anyway, even if it could have, and – apart from anything else – had decided some time ago that even resorting to such desperate measures wouldn't solve anything in any case. Because there were two Problems: the Simming Problem and the Chaos Problem.

The Chaos Problem meant that in certain situations you could run as many simulations as you liked, and each would produce a meaningful result, but taken as a whole there would be no discernible pattern to them, and so no lesson to be drawn or obvious course laid out to pursue; it would all depend so exquisitely on exactly how you had chosen to tweak the initial conditions at the start of each run that, taken together, they would add up to nothing more useful than the realisation that This Is A Tricky One.

The real result, the one that mattered, out there in reality, would almost certainly very closely resemble one of your simulated results, but there would have been no way at any stage of the process to have determined exactly or even approximately which one, and that rendered the whole enterprise almost entirely futile; you ended up having to use other, much less reliable methods to work out what was going to happen.

These included using one's own vast intelligence, pooled with the equally vast intelligences of one's peers, to access the summed total of galactic history and analyse, compare and contrast the current situation relative to similar ones from the past. Given the sort of clear, untrammelled, devastatingly powerful thinking AIs and particularly Minds were capable of, this could be a formidably accurate and – compared to every other method available – relatively reliable strategy. Its official title was Constructive Historical Integrative Analysis.

In the end, though, there was another name the Minds used, amongst themselves, for this technique, which was Just Guessing.

The mount was called Yoawin. It was old and in no particular hurry, though still strong and tireless. Well, as tireless as Tefwe needed it to be; she got weary and saddle-sore before it started showing signs of complaint.

Tefwe had chosen an old-fashioned saddle: tall and

unwieldy if you were planning on performing any fancy stuff, but comfortable. Comfortable for the aphore as well as her; you always had to think of your mount. They'd had intelligent animals for hire at the stables in Chyan'tya, too; ones you could talk to, both amended bio and what were effectively walking, talking slightly dumb drones made to look biological. She guessed talkative people might hire those. Maybe people who were so talkative they couldn't persuade other humans to ride with them. But a talking mount had always struck Tefwe as taking things a little too far. Aphores were quite smart enough, and sufficiently companionable to provide a sort of silent friendship.

They'd arrived in the middle of the night, on this side of the Orbital. She left at first light, riding out through the quiet town. There was some sort of festival happening during the day and some flower garlands, stretched across the street leading out of town towards the hills, had sagged with the dew during the night; she had to lift them out of the way to get underneath. One pale blue flower, loosened, started to fall. She caught it, sniffed it, stuck it in her hair, rode on.

The town was much as she'd remembered. It sat like a rough brush stroke along one side of the Snake river, cliffed on the shifting sands of tawny and grey-pink that marked the desert edge; a fragrant oasis of bell-blossom and strandle flower, even-cluss and jodenberry, the low, flowing buildings half submerged by their own orchards and groves.

Across the river, past some stunted, half-hearted dunes and the silted-up entrance to a long-dry oxbow lake, the brush and scrub of the low prairie began. The few scattered bushes looked like an after-thought to the land: quick, light scribbles of brittle-dry vegetation, prone to fires that in the right wind could move so fast you were better turning to face their heat and running straight through, because you'd never outrun them.

The river was very low; just a trickle at the bottom of the crack-dried muds and in-flowed spills of sand like fanned ramps. High season. The rains would come in a third of a year from now, falling in the Bulkheads, which were so far off that even in the clearest weather you could strain your eyes for ever and you'd never see them, night or day, not this far down in the thick of air.

A few tens of days later, after the rains started falling in the high lands of the Honn-Eynimorm Bulkhead Range, the river would swell, generally pushing a plugged mess of old leaves, scrawny twigs, gnarled branches, stripped tree trunks and the bleached hides and bones of dead animals before it, like a moving barricade of half-forgotten decrepitude and death.

She rode out across the Pouch, the bay of desert and patchy set-sand that lay between the river and the town on one side and the hills on the other. A pair of raptors wheeled high up, following her for half the morning, then found something else to watch, kilometres off anti-spinwards. She lost sight of them in the building heat of the cloudless day.

Her backside got sore; she glanded *numb*, rode on.

At the height of the day, a desiccant umbrel provided shade for her and the aphore, once she'd chased a snoozing misiprike away. It had been fast asleep; she'd had to clap her hands and holler to get it to wake while she and the suddenly nervy aphore stood, only ten metres away.

The misiprike had looked up, risen tiredly to its feet and loped off. It stopped once to snarl back at them as though it had only just remembered it was supposed to be a fearsome creature, then padded loose-limbed over the frozen waves of set-sand.

She fed the aphore, her stomach rumbling, then ate, drank. Even in the shade it was very hot; she and the mount snoozed.

She'd missed the descent; usually she liked being dropped onto the inside of an Orbital, rather than taking the conventional approach of coming up from underneath. A descent meant you got to see the overview of the place you were coming to; a real view, even if it was through a screen, not a pretend one.

She'd been born and raised on a planet. This was a rare thing, in the Culture; even rarer than being born on a ship, and that was pretty rare in itself. Things had been like this for millennia. Anyway, she ascribed whatever eccentricities she was prone to displaying to that oddity of birthright. She'd spent more time on Os than anywhere else – spent centuries living on them – but still she couldn't help but think of planets as normal and Orbitals as somehow aberrant, for all that the artificial worlds far outnumbered the number of naturally inhabitable ones.

In the end it was kind of unarguable that planets were natural and Orbitals were artificial, though she supposed that, when you thought about it, it was really no more natural to live on the outside of a huge, skein-warping sphere of rock, held to its surface – like the atmosphere – by nothing more than gravity than it was to live on the inside of an O, held there by spin, with the atmosphere held down by the same movement and stopped from spilling off the edges by retainment walls of diamond film and fate knew what exoticism of material and field.

She drifted in and out of her snooze, and, while still dozily waking up, asked her ancient pen terminal whether anybody had ever built a planet, or discovered a natural Orbital. Yes to the former, though rarely, and not for aeons. A straight no to the latter.

"There you are," she told Yoawin as she got her to stand and busied herself re-setting the animal's bridle. "Planets not guaranteed totally natural after all."

The aphore snorted.

That night, at the start of the hills – maybe a kilometre in and a hundred metres up, by a dry water bowl – Tefwe slept under the stars and the bright, lit band of the Orbital's far side.

That was the really unnatural sign of an O, she supposed. You might not notice the inside-out curvature at any time, or come to an access tube that would let you drop the hundred metres or whatever to the world's space-exposed under-surface, or see the sea or the clouds held ruler-straight against an edge wall, but, come the night, there would be the sure and certain sign that you really were pinned by your rotating frame of reference to the inside of a bracelet ten million klicks across: the far side, shining in its daytime while the side you were on had its back turned to whatever sun the whole O circled.

Well, unless the clouds on your side of the Orbital were really thick, she supposed, and fell asleep.

Come the morning, they left in the grey pre-dawn, despite Yoawin's protests. "Don't you spit at me, you addled stumble-hoof," Tefwe said, and spat back at it. "There. See how you like it." She wiped her face while Yoawin shook hers. "There. Now, sorry. Both of us sorry, yes? No more spitting. Here." She gave it some dried berries.

A series of tall cliffs kept them mostly in shade until nearly noon, letting them keep going longer. They ate, drank and dozed under an overhang.

The track just before the pass was very steep; she got off Yoawin and led the animal up the zigzagging path. Dry stones rattled under her boots and the aphore's hooves. At a corner in the trail near the top, one fall of initially just a dozen or so stones set off a small landslide further down. The fractious, rattling, rumbling sound of it echoed off the cliffs and slopes all around like dry thunder. Tefwe watched the dusty mass descend, to see if it would sweep away any part of the track, but it didn't, and the tumbling mass of stones and boulders slowed and slumped to a dusty stop on the shallowing slope some way above the valley floor.

From the pass, the plateau was only fifty metres below her, ringed by sharp peaks and ragged cliffs. Its surface was bright with salt lakes and thin wind-corralled whorls of pale sand. Yoawin panted. Tefwe patted the animal's snout and looked around as the hot wind swept her hair back from her face. She smiled, and felt the dried skin on her lips protest at the motion.

A couple of kilometres away, shimmering in the heated air, she could see the rocky outcrop where the drone Hassipura Plyn-Frie would be working on its sandstreams.

Tefwe reached up to where the flower she'd picked the day before had been, tucked into a coil of her hair, at least until this morning, thinking to leave it here at the pass. But her fingers closed round nothing; it had gone, already fallen.

xGSV *Contents May Differ*
 oGCU *Beats Working*
You appear to covet the behaviour of our superlifter siblings, and have become a sort of serial tug. Were you getting bored?

∞

A little. I also thought that – given the Ronte had been due to arrive at Zyse in particular significantly after the Enfolding – helping them to get to Zyse swiftly might help preclude the Liseiden, faced with an empty home

system devoid of both those it had belonged to and those it had been allocated to, being tempted to ignore the decision in favour of the Ronte by resorting to illegal pillaging. I simply wanted to remove that temptation by making sure the Ronte were in position at the time of the Instigation, thus ensuring a smooth handover.

∞

Thoughtful. However, it does rather make it look as though we favour one over the other.

∞

I appreciate that, however, all we are doing is favouring the rightful over those who might, wrongly, feel aggrieved and who, were this action not taken, have the means and the opportunity to act upon that feeling, with potentially disastrous results.

∞

Noble motivations, I'm sure. May I ask you to run any ideas for future innovations of a similar nature past the rest of us before carrying them out? Would you do that?

∞

I would.

Fifteen

(S -13)

"This is a closed system, of course," the blindfolded man said, feeling his way to the seat and then turning it, holding it angled away from the ancient-looking console and screen so that the septame could sit in it. Banstegeyn held the back of the seat but did not sit. The blindfolded man – by his uniform, a captain in the Home Regiment – talked to him as though he could see him. "It is unconnected to any other, and so its contents are unavailable elsewhere. I understand other such hermetic arrangements hold certain records it is as well are not readily accessible; however this one merely catalogues various pieces of equipment which are regarded as being best kept secret from the general mass of people, and indeed even the general mass of armed forces personnel."

"I see," said Banstegeyn, studying the captain's face. The man's eyes were concealed behind a thick metal strap cushioned with dark foam. According to Marshal Chekwri, who had personally driven him here to this anonymous if well-guarded warehouse on the capital's outskirts, this was perfectly normal and did not constitute some special arrangement made just for him.

When they'd first arrived and been introduced to the blindfolded captain, the marshal had produced a vicious-looking fighting knife and flicked it fast and straight at the captain's blindfolded face, eliciting, it seemed at first, not the slightest response. Though then the captain had smiled and said, "Ah, I felt the wind of that; were you really testing me, ma'am?"

Chekwri had just smiled her thin, humourless smile.

She'd stayed in an outer office as Banstegeyn had been led into the barely lit inner office, through a double set of thick doors.

"So," Banstegeyn said, still not sitting. "Do you know who I am, Captain?"

"No, sir. You must be above a certain rank to be here – exactly which depends on the service and regiment – but I don't know who you are. Your voice sounds vaguely familiar but I wouldn't be able to place it." He smiled, and his head tipped back a little so that now he seemed to be addressing a point somewhere above the other man's head. "For somebody who spends a large part of his working day as a blind man, I am remarkably bad with voices, sir." He shrugged. "It is a blessing in some ways."

"I'm sure."

"Please, sir; sit."

"Thank you." Banstegeyn sat down. The captain went through the controls for the system. They were simple enough.

"Any item below a certain size, such as would fit into this drawer . . ." the fellow pulled out a very long and heavy-seeming drawer in the console ". . . will be delivered into it. Larger items will be delivered into the pull-out hopper behind you, sir." He nodded at a section of the wall where there was a rectangular outline nearly two metres long with a substantial double handle.

"The screen should tell you how long it'll take to physically retrieve any item, sir, should you find one that meets your requirements, but please do be aware it could take some minutes; up to ten in some instances, and certain items require some assembly and . . . well, loading, frankly. A little patience may be required, sir, and possibly a little familiarity with whatever item is to be called for. I'll leave it to your own good judgement and that of the officer who accompanied you here whether any selected item is suitable." The blindfolded captain sighed regretfully. "I trust you've already been so informed, sir, but I'm duty-bound to inform you that any and all responsibility for the use of any items found herein rests entirely with your good self, sir, and once an item leaves these premises it becomes fully your property, to the extent that all record of it even having been stored here will be irrevocably wiped and deleted from the database held herein."

"I understand," Banstegeyn said. "Do I have to sign anything, or speak a form of words?"

The captain's smile was broad, tolerant. "Oh, absolutely not, sir. Officially you aren't even here."

"I see. Well, thank you. Sorry to put you to so much trouble."

"Not at all, sir. There's been very little demand lately; it's been terribly slow. Nice to have somebody requiring our services again. I'll leave you now, sir; press the blue button on the left of the console if you need any help."

Banstegeyn waited until the heavy doors had fully closed behind the captain before turning back to the screen. He took in a breath to tell it to wake up, then felt foolish. Of course; entirely manual, without the least semblance of voice-recognition, let alone even crude AI. He found the On button, thumbed it.

A simple in-holo screen, with a keyboard, or a stylus and writing tablet, if so desired.

He sighed. This might take some time.

T. C. Vilabier's 26th String-Specific Sonata For An Instrument Yet To Be Invented, MW 1211 – The Hydrogen Sonata – started with a single sustained note, right at the top of the range of the instrument which had had to be invented to play it properly, the bodily acoustic Antagonistic Undecagonstring for four hands. That single note was then joined by a faint, uncertain chord of slowly shifting harmonics, which was another way of saying that it started to sound out of tune after it got more than one note in. Fans and detractors alike agreed that this was a remarkable achievement, and also that the work as a whole was something of an acquired taste.

The single high note at the start of the work was meant to signify a solitary proton, specifically a hydrogen nucleus, while the following wavering pseudo-chord was supposed to embody the concept of a sole electron's probability cloud, so that together the first note and the first chord represented the element hydrogen.

Vilabier was thought to have been joking when he had

claimed that the work was itself merely the first note in a vast and incrementally more complicated cycle that would grow to encompass the entirety of the periodic table.

Regardless; after this simple beginning the work became furiously complicated and – initially at least, until playing techniques and prosthetic technology had sufficiently improved – almost unplayable. Initially, in this case, meant for several centuries. Many held that whether it was unplayable or not didn't particularly matter; what did was that it was completely unlistenable.

But that was, arguably, to take a somewhat doctrinaire attitude to what the word "listenable" meant.

"I like it," the ship said, through Berdle.

"*Really?*" Cossont said, standing and shaking herself, loosening all the over-tensed muscles that tended to result when one played the elevenstring with any gusto. She'd only tackled the first movement, and then purely because the ship had asked her to, and because she was feeling guilty about not having played the instrument for days. The ship had altered the acoustics of the big central lounge area of the module to make it sound sweeter. They were a day out from their destination, the cloud of Centralised Dataversities and associated other habitats, institutions and auxiliary resources in the Ospin system.

"Yes," Pyan said, "*really?*"

Pyan had been perfectly indifferent to the Hydrogen Sonata – as it was to all music – until it had realised that most people hated the piece, when it had decided to join in the chorus of disdain.

"I can see what it's trying to do, and it has a mathematical elegance to it that I appreciate," Berdle said. "Also, I've invented a form of musical notation that I think enhances its appreciation in the abstract, as a visual and intellectual internalised experience, without one actually having to listen to it."

Cossont nodded. "I can certainly see the point of that." She stopped, frowned. "You've invented a . . .?" She shook her head. "No, never mind."

"I agree with Mr Berdle," Eglyle Parinherm said. "However, I do detect a degree of discordant tonality."

The android had been activated hours earlier, waking instantaneously on the bed platform where he'd been stored. He'd stared straight up and, in a deep, controlled voice said, "Unit Y988, Parinherm, Eglyle, systems checked, all enabled. Sim status ready, engaged, chron scale subjective one-to-one."

"Hmm," Berdle had said. It had tried turning the android off and on again a few times since, but to no avail.

Cossont flexed her fingers, stowed the instrument's two bows in its case. "Discordant tonality about covers it," she said.

"While you were playing," Berdle said, "I found some screen of your mother."

"Oh, shit."

"Shall I . . .?"

"Yeah, I suppose."

Two days after they'd left the Izenion system, Cossont had suddenly realised she ought to let her mother know she was okay. She'd asked the ship to get a message to Warib telling her that she was alive and well but couldn't communicate directly.

"But I could arrange a direct communication quite easily," the ship had told her.

"Could you really?" she'd said, eyes wide. "Anyway, as I was saying: alive and well but not able to communicate directly . . . um, don't tell anybody I've been in touch, obviously, ah . . . hope you're well . . . should see you before the Instigation." She'd smiled at the very handsome Gzilt male that the avatar had become. "And tell her I've met an extremely good-looking and very powerful man, if you like. That'll keep her happy."

"Any customary sign-off?" Berdle had asked.

"Well, hers to me is usually, 'Well, if you're going to be like *that*!' followed by the screen going blank, and mine is usually, 'Um, you take care,' because it sounds, well, caring, without necessitating the use of the word 'love'."

"Hmm," the avatar had said. "Also, it's a little un-personalised. As it stands, anybody could be sending her this, and she might suspect she is being lied to by a third party."

Cossont had sighed. "I suppose. Well . . . tell her Pyan says hi, and . . . I'm keeping my natural hair colour."

And now the ship had found some screen of Warib.

"This is from yesterday afternoon, on one of the channels on the cruise sea ship your mother inhabits," Berdle told her, as a screen appeared in mid-air, level with where Cossont stood. She threw herself down into a chair. The virtual screen dipped, following her. Pyan flapped and flopped over to arrange itself on the lounger next to Cossont. Even Parinherm leaned over to get a better view. Cossont thought of requesting some privacy, then decided she didn't care.

The screen came to life with a roaming shot of her mother's apartment on the sea ship and a female voice-over saying, "We spoke to Madame Warib Cossont, of deck twenty-five, who believes her daughter may have been swept up in the current emergency and now, having just heard from her, fears for her well-being and even life."

"Oh, for *fuck's* sake!" Vyr shouted. She looked at Berdle.

"You did put in the bit about her not telling anybody I'd been in touch?"

"Of course," Berdle said. He frowned. "I thought I'd been entirely unambiguous. Even forceful."

Cossont just shook her head, looked back at the screen. There was an abrupt cut to a head-and-shoulders shot of Warib, sitting in her largest white couch with the sea and clouds behind. Small glowing figures in the top right corner of the screen read *S -13*, reminding any especially absent-minded viewers how many days were left to the Subliming. Warib was dressed in a blouse suit Vyr didn't recognise. It was a bit frilly and showy. "Madame Cossont," the voice continued, slightly altered in timbre and ambience now, "you recently heard from your daughter, didn't you?"

"Or somebody claiming to be her, yes. It's not like her to be so poor getting back to me, it really isn't. We've always been very close and kept in touch all the time and then she just seemed to disappear from the face of the planet, and apparently her bed hasn't been even slept in for days – many, I mean several days – and then, of course, she is in the Fourteenth, the regiment the Fourteenth, and she was always very active in the Reserve, *very* respected, and of course there's been this terrible, terrible—"

"Madame—" the voice of the unseen interviewer said.

Berdle looked at Vyr; she had one of her upper hands cupped over her nose and eyes, the other three hands all clasped tightly across her chest.

"—terrible explosion on this planet and for all I know – well, I thought, I assumed the worst, naturally, as any mother would. I wondered, 'Could she have been there, was that where she went? Did she know something?' as soon as I heard about, about the thing, but then there was nothing, just nothing—"

"Madame Cossont—"

"I'm sorry. I am just rattling on, aren't I? I do care, I worry so much about her . . ." She looked away to one side, put her hand to her mouth and balled it there, her lips tightening, her eyes blinking quickly. Her lower lip started to tremble.

"I can't watch any more of this," Vyr announced. "Turn it off. Please. What's the upshot?"

The screen disappeared.

"Oh!" Pyan said. "I was enjoying that!"

"Your mother relates," Berdle said, "that she received the text message you sent via myself and says she thinks you're 'mixed up in something'."

"Well," Cossont sighed, "she got that right, if nothing else."

"She says that she doubts it really was from you and describes you as, I quote: 'wittering about her hair, when that's never been something she's ever even cared about, I mean I've done my best, I always have, but anyway, it did strike me as highly suspicious'. End quote."

Vyr put both upper hands over her face. "Oh, for fuck's sake. That was supposed to . . . last time we . . . she said . . . oh, never mind." She took a deep breath, looked up. "Nothing about how my claiming to have met an extremely good-looking and very powerful man was even less likely to be true?"

"I didn't include that," Berdle confessed. "You left it to my discretion and I thought it best to leave it out."

"Probably just as well. She'd have assumed it was code for I've been kidnapped."

Parinherm looked suddenly alert and glanced around quickly. "You *haven't* been kidnapped, have you?" he said, and seemed to be tensed to leap up from where he sat.

"Excuse me," Berdle said, and the android went limp, relaxing as though deflated and settling back into the lounger.

"That is going to get tiresome," Cossont said, frowning at the unconscious android. "Can't you just re-program it or something?" she asked Berdle.

"Not so easily," the avatar said. "It has highly recursive, deeply embedded, multiple-level physical source coding check-sets worked down to the atomechanical level as well as a radically tenacious prescribed assume-simulation default with closely associated deacativatory protocols. It's a real tangle. Probably meant to be a safety feature."

"Certainly not a comprehensibility feature."

Berdle smiled. "I beg your pardon. I mean it's hard to re-program it without disabling it, potentially." The avatar shrugged. "There will be a work-around recorded some-where obscure, probably; I'll keep looking. Plus I'll just continue to think about it."

"What about the ship that's following us?"

"I don't see any need to test its top speed by trying to outpace it; better to keep that edge, assuming it exists. I've run a lot of sims for a fly-through of the Ospin system and an insertion into various of the dataversities and I'm confi-dent this can be done with minimal chance of the following ship spotting where you're inserted, unless it's a particularly remote unit." Berdle paused. "We can leave this another hour or two, but, given that you have effectively raised the subject, it would be helpful to know which of the dataversities or other objects we might be targeting."

Cossont nodded. "It's the Bokri microrbital; the Incast facility."

"Thank you," Berdle said, then smiled. "That shouldn't be a problem. It's in a relatively densely packed volume of the cloud. Plenty of cover." It looked at Cossont. "Would anybody – your mother, for example – know that you took the mind-state device to the Incast order on Bokri?"

She shook her head. "I didn't tell anybody." She sighed. "I put it in my private journal and General Reikl knew about that, but I suppose that all got destroyed when the Reg HQ was blown up."

"Probably," Berdle agreed.

Cossont sighed. "If this all goes horribly wrong, you'll have to contact my mother to tell her you've lost her little girl."

"If this all goes horribly wrong," the ship told her, "I too might be lost."

"Well, you've heard what she's like; death might be preferable."

"That," Pyan said primly, "is no way to talk about your mother."

Cossont looked at Berdle and said reasonably, "That, I think you'll find, is the only way to talk about my mother."

"These things accrete."

"Most things accrete that don't gradually crumble, rust or evaporate."

"I didn't mean to suggest there was any merit in the process."

"Indeed. Nor in its opposite."

"I'm glad we have finally found something to agree on."

"I'm not."

"I think you make a virtue of contrariness, or think to."

"You might be dismayed to know just how little what you think matters to me, Scoaliera."

"I doubt it. My expectations could hardly be lower. Also, I'm encouraged by your relative approachability and good humour on this occasion."

"I do believe my sarcasm-meter just twitched."

"A false positive, I fear. I was being entirely sincere."

"You say? Have I been imagining that I was the very exemplar of hearty, helpful bonhomie on our last meeting?"

"Possibly."

"Hmm."

The drone Hassipura Plyn-Frie was the size and shape of a large grey suitcase. A rather battered and dusty large grey suitcase. Its scraped, slightly dented casing glinted in the sunlight where it had been polished by the sand in the wind, or had been scraped against stones. If it was showing an aura field, it was being washed out by the brilliant sunlight. But probably it wasn't; it never had in the past, not as long as Tefwe had known it.

"Anyway, I am not persuaded that memories do only accrete," the drone told the woman. "Even without the intrinsic limitations of a conventional biological brain, what one forgets can be as important and as formative as what one remembers."

Hassipura had made its home in a tall, jagged outcrop of dark rocks that stuck out above the white waste of the salt desert like a diseased tooth. Through the machine's efforts over the centuries, the place had become a dry little paradise of directed cause and effect, an oasis of minutely ordered motion and an arid image of a water garden.

"I thought drones, like Minds, remembered everything," Tefwe said.

"Well, we don't." There was a pause before it said, "Well, I don't."

Tefwe and the drone were at the foot of the outcrop, just a vertical metre and a few shattered-looking boulders away from the surface of the desert. Tefwe was standing and Hassipura was hovering level with the woman's head, performing some maintenance on a fragile-looking raising screw. The raising screw was powered by the fierce sunlight falling on a small semi-circular array of solar panels part-encasing its lower quarter.

"I see," the woman said. "Do you choose what to forget, or do you just let things disappear randomly?"

"Scoaliera," the drone said, "if I chose what to forget, I would very likely have forgotten all about you."

The screw, one of a dozen or so at this lowest level of the rocks, was a couple of metres tall, and thin enough for Tefwe's fingers to have met, had she grasped it one-handed. The foot of the device lay in a pool of sand about a metre across; the slowly rotating screw twisted lazily in the dark-gold grains, raising them inside a transparent collar with a hypnotic steadiness to deposit the lifted material, a minute or so later, into another pool on a higher tier of the outcrop, where a second level of raising screws and sand-wheels like pieces of giant clockwork would transport the material further up, and so on, for level after level and diminishing tier after diminishing tier until a single last raising screw, buried in a tunnel inside the dusty peak of the tor, deposited a small trickle of sand to an overflowing pool at its very summit.

"That is ungallant, and, I suspect, also not true."

"Let us test that, shall we, should you ever come to visit me again?"

"I don't believe you delete memories at random."

"They are chosen at random and buffer-binned; whether they are finally deleted is a matter of choice."

"Ah. Might have thought so."

The drone had subtly sculpted the outcrop over the decades and centuries it had lived here, cutting channels, pools, cisterns, tunnels and reservoirs into the rock, building structures that at least resembled aqueducts and creating, had the whole complex been filled with water, what would have been a kind of secret water garden, albeit with rather steeply inclined canals and aqueducts.

But the outcrop held no water at all. Instead it was sand that moved within the tunnels and channels, sand which was lifted within the raising wheels and screws, and sand which fell in little whispering falls and moved liquidly down dry weirs.

"Whatever makes you think I'd wish to visit you again after being so roundly insulted?"

"That fact that I have insulted you just as roundly in the past to so little effect," the drone said smoothly, "for here you are. Again."

"You're right. I ought to come back just to annoy you," Tefwe said, squatting. She dipped her hand into the shaded pool where the rod of the raising screw slanted into the tawny grains. She let the sand fall back between her fingers; it slipped away almost as quickly as water would have. "It moves very smoothly," she said, inspecting her hand. A few tiny grains adhered to her skin, all in the lines of her palm.

"Please don't do that," the drone said, using invisible maniple fields to adjust parts of the diamond-sheet-covered solar panels.

"Why?" Tefwe asked.

"Moisture," Hassipura said. "And impurities such as salts. Your hands will have added a little of each to the sands."

"Sorry." Tefwe squatted and stuck her head down into the shade created by the solar panel, gazing at the pool of sand underneath. Inside its transparent sleeve, the turning screw seemed barely to disturb the surface of the sand, which appeared to flow in to fill even the slightest of hollows. She glanced up to see if the drone was looking, reckoned it couldn't see, then stuck a finger into the surface of the sand pool and took it smartly out again. The sand closed up round where her finger had been – running in, again, like water – to leave no sign that its surface had been disturbed.

"Will you stop doing that?" the drone said, tiredly.

"Apologies," Tefwe said. "How *does* it move so smoothly?"

"The grains are spheres," the drone said, clicking something back into place on the solar array. "They are polished, individually where necessary. I call the stuff sand because it starts out as ordinary sand and still has the same chemical composition as the raw material, but really the particle size is reduced almost to that of fines, and the polishing process leaves each grain almost perfectly spherical. See." The drone shifted in the air, humming very faintly.

Tefwe stood and straightened as a bright screen suddenly filled the air in front of her, seeming to dim a significant part of the sky and putting her in shadow. The drone had produced a holo display like a magically produced cabinet hovering in front of the woman. The holo showed two grains, highly magnified. One appeared to be about the size of Tefwe's head, and was jagged, crystalline, all straight edges, spires and juts; not unlike the rocky outcrop itself. It was rainbowed with diffraction colours. The other was pebble-sized, a glass-like shiny blond and seemingly a perfect sphere.

"Before and after," the drone said, shutting the screen off and letting the blast of sunlight fall upon Tefwe again. Her eyes adjusted, putting a black dot over the sun to reduce the glare. The sunlight was so strong her vision would have been affected by light coming in through the surrounds of her eyes, so they would be partially silvering, she suspected. Something similar had happened to areas of her skin, again to cope with the ferocity of the sun's glare. *Grief; I'm going silver*. She was, she realised, starting to look like a ship's avatar.

"You polish them all individually?" she asked.

"I have processes, machinery to do the gross polishing," the drone told her. "Then they are all inspected individually, by me. Any further polishing that is required I do myself."

"That seems obsessive."

"Meticulous care can seem so to those unwilling to recognise it for its true worth."

"I meant you might simply discard the rejects."

Hassipura gave the appearance of thinking about this. "That I would find offensive," it said eventually.

"What a strange machine you are," Tefwe told it.

"That is why I make my home here in the centre of a city in the midst of my dear fellow drones and so many, many delightfully gregarious humans."

"Is this really all you do?" she asked, gazing round the network of sand-canals, sandfalls, sand weirs, pools, lakes and whirlpools. She wanted to call the dry, canted bridges aqueducts, but couldn't. Silicaducts, maybe.

"Yes. Do you find it in some way inadequate?"

"No, it's beautiful in a way. You really have no water at all?"

"None. Why should I have water? I have no need for it, nor does the sandstream complex. Water makes paste and mud. Water clogs and makes the complex stop working. Here, water is a pollutant."

"Does it rain often here?"

"Almost never, thankfully."

"Still, shouldn't you have some water for guests, for visitors?"

"I try to discourage visitors."

"What about weary travellers? Or what if some poor devil

comes crawling across the sands, croaking for water?"

"Having lost their terminal, so unable to call Hub or anywhere else for help?"

"For the sake of argument."

"Then *I* would call Hub or somewhere else for help. Scoaliera, do I take it you're thirsty?"

"Not really, but I think the aphore is."

"You should have brought more water."

"I still have some. I'll let it drink shortly."

"You came from Chyan'tya?"

"Yes. Read my terminal for the detail."

The drone was silent for a moment. "Spat on you, did it?" it said. "Can't have been that thirsty."

"Patently."

"I'm going to be visiting various parts of the complex over the next hour or so. Do you have anything to let you float?"

"No."

"You'd better climb on top of me if we're still to converse, then. I take it you do still wish to converse. It would be too much to hope that you just happened to be passing by sheer coincidence and are now happy to be on your way."

"Thank you, I will. And of course I'm here for a purpose."

"I'd kind of guessed." The drone made a slow swoop to about mid-thigh level on Tefwe. She climbed aboard, sitting cross-legged on its broad back. It rose into the hot, dry air, heading up about ten metres to a sort of little depot of machinery set on a levelled area where the rock had been melted and allowed to cool. Patches were like glass, reflecting the sharp glare of the sun.

The aphore, nestling in the shade of a house-sized boulder, raised its head when it caught sight of her on the drone. It looked confused. Then it put its head back down to the shadow-dark sand and closed its eyes again. The drone lifted a small tube and appeared to inspect it, turning it this way and that in front of the high-magnification band running along its blunt snout. It replaced it, moved to another rack of what looked like miniaturised mining equipment.

"So, come far?" it asked.

"Far enough."

"Who sent you?"

"Bunch of ships."

"Will I have heard of any of them?"

She reeled off the relevant names.

"Is this SC?"

"Not generated. Some EUAs are helping out. Think they're bored. It's a bit quiet right now."

"Ah, Elements Usually Associated," the drone said, and managed to sound almost wistful. "And is the *Smile Tolerantly* really involved, actively?"

"No. It's more . . . wanted."

"And what do you want, Tefwe?"

"From you? To know the location of our old chum Ngaroe QiRia."

"Ah. I suppose I should have guessed. What makes you think I know that?"

"Oh, come on."

"All right. What makes you think I would tell you?"

"It's important."

"Why?"

"Long story. He might remember something that backs up a claim somebody's made. Claim that might make a big difference to a lot of people."

"You are going to have to do better than that."

"How long have we got?"

"All day."

"Okay." She told him the background. By the time she was finished the drone had carried her almost to the summit of the outcrop. From here, maybe sixty metres above the surface of the desert and the salt pans, she could see pretty much the whole network of the sandstream complex: all the silicaducts, channels and pools, lakes, pools and weirs and all the raising wheels and screws that lifted the sands from the base of the outcrop. From above, it looked even more like it was all done with flowing, dyed water; foreshortened like this, you couldn't see the relatively steep slopes required to make the sands move under gravity. The raising wheels turned slowly, scooping sand from one pool to deposit it in a higher one. The wheels in particular, seen en masse, made the whole outcrop look like a giant clock powered by sand and sunlight.

She could see the aphore, still trying to keep in the shade of the rocks far beneath as the sun moved across the sky. The animal was making thin, whinnying noises. Probably thirsty, Tefwe thought.

The high desert was flat and shining, dotted with dark outcrops like jagged islands on that sea of salt, hot sand and dust. The pale writhing column of a dust devil danced in the distance, like a ghostly impersonation of a waterspout. The view of the encircling mountains, all shimmering in the heat, was bleakly impressive. She did feel a little exposed though. The skin on the back of her hands had gone quite silvery-white under the sunlight. The sky above was a hazy shining blue; a cobalt blister like a vast, concentrating lens with her at the focal point. This stark, intense azure was the true colour of the desert, she thought.

Her stomach made a faint, delicate rumbling sound. She wondered when she had last eaten; her body was using the ambient heat to drive many of the processes that usually would have needed the chemical fires produced by food. Her real body, the one still Stored somewhere inside the *You Call This Clean?*, wouldn't have been able to do this, any more than it would have silvered up on prolonged exposure to harsh sunlight. Her own skin would have started to tan.

"I remember that Ngaroe had some affinity with the Gzilt," the drone said, once she'd told it all she knew. "At one time I thought he might have been one of them originally, many bodies ago."

"Seems he's still on his first."

"My, that is a long, long time to be in the one body," the drone said, sounding genuinely impressed. "I knew he was old, but *that* old? Really?"

"Apparently."

"He could still be lying. He used to lie a lot, I recall."

"He might be lying. But then he might not. Anyway, what do you think? Important enough to let me know where the hell the old fuck is?"

"What would be intended for him?"

"Just going to be asked what he knows. Nothing untoward."

"What if he is uncooperative?"

"Ha! When was he otherwise?"

"You know what I mean."

"Then I leave empty-handed. But at least we can say we tried."

"Nothing further?"

"Nobody's going to drug him or read his mind or anything. These are perfectly normal Minds involved here, with honour, self-respect and all that usual uptight shit."

"I will need your word on this."

"You have it. If he won't tell me, he won't tell me. End."

"My information is five years old."

"Barely yesterday, by QiRia's geriatric standards."

"He told me he was going to . . . lose, or donate, or abandon, or get rid of something – he used all four terms when we talked – then go to contemplate The Mountains of the Sound, on Cethyd, in the Heluduz system."

"Never heard of it."

"Few have."

"Just . . . these mountains?"

"He wasn't sure where exactly he'd be going but there's an Outworlders' Quarter, so probably there. Claimed he'd already been for a look and talked to . . . ah."

"Deleted at random?"

"Nearly. Still have it. Docent Luzuge. Somebody called Docent Luzuge. If he, she or it is still alive and active, this person would know where to find him."

Tefwe's pen terminal picked up the words. It was a lot smarter than the old pen terminals Tefwe had been used to, and the kind of smart that found it relatively easy to hide from the level of investigatory tech the drone had. The terminal had been effectively awake and evaluating everything it had been sensing since shortly before Tefwe and the aphore had arrived at the outcrop. It was getting jostled about in the bottom of a pocket in her thin shirt and so not seeing very much, but it could hear perfectly well. It made a transmission.

A satellite the size of a pebble, held stationary just above the atmosphere directly over where Tefwe was, which had been keeping station directly over her since she'd been Displaced to the surface at Chyan'tya, relayed the transmission to its home ship, the VFP *Outstanding Contribution To The Historical Process*, which, on hearing the relevant words, itself handed the information on to various other craft, including the *Contents May Differ* and the element of

350 IAIN M. BANKS

the fast picket fleet known to be nearest to the planet Cethyd, as well as making a general call through the usual network of trusted craft, just in case they knew of a still closer ship that hadn't been letting everybody else know its position.

"I wonder what he was leaving behind, and why?" Tefwe said.

"I wondered that too. I did ask. He wasn't forthcoming."

"Cethyd?" she said.

"Some civ-forsaken ball on the outskirts of nowhere, jealously guarded by well-teched barbarians. Known for The Mountains of the Sound. Aren't your implants working?"

"I'm leaving them off. Just got my terminal."

"Which has just been in touch with something overhead."

"Really? That's sneaky."

"You didn't know?"

"I should have guessed."

"This isn't the real you, is it?"

"No; spare body carried by an SC ship, altered to suit."

"I imagine another you will be popping into existence very shortly, somewhere near The Mountains of the Sound, on Cethyd."

"I dare say. That *is* where you think he is?"

"Yes," the drone said. "I'm too old to play those kinds of games. Your word stands, of course."

"Of course."

"Well; good hunting, to your next self. What happens to you – to this you – now?"

"Supposed to head back to the VFP. Naturally it wants to snap me back instantly, now, and be on its way, but I said you'd appreciate me making the effort."

"Well, I have. But don't let me detain you."

"Really?"

"Go immediately if you wish."

Tefwe thought. She could almost feel the VFP – doubtless listening – willing her to agree. "Later," she said, and half expected to be snatched away anyway as the ship's property, or to see a wrathful bolt of fire falling from the heavens to strike her, or at least the nearby desert. "Around sunset, perhaps. First I ought to let the aphore drink, but I'd like to see more of the sandstream. If it's not too much trouble."

~Ms Tefwe, sent the ship via some internal piece of augmentation which, obviously, she only thought she'd turned off.

"None at all," the drone said. "Though, *sandstreams*, in the plural, you should have said."

"There's more than one?"

~Ms Tefwe, the ship sent again.

"Many. Most of the outcrops you can see from here are similarly adapted." The old drone sounded proud.

"Really! I must see them."

~Ms Tefwe, the ship sent once more.

"We could visit two or three in the time. Soon I hope to start linking them, underground, and complete a programme of replacing all the external raising screws with internal ones."

"Not the wheels, though, I hope. I like the wheels."

~Ms Tefwe; kindly reply.

"Not the wheels. Those I intend to keep."

"How long will all that take?"

~Ms Tefwe . . .

"Many decades. Don't you think you should answer the ship?"

". . . Na."

Sixteen

(S -9)

xLOU *Caconym*
  oMSV *Pressure Drop*
Cethyd? Barely mentioned in my data reservoirs.
∞

    Will you down a current all-civs/systems overview? This is becoming ridiculous.
∞

Ignorance can be interesting.
∞

    Also fatal. I am not going to copy you the relevant data; get it all yourself. Anyway, Cethyd is a good choice, if he's trying to escape our attention. Home of the Uwanui,

under something called the Oglari Jurisdiction, themselves beholden to the Dolstre, who seem to have decided we're no friends of theirs. And the Oglari are just able enough and vicariously well up-teched enough to make a friendly visit tricky. Perhaps as well we have the SC fleet and its fellow travellers on-side. Nearest is a brother ship to you, a Troublemaker, de-fanged to VFP. Think it'll be up to the task?

∞

Indubitably.

∞

It is effectively weapon-free. And it starts as a Limited. No offence.

∞

We are of that generation of "Limited" that classes as nominatively camouflaged. We out-everything earlier GOUs. It'll handle whatever it finds.

∞

Hmm. Oh-oh, hello; incoming . . .

∞

xGSV *Contents May Differ*
  oLOU *Caconym*
  oGCU *Displacement Activity*
  oGSV *Empiricist*
  oGSV *Just The Washing Instruction Chip In Life's Rich Tapestry*
  oUe *Mistake Not . . .*
  oMSV *Passing By And Thought I'd Drop In*
  oMSV *Pressure Drop*
  oLSV *You Call This Clean?*

Hello all. Developments. Not all encouraging. The good news is that the two Delinquent GOUs *Headcrash* and the *Xenocrat* have arrived at Zyse. The neutral/slightly odd news is that the *Beats Working* has taken it upon itself to ferry the principal squadron of the Ronte fleet to Gzilt ahead of time, and the bad news is that the *Smile Tolerantly*, once an ancient GCU, is now what might best be described as a Culture-Zihdren-Remnanter hybrid.

∞

xGSV *Just The Washing Instruction Chip In Life's Rich Tapestry*

I think I speak for all of us when I say – relative to that last bit there – *what*?

∞

xGSV *Contents May Differ*

Well, quite. The *Smile Tolerantly* has been discovered in the Zihdren home system and now apparently describes itself as a tributary adjunct to the Z-R, with enhanced loyalties and a hybrid OS now including multiple elements congenitally associated with Z-R craft.

∞

xGCU *Passing By And Thought I'd Drop In*

"Enhanced loyalties"?

∞

xGSV *Contents May Differ*

The thinking is this actually means divided loyalties, though when pressed the vessel also expressed a preference for "dual loyalties".

∞

xLOU *Caconym*

Is there any hint it has access to the Z rather than just the Z-R?

∞

xGSV *Contents May Differ*

Sadly, none. In fact it specifically ruled that out. It was at pains to stress it was a level down from whatever parts of the Z-R get to pick up the mysterious but majestic crumbs of information and instruction that fall from the celestially elevated high table that is the Enfolded Realm. It would appear to have become devoutly eccentric, if not technically Deranged. It ceased communication with the ship which re-discovered it – its own old home GSV, the *Unreliable Witness* – after a few short messages, and was willing subsequently to reveal only that their exchange had already run over some (it is believed arbitrarily arrived-at) limit.

∞

xGSV *Just The Washing Instruction Chip In Life's Rich Tapestry*
So do we now need somebody specialised who can talk to it? Or a succession of them, each claiming their ration?

∞

xGSV *Contents May Differ*
Possibly. This is being looked into.

∞

xMSV *Pressure Drop*
And, a "hybrid OS"?

∞

xGSV *Contents May Differ*
Whatever that might be taken to mean. It has hinted that it has incorporated certain processing paradigms and substrate/software architectures from the Z-R into its Mind.

∞

xMSV *Pressure Drop*
My first – and, thus far, abiding – reaction is, That's diseased. But perhaps that's just me?

∞

xGSV *Contents May Differ*

No, not just you.

∞

xGCU *Displacement Activity*
Ditto.

∞

xGSV *Just The Washing Instruction Chip In Life's Rich Tapestry*
Okay. While accepting that that particular nugget of nonsense presents as a one-off random irrelevance, it still seems somehow pointedly symbolic of this whole enterprise turning up grisly unpleasantnesses that it might, in retrospect, have been better to have left stewing under their particular little rocks. Need we go on with this? Can't we just, for once, let the slumbering ogre be, and step lightly away?

∞

xMSV *Pressure Drop*
I might see some merit in that.

∞

xLOU *Caconym*
Well I don't. It is not seriously being suggested that we back off just because what we seek isn't falling into our laps, is it? We made an undertaking to help the Z-R. We stick to that.

∞

xGSV *Just The Washing Instruction Chip In Life's Rich Tapestry*
But *they* don't seem too concerned about us sticking with it. Why should we?

∞

xLOU *Caconym*
Because *somebody* around here has to keep their word and do the right thing.

∞

xGSV *Contents May Differ*

Let's vote on it. We can discuss details later, and/or set up different proposals, but just to clear the air here, the proposal is: we abandon the whole shebang regarding the attack on the Z-R ship and the BoT (and whether it's actually "T" or not) and go back to what we were each doing before this all blew up. Yes or no?

∞

LOU *Caconym* No.
GCU *Displacement Activity* No.
GSV *Empiricist* Abstain.
GSV *Just The Washing Instruction Chip In Life's Rich Tapestry* Yes.
Ue *Mistake Not . . .* No.
MSV *Passing By And Thought I'd Drop In* Yes.
MSV *Pressure Drop* No.
LSV *You Call This Clean?* No.
GSV *Contents May Differ* (Co-ordinator's abstention, but leaning towards Yes.)

∞

xGSV *Contents May Differ*

Clear enough. Does anybody want to resign from the group? . . . No? Any other comments? No? . . . Really? All right. As ever; back as and when with whatever exciting new snags start laddering the skein . . .

∞

xGSV *Just The Washing Instruction Chip In Life's Rich Tapestry*
  oGSV *Contents May Differ*

Worth a try. I appreciate you making the point about leaning towards Yes even though the vote was already lost.

∞

    Least I could do. Maybe thoughts will change with subsequent developments and we might vote again.

∞

I shall cling to that filament.

∞

xLOU *Caconym*
   oMSV *Pressure Drop*

"Pointedly symbolic"! What gibberish. And our group coordinator is "listing".

∞

    That was "leaning", as well you know.

∞

Still off-kilter.

∞

    Perhaps some of our colleagues worry we are starting to indulge in group-think, and to obsess.

∞

We are a group of Minds. Thinking is what we do. And obsession is just what those too timorous to follow an idea through to its logical conclusion call determination.
    However, they're still aboard, even if they might be sitting fretting in the lifeboats. Unlike the completely overboard idiocy of this "Hybrid OS" abomination.

∞

    First I'd heard of *that*. Some sort of weird Z-R mutant Mind. That's almost baroquely ... horrifying. Ghoulish, even. Positively Gothick. What could have possessed it?

∞

To do it? Who knows. But we know what possesses it now. The Zihdren-Remnanter.

∞

If this marks the start of a new, fashionable trend amongst ship Minds, I may Sublime myself shortly.

∞

Still, might yet yield advantage. Never mind the denials. Any sort of more direct link to the Z-R than we've been used to until now implies better access to the Z within the Enfold. An opportunity.

∞

Uh-huh. We'll see. Makes the *Beats Working*'s oddly enabling behaviour look positively normal, for sure. Giving pickup-backs to the Ronte. I mean, really. Mind you, they were going *so* slowly. It probably got bored. What do you think?

∞

I think there's a reason there are so few of the Scree class, despite the fact they're the smallest, energy-cheapest to build of all the Contact Units. Five humans is just too small a crew; they're almost guaranteed to go a bit mad. It's like the opposite of being outnumbered; the more humans you have aboard you, the better their eccentricities average out and you're left with something easy to model, anticipate and influence. You have safety in their numbers. Five bios and one Mind, in one teeny wee ship? Their basic insanity is going to manifest. And it's reality-distorting; infectious, practically. Always going to end badly.

∞

Yes, but you can always kick a human crew off at the next GSV if you *really* don't get on. Not as bad as becoming a "hybrid", with alien operating system shit incorporated. That's just . . . perverted.

∞

The Culture had a problem with the rump of the Zihdren civilisation that the Zihdren-Remnanters represented. It was the same problem they had with most other light-basking species. The whole comms and data network of such beings was not something truly independent of them as creatures; instead it was effectively an extension of them as a mass of interconnected individuals, and so the Culture, with its self-imposed embargo on reading the minds of other beings, regarded it as immoral to investigate even aspects of the Remnanters' existence as seemingly impersonal and banal as their data reservoirs without specific permission, something that had, to date at least, rarely been forthcoming.

It meant that the Remnanters were slightly mysterious as far as the Culture was concerned; they were less than perfectly known and understood, they were incompletely assessed, intrinsically beyond certain very useful forms of analysis, proof against being properly simmed and so, in theory, capable of surprising the Culture. This was a devil-ishly itchy, annoying thing for your average Mind – had there even been such a thing – to have to address.

It was just as well that the Remnanters were little more than a civilisational after-thought, an only-visible-at-high-magnification detail on the vast, ever-changing galactic map, and that – at least for now – there were only a few other similar species making any ripples in the big shared paddling pond of the big G; imagine – so went a popular nightmare scenario for ships of a certain disposition who worried about this sort of stuff – having to cope with the Zihdren them-selves when they'd been in their pomp!

On the other hand there were species/civs with no such compunctions who regularly investigated as deeply as possible into the minds of others – especially when they were as weird as the Remnanters – and would cheerfully share the information with anybody who asked.

As long as no favours were promised in return, the Culture

would – reluctantly, even a little guiltily – use that kind of information, just to keep from being too embarrassingly ignorant.

Scoaliera Tefwe woke slowly, as she had woken slowly a few dozen times, over the intervening centuries.

Only it wasn't really waking slowly; she was being woken.

All dark at first. Stillness and silence too, and yet the sensation that things were happening, both inside her head and body; organs and systems and faculties being woken, revived, checked, primed, readied.

It was at once reassuring and somehow disappointing. *Here we go again*, she thought. *Hmm*. That thought itself felt . . . familiar. She opened her eyes.

She was sort of expecting to see the word SIMULATION, however briefly, but it wasn't there. She blinked, looked around.

She was floating in some sort of suspensor field, in air, in a human or humanoid body dressed in some clingy but lightly puffed cover-all which left only her feet, hands and head exposed. She was held reclined in the air. It was as though she was sitting in an invisible chair. A boxy ship drone was at eye-level, looking at her. The room around her appeared to be medical unit standard.

"Ms Tefwe?" the drone said.

"Reporting," she said. She looked at her hand. It looked like her hand, though she knew enough to know that meant almost nothing. "A reverser field, please?"

The drone put a screen in front of her, showing her her own face. She touched the skin on her cheek, pressed her nose one way then the other. Looked like her face.

She remembered talking with the avatoid of the *You Call This Clean?* in a virtual environment. She remembered waking in reality in the medical facility of the *Outstanding Contribution To The Historical Process*, and she remembered the journey across the desert on the aphore, to go and talk to the old drone Hassipura Plyn-Frie.

She had stayed with it for a couple of days, calling in a supply drop from the Orbital's Hub to feed and water the animal at the end of that first day.

The VFP had been annoyed at her dallying but had not zapped her back to it without permission. The important part of its mission had already been carried out; it had transmitted the information on QiRia's location to the other interested ships. It could afford to let her spend a while with the ancient drone and its sandstreams.

Another ship, another VFP, the *Rapid Random Response Unit*, had been time-closest to Cethyd and had started out for the planet within a second of the information being picked up. It had started readying one of the handful of humanoid simulacra bodies it carried aboard, instructing the creature's physiological systems to alter the blank-basic body's appearance so that it would resemble Tefwe. The transfer of Tefwe's updated mind-state could wait until the last hour or so before deployment, hence the relaxed attitude the *Outstanding . . .* was able to take to Tefwe's delaying tactics.

The *Rapid Random Response Unit*'s flight time to Cethyd had been two and a half days; a lucky proximity, Tefwe guessed, given that the place was, as Hassipura had suggested, kind of off the beaten track, in a system called Heluduz in one of the faint tendrils of stars that lay on the very outskirts of the galaxy, spun out from the rim like the exhaust from a spent firework.

The place itself was nothing special; just a biggish rocky world with a thick though transparent oxygen/nitrogen atmosphere and a small majority of land compared to deep ocean.

After her surprisingly extended jaunt to see Hassipura's sandstreams, Tefwe had ridden off again on the aphore Yoawin. The ship had Displaced both of them as soon as they dropped more than a couple of metres beyond the pass, depositing a very confused aphore straight back into its stables in the livery at Chyan'tya.

Tefwe went back to the ship, where her mind-state was, finally, read and transmitted to the *Rapid Random Response Unit* half a day before it reached the planet of Cethyd, while it was still checking and re-checking its Displacer components, testing the system with dummy payloads and planning its brake points and loop-return profiles.

Tefwe shook her head. "Is this really necessary?"

"This would represent an absolute minimum," the boxy ship drone told her.

Tefwe looked down at herself. The ship had insisted she wear what appeared to her like a grossly over-spec'd suit. She looked, she thought, like she'd been dipped in a thick layer of sticky mercury.

The suit was only about five or six millimetres thick and seemed to weigh almost nothing, plus it thinned so much over her hands and especially her fingers that she half expected to see her fingerprints through the silver covering, but it was meant to be terribly effective. Well, once the helmet component had rolled up, it was just a roll round her neck at the moment, like a thick metallic scarf. Obviously the tech had moved on since the last time she'd needed to be protected at anything like this level.

"What exactly is this?"

"That is a full-survival/light-battle suit, two layer."

"What's a light battle? Is that a skirmish or something?"

"It will keep you safe and well, even if the Displace is very slightly off, and protect you against unwelcome attentions, should locals take exception to you."

"Why would they do that?"

"Who knows? Some people are just primitive."

"This isn't really about the locals, is it? This is in case the other lot – the Oglari – in case they spot me, or their bosses." Tefwe had woken with a full briefing effectively downloaded and digested inside her head.

"We are trying to protect you as well as we can, Ms Tefwe," the ship told her. "Ideally I would put you down in a more aggressively profiled suit and inside a supporting capsule – at least – with a full drone and missile screen, exactly where you need to be; however, our intelligence is that such a force, in such a location, would be very likely both to be sensed on emplacement and to give cause for severe diplomatic unpleasantness if discovered. Hence the suit."

"Can I put ordinary clothes over it?"

"They'll burn off if the Displace is even slightly out. The suit is able to mimic the appearance of clothing."

"I'd prefer ordinary clothes. Can't I carry them inside the suit or something?"

The drone made a sighing noise.

Eventually she got a kind of backpack that melded itself to the suit, containing some clothes and a few supplies.

"This increases both your mass and bulk," the ship told her through the drone. "Now I have to re-calibrate and skim even closer to the planet."

"How close you going?"

"Seventeen-five k."

"Velocity?"

"Forty per cent Crashed to fifty-seven kilo-lights at closest approach; sub millisecond window."

Tefwe whistled. "You're going to scrunch me up into a tiny little ball, aren't you?"

"If you were properly human, it would break every major bone in your body, and quite a lot of the others. Happily, you're not. You won't trauma, will you? I could put you under . . ."

"Not me. Tough as old space boots. Known for it."

"Good. The suit will be trying not to use any fields, including AG, so the landing could be a little bumpy."

"Kinetic."

"Kinetic?"

"That's how we used to express it in the old days."

"Hmm. Kinetic. That too is appropriate."

The *Rapid Random Response Unit* performed the start of a crash-stop, then – when it was, for a vanishingly brief moment, within less than a planetary radius of the world – used its heavy-duty Displacer to loose a balled-up Tefwe and a scatter of miniature subsidiary support components towards the planet. Then it continued on its way – slowing, in effect, more slowly – and started a wide turn that would bring it back to the system some hours later for a more stealthy approach to Cethyd.

Tefwe came hurtling out of the sky at a little under the speed of sound. The suit gauged where it was and what was happening to it, saw that it was heading for land with no large body of water available – which was sub-optimal, but never mind – and braked hard by spreading layers of itself like ribboned parachutes, scrubbing off ninety-five per cent of its speed in about half a kilometre of forty-five-degree flight. Tefwe felt herself tumbling, and the deceleration as a tremendous weight – oddly distributed due to the way she was packed, pressed into a contorted, maximally compacted ball that would have killed a basic human. The tumbling decreased. She felt her orientation steady and settle, and then the weight eased too.

She felt the impact as a dull thud on her back and knees, not sore at all, then the suit's voice said quietly, "Landed."

Tefwe started to un-ball as the suit unwrapped her, letting her spread herself out to lie looking up at an ochre sky visible between softly swaying stalks of some tall, bronze-coloured grass. She could feel her lungs re-inflating. They'd been collapsed to save volume.

"How we doing?" she asked when she had some breath to spare.

"We are doing well," the suit said. "No hostile interest detected."

"That's nice." Her conventional pain receptors came back on line, tingling once to confirm, then quieting down.

She sat up, dusted herself down, then, still sitting, unhitched the backpack and put on the clothes she'd had the ship make for her. They were supposed to make her look a bit like a pilgrim. A human pilgrim, specifically, because the locals here weren't human, though they were used enough to hosting humanoid pilgrims from nearby systems. Then she let the backpack collapse itself and stow into the small of the suit's back.

Finally, cautiously, she stood up.

Cethyd lay heavy beneath the orange-red sun called Heluduz.

"You used to look at my chest."

"Because of what was not there. Absence can snag the gaze more effectively than presence."

"What? Oh, breasts! Mammalian stuff. Of course. I thought you just thought I had a particularly fine and barrel chest."

"One way of putting it."

"Did you ever want . . . did you ever think about us, you know, fucking?"

"Which answer would insult you less: yes or no?"

"Neither. Either. I wouldn't be insulted."

"Then the answer would be, not really."

"Not *really?* So a bit, then. Ha!"

She was a little drunk. She was still going to leave the silver-grey cube with the Incast order – she was en route to the Ospin system now, in this fine clipper ship – but she'd thought she ought to at least turn the device on, make sure the old guy was in some sense still in there, and maybe ask his forgiveness. Maybe.

Too many cocktails in the bar. Thought she'd been doing extremely well with a handsomely chunky young fellow there – a serving captain in the Eighth – but then the girlfriend he'd neglected to mention had shown up – supposed to be a surprise for him; she'd got on at the last port a couple of hours ago, been waiting impatiently in his cabin since, wondering where he'd got to . . . Things had started to turn just a little ugly and so she'd made her excuses and left.

She had decided before she'd left home ten days earlier that one thing she definitely wasn't going to do during the voyage was turn on the device with QiRia's mind-state inside – she'd been adamant about that. He was an old fraud and even just giving the damn thing to her had probably been some sort of attempt to manipulate her; he was lucky she was paying him the compliment of physically taking the device to Ospin like some sort of warped pilgrimage or homage or something rather than just posting it to the Incast order. She'd brought her volupt with her; she would use the time constructively to practise.

But then, perhaps because of the cocktails, she'd changed her mind.

"The Gzilt never joined in the great genetic mash-up that the rest of the Culture proper thought appropriate to ensure everybody could breed with everybody else," QiRia's voice said. (In theory she could have seen him too, had his face look down on her from the cabin's screen; she hadn't chosen that option.) "As a result, the genes aren't in either of us to make us appear attractive to or feel attracted towards the other, beyond a very basic pan-human interest sparked at a distance or when clothes conceal the disappointing truth. Trust me; it is rarely an encouraging sign when the more apparel is removed, the less attractive a prospective sexual partner becomes. I wasn't keeping a tally, but if you'd been watching carefully I suspect you'd have noticed that I looked – glanced, more likely – at your chest more often when you wore a top than when you were naked from the waist up. The point is rather that we found each other interesting at all, sexual considerations removed. Again, you'll have to trust me that the difference implicit in a ten-millennia age difference is far more important than a difference in both gender and/or species."

"So you've never had sex with a Gzilt woman?"

"Ah. I didn't say that."

"So you *have*?" Cossont, lying on the bed, plumped up her pillow and made herself comfortable, staring at the screen. Maybe she should have put his face on the screen. Would he be blushing now? Did mind-states inside devices like this blush? Did QiRia blush? Had he? She couldn't remember.

"Technically, yes," the voice from the cube said, sounding unconcerned. "It was, again technically, unsatisfactory for both parties. The seemingly superficial physical differences become more . . . pronounced when one gets down to it, as it were. Sometimes, however, one indulges in that sort of behaviour as a sort of extension of friendship. Not with everyone; not all need such an expression. Most of the people I find interesting, and in that sense attractive, live more in the mind than in the body. Still, some seem to require such . . . confirmation. My impression has always been that the commitment to the act, its symbolism, is more important than the act itself, which, in its commission – or at least in the reflection upon it – tends to emphasise the differences between those involved rather than their similarities. I have done the same sort of thing with males of my own species type, despite not having sexual feelings specifically for them. Sometimes it feels only polite."

Cossont lay on her back, looked up at the cabin ceiling, both hands clasped behind her head. "Anybody I'd know?"

"Who? My sexual partners amongst the Gzilt?"

"Yes."

"No. Nor heard of. And besides, they're all long dead. As of now, I believe all my ex-lovers, of all species, are dead. One or two might be in Storage."

"That sounds so sad."

"Well it isn't. Feel free to feel sorry for me if you wish, for your own sentimental satisfaction, but not on my account. I have lived ten thousand years; I'm used to it. Lovers dying, civilisations dying . . . one develops a certain god-like indifference to it all, intellectually. Happily one retains the emotions that let one draw delight from life's enduring basics, like love, friendship, sex, sheer sensory pleasure, discovery, understanding and erudition. Even when one knows that in the end it's all . . . contingent."

"Really thought you were going to say 'meaningless', there."

"No. All things have meaning. Haven't we already been through this?"

"It's just that meaning doesn't mean what we think it means."

"Even your attempts at triteness cannot entirely hide the grain of truth in that particular assertion. We are all prone, in our ways. My own comforter at the moment, and perhaps for the next few centuries, appears to be homing in on the serenity offered by immersing oneself in an environment of all-pervading sound . . . for some reason. I really only meant to spend a year or so with the leviathids on Perytch IV, but then felt very . . . at home in that sonic environment; very content." The voice from the cube paused. "In the end it palled . . . but only relatively, and still it left its own . . . echo. An echo of desire, of need." Another pause. "I – the real me – may pursue that interest. For a time."

Cossont was silent for a while.

"You really are old, aren't you?" she said eventually.

"What makes you think that?"

"A young – younger – guy would have asked whether I ever felt attracted to you."

"No; a less secure, less self-sufficient, less sure-of-himself person might have."

She gave it a moment, then said, "So, what do you think?"

"About your feelings for me?"

"Yes."

"As a person I'm sure you found me profoundly interesting though not actually attractive. As a potential sexual partner, I would prefer to hope the very thought would have been at least slightly unpleasant. Don't feel you have to confirm or deny any of that. What other questions arising might you have?"

"How have you kept going, all this time?"

"Fortitude."

"Seriously. If I'm to take you seriously, your claims seriously: how? Wouldn't you want to kill yourself eventually, at some point, just at some really low point that you'd never have got to if you only lived for a century, like they did in the old days, or a few centuries, or whatever? Wouldn't that happen?"

"Well, not to me, obviously."

"But that's what I'm asking. Why? Why not? How come?"

"I told you before: I take a perverse delight in watching species fuck up."

"I remember. I've thought about that. I don't believe that can be all there is. There must be something else."

"Maybe I had something to live for."

"Okay. But what?"

"Or, maybe I had something to not die for."

"Hmm. Aren't they . . . ?"

"They are not quite the same thing. You may have to think about it. Anyway, my precise motivations needn't concern you. That I am as old as I've claimed, that you believe me; that does concern me. Not a great deal, but I would like to think you do believe me."

"Sometimes I do, sometimes I don't," she confessed. "When I talk to you I do."

"That will suffice. Anything else I can help you with?"

She smiled, though he couldn't see. "So, do we get more secure as we get older?"

"Some do. I have. Though I have also detected a sort of long-term tidal action in that and a lot of other emotional states. For real-time centuries I will feel, say, gradually more secure in myself, then for the next few centuries I'll feel less certain. Or over time I'll go from thinking I know pretty much everything to realising I know next to nothing, then back again, and so on and so on. Overall, it approximates to a sort of steady state, I suppose, and I am by now quite entirely used to such periodicity and allow for it. Similarly, I seem to oscillate between times of feeling that nothing matters, when I tend to act riskily, foolishly – often on a whim – and intervening periods when I feel that everything matters, and I become cautious, risk-averse, fearful and para-noid. The former attitude believes in a sort of benign fate, thinking I am just somehow destined to live for ever, while the latter believes in statistics, and a cold, uncaring cosmos, and cannot quite believe that I have lived as long as I have while ever thinking that life is just a hoot, and taking risks and behaving rashly is worth it just for the fun of tweaking the nose of the universe. The former state has a sort of cheery contempt for its opposite, while the latter is simply terrified of its obverse. Anyway, my point is: come back in a century or two and I might not seem so sure of myself."

"In a century – in a few years – I'll be with everybody else in the Sublime."

"Best place for all of us. I'd go myself but longevity has become such a habit."

"You don't want to be offered the chance to go with us, with the Gzilt?"

"You'd be my second choice, after the Culture itself, but no. Not really my choice to make anyway; my real self will take that decision and I'll be looked out wherever I am and taken away too, if and when the time comes."

"They say it's like the most brilliant lucid dream, for ever."

"So I've heard."

"Do you dream, in there?"

"No. Being switched off is exactly like going to sleep – you're not really aware of it happening, only of waking up again. But you wake after a dreamless sleep."

"I'm sleepy now," Cossont said, yawning involuntarily

just at the thought. "I'm going to switch you off. That definitely okay? You sure?"

"Entirely. Sweet dreams, Ms Cossont."

"Sleep well, Mr QiRia."

. . . She woke up. Still aboard the *Mistake Not* . . .

They'd be at Ospin in a couple of hours, bouncing into the microrbital belonging to the Incast Secular Collectionary order she'd donated the device to.

She remembered that evening aboard the clipper, umpteen years ago, and remembered a surprising amount of that conversation with QiRia's stored mind-state. She remembered lying with just two hands clasped behind her neck, travelling with the sensibly sized volupt – as elegant in form as it was in tone – rather than the hulking lump of half-unplayable preposterousness that was the twenty-four-string elevenstring.

She remembered fretting over things like pleasing her mother without giving in to her, and whether she'd find somebody as cute as that serving captain in the cocktail bar – though single.

This time, she was wondering whether a pursuing ship might be just about to blow them out of the skies, or whether some pre-alerted special forces ultra-commandos would be waiting for them at the Bokri microrbital to slice or blast them to pieces. Also, whether she'd live to see the Subliming, and whether she would, in the end, go along with everybody else into it.

Vyr lay in the darkness, top hands clasped behind her neck, lower hands clasped over her belly, thinking that, sometimes, not all change was for the better.

The image – of a tearful woman sitting with her back to a view of clouds and sea – was shown as though on a conventional screen hanging in front of him.

THE HYDROGEN SONATA   375

"... and then she just seemed to disappear, from the face of the planet, and apparently her bed hasn't been even slept in for days – many, I mean several days – and then, of course, she is in the Fourteenth, the regiment the Fourteenth, and she was always very active in the Reserve, *very* respected, and of course there's been this terrible, terrible—"

"Madame—"

"—terrible explosion on this planet and for all I know – well, I thought, I assumed the worst, naturally, as any mother would. I wondered, 'Could she have been there, was that where she went? Did she know something?' as soon as I heard about, about the thing, but then there was nothing . . ."

The screen went blank. Colonel Agansu nodded. "I see. And this lady is . . .?"

"She is Warib Cossont, mother of Vyr Cossont, Reserve Lieutenant Commander in the Fourteenth, the female her mother is referring to," the intelligence officer of the *7*Uagren* said. The IO, the colonel and the ship's captain were the only presences within the virtual command space.

"This may tie in with the unexpected presence of the *5*Gelish-Oplule* at Eshri," the captain told Agansu. "The ship's last known location was near Xown, and the last known location of Vyr Cossont was in the Girdlecity of Xown. If the ship made full speed from Xown to Eshri there would have been time for it to deliver Vyr Cossont to the Fourteenth's HQ anything up to two or three hours before our arrival and the attack."

"Was Vyr Cossont listed as one of those aboard the Fzan-Juym satellite?" the colonel asked.

"No," the IO said.

"However, that means nothing," the captain said. "There

was barely time for her to be registered and besides, if she was being summoned for some sort of secret mission she would never have been added to the official complement anyway."

"Where did this information come from?" Agansu asked.

"The screen clip came medium-ranks secret from Regimental Central Intelligence, flagged low probable relevance," the IO officer said. "But we then added it to a review of our own multiple-remotes sensor data following the destruction of the HQ, which indicated there's a fifty per cent chance that one of the larger medium-sized pieces of wreckage was a mostly intact though largely disabled four-berth shuttle. That being the case, there is then a sixty per cent chance that one or more viable biologicals could have been Displaced from the wreck to the *Mistake Not . . .*, the Culture ship we're following."

"Why was this information not extracted from the data at the time?" Agansu asked.

"The data from remotes," the captain said, "especially in a combat volume, is received erratically, sporadically and late. Real-time data has to be prioritised, Colonel."

"I see. This Lieutenant Commander Cossont; I can see no mention of her in any special forces or intelligence lists."

"We don't believe she is special forces or on a military intelligence secondment," the captain said. "We believe her semi-civilian status was not cover, but the truth. Her value to the Fourteenth's high command may have been opportunistic and sudden; the likelihood is it would only just have come to light before she was summoned."

"And what might the nature of that value have been?" Agansu asked.

"We don't know yet," the IO admitted. "Best guess is possibly related to the Culture individual Ngaroe QiRia, who is mentioned in the message from the Zihdren recovered at Ablate."

"There is record of an individual or individuals of that name having visited Gzilt several times in the past," the captain added, "though not for several centuries."

"And all this tells us what?" Agansu asked.

"Perhaps where Lieutenant Commander Cossont is heading," the captain said. "Until now the Culture ship has pursued a course which has made its final destination difficult to predict, even at a system level. However, within the last half-day, it has become almost certain that it's aiming for somewhere within the Ospin system. There is a record of Vyr Cossont travelling to the habitat of Bokri, within the Centralised Dataversities of Ospin."

"When?" Agansu asked.

"Sixteen years ago, three and a half years after she returned from a student exchange trip within the Culture. Her most likely destination within Bokri, we believe, would have been the Incast order. It is possible she deposited an article of some sort with them, possibly a mind-state; the cargo manifest for the vessel she travelled on is a little ambiguous on the exact nature of whatever she might have left there, though some sort of article classified as a 'self-powered general storage device, alien, vouched, sophisticated, capacity unknown' is mentioned as forming part of her luggage on the way there but not on the way back."

"We've started trying to get some answers out of the Incast order on this," the IO said. "Nothing so far; there are confidentiality issues. Also, they're just under-staffed." The image of the intelligence officer looked at the captain and the colonel. "With cooperative assets in place we could just hack them but as we're on our own with this there won't be much we can do until we physically get there."

"This is, anyway, all conjecture," the colonel pointed out.

"It is," the captain agreed.

"But it's the best conjecture we've got," the IO officer said. "Nothing else is flagging connections."

"The Culture ship is already running us about as fast as we can go, Colonel," the captain said. "If it starts bouncing around inside the Ospin system there's every chance it can either lose us, put somebody or something down anywhere it wants to without us being able to spot it happening, or both. I think the concatenation of this Cossont person and the Bokri habitat represents a serious lead and that it's worth following. I propose we try to follow the ship round Ospin if it does start dodging, but rather than lose it while we try to find out what it's been doing where, we assume it's heading for Ospin, and act accordingly."

Colonel Agansu thought about this. As ever, he was painfully aware that, even speeded up to the max, he was thinking so terribly slowly compared to the captain, the intelligence officer and the rest of the *7*Uagren*'s virtual crew. He was also aware that he would probably have to leave the easeful security of the ship, this vast, potent swaddling all around him, and become a walking-around figure once more; a soldier again. A soldier in a battle-worthy combat suit, so still encased in layers of power and protection, but still, just a soldier, toting a gun, even if the combat arbite was at his side to back him up. In a way the prospect filled him with longing, just at the thought of fulfilling his duty, but in a way it filled him with a dread he could never admit to anyone.

Eventually he said, "Very well. I agree, Captain. Please commit to that. Let Marshal Chekwri know about Lieutenant Commander Cossont—"

"We've already copied to her," the captain said.

"Good," Agansu said. "I think it obvious that all possible avenues of research and confirmation related to this should be pursued urgently, including somebody trusted, if available, interviewing Madame Warib Cossont."

The thing looked like a very delicate, golden version of a lace condom; a jewellised version of something from ancient history made pointless by its openness.

Orpe stared at it lying there in its luxuriously cushioned case, nestled amongst lip-like folds of purple-stained gold-cloth like something illicit; half obscene, half sumptuously beautiful. She held her hands up near her face, away from the opened case, as though nervous, even as her mouth opened and her large eyes drank in the look of it.

"Oh, I don't . . . It looks so . . . I'm not sure . . ."

"Let's just try it, shall we?"

"What does it . . . do? What is it for?"

"I wear something similar; very similar. They both sink very slightly into our flesh, half a hair's breadth. And only we know that they are there. When we make love, when we couple, and they touch, they add to the pleasure. It's as simple as that."

"Can they . . . are they, might they cause . . . harm?"

"No no no. They are for pleasure, purely. They are better than surgically sterile, and have no effect except when paired with their twin, the other half of their matched pair, when they create a more intense ecstasy." Banstegeyn smiled, ran his fingers down amongst some of the ringlets in her hair, touched her cheek. "There are many similar paths to the same effect, my love, just through drugs, implants, augmentations . . . but the beauty of these is that they are made for each other, and have no other effect, even if," he smiled regretfully, "one has other lovers. They can't be felt, they can barely be seen, even if you look for them, and everything else that would ever normally happen, there, can still happen – people have happily given birth, even, though I understand that is not advised – yet the wearer knows they are there, and the wearer of the other half knows that it's there. It is about . . . commitment, you might say, and I would say a kind of tying, a bonding, between us."

She looked at him shyly. They were alone in the dark cabin of a quietly purring skiff on a perfumed lake in a private pleasure garden on the outskirts of M'yon, at a party being thrown by a family long grown rich on government contracts. They had both worn masks and plain cloaks, like everybody else at the party. "And is there one for you, then?" she asked.

He smiled, opened the case further, revealing another level, where a slightly slimmer version of the piece lay, also glittering like a narrow pocket of lace made of liquid gold salted with tiny jewels. "There!" he said, as he smiled and she smiled. "One each."

She touched the one that was his, stroking it with one finger. "They are not . . . permanent, are they? They can be taken . . . out, off . . . ?"

"Yes. Most easily, by touching the cloth of the case to any part of them. You may keep the case. I'll wear mine for ever, I swear."

She made a delicate, laugh-like noise through her nose. "How do we . . . put them . . . ?" she asked.

He laughed, almost silently. "How do you think. Shall I put mine on, first? Perhaps you might like to do that?"

"Mmm, perhaps," she said, smiling, lifting the male piece of the two from its ruched nest. It hung from her fingers, golden in the subdued light, perfectly draped. "How . . . limp it is," she said, and pressed herself against him, beginning to undo his clothes. "That will not do, now, will it?"

"Not at all," he agreed, and lay back, exhaling, allowingly.

The tramway led tilted into the sky for a long, long time.

She'd been put down as close to her destination as the ship had dared, but it had still meant a hike through thick fields of chin-tall bronze-coloured grass to a dusty dirt road and then a longer tramp to a deserted tram stop in the middle of the plain.

From the platform, while she waited, she looked in the direction of the mountains, but they were too far away. A smudge of orange-white, high in the sky to the east, might have been clouds above the mountains, but the range itself was submerged in the atmospheric haze.

She was on her way to Ahen'tayawa, a hearkenry on the slopes of Mount Jamanathrus in the Querechui range, Cethyd.

Another traveller came along the road from the opposite direction in a ramshackle three-wheeled vehicle that bounced over the tracks in a cloud of dust. The single passenger got out, lifted a bag, then the contraption drove itself away again, heading back the way it had come. The traveller stopped suddenly on seeing Tefwe, then bow-nodded, chose a sitting area of the platform at the other end from where Tefwe stood, and folded itself compactly into a resting configuration, the rhombus of its patterned head-part lowered over the complex of creased planes it used as upper limbs.

The Uwanui were mattiform. Most people, most of the time, would have called them *folds*, though this term could be insulting, depending on the language the term was expressed in and the species it was being used to describe; they looked like tall, dark, angular, multiply poled tents, complexly folded. Their rhomboid head-parts, patterned with eye bands and ear spots, cut by a slit that was their mouth, looked like oddly tilted flags above the tents of their bodies. Origami creatures; beings of the crease.

The tram arrived, rattling. It was three carriages long with an open upper deck perched above the middle carriage. She and the dark fold got on.

The tram was mostly empty. It climbed steadily up a slope of tilted plain, stopping to pick up or drop off a few travellers. Those that saw Tefwe all stopped and stared at her for a few moments, then ignored her. Nobody chose to sit close to her.

The sound built very slowly; it would have been hard to know when it first started to become distinct from the noises of the rattling, swaying tram and the wind moving over the surrounding fields of tall, bronze-coloured grasses and occasional thick-trunked coppery trees. She became aware of the sound when she realised that she'd been assuming for a while that somebody was humming monotonously just behind her, only there was nobody there.

"Is that . . . *the* sound?" she sub-vocalised to the suit.

"Yes."

The tram clattered to a stop at another station, and now she could hear the sound properly, distinctly; it was a low booming collection of tones like very distant and continuous thunder, all the individual claps rolled together and coming and going on the wind.

She got up out of the uncomfortably tilted seat and went to the front of the tram's middle carriage, heading upstairs to get a better view. There were more of the locals here; they parted as though to let her through to the front, but she bowed, gestured, hung back. She could see well enough.

The mountains rose out of the hazy plain ahead like a dark storm of rock, the higher massifs draped with cloud, the highest peaks capped in orange-white ice and snow.

The sound swelled and fell away with a sort of tantalising grace, its strength implicitly influenced not just by the light breezes circling round the tram but by mightier winds blowing tens of kilometres away towards the far horizon and kilometres further into the sky. The sound, she thought, was like something you might have heard from an enormous choir of basses singing a slow, sonorous hymn in a language you would never understand.

The tram station in the foothills possessed a sort of modest, ordered busyness to it, full of the dark folds moving about it with their odd, side-to-side, flip-flopping walk. The station connected with a whole fan of cogged funicular lines, winding up into the mountains like something being unravelled. The sound here was a little louder, still coming and going on the wind.

The line she took rose curving away along the side of one mountain, traversed a tall viaduct to the flank of another, went squeaking and squealing through a long tunnel, then ended up at another small station where three cable-car lines terminated. A signpost told her which to take. The sound was a little louder, here; loud enough so that sometimes on the swirling winds you thought you heard a single note or collection of notes and then heard the same again, echoed from some distant cliff.

The funicular car had had less room than the tram, and the cable-car gondola had even less room than that; the locals almost had to touch her. Part of her briefing download had been a rough understanding of their language. Mostly, amongst themselves, they expressed surprise that she didn't seem to smell.

The cable car rose over a dark valley of shales and scree, then over a tilted plain of tumbled rocks interspersed with low, scrubby bushes. Finally the gondola parked in a bare, echoing shed, and disgorged. They were high now, and it was cold. The sound was very loud, and rich; she felt she was starting to feel it in her lungs.

She hung back to let everybody else go ahead of her, then tramped up a well-worn path through a field of higher-than-head-high boulders, all smooth and round. Stepping stones took her across an icy patch of marsh to a sort of absurdly steep stairway built into a twenty-metre cliff of naked rock. It was so steep it was nearly a ladder. She used the ropes on either side and climbed, following a lumbering local with a giant woven basket on its back; it heaved itself up, corner feet fitting into the creased steps, its elongated prehensile side-corners curling round the thick ropes like hands. It achieved the cliff crest with obvious effort, hauling itself over a low wall.

Tefwe followed, clambering further up and then over into the wave-wash of vast, bone-battering sound. She felt her ears closing up, reducing the immediate impact of the colossal noise, but she could still feel it through her head, through her teeth.

She stood in the side-on evening light, looking slightly downhill to the hearkenry.

The Ahen'tayawa hearkenry on the slopes of Mount Jamanathrus was a collection of modest, low buildings scattered across the stony ground to the rear of the open-fronted cells that formed a long curve facing the mountain itself, which rose – steep, sheet-smooth – from the high plain ahead, its summit obscured by broad rivers of orange-white cloud.

The sky-filling, soul-battering, ear-splitting sound came from the Timbrelith Caverns: tens of thousands of enormous tunnels bored into and through the tops and flanks of this part of the Querechui Mountains millennia ago by long-departed aliens many centuries before the Uwanui had colonised this part of their world. As was so often the case with enigmatic alien artefacts, the general assumption was that the work must constitute Art.

The Sound was the result of Cethyd's prevailing Belt Winds coming thundering through and across those colossal pipes, creating a noise like an orchestra of hundreds of gigantic organs all playing a changing selection of most of their available notes at the same time, with all their stops pulled out. It varied according to the strength and direction of the various winds, how the gusts curled and twisted around the peaks, and whether the local jet-stream was scouring across the peaks of the mountains as well; when that happened – fortunately only every few years – the Sound could reach pitches and strengths that could deafen people kilometres away and bring down buildings in the surrounding hearkenries.

Ahead of Tefwe, the lumbering local with the basket made its slow, painful-looking way down to the only two-storey building, at the centre of the complex. It disappeared under an archway. She followed it. Two folds stood in the centre of the archway, blocking her way and that of the local with the heavy woven basket. One wall of the archway was grubby white, smudged everywhere with grey. The basket-carrier was just finishing writing WATER, GRAINS on the wall, using a thick stub of charcoal. The two folds stepped aside, let it pass, then stood where they had before, blocking the way.

Tefwe bowed, then picked up the lump of charcoal. It was almost too big to hold one-handed.

She took a breath – the thin air she breathed vibrated with

the Sound, like something made liquid by it – and wrote, in the local language, GREETINGS. MAY I SEE DOCENT LUZUGE?

One of the folds nodded, turned and walked away. The other stood in the centre of the archway, impassive, as still as though it had been carved from rock.

Tefwe got to stand there listening to the Sound, wondering if it was magnified in some way by the archway. She thought she could feel it echoing through her feet and legs, thrumming up through her like a never-ending earthquake.

Eventually two folds appeared; one was smaller and paler than the other, which she guessed was the guard that had gone to fetch this one, who confirmed its identity by taking the charcoal gently from her hand and writing, I AM LUZUGE.

It handed her back the charcoal. She wrote afresh; GREETINGS. MY NAME IS TEFWE. MAY I SEE NGAROE QIRIA?

Luzuge motioned one of the other folds to come forward and look at the names she had written, then indicated that it should go. It did, and she was left looking at the two folds, Luzuge and one of the guards, both of whom rested in front of her in their stood-sitting/parked configuration until the first one came back. It touched Luzuge hand-part to hand-part with a sort of rippling motion, then Luzuge nodded to it and it went to the wall. It rubbed out her original greeting and request to see the docent and wrote, FOLLOW.

She followed it along a dark, cold, gradually curving corridor at the back of the cells. Almost at the end of the corridor, the fold opened a heavy wooden door and gestured her to enter.

She was in an open cell with a perfect view of Mount Jamanathrus. In front of her was a low wall, about knee-height on her. The cell was bare apart from a small wooden set of drawers in one corner and a crude wooden seat in the middle, on which a man in dark robes sat. The cell was shaped so as to maximise the Sound, the rear wall bowed and the corners only really there at ground level; above the floor, the walls curved in to meet each other, forming arches that met in a sort of shallow dome above.

The man in the dark robes half turned both body and head towards her. He looked like QiRia, though he appeared smaller, reduced; like something boiled down to its essence. His skin, visible on his face and hands and feet, had gone a dark red-brown, again like something undergoing a reduction in the bottom of a pan. He wore what looked like dark glasses. They had no glass or anything else transparent in them that she could detect; instead they were slatted, like half-open blinds. Tefwe wasn't sure how to greet him so was leaving the choice to him; he had never been very forthcoming physically, even as a lover. If he approached her they might hug, but it was not something she expected.

She saw his mouth move but she could hear nothing over the vast, enveloping Sound. It filled the cell like a god bellowing in her ear.

She shook her head, though he wasn't really looking at her. He reached to one side, picked up a cord lying on the floor and pulled it. The cell started to go dark as some sort of covering began rolling down over the single open window. The noise reduced a little. Then he got up and went to the side of the window, swinging in a heavy, wooden, two-part shutter. Tefwe did the same at the other side. The cell was almost completely dark now; her eyes were working mostly on infra-red. The Sound was reduced less than the light. It was still there, especially the deepest, most resonant and longest notes, but when QiRia put a thick wooden bolt across between the two shutters to secure them, she heard the clunk it made. It was, she realised, the first thing she'd heard that wasn't the Sound in quite a long time. Her ears relaxed a little.

QiRia had sat down in his crude-looking seat again. She sat by the low wall in front of him, under the shutters. At first she thought he wasn't going to look at her, seemingly gazing over her head as though still staring out towards the mountain, then he lowered his head.

"So, Tefwe," he began, speaking Marain, his voice little more than a croak. He coughed, cleared his throat, started again, voice louder and assured. "So, Tefwe, let me guess. You just happened to be in the neighbourhood."

"Hello, Ngaroe. It's good to see you again. How are you?"

"I'm well." He smiled. It was hard for her to read his expression behind the slatted glasses, but she reckoned it was a genuine smile. "You?"

"Also well, though it's complicated." She looked around the bare little cell. "What is it that you *do* here, Ngaroe?"

His eyebrows went up a little at this. "Isn't it obvious?" he asked mildly. "I listen."

"You listen?"

"Yes. That's . . . that's all I do. I sit here and . . . well," he said, smiling – this was, Tefwe was already thinking, the most smiley and un-prickly she could remember seeing the man – "calling it 'listening' doesn't really do it justice. I sit here and . . . absorb the Sound. It becomes part of me, I become part of it. It is . . . magisterial, bliss-making, overwhelming. I am . . . transported by it, Tefwe. Here, the locals treat it as a religious experience. I don't, of course, but I'd still claim it is as important to me as it is to them. As . . . profound." He gave a small laugh. "You're lucky, you know. It comes and goes. Right now I am like a sleeper near the shallowest part of a sleep-cycle, so I can come out of the trance of listening and talk to you. I . . . I almost welcome the break. A week from now, though, and I'd refuse even to talk to anybody, no matter who they might be, how far they'd come or how urgently they needed to see me, and in two weeks I would be so far under I'd be incapable even of acknowledging the presence of one of the helpers come to tell me I had a visitor. That's when they have to feed me water with a sponge and try to get me to swallow crumbs of cake." He smiled his beatific smile again. "But you said that 'it' – that is, how you are – was complicated. In what way?"

"It's complicated because in a sense I'm not really here, Ngaroe," she told him. "I'm still Stored – technically, basically – on a ship called the *You Call This Clean?* a long, long way from here. What you see in front of you is a copy; I feel entirely like me inside here, but the truth is I'm embodied inside a ship's blank-body, appropriately customised."

"Hmm. So, let me see, I think only Hassipura knew where I'd hidden myself this time. Have you been to see it?"

"Yes. It still builds sandstream complexes on a life-forsaken plain in the middle of nowhere on an O called Dibaldipen; the kind of barren wasteland on an Orbital that designers pretend they meant to happen all the time but which is really the result of over-artistic weather-pattern modelling and which secretly they are thoroughly ashamed of and embarrassed by." She paused. "Though I was in yet another copied body then, still it feels exactly as though that was me, riding out across the desert to talk to the recalcitrant machine. It, ah, it sends its regards, by the way." She shrugged. "It was being sincere and un-ironic, as far as I could tell."

QiRia smiled. "Yes, I visited it there," he told her. "Honn,

Dibaldipen. Dusty . . . Anyway. What has caused this prolif-eration of Tefwes, Tefwe?" he asked.

"Oh, there's a flap going on. They need me to ask you something."

"Who's 'they'?"

"A fairly standard ship collective handling the latest budding emergency."

"SC?"

"No. Though some SC-associated ships helped get me to Hassipura and now to you."

"Should I be worried or flattered?"

"Flattered."

"Hassipura told you where I was . . . willingly?"

"Yes."

"How easy was it to convince it?"

"It took time, but that was mostly just showing it the respect it believes it's due. That drone demands a certain ceremoniality in such matters."

QiRia smiled again, nodded. "And you left it well, functioning?"

"Entirely. Anyway, it still has surprisingly many ambitions in regard to its desiccated hobby."

"So, what is it you want of me?"

"We need you to confirm or deny something. It will take a little while to explain."

"I have the time. Do you?"

"Of course. It's about the Gzilt."

"Ah-ha!"

"They're about to Sublime."

"I know. I trust that all goes smoothly."

"Ah, well," she said, and told him all she had been told. He sat forward, listening, nodding now and again.

"So," Tefwe said, "the Z-R seem to think you might be

able to confirm what the message from the Zihdren themselves is claiming: that the Book of Truth is a lie, part of somebody's experiment in applied practical theology or something. And we – the Culture – have been asked to help the Z-R with this, plus we have a kind of obligation to the Gzilt to do the right thing."

"But how much difference might it make?" QiRia asked, sounding sad. "Knowing the truth of it, if it is true?"

Tefwe shrugged. "I don't know, Ngaroe. I'm not sure anybody knows. But we can't just let it go. I guess the truth always needs to be chased down. I'm helping with the chasing, and you have the answer, or part of it. If you remember. Do you remember?"

He just sat there smiling at her, silent. The Sound, outside, a vast shadowy symphony of meaninglessness, still seemed to fill the small, night-dark cell.

Her throat was a little sore, she realised, from having to keep her voice raised for so long. She cleared it, said, "I remember that you told me you forgot nothing, remembered everything, had it all stored within you, sometimes multiply, in exhaustive, awful, boring, terrible detail. Detail ghastly for its sheer everlasting banality." She paused to give him time to speak, but still he didn't. "It would be good to know what you know about all this, Ngaroe. You always seemed to feel something for the Gzilt. It might help them to know whether this is the truth at last, or another lie." She paused again, but still he kept silent. "Even if we find out something that it might be best for them not to know, at least *we'll* know. At least we'll have the choice."

"But who would we be to make that choice?"

"Their friends."

"Really?"

"The Culture has no selfish interests in this, Ngaroe," she

said, trying not to sigh, though doubting that he'd hear her if she did. She could sense that they were already starting to gravitate back to some of the arguments they'd had centuries ago. They had ended inconclusively then – unless you counted mutual annoyance as a conclusion – and she thought it highly unlikely they'd end up any different this time.

He looked unconvinced, eyebrows rising again. "The Culture has an interest in everything it touches," he said. "I thought we'd agreed that at least."

"Maybe so, but no *selfish* interest. We just want to do the right thing by people we've historically felt close to."

"Ah. That old excuse."

"Will you stop that?" She could feel herself starting to get angry with him again, and that was not going to help. "It's not an excuse. It's just the truth."

"One person's truth," he began.

"Oh, fuck," she said, looking away and crossing her arms. "Here we go . . ." She looked back when she realised he was laughing. "*What?*" she demanded.

"I can't help you, Tefwe," he told her. He was looking down now.

"What? Why not?"

"I just can't." He reached down by the side of the chair, felt for and found the cord there, and started pulling it. She could hear the matting that had rolled down over the cell's open window earlier as it was pulled back up again. The Sound pulsed back into the room, filling it like an avalanche bursting into a cabin an instant before it was swept away entirely.

"Because," he said, shouting, "I got rid of those memories some years ago." He completed hauling the sound-deadening matting back up and sat back again as though exhausted, like somebody long deprived of the sunlight finally being allowed to face directly into its warmth again. He took a deep, satisfied breath and shouted, "So I don't have them any more. Not here. Not on me, not in me. They're gone." Tefwe's ears had mostly closed up again, assaulted by the noise. She wasn't sure she could really hear what QiRia was saying any more; it was more that she was lip-reading. There was a fraction more light getting into the cell now, around the still-closed shutters.

"But why?" she shouted.

"Fear, Tefwe," he said, shrugging. "I was frightened that what I knew would be enough to cause me trouble, given what was going to happen; given the Subliming. So I made sure that the memories became encoded in just one place – two places. Then I saw an old friend who relieved me of them." He shook his head. "Now I have no idea what I used to know. I'm sorry."

"So . . . where are . . . where were those memories?" she asked, yelling. "Where *were* they encoded?"

He reached up to his face with one hand, took off the slatted glasses. The heat coming off his skin, differentiated according to the various surfaces on his face, plus the small amount of evening light leaking round the edges of the shutters, meant her eyes could see quite well enough.

In the very first instant, she wasn't sure exactly what she was looking at, or what was wrong with his face. Then she started to realise. She felt herself frowning and sitting further forward, to see properly and to make sense of what it was she was seeing. Though she thought she knew now, and thought she should, really, have known all along.

At first she thought that where his eyes had been he now had a pair of belly-buttons, but that was just her first, instinctive reaction. Looking closer, thinking it through, she realised that what he actually had in his eye sockets, in place of his eyes – quite neatly integrated, looking for all the world as though they belonged there – was another pair of ears.

Ngaroe smiled, though it was a thin smile this time; perhaps even a mocking one. The Sound, though baffled by the heavy shutters, seemed to rise suddenly then and shake her to her core, making her synthetic lungs resonate and her carbon bones vibrate and her own augmented eyes quiver and water in their sockets. It all but drowned out his voice.

Through her tears she struggled to lip-read what he said in reply to her question about where the missing memories had been encoded:

"Take a guess, Tefwe."

Seventeen

(S -8)

xLSV *You Call This Clean?*
   oLOU *Caconym*
   oGCU *Displacement Activity*
   oGSV *Empiricist*
   oGSV *Just The Washing Instruction Chip In Life's Rich Tapestry*
   oUe *Mistake Not . . .*
   oMSV *Passing By And Thought I'd Drop In*
   oMSV *Pressure Drop*
   oGSV *Contents May Differ*

Hello. Bad news. Mr QiRia has been tracked down but would appear no longer to have the information we seek.

See attached report.

∞

xGSV *Contents May Differ*

Ms Tefwe seems to have been unable to take any steps which might have confirmed whether he was telling the truth or not. Are we simply going to take his word for this? I had gathered that the gentleman was/is notoriously unreliable.

∞

xLSV *You Call This Clean?*

Correct. However, determining whether he was telling the truth or not would have meant kidnapping Mr QiRia. That would have been difficult and wrong. And it is hard to see what his motivation might be in lying about this. He certainly had the ability to compartmentalise his memories in the way described, and his eyes were genuinely missing. As the report's appendices make clear, Ms Tefwe carried analytical capacity which independently verified both that this was the real person and that his eyes had been surgically excised. Short of removing him entirely from the hearkenry to carry out a full body scan, it is not easy to see what more could be done. I think we have to take this as it appears.

∞

xGSV *Just The Washing Instruction Chip In Life's Rich Tapestry*

And it appears that the problem recedes over the horizon once again, its solution still out of our reach. Are we really determined to pursue this chimera regardless of cost?

∞

xGSV *Contents May Differ*

I suspect the consensus remains much as it was. Has

anyone changed their opinion since the last vote? . . .
No? All right, then; we are as we were.

∞

xGSV *Just The Washing Instruction Chip In Life's Rich Tapestry*
Thinking, I hope, of what we do if and when we discover whatever there is to discover. Personally, I would vote for not telling the Gzilt, no matter what we find, and I suspect I am not alone in feeling that way. Which is why I question the point of looking so insistently in the first place. I don't want to appear presumptuous, but perhaps we might all think a little along these lines?

∞

xLOU *Caconym*
Gee, thinking ahead. Whom'd a thunk a *that*?

∞

xGSV *Contents May Differ*
Mistake Not . . ., it would appear to be up to you and Lieutenant Commander Cossont.

∞

xUe *Mistake Not . . .*
Yup. Little busy.

The elegance of conventional Orbitals lay in the fact that their diameter – they were usually about three to four million kilometres across – meant that the speed you had to rotate them at to produce what would feel like standard gravity to your average Culture person – not to mention a generous statistical spread of non-Culture humanoids and other species – also automatically produced a day/night cycle that was right in the middle of what the Culture regarded as the acceptable spectrum of values.

The artificial, inside-out worlds usually orbited their stars on roughly circular paths, generally following orbits set between those of any planets present, though sometimes taking up the same orbit, socketed into safe, non-collisionary lock-step tracks in and around the planet's Trojan points. Some Orbitals flew more ellipsoidal paths, swinging further out and closer in to their star, to produce seasons, if desired. Spinning them almost but not quite edge-on to their parent sun prevented the far side from eclipsing whatever part lay in sunlight at the time.

The Culture hadn't invented Orbitals like this, but it had taken them up with an enthusiasm nobody else had ever displayed, the Minds attracted both by the grandiosity of the concept – this was engineering on an epic scale, and even the skinniest full O had the surface area of twenty or thirty standard one-G planets – and by its sheer chronocyclic, material-frugal elegance; compared to planets, Orbitals represented a very matter-cheap way of providing generous amounts of pleasantly rural and even wild-looking living space, plus you could usually build your Orbitals from exactly the asteroidal debris you'd want to get rid of in a solar system anyway, to stop bits of it flying around and hitting your fancy new worlds.

Microrbitals were, as the name implied, much smaller versions of the same basic idea; they could be any diameter you wanted because the spin speed wasn't rigidly linked to both the force experienced at their surface and their day/night cycle. You spun a microrbital at the appropriate rate to produce whatever apparent gravity you required, set it circumference-on to the sunlight, then put a suite of angled mirrors at its centre to reflect the light, rotating these independently to give you the desired light/dark periodicity.

The microrbital of Bokri was tiny; barely more than a thousand kilometres across. This was so small that the retaining side walls of sheet diamond which kept the atmosphere in would have met in the middle had the world been filled with a significantly denser atmosphere or spun much slower. As it was, the central mirrors were so close to the top of the walls that they rested on struts running along their inside edges so that the whole assemblage looked like the axle and spokes of a giant wheel.

The world was almost as long down its axis as it was wide and was conventionally arranged – by the relaxed, abundantly provisioned standards of a post-scarcity humanoid civilisation – with parkland, forests, lakes and aesthetically pleasing built-up areas and isolated grand architectural statements spread across its nearly three million square kilometres of interior surface.

The Gzilt had never entirely turned their backs on the ideas of both private ownership and money, though the latter had been demoted to being of mostly ceremonial value and both had been detached from what most people regarded as being the most important measure of a person's worth; there had been enough of everything to go around everybody in the Gzilt civilisation for many millennia, and while a degree of self-interest and acquisitiveness was taken as being only natural, outright self-obsession and full-on greed were regarded as signs of weakness of character, if not a symptom of actual psychological damage.

The Bokri microrbital was joint-owned by a group of Secular Collectionary orders: institutionalised obsessive, only para-religious organisations, each devoted to one or other aspect of preservation.

One order collected ancient farming implements, another chemical rockets and antique space craft, while another had specialised in household dust; its sheds and warehouses were packed with billions and billions of vials and other containers collected from worlds and habitats throughout the Gzilt realm over thousands of years and filled with nothing more than the sort of stuff that collected in the corners of rooms and cabins and which had been picked, swept, sucked or electro-staticked up by volunteers or enthusiasts to be sent to the Little Siblings of the Detritus, on Bokri.

This had seemed idiotic, even perverse to many people, right from the start, but had turned out to be surprisingly if modestly useful, providing the raw material for many an undergraduate paper on, for example, changing patterns of casual domestic ambient surface debris through the ages.

The Incast were a philosophical order dedicated to storing as much of the disputed, superseded or just plain long-proved-wrong knowledge that the Gzilt civilisation and species had built up over the millennia, and any artefacts associated therewith. Housed in multiply backed-up and distributed memory storage facilities across Bokri and various other microrbitals throughout the Ospin system and beyond were entire libraries of ancient conspiracy theories, crackpot physics hypotheses, unutterably antique speculations on anatomy, chemistry and astronomy, and – as a sort of sideline – devices holding the mind-states of untold numbers of individuals and group-minds – mostly Gzilt but from other species as well.

Some were static back-ups for the dynamic originals, held and running elsewhere, some were being retained under the instructions of the people whose personalities and memories they held encoded, to be re-energised and their inhabitants woken at some specific date or when something especially noteworthy occurred to the Gzilt – the Subliming naturally representing pretty much the ultimate example of that criterion – and some had effectively been lost or abandoned.

In the Culture, stuff like this would be collected by Minds

with an interest in just such societal flotsam and jetsam and stored in the specially adapted bays and hangars of GSVs, or in the subsidiary structures of Orbital Hubs. In the Gzilt, the Centralised Dataversities of Ospin were the place; they acted as the sump, the filtered, partitioned bilges of the civilisation.

The main Incast Facility within Bokri lay in the centre of a broad, circular lake; it was a spherical building a kilometre across looking like a sort of reversed image of an iceberg, with barely a tenth of its bulk seemingly lying beneath the surface of the lake. It was mostly white, wore its multi-storey nature on its surface with obvious horizontal divisions but possessed relatively few piercings, windows or balconies.

It was generally reached by an evacuated travel-tube system set on a long, elegantly thin bridge extending from the shore of the lake, a kilometre away. The *Mistake Not . . .* reckoned they didn't really have the time to indulge in such niceties, so deposited Cossont, the android Eglyle Parinherm and its own avatar Berdle near the centre of the building, Displacing them neatly into an empty elevator car and using a small collection of similarly dropped-off comms and effector gear to start interfacing/interfering with the facility's own administrational data complexes.

The ship itself, though much slowed for its erratic transit of the system, hadn't paused as it passed Bokri. It had already taken a wild, almost jagged route through the cloud of habitats and dataversities, pinging from one to another like a ball down a nail-board, just to confuse anybody following; having got Cossont and the others to their destination, and feeling fairly sure that it had indeed shaken off any pursuing craft, it raced off to continue its eccentric join-the-dots loop through the system.

It had promised to be back within the hour; that ought to be long enough.

"Still not getting anything?" Cossont asked the avatar.

Berdle shook his head. "Pinging away merrily," he said quietly, "but nothing's answering."

The avatar and the various pieces of gear the ship had Displaced into and around the facility were trying to locate the device with QiRia's mind-state inside it by sending out signals it might respond to, assuming it possessed any normal Culture processing. The *Mistake Not . . .* had tried to contact the *Warm, Considering* – the ship believed to have helped QiRia encode his mind-state within the cube – to get whatever technical details about the device it could, but the other ship had yet to reply. From what it could gather, nobody willing to tell even knew where the *Warm, Considering* was.

"Why exactly are we here?" the android Parinherm asked, looking round the pleasantly wide, softly carpeted and very slightly curving corridor they'd found on exiting the lift. The corridor's white-with-a-hint-of-blue walls glowed very gently with the fake daylight of a lightly overcast day and were covered in thin grooves, some of which indicated doorways with hermetic-quality shut-lines.

"You are here to protect Ms Cossont," the ship's avatar explained, also looking round. "She is here because she is looking for something."

"May I help?" the android asked brightly. Like Cossont and Berdle, it wore well-cut if nondescript civilian clothes. Cossont wore a thick necklace of what looked like brushed silver.

"Just be prepared to step in to protect Ms Cossont," Berdle told it patiently, "in case I am unable to."

Parinherm stared at the avatar. "You are remarkably opaque to my senses," he remarked. "What are you?"

"An avatar, Parinherm," Berdle said, smiling. "Surely you guessed that?"

"Yes," Parinherm said, nodding. "Good to have it confirmed. Would this be a joint Culture–Gzilt scenario?"

Berdle nodded. "Feel free to treat it as such."

"And I," Cossont said, "am a human. With a low boredom threshold. I'm almost starting to regret leaving Pyan back on the ship." She spread all four arms. "Can we . . . *do* something?"

Berdle nodded. "We're going to have to," it said. "There's nothing coming back." He smiled at Cossont. "This will require you to make an official request to locate and retrieve your property from the facility."

"Yippee. Do I have to fill out a form?"

"You have to submit a formal application five days in advance," Berdle told her.

She stared at him. "Five *days*? I assume you have some clever—"

"The formal application was emplaced two seconds ago," the avatar told her. "Suitably, if illegally, back-dated." Berdle bowed. "Please follow me," he said, turning on his heel.

"Ms Cossont," the Executive Recoupments Officer said, coming to stand before them. He nodded at her companions, bowed to her. The waiting area was extensive, pale, lush with potted plants, filled with the sound of water trilling in fountains and pools and dotted with very comfortable seating. Cossont lounged in what she trusted was a suitably proprietorial fashion, upper arms spread, her lower set concealed by her formal jacket, legs crossed, a small shoulder bag lying on her lap. Berdle and the android had chosen to remain

404   IAIN M. BANKS

standing, looking slowly about all the time. "May we offer you a beverage?"

"No, thank you."

"I wasn't even aware there were any arrivals today," the Incast officer said, glancing at a projected screen hanging in mid-air down and to one side of his straight-ahead sight-line.

"Ms Cossont arrived by private craft," Berdle said smoothly.

"Ah, I see," the officer said. "And you've come in from . . .?" he continued, looking at Cossont, who was listening on her earbud as Berdle said, "Please, let me," to her at the same time as he said, to the officer, "Ms Cossont's application to retrieve her property is in order, I take it?"

The officer was dressed in vaguely ecclesiastic-looking pale robes. He looked from Cossont's stony expression to Berdle's agreeably open one. He checked his screen, one hand moving and his eyes flicking. ". . . Yes, yes, it's all in order." He smiled emptily at Berdle. "The object has been located and is being retrieved as we speak."

"Splendid," Berdle said quietly.

The officer looked back to Cossont. "We usually ask our clients if there is a particular reason for them wishing to recoup an object."

"Again, allow me," Berdle said to Cossont as he said, "How commendable," to the Incast officer. "What is the most common reason given?"

"Ah," the officer said, distracted again. "Sadly, due to client confidentiality strictures, we are unable to share that information."

"What a terrible pity," Berdle said, looking sympathetic. He put one hand gently on the officer's forearm and said, "I am sure then that you will fully understand that Ms

Cossont has equally valid reasons for being unable to share with you her reasons for being unable to share with you the information that you seek and request. I trust I am not mistaken in proceeding on the assumption that this request is of a non-compulsory, voluntary opt-in nature?"

The Executive Recoupments Officer looked like he was processing this. After a moment he said, "Well, indeed." He glanced at his screen. "Excuse me; the requested object is in transit." He smiled at the unresponsive Cossont. "I'll fetch it. One moment." He turned and walked back to the curved sweep of desks where they'd found him earlier, sitting with his feet up, listening to music.

Berdle watched him go, then turned back to Cossont, who raised her eyebrows.

"All going smoothly," Berdle told her through the earbud.

Parinherm was staring intently at a water feature ten metres away. The feature's central fountain closed down suddenly, collapsing with a sort of relaxed decorum; the watery tinkling sounds filling the reception and waiting space quietened very slightly.

~Parinherm . . . Berdle sent.

The android turned to look at the ship's avatar. ~Just testing, he replied.

~I trust the test has been completed to your satisfaction.

~It has.

~Then, if you'd be so kind . . .

~Certainly.

The fountain burst into life again, leaping higher into the air than it had before and causing some water to go splashing over the edge of the pool and onto the carpet.

~Oops.

The fountain settled back to normal.

The Executive Recoupments Officer returned holding a

406 IAIN M. BANKS

white half-metre cube. "Here we are," he said, presenting it
to Cossont with a bow.

"Thank you," she told him, glancing at Berdle, who came
forward and accepted the box as Cossont rose to her feet.

"Ms Cossont herself will need to open the . . ." the officer
said, as Cossont opened the box, looked inside and lifted
out a silver-grey cube.

"Also, the storage container remains our . . ." the officer
said, as Berdle handed the white box back to the officer and
Cossont slipped the cube into her shoulder bag.

"Thank you for your help," Berdle told the officer. "We'll
be on our way."

"My pleasure," the Executive Recoupments Officer said,
as the three walked towards the elevators.

"We still have two-thirds of an hour before the ship
returns," Berdle said through Cossont's earbud as they
stepped into the lift. "I thought we might leave the facility
and find a hostelry of some sort on the lake shore, to wait
there."

Cossont nodded as the doors closed.

The car started its descent, then its soft lighting seemed
to flicker delicately. It drew smoothly to a stop, settling,
finally, with what Cossont heard as a single click and the
two non-humans present both heard as three distinct snicking
noises. A background susurrus Cossont had hardly noticed
consciously ceased, suddenly.

The android and the avatar exchanged looks.

"Ah-hah!" Parinherm said, with a smile.

"This is," Berdle said aloud, and then seemed to think
about what it was, "un-promising," he concluded.

~Is that you? he was asking the android at the same time.

~Facility mainframe / material systems / motile systems /
general elevator control suite / basement-to-mid-section shaft

complex / core-central / faults / fault notification / fault confirmation / fault over-ride / safe fault work-arounds . . . ?

~Yes, all that. Please leave that to me. You're getting in the way. And stop trying to remove the block on the car's external AV feed; I did that nearly a quarter of a second ago.

~Very well. What may I do?

~Please remain/be on full alert within the immediate physical environment with particular regard to extraneous anomalous audible and general vibration signals, extending your sensor/effector abilities no further than the elevator car's and the shaft's own monitoring and activation circuits. I'll continue monitoring and trying to affect further afield.

~My on-board expert systems precedents set indicates strongly we might be in a definitional pre-attack phase and so close to the point at which some sort of physical measure may become advisable.

~Agreed. Currently eliminating all chances this could be happenstance before taking any irretrievably physical action.

~We should warn/prepare Ms Cossont.

~Also agreed. I am in the process of interrupting her.

"'Un-*promis*—'?" Cossont was saying as Berdle talked over her, saying,

"Strong likelihood this is hostile. I'm activating your eSuit and neck-helmet. Please do not be alarmed and remember to put all your weight first on one foot and then the other."

"'—*ing*'?" Cossont finished, as something happened all over her body.

Her underwear consisted of a millimetre-thin body suit which only left her feet, hands and head uncovered. The ship had insisted she wear it, and that they perform a drill before she left to see what would happen if it deployed. Before her eyes, even before she'd put it on, the eSuit had grown an extra set of arms as easily as though it was a big complicated balloon the ship was blowing up, and these had been the last bits to unstick themselves and inflate.

As it had during the practice on the ship, the suit puffed up a little all over, while the thick hems at ankles and wrists unrolled, the suit quickly covering all her hands and fingers in thin gloves and slipping between her feet and shoes in turn as she did as she'd been told and performed a side-to-side stepping motion to allow this to happen; what felt like thin bootees now enveloped her feet.

The thick necklace had unrolled at the same time, extending quickly downward to bond with the collar of the suit while blossoming and closing round her head before shrinking back again to rest lightly on her scalp and most of her face, leaving her eyes, nostrils and lips free under small bulges in the material; the bulges over her eyes were transparent. The first thing she did was tear off the restrictive formal jacket, freeing her lower set of arms. She got tangled in the strap of the shoulder bag, finally setting it securely back in place over her head.

~The problem is located in the primary shaft control node, Berdle told Parinherm. ~It is under continual and dynamic effector load from apparatus it is beyond the abilities of our local assets to counter. I am sending a missile component to the location to attempt some sort of intervention.

~A missile? Are we escalating to—?

~Your pardon. Missile as in, for example, scout missile. Decimetre-scale, field-powered, non-expendable.

One hundred metres away horizontally from the arrested lift and fifty metres higher, within a service space in a suspended ceiling over a dark, unoccupied lecture theatre, a stubby cylinder the size of a fat pen jerked into motion. It lifted and stabbed forward, flourishing an angstrom-fine cutting field that sank into and peeled back the thin metal covering of an air duct.

The missile was one of three Displaced into the spherical Incast facility by the *Mistake Not . . .*, along with various other bits and pieces of potentially useful equipment, almost all of which were rapidly redeploying to suit the current situation.

The missile slipped into the duct and accelerated hard, within metres achieving speeds which caused a wave of expansion and compression to travel down the ducting with it, making the duct's metal creak and its supports groan. Razor-sharp grilles inside the ducting, stationed every few tens of metres to stop animal pests using the ducts as runs, were despatched in field-sliced showers of glittering shards, barely slowing the device at all.

"Fuck," Cossont breathed, looking from Parinherm to Berdle. "This isn't good, is it?"

"No, it isn't," the avatar agreed, then its head flicked – impossibly fast for a real human – towards the lift's manual control panel, an instant before a gentle beeping noise came from the speaker grille.

Parinherm seemed to be about to speak, but Berdle held up one finger. In a neutral voice, he said, "Yes?"

The missile came to the end of the useful part of the air duct in a last burst of grille components, exiting into a parallel elevator shaft, flying straight across as it twisted and slowed, bouncing off the shaft's ceramic surface hard enough to leave a crush-indentation then pulsing up the shaft at maximum acceleration, towards the under-surface of an ascending elevator car. It adjusted its course, jolting across the shaft, aiming for near one corner of the car and bursting through it.

It had time to register three humans present in the lift through the shower of debris, then it was bursting out through the roof. It used its already deployed cutting field like an air-screw to provide a tiny amount of extra lift, then as a fender to cushion the next blow on the roof of the shaft as it twisted and turned again and darted down an access tunnel to the next shaft, braking hard at the last moment as it neared the offending control unit. Below, in the shaft it had just left, it could hear screams. These would likely be associated with its incursion into the elevator car two seconds earlier and probably indicated extreme surprise as well as some shrapnel injuries.

"Is that Ms Cossont, Vyr, Lieutenant Commander, Reserve?" a male voice asked from the grille in a conversational tone.

~Getting some air movement, compression, in the shaft out there, Parinherm sent.

~That's my missile, Berdle sent back at the same time as he said, "It is not," to the grille. "Why has this lift stopped?"

"Ah. Then I must be addressing one of the two gentlemen who accompanied the lady. My name is Colonel Agansu, of the Home System Regiment, on special secondment, unspecified. I'd like to talk to Ms Cossont."

"Did *you* stop this lift?" Berdle said, voice clipped and severe. "Set in motion again immediately."

Fifty metres over Berdle's head, the missile floated in mid-air in front of a control unit barely bigger than itself, inspecting the quivering cage of bizarrely spectrumed energies enclosing the unit and the cables leading to and from it.

~Effector-targeted component and ancillaries highly ext-shielded, it reported to the avatar. ~Actions to control/defeat unclear.

Berdle briefly reviewed the poor-quality video the device was sending, and the missile's available weaponry. It was the least well armed of the three that had been Displaced, reducing the options. ~Close-entrain all 2-mm mini-rounds, the avatar sent. Set for point, centred, kinetic assist.

~Copy, the missile sent, and squirted all its tiny shells at the field-wrapped control unit at once, far too close together to work properly had they been travelling further than a few tens of metres; as they were travelling less than a metre before impact and detonation, this didn't matter. It used its maniple and cutting fields to kick them forward at the same time, imparting a little extra kinetic energy and throwing itself backwards as a result. Light erupted around the control unit, temporarily blinding the missile as it extended its forward fields to fend off the blast wave and pieces of debris and used its rear field components to help cushion it against the blow as it hit the far side of the shaft it had flown up seconds earlier.

"First I need to talk to—" the voice from the grille was saying.

~Wow! Parinherm sent. ~Sub-gramme AM explosion fifty up! Correction; series of same but smaller.

The air in the lift seemed to pulse gently as the shock wave travelled down the shaft's structure. Berdle put his hand out and took hold of Cossont's elbow. She appeared to have noticed the pulse of infra sound and was opening her mouth to speak as the thud from above came. The blast wave slammed down onto the roof of the car, sending the human, avatar and android briefly up into the air as the whole lift was rammed down a notch on its trio of side ratchets; the three dropped to the floor again, steadied themselves.

~Debris approaching you, the missile sent. ~Medium sub-sonic. It sidled back through the dust and smoke choking the debris-littered access tunnel to inspect the control unit. ~Target unharmed.

It's a ship, Berdle thought. *The unit's being effectorised by a ship, or a unit as strong as one a warship would carry.*

~Pause, he told the missile. ~Prepare full personal destruct, immediately under unit.

"Wh—?" Cossont had time to say, before a series of titanic claps shook the elevator car from above. Her helmet had inflated itself and gone to triple layer above the crown of her head. Berdle watched the lift's ceiling dent in a couple of places.

Fifty metres above, still in a storm of smoke and dust and a faint snowfall of ceramic flakes filtering from the shaft's summit, the missile positioned itself carefully.

The voice of Colonel Agansu, from the grille, did a little better than Cossont, getting out the whole of *"What—?"* before matters proceeded.

~That's a scout missile? Parinherm asked Berdle. ~Really?

~No, that's a knife missile, Berdle replied. ~And expendable, as it turns out.

The roof/ceiling above would take more, the avatar decided, and the elevator car appeared structurally sound.

Alarms were warbling in the distance, and the local networks, where not under attack, were buzzing with sudden traffic. The Incast facility was not without protection or resources, and was fighting back as best as its automatics knew how against the effector onslaught from outside and inside its walls. That the other side had such powerful assets in place so quickly was not a good sign though, the avatar knew.

~We'll need to protect Ms Cossont physically now, from above, Berdle told Parinherm, double- and then treble-checking the state of the missile's anti-matter battery before – to the missile – sending the signal, ~At 35 per cent AM yield; prepare, confirm.

~Copy 35 per cent AM yield.

~Enact.

The knife missile blew itself up.

Cossont felt herself go utterly limp, from the outside in, somehow. Had she had the time, she'd have worried about her bowels relaxing, but instead she was fascinated to find that she now had no control whatsoever over any of her major muscles, which, having been lost to her, now seemed to have developed minds of their own and taken the decision to roll her up into a foetal ball, while Parinherm and Berdle, perhaps similarly afflicted, were arching over the top of her. If she'd seen this done on stage, she thought, it might have looked quite an elegant ballet move.

"Blast-from-above-coming-apologies," Berdle said in her earbud, talking very fast and clipped.

There was an almighty crack of sound, she felt briefly weightless, though still held down by the two bodies spread over her, and then the floor came smacking up towards her, slapping her feet, creaking her bones and making her insides feel bruised. Her chin, on her tight-together knees, tried to bury itself between her calves. The shoulder bag with the cube in it pressed painfully into her back. It all went very dark. She expected to find her ears ringing but they weren't. Something cracked above her, making the whole lift shudder.

"Okay?" Berdle asked her, as the avatar and the android pulled up away from her and her suit started bringing her quickly to her feet. Standing, she suddenly found she had control of her body again. There was a haze of dust in the car, and the centre of the roof had caved in to the extent that the three of them had to stand back near the walls.

"Yeah," she said. "What was—?"

"Knife missile self-destructing directly above us," Berdle said. "Excuse me." The avatar squatted, his hands seemed to sink into the surface of the soft plastic floor, and then he pulled back. There was the sound of tearing, protesting metal, and Berdle's feet sank deep enough into the plastic tiles to cause ripples round the soles of his shoes, which themselves seemed to be deforming. Parinherm jerked suddenly, seemed to stagger.

Cossont stared at it. "You okay?"

~I just tried activating some AG, Parinherm sent to Berdle. ~I think I got targeted; non-viable. "Fine!" it told Cossont brightly, at the same time.

~Our adversaries are able to manipulate the topography of the local gravitational environment, when we give them a target, Berdle told the android.

Parinherm thought about this. ~Neat, he sent.

~The other Displaced components are experiencing the same problems, Berdle told the android, ~only the knife missiles are unaffected. AG is a little subtle for their purposes; they just use naked force fields.

Pulled by the avatar, a giant flap of metal and plastic came peeling and screeching back from the floor, showing the shaft underneath, sinking away into darkness several hundred metres below.

Berdle dropped head-first into it, his feet remaining hooked onto the floor.

~Parinherm, the avatar sent, along with a simple diagram of what it wanted the android to do. ~If you would.

~Certainly, Parinherm replied, and dropped through the hole too, also head-first, feeling Berdle catch his ankles as he fell past and then cooperating in a swinging motion that within two oscillations allowed his hands to reach the upper edge of an open doorway where a tiny missile the size of a human thumb was floating, two delicate-looking outstretched field components fending off the twin doors, which were sliding back and forth continually, trying to close.

"Vyr," Berdle shouted. "Make sure the cube is secure within your bag, then climb down my body. Lie on my back and hold on very tightly. The suit will help."

"*What?*" Cossont said, kneeling by the side of the hole in the lift floor and staring down the bottomless-looking shaft. Berdle was stretched across the shaft at forty-five degrees; she couldn't see Parinherm at all.

"Climb down me first," Berdle said reasonably. "We'll tackle the rest as we go."

Quaking, Cossont checked the shoulder bag was fastened, then lowered herself down the body of the avatar, feet first, holding on to his legs, then turned round on her knees on the slope of Berdle's back. She had never been more thankful for having four arms. Also, the suit did seem to be helping, but not as much as she'd have liked. She lowered herself to lie on his back, shaking, blood pounding in her ears. The bag slid round her shoulder, hitting Berdle on the head. Her hand was shaking as she went to grab it.

"Sorry!" she yelled.

"No, I'm sorry," Berdle said. "Are you afraid of heights?"

"No," she said through clenched teeth, "just of dying generally." She put the bag over her shoulder again and hugged the avatar from behind, so hard that had he been human she'd have worried about cracking his ribs.

~Okay? Berdle sent to Parinherm.

~Ready.

The little missile floating between the doors on its gyre of fields withdrew, letting the doors start to close as Parinherm let go of the top lip of the doorway and immediately flicked his hands around to grasp the edges of the closing doors.

~Secure hold, the android sent as the doors pressed into his fingers.

"Really tight now, Vyr," Berdle said quietly, then brought his feet together, letting him and Cossont fall from the under-surface of the elevator car. They pendulumed in the air, their combined mass sending them both swinging thudding into the shaft wall. The avatar took most of the impact and the suit's gloves protected Cossont's hands, but it still hurt.

Parinherm, fingers jammed, now had his own weight and that of the two people clinging to him on his arms, hands and fingers, which were being forced to slide down the narrow gap between the almost fully closed doors. Even in a fairly optimistic, human-flattering virtuality, Parinherm thought, a real human would be screaming head-over-heels down the shaft at this point, the bloody stumps of their fingers still trapped between the doors.

Happily, I am not human, Parinherm thought, *and this is only a simulation.*

~Climbing, Berdle sent, and quickly hauled himself up the android's body, hand over hand, taking Cossont with him. He stood braced on the lower lip of the doorway and swept the doors open – Parinherm dropped a metre but held on to the lower lip easily enough – stepped forward and turned to let Cossont jump off his back and then stooped to grasp the android's hand just as, with a creak and a sudden rush of air, the elevator car dropped down the shaft in front of the open doors, hit and severed Parinherm's fingers and then shuddered on downwards to sweep the rest of his body away.

~Damn, the android sent. ~I was enjoying that!

Cossont caught her breath, started forward towards the open shaft, looking down at the fast-retreating roof of the battered lift as air sucked out all around her.

Berdle reached, pulled her backwards, away from the shaft. "You know," the avatar said, stepping round her and looking out from the alcove where the lift doors were set, then taking another step out into the gently bowed corridor, "Parinherm will probably be okay, but we have to—"

Something seemed to strike the avatar full in the upper abdomen; Berdle was jerked backwards as a blinding light burst out all around him and something exploded further down the broad curve of corridor; Cossont was sent flying back towards the open doors and the shaft, staggering and skidding right to the edge, all four arms windmilling desperately as she stood teetering, heels-on to the drop. Her eyes were going crazy, reacting mostly too late to the star-burst of light that had erupted from the avatar, filling her vision with black dots. Berdle still seemed to be there, in front of her, his body shuddering, wrapped in flames.

She felt herself start to tip backwards, into the void.

"Oh, fuck," she heard herself say, and thought what pathetic words those were. And not even remotely original and unique, she thought, as she canted backwards, arms still hopelessly wheeling.

Berdle, enveloped in fire, stepped forward and caught the strap of her shoulder bag one-handed. He stopped her, held her, then grabbed her round the waist with his other hand and pulled her forward, back into the alcove.

"Best get down," he said, kneeling within the alcove. She dropped to her haunches, taking cover behind the metre of wall between the jammed-opened doors and the corridor. Berdle stripped the remains of his burning clothes off and threw them down the elevator shaft. His skin had gone silvery. There was no mark on his back at all; she'd have expected an exit wound. Actually, she'd have expected him to be blown in half.

"What the *fuck*?" she asked. She was trying hard not to shriek.

"Didn't quite see that coming in time," Berdle said, turning and grinning at her. "Managed to . . ." a hole appeared, instantly, in his back; she could see straight through his body to his silvery thighs. The hole was big enough for her to have put her fist in. The smooth hole closed up again, just as quickly. ". . . but not quite fast enough; caught some round the edges. Sorry about that." He nodded at the floor. "Lost the scout missile." Cossont looked at the floor, where half of the little scout missile that had been holding the doors open earlier lay, gently smoking.

The avatar put one finger to the edge of the alcove, flicked it out and brought it back just as another bright beam came lancing past where his finger had been an instant earlier. The edge of wall flared and a heavy detonation came from somewhere past them down the corridor; a blast of light followed by a body-shaking tremble beneath their feet and a pulse of blast, forcing Cossont to lower her head briefly. Grey smoke was drifting along the ceiling and a whole spectrum of alarms went squawking, warbling and howling all around them.

Then there was a dull, seemingly very distant thud, almost infra-sound deep. The ribbon of dark smoke in the lift shaft, extending from the burning clothes Berdle had discarded, trembled in the column of air.

~Oof! Hit bottom, Parinherm sent. ~95 per cent disabled, but still alive! End-run, I'm guessing. Nice working with you. Powering dow—

"Parinherm is still alive," Berdle told Cossont. "We are being fired at by some sort of military arbite stationed just at the line-of-sight curve-limit of the corridor to the right. To the left, eighty metres away, one corridor higher, advancing this way at jogging speed, is a Gzilt person in a full battle suit armed with a laser assault rifle. This may be the Colonel

Agansu person who contacted us earlier. I have two knife missiles to the left, within this corridor. They are holding fire while Gzilt civilians on a tour are evac— Wait. I'm being contacted. Excuse me."

~Android/avatar entity, this is Colonel Agansu. Do you read? Come in.

"Colonel Agansu wishes to talk," Berdle told Cossont. "Given our situation and the time we have to wait for the ship to return, I believe keeping him talking is to be preferred to having him or his adjuncts shooting at us."

"The ship," Cossont said. Her teeth wanted to chatter. She tried to stop them. "How long? It was still two-thirds of an hour away—"

"It is returning a little faster now," the avatar said. "Though we still need to stall the Colonel. I intend, therefore, to engage him in conversation."

"You engage away," she told him.

~Android/avatar entity, in the corridor, this is Colonel Agansu. Do you read? Come in.

~Colonel Agansu, Berdle sent. ~To what do we owe such destructive attention?

~Ah. And who might I have the pleasure of addressing?

~You knowing my name; is that really necessary, Colonel?

~My knowing it is strictly speaking unnecessary, I'll grant, Agansu sent. ~However, purely for form's sake, we might as well exchange names; sobriquets, at least.

~I fail to see how this will make any material difference to our exchanges, of information or fire.

~I don't mean to imply we are at all likely to become friends, sir. But a degree of civilised politeness should not prevent us discharging our duties.

~Or our weapons.

~Of which you seem to possess rather few, following the

destruction of your knife missile, not to mention the demise of your fellow at the bottom of the elevator shaft. I am somewhat tempted to send the arbite up the corridor towards you, just to see what you are able to put in its way to stop it; however, I am aware that Ms Cossont is relatively vulnerable compared to your good self, and may come to some harm in any resulting fire-fight, even while you might remain quite hale and hearty. The arbite is already in a state of some confusion following what it thought was a centre-body 100 per cent kill-shot which you seem, nevertheless, to have survived. Is Ms Cossont well?

~Well enough.

~You know, I think I am going to—

~My name is Berdle, Colonel Agansu. Interesting to make your acquaintance.

~Likewise, Berdle.

~I did ask, earlier, to what we might owe such destructive attention, if you recall?

~Indeed you did, Agansu sent. ~Well then, Berdle, the answer would be: to Ms Cossont, and possibly the device which the facility's records show she recovered a few minutes ago. As I said earlier, I would like to talk to Ms Cossont. Face to face; human to human. Also, I think it might be germane if I were to be allowed to inspect the device she retrieved. I strongly suspect you will have to accede to my requests in time, Berdle. We do rather have you at a disadvantage, wouldn't you say? There was a pause, and then the colonel sent, ~I certainly would.

Berdle looked at Cossont, glanced at the ceiling and said quietly, "The person in full battle gear – who I'm assuming is Colonel Agansu – is now almost overhead, possibly ready to make ingress here, either down the shaft behind you or straight through the floor. The tour party near the combat

arbite's position is still not quite clear of the likely destruction volume, were I to let the two knife missiles off the leash.
Excuse me; I must let Colonel Agansu talk at me some
more."

~You might benefit from being a little more cautious,
Colonel, Berdle sent. ~We are less at a loss than you appear
to imagine.

~Are you really? The colonel sounded amused.

~We are. We are currently mustering and preparing our
forces, Colonel. You have my word.

~I'm sure I do, Agansu said, with mock seriousness. ~And
that it is worth everything in the current situation, I feel
certain. Nevertheless, the fact remains that you do not benefit
from the presence of a friendly ship nearby, whereas I do.
As well as, as you may have noticed, a very capable combat
arbite.

~Yes. I trust the combat arbite is not in any way . . .
precious to you, Colonel?

Berdle heard the colonel laugh. ~Ah, dear. How fine the
line is between acceptably defiant bravado and hopelessly
delusional boasting. You were doing so terribly well up until
that point.

~I am sorry to be such a disappointment to you, Colonel
Agansu.

Berdle glanced at Cossont again. "The tour party near the
combat arbite's position is now clear of the likely destruction
volume and the knife missiles are cleared to fire," the avatar
told her. "Due to the nature of the munitions being used,
the corridor is about to become extremely bright. We are
trying to keep damage to a minimum, but – ah; here we
go . . ."

The air in the corridor seemed to fill and streak with
fanned white light, intensely bright; it almost looked like

the smoke-hazed air was being lit by lasers, but something about the quality of the light itself and the way the smoke in the corridor was tugged after whatever it was that was making its way down the corridor argued against this. Cossont had never paid all the attention she might have in weaponry identification or whatever they'd called it back in military academy.

It really was astoundingly bright; it was as though part of the surface of a blue-white sun had suddenly appeared in the corridor, searing, bleaching everything. The light cut off; what had seemed like a brightly lit space in front of them suddenly looked dull.

An instant later a series of colossal, still greater outbursts of light – just barely distinguishable as being made up of hundreds of small, searingly bright flares rather than being a single massive eruption – made a white sun of the end of the corridor to their right. In the instant between the light and the trailing sound of the fusillade, what probably was laser light came flicking through the hazed air, filling the patch of corridor Cossont could see with sparkling bars of cerise light.

Explosions shook and battered her from both sides. She put her head down, wondering if she'd have had any hearing left without the suit.

Something touched her on one ear and Berdle said, "We have only one knife missile remaining to our left now. The person above us is either waiting or hesitating. I have instructed the remaining knife missile to mount a frontal attack; it will fly past us at just under ceiling height in approximately six seconds and fire over us and through the lift-shaft doorway. The munitions being used, though tiny, are both powered by and payloaded with anti-matter, so some radiation exposure at such close quarters is inescapable.

Immediately after the missile has passed, you must stand and grasp me as you did before, from behind, arms round my body. Preferably legs wrapped round mine over my shins, too. Keep the bag with the mind-state device in it at your side, not over your back, do you understand?"

She nodded. More bars of pink light filled the air in front of the alcove, creating a screaming, tearing noise as the laser light impacted the swirling smoke and dust particles. Her mouth had gone very dry.

There was a further furious burst of cerise light and then the impression of almost invisibly quick motion high up, as though the corridor ceiling itself was rippling. Then the eSuit just turned the lights off; everything went completely dark while sound and blast-fronts seemed to detonate everywhere, pummelling her body from every side.

"Up!" Berdle shouted through her earbud. The suit helped her stand, she gripped the avatar from behind with three arms, brought her legs round his at the knee, made sure the shoulder bag was at her hip with her remaining hand and then put that round the avatar's body too. She could see again. The corridor was full of light, both white and pink.

Then something seemed to erupt from Berdle's chest and they were both flung away from the corridor and through the shallow alcove and into the lift shaft.

Cossont experienced what felt like the start of her head getting ripped off, then somebody slammed a sledge-hammer the size of a ship into her back and she blacked out.

Awake again; sore-headed, sore-backed, aching all over. She seemed to be still on Berdle's back, looking over his shoulder through a ragged, dusty gap across the elevator shaft to the doorway on the far side. Through the smoke and dust there, a thing lumbered like a bad dream of a man; massive, reverse-kneed, arms thick with weapon clusters, saucer-headed, it stood, straightening a little, seemingly looking straight at them. If the little knife missile's frontal attack had caused it any damage, it wasn't visible. Cossont didn't recognise the model; frankly it looked retro. Something rotated on its chest.

Then – silently, because her hearing didn't seem to be working properly – another explosion seemed to go off just above the part of the shaft she could see, and debris rained down, falling past and showering into the depths. A man in a bulky glittering suit and holding a large gun, also seemingly made of mirror stuff, came floating down, as though sitting in an invisible chair. He looked very relaxed.

Cossont looked around. She and Berdle seemed to have been blown through a wall and into a storage area; everywhere she looked in the dusty gloom she saw towering stacks of shelves full of pale boxes similar to the one that had held the glittering grey cube with QiRia's mind-state inside. They had ended up crumpled together in the remains of a set of shelves, half lying, half held standing by the twisted debris around them.

A couple of the pale, half-metre cube boxes came tumbling from somewhere overhead, bouncing and clattering down to join the jumble of debris already covering the floor. The combat arbite illuminated each of the falling boxes in turn with a thin beam of laser light from its weapon clusters, but let each fall and bounce without firing at them.

Cossont looked idly, groggily down at her hip. The shoulder bag wasn't there. It must have been ripped away.

Shit, she thought.

The man in the glittering suit was floating, stationary, in the middle of the elevator shaft, looking in at them. He tipped his head to one side, as though wondering what to make of them. The combat arbite shuffled to one side, to keep a clear field of fire.

"We really are fucked, aren't we?" Cossont said, her voice sounding odd inside her head and the helmet. She could taste what was probably her own blood in her mouth.

"Not necessarily," Berdle replied through the earbud, sounding, as ever, relatively unconcerned. "Still one knife missile left."

"But I thought it . . ."

"It left. It was not destroyed," Berdle told her. "It went the long way round the building. I suspect they assumed any combat missiles we had left would just burst through anything in their way; certainly that would be the first thing to occur to a knife missile. So – although this has taken longer, nevertheless – the element of surprise is with the missile. Here we are; that'll be it now," the avatar announced, as light erupted all around the combat arbite.

The man in the glittering suit started to whirl round to where the combat arbite was throwing its arms up and disappearing and disintegrating inside a consuming torrent of white fire. Then the view went dark.

More battering and pummelling. It was like being slung into a big metal drum with a bunch of sharp rocks and being kicked down a steep mountainside studded with boulders.

"The knife missiles in use here are from the Miniaturised Drone Advanced Weapon System," Berdle told her as floor, the shelves and the air itself all seemed to shake and quiver and beat. "Though it bears mention that it was 'Advanced' rather a long time ago. Still. And AM power is *very* crude, really. Raw, ragged stuff. Not really suitable for this kind of civilian-environment, in-structure work – far too battlefield – but it was all I had. Interestingly, the nanomissiles doing the damage are only a millimetre long and a tenth of that in diameter; too small to see for most unaided eyes; astonishing what you can do with anti-matter. There. Oh. Here—" Just as the battering seemed to be tailing off, there was another single, thudding, titanic impact, then Berdle said, "Ouch. Bet that hurt. Oh well, down you go . . ."

The view came back. The elevator shaft and the lit corridor beyond were full of dust and smoke. The doorway where the combat arbite had been standing was no longer a neat rectangle; it was practically circular, and most of the shattered, ragged edges were glowing. One or two shattered bits of machinery lying smoking, flaming or sputtering on the floor of the corridor might have been parts of the arbite. Of the man in the glittering suit, there was no sign. Something flashed briefly in the shaft.

"Yes, I wouldn't go sticking your head into the lift shaft," Berdle said, over a distant cacophony of alarm noises and some deep booming noises coming from the shaft. "Colonel Agansu is down there, largely disabled but patently still capable of firing." Berdle stepped out of the compacted debris of the shelves they'd smashed into, taking Cossont with him. He peeled her arms away, then turned to face her as she stood, swaying slightly. She suspected the suit was doing most of the work involved in keeping her upright.

She focused on the avatar. The whole front of his chest was a shallow silver bowl. It swam back into shape only slowly. "Hmm," the avatar said, looking down at this as another bright flash lit up the elevator shaft behind him. "Powerful laser your man had." He stooped, came back up holding the shoulder bag with the cube in it. "Here." He tied a knot in the burst strap, almost too quickly for her to see. "You okay?" he asked.

Cossont cleared her throat, nodded. "Fucking peachy."

Berdle looked innocently pleased. "Good. Well, there

don't appear to be any other forces wishing to engage with us, so we may be through the worst of it." There was another flash of light in the shaft behind.

"Shouldn't you be finishing off this colonel guy?" Cossont asked.

Berdle shook his head. "No need. I have a scout missile down there with him, monitoring. He shouldn't cause us any more trouble."

"What about Parinherm?"

"I've tried contacting; he's powered down. We'll try and Displace him too when the ship gets back. Walk this way."

Cossont, following the avatar, stepped shakily into a debris-strewn corridor between towering shelves. It seemed to stretch for ever into the distance. Something zipped past her from behind, coming through the smoke at head height and making her flinch. The thing stopped right alongside Berdle.

It was a thin cylinder about as thick as a thumb and as long as a hand, its front end shaped like an angular, blunted arrowhead and its dull silver surface marked with hair-fine dark lines and tiny dots. Berdle cocked one silvery eyebrow at it and said, "Yes, well done. So that Ms Cossont might be included in the conversation. Oh, both our lives. Inelegant use of rather too many nanos, though. Well, so you say, but it could have been accomplished more economically. Even so; had there been a whole section of those things, could you successfully have taken on all of them too? Well, there you are then."

The missile moved off so fast it was as though it was a shell in a perfectly transparent gun barrel; it just disappeared, leaving behind only an after-image and the vaguest of impressions it had headed away in the direction its sharp end had been pointing. Berdle's head jerked back in the blast of air and Cossont was only saved from being blown off her feet by the avatar reaching back with one silvery hand and grabbing her by the bag's strap again. The thunder-clap echoed off the surrounding shelves and the ceiling.

Berdle shook his head as he resumed walking. "Knife missiles," he said over his shoulder, with what sounded like affection.

"Yeah, knife missiles," Cossont agreed, like she knew what she was talking about. She glanced back, but could see little through the smoke. "You sure there's nobody else coming after us?"

"Not completely, no," Berdle admitted, "but there doesn't seem to be." He sounded thoughtful. "The Gzilt ship present here is at least a sixth-level heavy cruiser, possibly a seventh-level battle-cruiser; that'd mean between one and three platoons of marines available, at least, but they aren't being used. So that might say something about the secrecy and . . . well, authorisation of the mission involved." He shrugged. "Anyway. Onwards; I should warn you there will be some tramping, and we may have to hide."

The ship was led a merry dance, trying to get sufficiently close to the microrbital for long enough to get its avatar and the human off. Quickly getting the measure of each other, and each correctly guessing that its opposite number had no intention of being the first to open fire, neither ship resorted to serious targeting behaviour or the sort of hair-trigger weapon-readiness status that might have led to a misunderstanding. The whole tussle was conducted without signalling, as though neither vessel wanted to admit it was actually happening.

Eventually the *Mistake Not . . .* outwitted/out-field-managed the Gzilt ship and snapped the two humanoid figures off the habitat and back inside itself. It saw the Gzilt ship Displace/disloc one human-size entity off the little world a moment later. Having successfully retrieved its two primary Displace targets, the *Mistake Not . . .* tried to get a lock on the remains of the android Eglyle Parinherm, but found it had been beaten to it; a disloc field from the Gzilt ship was already starting to envelop the creature's crushed and broken body at the bottom of the elevator shaft.

Before the Gzilt vessel could complete the operation, the *Mistake Not . . .* applied a spatter of plasma fire to various parts of the android's body, cauterising all processing and memory/data storage nodes within the machine.

∞

xUe *Mistake Not . . .*

　oGSV *Contents May Differ*

Right. What? . . . Oh; the stuff from the *You Call This Clean?* . . . Okay. The memories were in his eyes and they've been removed. How severe with himself. Just as well we successfully retrieved Mr Q's mind-state, then. At no small risk to life and limb, I might add.

∞

　Congratulations. With what result?

∞

Just about to find out . . .

Cossont felt sleepy, sore, elated, all at once. Her pain-management systems were telling her to move gently, slowly, with no sudden movements. She would be bathing rather than showering, she had already decided, but first, the ship had insisted, they needed to talk to the stored mind-state inside the silvery grey cube.

The *Mistake Not . . .* was powering away from the Ospin system on a wildly erratic course, having decided – after its jinking, ducking and diving, field-to-field tussle with the Gzilt ship – that it was the faster. So far at least, the Gzilt vessel had shown no sign of following.

Cossont sat down in the lounge area of the shuttle that had become her home over the last few days, clad only in the eSuit with its hands and feet components retracted to cuffs again and the helmet collapsed back into its necklace form. Pyan had gone ooh and ah over her and wrapped itself round her neck, rubbing gently at her bruised skin. Berdle, back to looking like a handsome Gzilt male again, entirely gave the impression he'd just strolled out of a grooming parlour; not a hint of tiredness or a hair out of place.

"You *have* been in the wars, you poor thing," Pyan told Cossont, wrapping itself tighter.

"Yes. No need to throttle me."

"Apologies. There. And where is that silly android?"

"We had to leave him behind," Cossont said, glancing at Berdle as she extracted the silver-grey cube from the battered shoulder bag. "Under a wrecked elevator car at the bottom of a lift shaft."

"The Gzilt ship disloc'd him aboard itself," Berdle said. "It took Colonel Agansu too."

"Were they both still alive?" Cossont asked.

"I think Agansu was," the avatar said.

"Not Parinherm?"

"No." Berdle shook his head, held Cossont's gaze until she looked away.

She put the silvery cube on the low table in front of her, then reached out, touched it on.

"Ngaroe?" she asked.

"Ms Cossont," QiRia's voice said immediately.

Cossont realised she had been tense, hunched over the

table. She relaxed a little. "Good to speak to you again," she said, smiling.

"How long has it been? Oh. Quite a few years, I see. And are we on . . . a Culture ship?"

Cossont wasn't sure what to say. She glanced at Berdle, who shrugged, unhelpfully.

"Yes," she said. "Umm . . . I didn't realise you could . . ."

"I'm not completely without senses in here," QiRia's voice said. "I may only be switched on for fractions of an hour at a time, but I can tell roughly what my circumstances are, how much time has elapsed since I was last activated, and I have sufficient appreciation of the radiative and general sensory ambience of my surroundings to tell when I am, for example, on a ship."

"We were on a ship the last time we spoke," Cossont said.

"I know. So what? Hardly remarkable. But this is a Culture ship; a GCU or a warship or something similar. That is remarkable. So I remarked upon it. That it? We done? You going to shut me off for another sixteen years?"

"No, no," Cossont said quickly. "Sorry. Very sorry. But . . . look. We need to ask you something."

"Who's 'we'?"

"Hello, Mr QiRia," Berdle said pleasantly. "My name is Berdle. I'm the avatar of the ship you're on, the *Mistake Not* . . . Pleased to meet you."

"Yes. Delighted. You sound stressed, by the way, Cossont."

"Do I? Well, it's been—"

"Yes. That's why I said it," the voice said, with only a touch of acid. "Berdle, I'd like to interface. May I see through your eyes, or some other visual sensor immediately hereabouts?"

"Be my guest," Berdle said, and looked first at Cossont, then in a steady sweep round the rest of the lounge.

"Cossont! You have four arms," QiRia's voice said.

"To play the elevenstring," she said.

"Ah. You weren't put off playing it by the *Warm, Considering* after all. Good for you. So; what is it you want to know?"

She took a deep breath. "Ngaroe, we need to ask you something about . . . long ago. Going right back. It is . . . it's very important. It might affect how the Subliming goes. Our Subliming. The Gzilt Subliming." She took another deep breath. "There was a message, a signal from the Zihdren, saying that the Book of Truth might all be a lie, and you were mentioned as—"

"Wait, wait, wait," QiRia's voice said. Cossont fell silent. "*How* far back? Are you asking me to remember things from—"

"The time of the conference that set up the Culture, sir," Berdle said.

"Ah," QiRia's voice said. "That far back. Can't help you."

"What?" Cossont said. She and the avatar exchanged looks.

"I said," the voice from the cube told them, slowly, "that I cannot help you. My memories only go back to . . . about seventy years standard after that time. The memories in here begin at midnight on the 44th of Pereid, 8023, Koweyn calendar. Before that, I've nothing."

"*Seriously?*" Cossont said. She could hear her own voice start to rise in tone and volume. "You're missing—?"

"Must ask you to check, sir," Berdle said, in a pained voice.

"Check for yourself. You're a ship; you'll have the ability. I'm giving you permission. I'm not a biological, not in here, so take a look for yourself. Scan all the data in this cube. Go on; feel free."

"You're sure?" the avatar said. He looked at Cossont, who found it was her turn to shrug.

"Yes!" QiRia's voice said sharply.

Berdle sighed. He smiled at Cossont. "This might take a moment," the avatar told her.

She sat back slumped in the seat, rubbed her face with two of her hands. She sighed heavily. "Take all the—"

"Ah," Berdle said, sounding resigned. He looked at Cossont. "I'm afraid it's just as Mr QiRia's mind-state has claimed."

"Told you," the voice from the cube said.

"The memories aren't *there*?" Cossont felt suddenly tired, full of aches, and depressed.

"I'm afraid not," Berdle told her. "And even the memories of the times when Mr QiRia thought back to those times, before the source memories were edited out, have been expunged, too." Berdle looked at the cube. "That's quite a thorough job, Mr QiRia."

"Sounds like it," the voice agreed.

Berdle smiled faintly, shook his head as he said, "Would you have any idea why you—?"

"No. None at all. Guess I must have thought I had something to hide. If so, glad I've done a good job of it, or made sure somebody else did."

Cossont was sitting, looking deflated, eyes closed, shaking her head gently. "They can't just have gone," she said, as though to herself. "They can't just have gone." She looked at Berdle. "What now? Can we look for . . . the real QiRia, for the old guy himself? He might . . . he should still know." She shook her head again. "Shouldn't he?"

"We've already tried that," the avatar told her. "They found him, but he'd had the memories encoded site-specific in his body, and then had those sites removed."

"What?" Cossont said, frowning.

"Mr QiRia looks like this, now," Berdle said, and a screen appeared in mid-air, of a man in a dark room, wearing a pair of dark, slatted glasses. "The person who tracked him down," Berdle said; "their suit took this." The screen image moved and the man took off the glasses, revealing that it was QiRia, but also that where his eyes should have been, there were the inner parts of ears.

The clip looped and the screen split to show different versions of the same sequence, in infra-red, slow motion, with the eye sockets zoomed in on, and combinations thereof.

Cossont just stared.

"How *gross!*" Pyan said.

"What are you looking at?" QiRia's voice asked.

Cossont reached out and turned the cube off, then slumped back in her seat, eyes closed again. She had a feeling she might be about to cry.

"Do you remember this?" Berdle said softly, and when Cossont opened her eyes again the screen was showing a view that looked familiar, though at first she couldn't quite place it. It was of a man looking slightly lost in what might have been a transit lounge. Then he left, following a modest amount of luggage on a float-trolley.

Of course: QiRia, arriving on Xown, five years ago. Then a similar set of images which seemed to show him in the same place, dressed similarly but wearing big dark glasses. If anything, he looked even less sure about where he was going this time. The images faded away and the screen went dark.

"And this?" The screen shone out again to show Ximenyr, the man with the many penises on the airship *Equatorial 353*, in the Girdlecity. It was almost exactly the view she recalled having at the time, though then the view flicked round and showed Cossont's own face, before flicking back to the man in the bed again. So this had been Berdle's point of view. This was the sight through his eyes, recorded.

"Mr Berdle, Ms Cossont," Ximenyr said in his deep, thick voice. "Pleased to meet you." He opened his mouth and a long tongue snaked out and delicately licked at first one eyebrow then the other, shaping them both neatly into place. The tongue disappeared again. He opened his eyes wide; he had bright, pale blue irises. His eyeballs went back into their sockets, the blue irises disappearing. They were replaced from below by dark red irises which rolled into place and steadied. "Excuse me," he said. "These pupils work better in daylight." He smiled widely, showing very white teeth.

Cossont was nodding now. "Mr Ximenyr, the body-amendment specialist," she said.

This would be why QiRia had looked like he had, the second time in the transit lounge; wearing big dark glasses, seemingly – perversely – less sure of his surroundings than before: he'd been blind.

The screen view now was doing something she hadn't done at the time, zooming in to a close-up of Ximenyr's face; the teeth and the eyes at first, then down, to the necklace of trinkets adorning his neck.

The view came to rest and freeze on the tiny – at the time deactivated – scout missile that the ship had sent into the man's bed-chamber. It was resting on Ximenyr's chest between what looked like an android's thumb and a thick crystal cylinder, striped with encrusted jewels.

The frozen image jerked to one side, zoomed in further on the cylinder, showing a hazy view of what looked like semi-transparent crystal with what might have been a pair of berries inside. They were pale green, and looked like they were floating in some sort of off-white surround.

"What colour were Mr QiRia's eyes?" Berdle asked.

Cossont still had to think, just to be sure. Then she remembered. "When he was there, they were the colour of the ocean on Perytch IV," she said. "The ocean could be lots of colours," she told the avatar, "but mostly, in daylight, it was the colour of beach jade. Pale green." She nodded at the extreme close-up of the jewel-encrusted cylinder with its imperfectly transparent little windows and the two soft-looking things inside that might have been berries. "That colour."

Eighteen

(S -7)

She should never have trusted herself. She ought to have known what she was like. Well, she did know what she was like, but she should have paid more attention or taken the issue more seriously or something.

Scoaliera Tefwe, still within the virtual environment of a substrate housed within the LSV *You Call This Clean?*, looked at the two holo images of herself facing her and scowled. "So. Neither of you?"

"Certainly not me."

"Certainly not me."

They didn't say it at quite the same time, but then the ships they were housed within were at quite different distances.

The original Scoaliera Tefwe, who thought of herself as the real one – but then, both the others would as well – sighed in exasperation and flicked the images off.

"Huh," she said.

"I have their experiences, all the sensory data they collected," the *You Call This Clean?* told her. "They can't stop you reviewing those."

"That," Tefwe said, "will have to do."

"There's a surprise at the end," the ship told her. "Shall I warn you?"

"What, and spoil the fun? Why no."

So she watched herself take the aphore from the stables at Chyan'tya, by the Snake river, with its smells of bell-blossom and strandle flower, even-cluss and jodenberry, then head out across the Pouch to the hills. She saw the pair of raptors wheel across the blaze of blue sky, could taste the heat in her mouth at the day's peak, and lay panting with the mount in the shade of the desiccant umbrel.

She went up into and then through the mountains. She skipped her other self's memory of sleep; it saved time but also it felt like an intrusion too far, even though this person was still and really herself.

She met with the drone Hassipura, surveyed its intriguing but somehow pathetic little empire of tunnels, channels and pools of scald-dry sands. She heard where she – yet another, sequential version of her – might find QiRia, and left.

She watched herself – there was always that distance at first, like watching a play or a film, before you lost yourself in it – as she stood up within the tall sways of bronze and copper-coloured grasses, then walked to the deserted station and waited for the rattling train-tram thing.

She could smell the air, and sense the locals, the folds, trying not to stare at her. She was carried on up into the mountains, into the vast echoing kingdom of the Sound, and waited to be allowed in to the hearkenry, then followed the Docent Luzuge, and was, finally, granted her audience with the elusive Mr QiRia.

The eyes – the sockets that now housed ears – came as a shock. That certainly counted as a surprise.

She – her other self – didn't get long to gawk at the man's mutilated face. There was some commotion outside, audible over, or at least through, the crushing weight of the Sound.

The door at the rear of the cell was thrown splintering open and some sort of shining, multi-limbed drone, all angles and barbs, came tearing in and halted by QiRia's seat. It drew itself up as though to strike. QiRia had jumped when the door had been thrown open and was turning towards the machine, which screeched, "Arrest! Surrender self!" in a metallic scream pitched so high it cut right through the Sound.

Tefwe's suit had gone to full deployment the instant the door had started moving, covering her head in a close-fitting semi-transparent helmet. She jumped up and threw open the shutters, letting the Sound roll in. There was a white flash and she felt something hit her hard in the back, though without causing pain. She threw herself through the matting curtains and out of the window, landing on the cold slope of scree outside and hurtling in a zigzag down towards the nearest cover – a dark mass of metre-high boulders. "Ship!" she yelled. "You getting all this? Get me off here!"

"Suit lower dorsal area seventy per cent compromised," the suit told her solemnly. She could feel heat bleeding through where the blow from behind had hit, making her back warm.

"Shit!" she said as she dived for a gap between two of the boulders. She never got there. A second, much more powerful shot – from above, from a weapon platform she hadn't even known was there – hit her between the shoulders and blew her neck and head off.

Most of her landed in a bloody, fiery, smoking heap just before the collection of boulders; her head flew further and thudded off the top of one of the boulders, bouncing to the ground just beyond. Then the view, from the scout missile or whatever had been accompanying her, flashed once and disappeared too.

The *Rapid Random Response Unit*, suddenly subject to the aggressive attentions of a small flotilla of Oglari vessels, executed a very risky manoeuvre, succeeded in snapping Tefwe's still-just-about-alive head back to itself and then flared wildly off at its highest possible, engine-field-addling acceleration.

The whole incident caused some highly vocal distress and outrage for the Oglari, allegedly entirely on behalf of their valued allies and grateful charges, the Uwanui. Apologies for the misunderstanding were dutifully expressed by the *Rapid Random Response Unit*, its home GSV and other respected Culture worthies, but further favours and indulgences were now owed or at least expected by both the Oglari and the Uwanui.

Apparently, neither Contact nor Special Circumstances was particularly impressed with these developments.

"These things accrue," Tefwe muttered to herself.

"All on-boarded?" the *You Call This Clean?* asked.

"I experienced everything the other two experienced, so I suppose so," she said. "But I got *killed*, for fuck's sake."

"That was the surprise."

"Thanks. Think I'll go back to Storage now. Full asleep. No dreams."

"Certainly."

"And next time you want to wake me up—"

But the ship had already started putting her under. It strongly suspected that there had been only one more word to come in that sentence of Tefwe's, and that it would have been the word "don't".

Yes, but . . . plausibly deniable, the ship decided.

"Of course we're close. We've always been close. We're mother and daughter. You might not understand; you're a man. Men rarely do. It's a different thing. You really have to be a mother to understand, frankly. Even some daughters don't understand, to tell the Prophet's truth. Not that I'm saying Vyr doesn't. That would be going too far. But she is independent. Very independent. But I'm not complaining; I'm not the complaining sort, not at all. That's how I raised her, you see? That's what I wanted for her. I always meant her to be her own person, not tied to my purse strings. And she hasn't wanted to become a mother herself, what with the Subliming, obviously. Or really had time, for that matter. Very busy. She's always been very busy. And not always with things that she can tell me about either, if I'm telling the truth and you know what I mean. You know. Well, I'm sure you do, in your type of work. I'm not saying she was some sort of secret agent or anything, but you could tell – well, I could tell, being her mother, as I say, and I do have a gift for these things even if I say so myself, though it's not just me, not really; it's all my friends, I'm very modest, they're the ones who'll tell you I have a gift, almost a sight for these things . . . but there were things she obviously couldn't tell me, things that were secret that it was best for me not to know I suppose. I'm not surprised, I'm really not. She's very bright, very capable girl, very able to take care of herself, and trustworthy. And loyal. Loyal, too. Very loyal. She takes after me in that way, it's part of the bond we share."

"It's just that according to the logs of the ship here, she doesn't seem to visit very oft—" the first young man started to say, before his companion held up one hand to stop him.

She'd already forgotten their names, but the one who'd just been talking was the nicer of the two because he smiled more and looked at her properly and just had a nicer manner. The other one was even younger – barely more than a boy – and harder-looking somehow and didn't even seem to have noticed let alone appreciated the very flattering and daringly clingy lounge dress she'd worn especially.

Inter-Regimental Intelligence on Trimestal Secondment! How grand did that sound! And they were interested in her little girl! In a good way, obviously; they had been very polite and deferential ever since they'd called the apartment from their aircraft on their way to see her, and even the small, hard-faced one who was probably only interested in boys anyway had been scrupulously courteous and mannerly from the instant he and the nice, jolly, fuller-faced one had crossed the threshold of the apartment.

Apparently, though they couldn't confirm or deny anything, naturally, Vyr was still alive. And not just alive, but involved – the implication seemed to be – in something important. Her little girl! Well, it was no surprise really. She'd always known, at the back of her mind, despite all the silly, niggling things that the girl had done and said over the years, that Vyr would live up to the promise she'd shown when she was younger, and make her mother proud of her. It had only been a matter of time.

In fact, all the times she hadn't bothered to visit or get in touch and had seemed indifferent or intolerant or just seemingly wanting to be hurtful on the rare occasions when she *did* deign to show up suddenly made complete *sense* now; she'd just been trying to protect her mother! She should have known that's what it had been. Of course she'd loved and respected her old mum; how could she not? She just hadn't been able to bring her into her secret life in case it jeopardised her safety. Logical. Loving and sensible at the same time. Well, frankly, about time!

Warib could feel herself getting quite excited with all these thoughts; her breath was coming rather quickly and she wouldn't be at all surprised if she looked flushed and even more youthful to these two very well-dressed and immaculately groomed young men. The younger, harder-faced one was saying something. She really ought to concentrate; her attention had drifted there – not like her at all.

". . . her being involved in something secret?" he said, eyes narrowed but a small smile – finally! – on his lean face. "Did I understand that right? Did you . . . ?"

"Well, I can't say too much. Obviously," Warib said. "Oh, thank you, dear." She accepted a health drink infusion from Garron. Garron had been a little brusque with the two young men initially – they were both probably even younger than he was – but that was all right. He'd even offered everybody drinks, which was a lot better than his usual What-am-I-just-a-steward-to-you? attitude. "But she'd always been so outstanding, it would only be sensible for the regiment to put her talents to good use. I mean, she would never actually tell me anything, but," Warib winked at the two young men, "a mother can tell. I think especially when you're very close – almost embarrassingly close! – in age to your daughter – oh, dear! – I think you can tell when there's something going on she's not telling you about. I can't say any more. I don't *know* any more, in the conventional sense of knowing, but, trust me; I know."

The young, hard-faced one nodded. "That's very interesting."

Warib smiled, relaxed. She was much less worried about Vyr now.

xGSV *Contents May Differ*
　oLOU *Caconym*
　oGCU *Displacement Activity*
　oGSV *Empiricist*
　oGSV *Just The Washing Instruction Chip In Life's Rich Tapestry*
　oUe *Mistake Not . . .*
　oMSV *Passing By And Thought I'd Drop In*
　oMSV *Pressure Drop*
　oLSV *You Call This Clean?*

Well, I think we've all looked at the relevant signal streams by now. It would seem Mr QiRia really is going to some lengths not to let us know what happened in the way back when. The *Mistake Not . . .* has already thrown itself about – again – and is now heading straight back to Xown and the Girdlecity; however, I place this out there just in case there is anybody who knows of anything closer . . . No? Really? Nothing else within five days? No, then.

∞

xMSV *Pressure Drop*
Did our friend the *Mistake Not . . .* not leave any sort of presence at Xown?

∞

xUe *Mistake Not . . .*
The *Mistake Not . . .* did indeed, because the *Mistake Not . . .* is not a complete idiot.

∞

xMSV *Pressure Drop*

I certainly didn't mean to suggest that you were. Would any of these items still on Xown be able to procure these two pieces of soft hardware independently?

∞

xUe *Mistake Not . . .*

Not by themselves. The gentleman in possession of what we *assume* are Mr QiRia's eyes, which we *assume* are genuinely where his memories are, appears to have non-trivial resources to command in the field of surveillance and remote presences. The items I left in the vicinity might be of some assistance in getting hold of the objects in question, and a certain amount of preparatory work might be accomplished, but they would not be sufficient in themselves.

We could, of course, just send a message to Mr Ximenyr asking him to sell, trade or just out of the goodness of his hearts gift us the objects concerned and put them aside until I'm able to get there to pick them up; however, I imagine we might all feel that could serve to alert him – and possibly others – to their mooted importance.

Or we might ask some remaining element of the Fourteenth Regiment – its innocence/on-sidedness presumably taken as read following the attack on its HQ – to help us, but that takes control away from those we entirely and implicitly trust, and might be seen to confer potentially too much power on a Gzilt person, group of people or entity regarding the release or not of the information Mr QiRia's ocular out-board data storage devices may or may not contain. I think that covers all the available alternatives to my heading back as fast as my little engine fields will carry me to Xown and trusting to my own abilities to retrieve the situation.

∞

x*GCU Displacement Activity*
Speaking of Gzilt people potentially having too much power through access to what may be contained in Mr QiRia's memories; what of Ms Cossont?

∞

x*Ue Mistake Not . . .*
Ms Cossont has been no trouble so far, and of some use. Also, having been allowed to look inside the device holding Mr QiRia's mind-state, with his permission and indeed at his insistence, I've discovered that to access his memories is by no means simple; his cooperation may well be required to make sense of the encoded data we're looking for, certainly if it's to be done quickly and without fault. As he appears to have, at the least, a sentimental attachment to Ms Cossont, we need to keep both him and her with us. In any event, I wouldn't imagine that she would either harbour the desire or be in the position to affect matters materially.

∞

x*GCU Displacement Activity*
So you're vouching for her.

∞

x*Ue Mistake Not . . .*
Yes. As much as one can for a bio.

∞

x*GSV Contents May Differ*
Good. Meanwhile, we are faced with the problem of this disputed preferred Scavenger status between the Ronte and the Liseiden. Just because they've been taking their time crawling through space doesn't mean they have gone away. On the contrary, their most powerful fleet sub-units have each been crawling their way to the same

place, Zyse, and are due there in the next day or two. Given what the avatar of the *Passing By And Thought I'd Drop In* has had to report on what still seems like a delicate political situation, this is not encouraging. Any thoughts?

∞

∘GSV *Just The Washing Instruction Chip In Life's Rich Tapestry*
Yes. I think we should be glad those two Delinquents are there, not to mention the *Passing By . . .*'s pair of Thugs.

∞

×GSV *Contents May Differ*
I was looking for something a little more constructive.

∞

×MSV *Passing By And Thought I'd Drop In*
My responsibility. My avatar continues to seek audiences with the various personalities involved, especially Septame Banstegeyn. However, he is proving a hard man to pin down; he can't be quite as busy with his official responsibilities as he claims, but he certainly appears to have plenty of other interests with which to fill his remaining time. As a result, sadly, for now, I am no more able to suggest anything more constructive than is the *Just The Washing Instruction Chip In Life's Rich Tapestry*.

∞

×LOU *Caconym*
  ∘MSV *Pressure Drop*
The *Passing By . . .* would appear to be of the Effectively Useless persuasion. It needs – it has needed throughout – to be much more aggressive in monitoring these "various personalities involved, especially Septame Banstegeyn"; and – indeed – *especially* Septame Banstegeyn. It should not be lodging polite requests

to see these people if-they'd-be-so-kind-when-they're-able-pretty-fucking-please; it should be spying and eavesdropping on and bugging the fuck out of the fucking lot of them. This is what happens when you let an antiquated academic with a special interest in a civ take on any sort of serious role involving them because it "understands" them. It doesn't just understand them; it identifies with them, mimics them – it wants to fucking *be* them. Not good enough.

∞

To be fair, this posting did look like a sinecure until all this Z-R shit hit the impellers.

∞

These things always do. Perhaps the lesson is that there are no sinecures, just matters of potentially grave consequence we happen to get away with most of the time. Can we ask the *Empiricist* to lean on the *Passing By* . . .? These big System-class fuckers are supposed to cast a long shadow ahead of them, or what use are they?

∞

I'll make the suggestion. Back to the general babble.

∞

xGSV *Contents May Differ*
  oLOU *Caconym*
  oGCU *Displacement Activity*
  oGSV *Empiricist*
  oGSV *Just The Washing Instruction Chip In Life's Rich Tapestry*
  oUe *Mistake Not . . .*
  oMSV *Passing By And Thought I'd Drop In*
  oMSV *Pressure Drop*
  oLSV *You Call This Clean?*

Well, we must await further developments. Let us hope nothing too momentous occurs in the meantime.

The first part of the ship dance "The Approaching Eclipsing of One Sun by Another" was performed with due ceremony on the achievement of the Gzilt system outskirts, with the Gzilt home planet of Zyse only hours away. The dance was augmented with the participation of the Culture ship *Beats Working*. This vessel's accrued inferred alien cachet value (positive), honorary, had, by general acclaim within the fleet and squadron, now become so great that it might actually be embarrassing for it to be informed of the level to which it had ascended so rapidly.

It was probably and arguably already over the limit that even as august a being as Ossebri 17 Haldesib, holding a position as elevated as Swarmprince and Sub-Swarm Divisional Head and Fleet Officer in Charge, could be properly expected to confer-by-informing. It was decided therefore to allow the Culture ship to continue to accrue inferred alien cachet value (positive), honorary, for the meantime, while still not disturbing the metaphorical airflow-through-the-hive by informing the vessel of this distinction.

Regardless, Gzilt and Zyse now lay ahead, and close.

"Hello again. Sorry for being so . . . abrupt."

"That's all right. I take it we're still aboard the same Culture ship, the *Mistake Not . . .*"

"Yes, we are."

"So, what were you looking at that disturbed you so?" the voice from the silver-grey cube asked. "Or are you going to turn me off again?"

"We were looking at what you'd done to yourself."

"Really? What? . . . Come on; tell me. The version of

me in here and version of me that did whatever I did to myself are less than twenty years apart. When you've lived as long as I have, that's nothing. I won't have changed much in between. Effectively I'm the same person. Tell me."

"You'd put your earliest memories into your eyes, then had those removed," she said. "You went to Ximenyr, in the Girdlecity, to have it done. You had extra ears put where your eyes should have been."

". . . Well, that's certainly taking my predilection for the audible over the visible to an extreme." The voice sounded genuinely amused.

"It just seemed . . . drastic. Shocking," Cossont said. "It looked like . . . like self-mutilation."

"It's my body to mutilate as I see fit, Cossont. And, from somebody currently possessing four arms, that's an odd criticism." Cossont opened her mouth, but then the voice went on. "This wouldn't have been on a place called *Cethyd*, would it? In the Mountains of the Sound?"

"Yes."

"Ha! Makes sense. Heard about that place quarter of a millennium or more ago; been meaning to go ever since. Good for me for taking it seriously enough to dedicate more than the standard proportion of sensory equipment to the task. I admire myself."

Cossont, lying on her bed with the cube sitting on the pillow next to her, raised her eyebrows at that, but let it pass. "An old friend of yours called Tefwe went there," she said, "to try and persuade you to talk about what had happened back when the Culture was coming together and the Gzilt nearly joined but didn't."

"Huh. So much for swearing old lovers to secrecy and respect for one's privacy."

"But what the hell were you thinking? Taking out your own *eyes*? Leaving them with *Ximenyr*?"

"Did I? I bet it seemed like a good idea at the time. Also, less obvious than leaving the data with all the other informational detritus orbiting Ospin. For example."

"What were you – what are you trying to hide, though?"

"Who knows? Maybe I'm better without the memories. So: we're heading for Xown?"

"Yes," Cossont said quietly to the cube. "We're going to see Ximenyr, in the Girdlecity, to try and get your eyes, your memories back."

"Interesting that I didn't want the memories destroyed, just . . . parked."

"Whatever they may be."

"Whatever they may be . . . Of course, just because the eyes are there doesn't mean the memories are too. I could have had those wiped . . . It's gone very quiet out there. Hello?"

"That would be a joke too far, Ngaroe."

"All the same. I wouldn't put it past me."

"This. I love this, when you are over me, when I can barely see you or touch you but I know that you are there and just a breath away and I feel each exhaling is like a warm breeze across the land, when I can hear each beat of your heart over mine, when you are close enough that I can feel the heat of you on my skin. Then you are my presence, over and above me, like a promise. I live for these moments. I die at the thought they might stop in the Sublime."

"You say the sweetest things to me. I wish I could say such things to you, so beautifully."

"You draw them from me, you are their muse, their true creator; we make them between us. I am a hopeless stumbler and stutterer, always have been, with anybody else. So you must take half the credit. At least."

"If you say I must, I must, but I feel embarrassed that you say, that you give so much and I can't give you the same."

"Words are just one language, Virisse. Just one way of expression. You speak with your eyes, you speak with your sweet tongue and gentle fingers, with your whole body. Like this, and this. What?"

"No, I just, no; here, come here, hold me, hold me like this. Here, I'll . . . Be my presence, hang over me, embrace me. I need you. Do anything for you. I give myself. I need to give myself. Oh, you don't hate me for being so needed, do you? I am. I know I am. My own needing, it betrays me."

"Oh, my darling. I love that you need me as much as I, desperately, need you. But don't distress. What is it? What can . . . ?"

"You don't think they're lying to us, the Sublimed, the Presence; you don't think they're lying to us, deceiving us, do you?"

"What? Is that . . . ? Not for a moment. Oh, be calm, Virisse. Of course not. Do you think I would risk losing you? If I thought for a moment there was any danger they lied to us, that what we're offered isn't true, that we might simply die or be blown away like mist, I'd never even think of this, for myself, for you, for us, for all the people."

"Isn't it like a threat, though, this thing, hanging over us? I look at it some days, hanging over the city, over us, and it makes me shiver."

"It used to make me catch my breath, sometimes, I'll give you that. What can I say, Virisse? Promises take many shapes, and the more . . . momentous they are, the more they might look like threats. All great promises are threats, I suppose, to the way things have been until that point, to some aspect of our lives, and we all suddenly become conservative, even though we want and need what the promise holds, and look forward to the promised change at the same time. So we have that great grey shape hanging over us, over the parliament itself, as a reminder that this is where the final decision was taken, this is where we made up our minds. And it reminds us that there are powers and forces beyond us, that we are in the process of surrendering our full authority in this, and of taking a great new leap."

"Is it too late?"

"What? I'm sorry, my love, I didn't—"

"Is it too late? Can we still unmake our minds?"

"Well, no, it isn't. We can all change our minds, right up until the last moment."

"Must there always be forces beyond us?"

"Oh, my love, there always have been. The Sublimed have been there for ten billion years, the Elders too; we are just one species, not here for the longest time, then here for a while, then gone again, just like everybody else. But we've always known there is something worthwhile in just being ourselves, in being us as well as we can. We've found, been given a way, to symbolise this, in the Book of Truth, but the real truth is that every species feels the same thing, and every one is right.

"We all think we're special, and in a way we are, but, at the same time, that feeling of being special is one of the things that's common to us all, that unites us and makes us the same as each other. And when that feeling of . . . specialness is questioned, we feel threatened, naturally. We all do. I do. We have the Subliming drawing near, and we seem to be collecting alien warships, with Culture ships already arrived – two more this evening, the *Empiricist* tomorrow – and the Liseiden and the Ronte arriving in days, both seeming to think the other is the interloper while we feel they both are. The eyes of the galaxy are on us, and this ought to be a time of quietness and reflection and measured preparation, a time of looking back with gentle pride on all we've achieved, and yet . . . we have a regiment HQ attacked and thousands killed, and an undignified scramble going on over our heads over our spoils, and all sorts of absurd rumours and stories swirling about, but we—"

"I just worry. I worry that we've swept ourselves along somehow, got all too excited over something we haven't thought through, that . . . that . . . people have persuaded us to do something we're still not ready for."

"Well, Septame Banstegeyn is a very persuasive man, I'll give you that."

"I didn't just mean—"

"No, you did. And I know what you mean. But you have to see that we become . . . symbols for ourselves. One person can seem to be the instigator, the power behind some . . . great powerful current within a society, but they're not necessarily producing it; they may be at the front, and they may have some small, immediate influence over its direction hour by hour or day by day, but really they are swept along by it too, by the force of all those people behind them, by the idea they all represent and are all borne along by. But, Virisse, what talk is this for the bed? We have so few of these opportunities, my love, let's not waste this one in worry. Let's sweep each other away, like this . . . and this . . . and this . . ."

"Yes. Yes, you're right. I'll be your spoils, fight over—"

"Ow! What—?"

"What?"

"I don't know. My finger. A jab, like a thorn. My love, *there*? Of all places? Why, what *have* you been doing?"

"What? Don't laugh! No, what? Let me see!"

"Here. My finger. See? Poor finger."

"Let me see, let me see!"

"Ah, so pleasantly engaged, so sharply interrupted."

"Let me—"

"Oh. Worth one tiny injury for such a sweet kiss. You make me swoon . . . Oh, wait a moment, you really are. I really am . . . swoon. My. My head is quite . . . quite . . ."

"No!"

"It's all right. I'm just, it's just . . . Oh . . . I'm glad I'm lying dow—"

"No, Sef, no! Say . . .! Oh. Oh, of course; me too. I should. Should have . . . he . . . how could . . .? Oh, the fool . . ."

"Going dark . . . What, you too? My love? Have we . . .? Is this some . . .? Are we being . . .? Are we be—?"

"Doesn't know. Oh, the cruel, the stupid!"

"Not, not feeling . . . so good. Where's my – it was here. I need to call – Oh, fuck, I'm really . . ."

"I'm so sorry, I'm so, so sorry. Please . . ."

"Never – it doesn't . . . just hold . . ."

"I'm sorry! I'm so—"

"Just hold . . ."

"So sorry . . ."

"Just . . ."

"So . . ."

"**W**asn't *anything* found?"

"Mere traces, Septame. Some form of highly sophisticated, very hi-tech device, already starting to dissolve into her flesh and blood the moment after it had delivered its payloads."

"Payloads?"

Physician General Locuil nodded. "The first, almost certainly, into the president. The second, into Ms Orpe. Possibly a few seconds apart, perhaps almost at the same time. There is so little left of the device – so little not turned into its constituent molecules, at any rate – it's hard to tell, but the likelihood is it was something tuned to Sef's own genes, something that would only activate at her touch. Then, once it had delivered the toxin into her, it would deliver its second payload into the carrier, into Orpe." Locuil held up his hands in a gesture of helplessness. "To stop her talking, we have to assume. We also have to assume that she knew the device was in there, but didn't know it would kill the president. She might have thought it was going to drug her, or – given where it was – she might have thought it would, you know, enhance things for her, for both of them. We can't know."

The physician general sighed, sat back. He massaged his face with one hand. He sat across the septame's desk from Banstegeyn. Marshal Chekwri sat nearby; no others were present in the septame's private study in his town house, though both the marshal and the physician general had staff waiting in an ante-room along with Banstegeyn's own people, including Jevan and Solbli.

Outside, it was almost dawn.

The two bodies had been discovered by the president's own security team when her comm bracelet – taken off, lying by the bedside – had finally registered that the local sets of vital signs had altered anomalously. Both women had been beyond saving for many minutes before they were discovered, the fast-acting targeted synthetic neuro-toxins still multiplying within what was left of their brains and nervous systems, even as they gradually dissolved. A medical team of the best people and most exclusive machines had been working all night, trying to work out what had happened.

"But, the thing, this . . . how would it know to, when to . . . to activate?" Banstegeyn asked, aiming to sound bewildered without seeming too naively stupid.

"It would be monitoring everything it came into contact with," Locuil said wearily. "As soon as it sensed any genetic material belonging to the target – the president – it'd arm, check that there was an actual bit of body there to accept the micro-barb, then spring out, deliver. In a way it's quite old tech, Septame."

"But it would have to have a sample of . . . of the . . ."

"It would need a sample, or rather the *results* of a sample, of Sefoy's genetic material. But you could get that almost anywhere, Septame: from a glass, from one of the president's hairs, from any article of her clothing; you could get that from just having shaken her hand or having brushed her cheek with your own."

"Everyone she's ever met throughout her life would be a first-order suspect," Chekwri told Banstegeyn crisply. She turned to Locuil. "I assume you're already cooperating with the cops?"

Locuil nodded. "Second call her security people made."

"Truth is, though," Chekwri said, "this looks like one of ours."

"You mean the device that was used?" Banstegeyn said.

Chekwri nodded. "We had stuff like this. Once, long ago." She flexed her eyebrows. "Back in what you might call the interesting old days. It was all supposed to have been got rid of, but . . . maybe some of it wasn't. Maybe somebody kept some of it somewhere. Or kept the knowledge and the means to make it."

Banstegeyn looked steadily into Chekwri's eyes as she said this, and the marshal returned his gaze just as levelly.

"Or somebody invented a brand new one," Locuil said. "The fact remains the president is dead. Not to mention her AdC. Not to mention in . . . delicate circumstances. But what really matters is, the president is dead. What's to be done about it?"

"The protocols are clear," Banstegeyn said. He was aware that he looked dreadful; tired, unkempt. That was good. His voice was hollow, flat. He was keeping it that way. "The longest-serving trime becomes acting president, the longest serving-septame becomes an acting trime—"

"Prophet's spit," Chekwri said, almost spluttering. "Int'yom as president, even for six days?" She shook her head.

"Yes," Banstegeyn said, as though not noticing. "And so on down the levels, while a clone of Sefoy Geljemyn is grown, and elections for a new president are set in train."

"That might look a little pointless with the Subliming so close," Chekwri said.

"A vote of the whole parliament would be required to alter the protocols," Banstegeyn said dully, letting the tiredness into his voice. "Eighty per cent approval required for any changes. We'd struggle even to form a quorum with the people we could call back from out-system in time." He shook his head, wiped his eyes. "I think we have to stick to the rules, act as though there will be an election within forty days, even though there won't be one."

"Or in case there is," Locuil said. The septame and the marshal both looked at him. He shrugged. "In case this whole situation – the attack on the Fourteenth, the president being assassinated – leads enough people to want to postpone the Subliming." The other two people in the room continued to stare at him. "Well, it's plausible," he said.

"That would be a catastrophe," Banstegeyn said.

"Would it?" Locuil looked unsure. "Just a postponement. Not a cancellation."

"The septame is concerned that one might turn into the other," Chekwri said.

"Everything has been put in place, everything planned, everything set up and aimed, focused on the one single day of Instigation," Banstegeyn said. "We can't go back." He shook his head. "We go or we don't, but a . . . a postponement? I don't think so."

"Well, you're going to have a lot people wondering who did these things," the physician general said. "The attack on Eshri, the president's assassination. These are big loose ends. People will feel . . . I don't know; dissatisfied, heading off into the Sublime not knowing who had it in for us." He looked from Banstegeyn to Chekwri. "Don't you think?"

"Perhaps Subliming will look like a blessed relief from such worries," the septame suggested. Neither the marshal nor the physician general looked like they were buying this.

"Well," Locuil said, rolling up his screen and putting it back into his jacket pocket, "the first leak was over an hour ago. The news channels are spasming, or frothing, or whatever it is they do. I have a press conference to attend." He stood. "Septame? I'm assuming you'll want to be there too."

Banstegeyn nodded. "Of course, Locuil. Can you give us five minutes? There are developments regarding Eshri and our Scavenger friends that the marshal and I have to discuss. Briefly, though; literally five minutes." The septame glanced at his time-to. "Any longer and feel free to knock on the door. Do you mind?"

"Yes, all right. Five minutes, Banstegeyn," the physician general said, frowning. He left the room; a babble of noise from the various staff members in the ante-room swelled, then subsided.

The septame looked at the marshal for a few moments. She gazed back, then slowly raised her eyebrows. "I'm sorry, Septame, were you expecting me to say something just there?"

Banstegeyn smiled thinly. "No. Good. Right." He clasped his hands on the desk in front of him. "The physician general is right, though."

"I should hope so, on medical matters at least."

"Come on, Chekwri; you know what I mean. On people needing answers. We need to give them answers."

"Do we? What answers?"

"What happened at Eshri, what has just happened here. He's right; people – some people, at least – won't want to go, won't want to Sublime with all this going on, unsolved."

"So we give them a solution?"

"We do." He nodded his head to one side.

They walked across the study, to the short corridor that led to the bathroom and a small private sitting room. Banstegeyn closed the door behind them, shutting them in the two-metre-long corridor, lit by a single light.

"It's very simple," Banstegeyn said. "The Ronte are our fall guys."

Chekwri looked sceptical. "For the prez, too?"

"We say she had found out how they had been threatening us; that Eshri was their first shot, an example of how they would deal with us if we didn't let them have their way. Geljemyn was about to remove preferred Scavenger status from them by presidential decree, so they killed her. We tell them to get out of our space, sling as many as we can find of them here into prison or just ship them out too, and all our problems are solved."

The marshal looked distinctly unconvinced. "They're still a little . . . underdeveloped for convincing bad guys, Septame. In terms of ships they're barely out of rockets and you think you're going to convince people they could do this sort of stuff to us? That's almost as bad as not knowing at all. At least so long as we're in the dark we can pretend it's somebody bigger and badder than us. This . . . just suggests we're weak."

"Blame it on all the ships that have already Sublimed, and hint that the Ronte must have had some higher-tech help."

"Like the Culture?" The marshal's expression was something close to contempt.

"They have helped the Ronte, haven't they?"

"They've given a handful or two of their ships a tiny boost. One ship and an act of charity. Patronising, almost. Hardly a mutual aid pact."

"So, no, we don't try to implicate them. Certainly not directly. Just hint. People will come to their own conclusions. That's all we need. And besides, the Ronte and the Liseiden have backers, mentors; them, perhaps. They might be blamed. You can do this, can't you?"

"Of course I can *do* it, Septame." Chekwri smiled. "I have a whole regimental intelligence service that's developed a fine line in rumour-mongering and story-placing over the last few years, and the ear of every media player you've courted so assiduously over the decades; they will ask the questions we've suggested, they will listen, and they will repeat what we tell them. The issue is whether people believe it. I might even have to seem to oppose you, a little, by speaking up for the fleets – given that I am in charge of the Combined Regimental Fleet Command, after all. They'll expect me to support them, and I'll have to."

"Do whatever it takes," he told her.

"Depend upon it, Septame." The marshal looked at Banstegeyn's time-to, turning her head over to one side to read the upside-down figures and hands on the piece of jewellery adorning his chest. "Our five minutes are almost up," she observed. "Excuse me." She turned, took a step.

"I did what had to be done," he said. "You believe that, don't you?"

He hadn't really meant to say this. Not to her, not to anybody. He was surprising himself here. That wasn't good.

Chekwri turned, looked at him.

"It doesn't matter what I believe, Septame," she told him coolly. "All that matters is what you tell me to do."

He shook his head, gave a half-laugh. "Do you lose any sleep at all over any of this, Chekwri?"

The marshal raised her eyebrows. "I sleep like the drugged, every night, Septame. I'm just a humble military officer obeying orders. Nobody's ordered me to worry. Or to lose sleep."

A bitterness seemed to fill his mouth. "It had to be done," he told her.

"Of course, Septame." Chekwri shrugged. "I never liked her anyway. Pleasant enough, but . . . too weak for the position she held. Too . . . accommodating." Her eyebrows flexed again. "Still, eh? She died in the arms of somebody who really loved her. They both did. That's something. In the circumstances, it's almost kind." She nodded to one side. "I think I can hear the physician general knocking. We'd best go."

"There was one more thing, Septame," Locuil said, as they sat in the back of the aircraft hopping them from the diplomatic quarter to the parliament for the press conference. Chekwri had taken her own flier back to the Home System regimental ground HQ.

"What?" Banstegeyn asked.

"Excuse me," the physician general said, and reached forward to click a switch. The night-dark privacy screen rose silently between them and their respective senior staff members, sitting across from them.

Locuil leaned over, and, very quietly, into Banstegeyn's ear, as the flier levelled out, said, "Ms Orpe was pregnant."

"*What?*" Banstegeyn said.

"Only by about forty days; it would not have shown even at the time of the Subliming."

"Are you—?"

"Entirely sure. No question of doubt."

"But . . . Would she have . . . ? She must have known . . ."

"She certainly would have known. And she was no primitivist in her elective physiology. She had all the standard medically advised augmentations and amendments. The pregnancy must have been deliberate, Septame. It must have been willed."

Banstegeyn stared forward at the dark material covering the privacy panel, then looked away, to the side, out of the dull outward-mirrored windows of the aircraft. He watched the city sliding past. They crossed the river. The lowest tier of the parliament gardens rose walled above the troubled surface of the waves. The first few buildings and pavilions would appear in a moment. What had she been thinking of? What did she think she'd been doing? Had she gone completely mad?

"Why would she—?" he said, then – suddenly realising – stared at the physician general. "Has it – the embryo – has it . . . do you know who . . . ?" He was babbling. This was not him. He pulled himself together. "Has it been . . . analysed?"

"The products of conception have been removed," Locuil said, his voice barely more than a whisper. "Privately, as it were. So that these do not presently form part of the judicial or evidential material held by the security forces. And they have not been analysed. Of course, they would need to be, for the identity of the—"

"It might be best if it was . . . that is, if it . . . it might be for the best for all concerned if it was . . . if all that disappeared."

The physician general sat back, nodded. "I'll see what I can do, Septame."

He thumbed the privacy screen down again.

Banstegeyn felt his stomach lurch. The aircraft began its steep descent.

*

xGSV *Contents May Differ*
  oLOU *Caconym*
  oGCU *Displacement Activity*
  oGSV *Empiricist*
  oGSV *Just The Washing Instruction Chip In Life's Rich Tapestry*
  oUe *Mistake Not . . .*
  oMSV *Passing By And Thought I'd Drop In*
  oMSV *Pressure Drop*
  oLSV *You Call This Clean?*

The avatar of the *Passing By And Thought I'd Drop In* reports that the president of Gzilt, Sefoy Geljemyn, is dead and may have been assassinated.

∞

xLOU *Caconym*

Just looking at the feeds and the official in-system signal streams available, it looks pretty damn certain she was assassinated. One might have expected that our colleague the *Passing By And Thought I'd Drop In* would know and be able to confirm this by its own direct channels, rather than still be speculating like some out-of-the-loop news concern consisting of a couple of dodgy float-cams and a single reporter hopping round their apartment trying to get their pants on and brush their teeth at the same time, while staring goggle-eyed at the breaking news screens of the big boys.

∞

xMSV *Passing By And Thought I'd Drop In*

In a matter of such consequence, I thought it best to take a cautious approach and wait until the exact nature of the president's death had been officially announced by the rightful authorities. The *Caconym* is welcome to take over my role here, if and when it ever arrives in Gzilt.

That will, as I understand it, be some considerable time after the Subliming has taken place, though, doubtless, regardless of how that goes, the *Caconym* will take the opportunity to lecture any Gzilt remaining behind on how they got their whole Subliming strategy wrong anyway.

∞

xGSV *Contents May Differ*
I'm sure this comes as a shock to all of us and we are bound to react to the news in different ways, including blaming ourselves; however, once that is out of the way – and the sooner the better, I'd suggest – the question is going to remain: what can we do now?

∞

xLOU *Caconym*
Might I suggest the *Passing By And Thought I'd Drop In* takes a rather more robust and less respectful attitude to the Gzilt establishment? Treating the Gzilt as slightly eccentric but much-loved relations, worthy of being indulged as we might indulge other elements of ourselves, might be all very well when they are behaving as we might behave; however, when they start wasting Z-R ships, major command and control elements of their own military *and* their head of state, such indulgence starts to look, at best, like blindness born of self-deception.

∞

xMSV *Passing By And Thought I'd Drop In*
I can assure the *Caconym* and the others of the group that in a situation of such import, with the Subliming so close and yet so threatened, and a degree of panic and chaos seeming to infect even the highest echelons of Gzilt society, the last thing I shall be doing is indulging in any "blindness" or "self-deception". I have already begun a more rigorous and assertive overview of the

situation by various different methods and strategies. However, I might remind those who seek to tell me how to perform my task here that in a set of circumstances of such delicacy and sensitivity, being discovered to be behaving in what might be taken by our hosts as an aggressive or even threatening manner might only inflame matters further and make any contribution we may wish and be able to make to the solution of the problem itself problematic. This is not some bunch of lo-techs still struggling with the concept of four-dimensionality; this is an equiv-tech civilisation as old and as capable – point-by-point, if not in overall puissance – as our own and entirely able to prevent, discover and/or deal with the vast majority of any surveillance measures – for example – I might be able to emplace. It is also far from impossible that Gzilt is effectively under attack from outside and needs and expects our support, not our intrusive suspicions.

∞

xLOU *Caconym*

Had the *Passing By And Thought I'd Drop In* been taking a more intrusive and suspicious approach from the start – bugging/hacking/whatevering the relevant players – we would almost certainly *know* by now whether they are under attack from outside or not. And I bet, by the way, that they're not.

∞

xGSV *Contents May Differ*

I'm sure all these points are well made. Perhaps we ought to wait and see what the response of the Gzilt hierarchy itself is to the president's death before we decide what might be done next.

"Our Intelligence agencies have further, ah, determined, that these same people, the Ronte, have been directly responsible or, through their agents and abettors, been indirectly though culpably responsible for both the attack on the, ah, head-quarters of the Fourteenth regiment, on the Fzan-Juym moon of Eshri, Izenion. Izenion system. And the tragic, despicable murder, assassination . . . of President Geljemyn. Also, for attacks on two fleet warships, one at Eshri and another at the planet of Ablation. Excuse me. Ablate. The planet of Ablate, too, was attacked. And so, accordingly, we are resolved to resist the arrival of the Ronte fleet with all force and demand their surrender. Surrender of their agents and representatives, here. Here on, ah, Zyse and elsewhere. Our security forces are already, this day, carrying out the, ah . . . such, ah, actions. Being carried, ah . . . out. Thank you."

The new president and extremely old politician – Trime Int'yom, until a small ceremony in the president's office a few minutes ago – fell silent. He looked uncertain; a small, old man with nervous eyes and skin that had had to repair itself under the light of too many different suns. The first questions were being shouted out by the media people. Acting President Int'yom asked for the first one to be repeated, then held up one hand as he consulted with his staff, four of whom were standing behind him on the podium and looking just as nervy.

"Dear Scribe's piss," Trime Yegres sighed, turning to Banstegeyn with his hand partially covering his mouth. "Gets the Ablate thing wrong twice and then barely remembers the name of the planet he's fucking standing on. Worthy successor, eh?"

The septame nodded, after a moment.

Yegres frowned. "You all right, Banstegeyn?"

"Just . . . shocked, Yegres," he said. He looked at the mass of cameras, in case any were aimed at him. At least, in here, only hand-helds were allowed and you were free from the threat of a float-cam poking a lens up your nose. One or two cameras might have been trained on him and Yegres. He kept his blank, shocked, almost uncomprehending look going, gazed downwards again.

"You, shocked?" Yegres sounded surprised. "Whatever next?"

"Who knows whatever next?" Banstegeyn said.

Yegres sighed. "This is very early for this sort of thing. I didn't even manage breakfast. Too much to expect assassins to show more tact, I suppose. My belly's empty as the new president's head." Yegres exhaled loudly. "And the old one's, from the rumours of what the poison did to her. And that lovely girl, her AdC . . . Orpe, wasn't it?"

Banstegeyn nodded. Yegres looked at the septame, leaned in towards him and put his hand over his mouth again. "Always thought she might be a bit keen on you, you know. Was that . . . was I . . .?"

"Septame," a voice said from the other side of Banstegeyn, as the avatar of the *Passing By And Thought I'd Drop In* appeared suddenly. Banstegeyn took a deep breath. He'd have sworn the silver-skinned creature could slide through spaces it shouldn't have been able to, insinuating itself through a press of bodies almost as though they weren't there. Still, at least now he had an excuse not to answer Yegres. "We are *deeply* sorry," Ziborlun continued, speaking very quiet and close to his ear, "to hear of the death of President Geljemyn and wish to extend both our sympathies and an offer of help – any help at all – to the Gzilt people. I do hope you and I can talk further, soon. I may have information that I can share only with you. Thank you,

Septame," the creature touched him once on the forearm, slipped away again.

Yegres leaned out, looking across Banstegeyn. "I assume that was condolences," he muttered, "but it looked more like a betting tip."

". . . It is not known, at this moment in time," the acting president was saying, "precisely and exactly who is responsible, beyond a . . . a reasonable belief that the Ronte, and their, ah, their agents and their, ah, abettors are, ahm, behind whoever that person or persons might be. So. There we are. Yes. You. What?"

Banstegeyn sighed. "How did this moron get to be a trime? Or a degan? Or a thirty-second, for that matter?"

Yegres cleared his throat. "You promoted him, old son."

The septame stared at the older man. "What?" he whispered.

Yegres shrugged. "Oh, every available opportunity, maestro; gave him a helping hand whenever people wanted to kick him upstairs, which was often. Eventually you kicked him up above yourself, made the old duffer a trime." Yegres looked at him blearily. "Fuck me, Banners, you're not starting to forget which useful dipsticks you've supported over the years because they'll always agree with you, are you? Prophet's piss, you'll be forgetting me next." He shook his head, glanced at his time-to and muttered, "Wonder if the bars are serving yet . . ."

"This is much more satisfactory," Team Principal Tyun told Cultural Mission Director Keril. Jelwilin Keril had been invited back aboard the Liseiden flagship, the Collective Purposes vessel *Gellemtyan-Asool-Anafawaya*, to be congratulated for whatever part he might have played in the recent turn-around in the fortunes of the Liseiden.

Keril floated in his transparent bubble within the ship's command space, a genuine smile anchored on his face. He was sure that this expression, even if it was first-principles meaningless to the Liseiden – indeed, even if it was by some misfortune first-principles threatening to the Liseiden – would be suitably translated by the aquatic creatures' AIs and its happy import transmitted to the Liseiden officers.

"I am very glad, sir, that your faith in me – and my faith, in turn, in Ambassador Mierbeunes – has turned out not to be misplaced. We are your faithful agents and servants, Team Principal, and are glad to have been able to fulfil this part of the mission we undertook for you."

"Sir, is it true the Culture are suspected of having helped the Ronte?"

"I . . . Well, I'm not, that is, ah . . ." the acting president said, with the glazed look of somebody listening to something being said on their earbud. He raised one hand and appeared to be about to press his earbud further into his ear, then seemed to change his mind. "Excuse me." The acting president turned and consulted his staff. He turned to face the front again. "Well," he said. "There are rumours, apparently. Ah. There has been help of one ship, Culture ship, helping the fleet that has been approaching Gzilt. It is just one ship, and I'm sure our own fleets, own ships are entirely, ah, capable."

"Sir, what about the GSV *Passing By And Thought I'd Drop In*, and the other Culture warships now stationed directly over Zyse itself?"

"Well, I can't, I don't . . . Excuse me," he said, turning away again.

The screen cut to a different view, going back to the mass of media people again and zooming in on somebody shouting, "Sir, could this delay the Subliming?" while the acting president was talking urgently with his advisors.

Somebody else shouted out, "Sir, will you be putting yourself forward as a candidate, and will there even be an election?" and yet another person yelled, "Has President Geljemyn's back-up been woken up yet?" After that, more shouting made it difficult to hear individual questions.

Berdle, sitting beside an open-mouthed Cossont, looked at her and said, "Well, this is interesting."

Cossont, not long woken, dressed in a loose, voluminous robe, just stared at the screen. "The president's *dead*?" she said.

"No," Berdle told her, "that's the new one." The avatar nodded at the old man on the screen. "Seems to work a bit like having a king; there always is one, no matter how many you bump off. Until you have a revolution or something."

"She's *dead*?" Cossont repeated.

"President Geljemyn is no more," Berdle agreed. "And we – the Culture – appear to be in the frame somehow. That seems a bit unfair."

"I liked President Geljemyn," Pyan said, draping itself round Cossont's shoulders. "She had a nice smile. Who is this old person again?"

"New president," Berdle told it. "Acting President Int'yom."

"I see. No, he hasn't got such a nice smile."

"You're right," Berdle said. "He hasn't, has he?"

"No! He just *hasn't*, has he? It's just not there for him."

"I *know*," Berdle agreed, smiling.

Cossont looked from the screen to Berdle. "What the *fuck* is going on?"

The avatar shrugged, looked serious. "Long story. Power struggle, I suppose. Though that seems a little pointless, if everybody's going to Sublime soon anyway. Though they might not be, now." Berdle looked at Cossont. "And whether they do or not might come down to what happens when we get back to Xown and the Girdlecity, in about three days." The avatar assumed a look of some thoughtfulness. "Bit of a responsibility, really."

Cossont shook her head, looked back at the screen. "Oh, *fuck . . .*"

"'Rescinded'! What can be 'rescinded'? We had an agreement! We have done nothing! What have we done? Tell us what we have done! Prove anything!"

The individuals of the Ronte delegation were being dragged, inert, out of the adapted house in the diplomatic quarter that had been their home. As many media trucks were present as security vehicles.

The individual Rontes in their exo-suits had been covered in grapple nets by the security para-militaries after being effector-stunned in the early morning raid. The nets were supposed to disable their exo-suits and leave only basic life-support working, but while the aliens and their suits themselves were just dead weights being hauled out across the garden to the waiting police fliers, some sort of float-cam or drone device controlled by the aliens was still functioning, hovering over the scene and dodging attempts to shoot it by the security people.

"This is a diplomatic mission! On what authority do you—?" A small Gzilt security drone succeeded in landing a bore charge on the Ronte device, which jerked, went silent, then fell trailing smoke to the ground and thudded into a flowerbed.

The last exo-suited Ronte was bumped and dragged into the security flier. The ramp closed and the craft took off.

"I am standing here with Ambassador Mierbeunes of the Liseiden," a reporter said to a float-cam. "Ambassador

Mierbeunes, are you surprised to find the Ronte being treated in this way, while your own clients have been declared the new allies of the Gzilt?"

"Well, while I entirely understand the many and various pressures which are brought to bear on an alien delegation of this nature . . ."

"Has the Culture helped the Ronte or not?"

"Yes. Specifically, one of our ships helped a squadron of twelve of their vessels get from where they were to the Gzilt system outskirts. They've since turned about."

"Twelve ships? Is this an invasion force?"

"Hardly, Mr . . . Kresele, isn't it? No, their ships and weapons are quite primitive. Check the specs; freely available. And why would the Culture be helping anybody invade anybody else, let alone help anybody invade the Gzilt, who have been our friends for millennia? And why would anybody invade a people about to Sublime in the first place? Come now; at least try to make sense here. Yes, ma'am. Ms Aouse, isn't it?"

"Yes. Hi. Have you helped the Ronte in any other way?"

"Certainly not, as far as I know. And I would have been told."

"So you could have been helping them."

"To do what? Destroy the Fourteenth's HQ? That's ridiculous. That was not them. And it certainly wasn't us."

"Who do you think was responsible, then?"

"I don't know. But it's more likely that one of your own ships gone rogue, rather than the Ronte or the Culture, destroyed the Fzan-Juym, and I leave it to you to judge how absurd a proposition that is."

"Ziborlun! Was the Culture ship working in league with the Ronte acting on orders, and, if so, whose?"

"Oh. So we've gone from 'helping' to 'working in league with', have we? I see. The ship – the *Beats Working*, a tiny ship with a crew of five humans – had no orders. It still has no orders. It was doing what it and its crew thought was the right thing, at all points, including when it offered to help the Ronte get here faster. And at that stage, let's not forget, the Ronte still thought you were their friends and, apart from anything else, wanted to get here in time to help celebrate the Subliming."

"Somebody must have issued the orders."

"No, they didn't. There were no orders. You have much work to do, Mr Diria, understanding how the Culture works. Yes, ma'am. Ms Zige, isn't it?"

"Has the Culture been spying on Gzilt?"

"If we have, obviously not enough, because we seem to be as confused as everybody else about what the hell is going on here. Yes; gentleman at the back."

"Who's that smart-arse?" Cossont asked, scowling at the screen from within the heavy robe. "Looks like a ship's avatar."

"That's right," Berdle said. "Ziborlun. The avatar of the MSV *Passing By And Thought I'd Drop In*." Berdle seemed to hesitate, then said, "Ah. I don't think you're going to like this."

"What?" she said.

The image switched to yet another press conference and a senior policeman flanked by two First Regiment Intelligence and Security officers. Somebody's face was shown on an insert on the screen. Cossont knew she knew the person for about half a second before she realised; it was her own face. "We would be very interested in interviewing Ms Cossont," the head cop was saying. "And, yes, she is a contributory suspect in the matter of the destruction of the regimental headquarters of the Fourteenth Regiment, on Eshri."

"*WHAT*?" Cossont yelled, jumping to her feet. Pyan had to hang on tight to stay round her shoulders.

"Told you you wouldn't like it," Berdle said.

"Oh, Vyr, are you an *outlaw*?" Pyan said, sounding excited.

"But I haven't *done* anything!" Cossont shouted.

Berdle looked at her, head tipped. "My, you really are naive, aren't you?"

The ship dance of triumph that had been "The Approaching Eclipsing of One Sun by Another" was abandoned in mid-final formation. On confirmation of the humanoid treachery, all ships somersaulted about, went to full power and simultaneously began a maximally tight zooming loop, twisting as they turned so that at all points throughout the manoeuvre their drives were presented towards their earlier destination, the planet Zyse in the system of Gzilt.

The drone Jonsker Ap-Candrechenat, representative of the Culture ship *Beats Working*, was accepted again within the command space of the Interstitial/Exploratory vessel *Melancholia Enshrines All Triumph* – arriving by the quicker though most alarming method of Displacement – and made a show of prostrating itself before the Swarmprince and Sub-Corporation Divisional Head.

Ossebri 17 Haldesib regarded the Culture machine for some time before saying, "Device, there are those amongst my officers who would have us attack you, believing you to have been complicit in a deception upon us. They believe that you were both leading and hurrying us into a trap, and that, as such, neither you nor your ship should be suffered to live."

"If the Swarmprince so desires, I shall absent myself immediately, return to my ship and depart along with it. The

478   IAIN M. BANKS

Swarmprince should know, however, that we have engaged
in no such deception at any point, and have at all times done
all we could to cooperate with and to aid the Ronte fleet
and squadron. Had we been engaged in any plot to deliver
the squadron to a place of jeopardy, all those complicit would
surely have brought the squadron further into the Gzilt
system, where the threat to it would have been by that
measure enhanced, before the trap was sprung, instead of
timing matters such that the squadron has – happily – had
time to deflect from its earlier course and instigate its current
re-disposition."

"'Deflect from its earlier course and instigate its current
re-disposition'," Ossebri 17 Haldesib quoted. "Does the
Culture machine possess any other especially pretty ways of
saying 'run away' or 'escape like a shamed, pursued prey'?"

"Swarmprince, we attempt to respect your customs and
protocols and the ways that you express yourselves. If I fail
to do so as well as I might, I apologise. Yes, we are running
away. I run with you, being determined to stay with the
squadron and fleet for as long as you wish me to. The instant
you wish me gone, I shall be."

"You say you respect us, yet you ignore my earlier threat
to attack you. Is that not an insult, even if disguised by
ignorance?"

"It is not, Swarmprince. It reflects my belief that I personally would probably be able to frustrate any attempt by
you to harm, disable or imprison me, and that the *Beats
Working* would similarly be able to escape unharmed should
any hostile act be directed at it. We could, of course, be
wrong on both counts, but we think not. To accept what
we regard as this truth only reinforces our desire not to
dwell on the unpleasantness of threats delivered by those
who were so recently friends, whom we still value, and

whom we hope will swiftly accept us as true and trustworthy friends again."

"Then kindly leave us, both personally and in the shape
of your ship. We shall make our own way to a place of
safety. If what you claim is true and you meant us no harm
by delivering us so expeditiously into the jaws of our enemies,
you may accept our apologies. If not, then know that the
Ronte make implacable foes, and the memory of a betrayal
against one group becomes part of the memory of all. You
are dismissed."

"May I—?"

"Whatever it is, you may not. I said you are dismissed.
Go."

The Culture machine dipped its front portion in what was
supposed to be taken as a respectful bow, then the whole
machine was enveloped by a silvery sphere of fields beyond
the ken of the most sophisticated analytical devices the
Collective Purposes vessel possessed, the sphere shrank to
a point and disappeared, and the machine was gone.

The Navigation and Targeting team reported that the
Culture ship began to depart in the same instant, pulling
slowly away and then, effectively, disappearing.

"A signal from the Culture ship, sir," the communications
officer said. "From the drone Jonsker Ap-Candrechenat."

"Show."

The drone appeared on screen.

"Swarmprince," the drone said, "my apologies for intruding
again so immediately; however, what I wished to say and still
have to say is important: a five-ship formation of Gzilt war-
craft including one capital ship has left Zyse, heading in your
direction. Our initial simulations indicate that they intend to
make a show of force and be seen to be seeing you off, rather
than intending to offer battle. We believe similar though

smaller Gzilt formations have been disposed to carry out similar actions wherever else Ronte forces have been en route to their destinations.

"Of more concern for your own squadron are two forces of Liseiden ships, both consisting of four vessels, each at least as heavily armed as your squadron flagship. These are believed to be converging on your entry point into the Gzilt system. The *Beats Working* continues to pull away but remains at your disposal and will respond as quickly as possible to any signal from you. Thank you and good luck."

The screen blanked out.

"Signal all squadrons and elements to turn about," Swarmprince Ossebri 17 Haldesib said. "Have them find places of safety according to existing fleet orders and prioritise eluding Liseiden units over those of the Gzilt and the Culture, though all are to be avoided, in that order. Senior Navigation Officer, you and I shall submit our codes to the AI to unlock our own sealed orders."

"Sir."

The sealed orders indicated that in the event of an emergency of the type now facing them, the squadron should make its way to the nearby system of Vatrelles, five days distant at full speed, to await further instructions.

The Swarmprince issued the appropriate orders, then turned to his communications officer. "Signal the Culture ship that it may remain at its current distance from us if it wishes. We may have need of it yet. Convene a full consultation with all senior officers, AIs and expert systems."

Twenty

(S -3)

The General Systems Vehicle *Empiricist* felt it was arriving in Gzilt at a bad time – a bad time that was meant to be the start of a (brief) good time, a momentous and celebrated time but which had somehow gone wrong. Well, in the end, there was no helping this. Sometimes you just had to adopt the attitude summed up by, *Too bad*.

The ship was about as big as standard Culture vessels ever got; a System-class that had beefed up over the decades and centuries for what had always seemed like sound operational reasons at the time until it had become one of the most impressively large, commodious and populated examples of the class that was already the most impressively large, commodious and populated the Culture possessed.

The design of the System-class made such self-augmentation easy; the ships had no single outer hull surrounding their hundreds of individual components, just colossal bubbles of air held in place by field enclosures. Adding new, self-manufactured bits was so simple it was, for some ships at least, apparently, tantamount to compulsory, and it was only a sort of residual decorousness and a wish not to be seen as too self-indulgently ostentatious that prevented certain System-class vessels from going expansion-mad and growing to the size of planets, or at least moons. That sort of indulged obsessiveness was what simming and strong VR was for; you could convincingly imagine yourself being any ludicrous size without actually committing to such mono-mania in reality.

Doing away with a physical hull – or treating the exterior of every component as a hull, depending on how you looked at it – had been no great leap for GSVs. Ships thought of their multiple-layer field-complex enclosures as their true hulls anyway. That was where all the important stuff happened in relation to the outside: that was where the sensory fields were, where any stray impacts were absorbed, where concentric layers of shielding tuned to various parts of the electro-magnetic spectrum lurked, where holes could be opened to allow smaller units, modules and ships to enter and depart, and – especially in the case of the larger vessels – where atmospheric pressure was kept in, and sun-lines could be formed and controlled to provide light for any parkland carried on the top of the ship's solid hull.

Frankly the material bit inside was just there to provide a sort of neat wrapping for all the truly internal bits and pieces like accommodation and social spaces.

Comfortably over two hundred kilometres long even by the most conservative of measurement regimes, fabulously, ellipsoidally rotund, dazzling with multiple sun-lines and tiny artificial stars providing illumination for motley steps and levels and layers of riotous vegetation – belonging, strictly speaking, on thousands of different worlds spread across the galaxy – boasting hundreds of contrasting landscapes from the most mathematically manicured to the most (seemingly) pristinely, savagely wild, all contained on slab-storeys of components generally kilometres high, each stratified within one of a dozen stacked atmospheric gradients, the ship's cosseted internals were riddled, woven and saturated with domesticated, tamed and semi-wild life in hundreds of thousands of smaller enclosed habitats, while its buzzing, external, bewilderingly complex archi-geographic lines were made fuzzy, imprecisely seen by near-uncountable numbers of craft moving within that vast, elongated bubble of air – from smaller classes of GSV through other ships, modules, shuttles and aircraft all the way down to individual humans in float-harnesses, single drones and even smaller machines, as well as thousands of species of winged and lighter-than-air bio-creatures – the *Empiricist* was, in sum, home to hundreds of billions of animals and over thirteen billion humans and drones.

The people of the Culture, better than ninety-five per cent of them housed across the vast, distributed bucolic hinterland of the Orbitals, scattered throughout the civilised galaxy like a million glowing bracelets, were used to thinking of the GSVs as being their true mega-cities – albeit determinedly highly mobile, high-speed mega-cities – but GSVs like the *Empiricist* were on another level and of another order entirely; they held the populations of worlds, of entire inhabited stellar systems. Zyse, the Gzilt home planet and the giant GSV's destination, held over three billion people. The whole of the Gzilt system added another twenty billion, in part-habiformed worlds and moons, microrbitals and other habitats. The *Empiricist* arriving was like another half a solar system of people being added, like another four mature, substantial planets' worth of souls suddenly coming to visit.

Preceded by a ceremonial screen of smaller craft – including a couple of GSVs, each home to many millions – the gradually slowing *Empiricist* first met with a couple of Gzilt navy ships – effectively sweeping the two cruisers up with it as it proceeded resplendently past the rendezvous point – then, as it slowed still further, gradually attracted hundreds of civilian welcoming craft too.

Had not so many locals been Stored – and had all been well within the Gzilt body politic – it supposed it might have attracted thousands. The ship's septet of semi-independent Minds became graciously, easily busy with welcoming signals and media requests.

The *Empiricist* approached and then inserted itself into a specially cleared orbital band high over Zyse. It had started slowing almost a day earlier; now it was down to the sort of velocity required for a stately orbit of the world every couple of hours, allowing plenty of time for people on the ground to look up and see it gliding smoothly, glitteringly, statuesquely overhead, and reducing the time it would take to ferry people to and from the planetary surface.

∞

xGSV *Empiricist*
  oLOU *Caconym*
  oGSV *Contents May Differ*
  oGCU *Displacement Activity*
  oGSV *Just The Washing Instruction Chip In Life's Rich Tapestry*

oUe *Mistake Not . . .*
oMSV *Passing By And Thought I'd Drop In*
oMSV *Pressure Drop*
oLSV *You Call This Clean?*

Arrived over Zyse. Good to be here, finally. Mostly. Been thinking; going to keep my two Delinquents, *Headcrash* and *Xenocrat*, close by. They are conveniently hereabouts, after all, and the political atmosphere locally does seem a little . . . odd. Well, poisonous, to be blunt. How was this allowed to develop?

∞

xMSV *Passing By And Thought I'd Drop In*
Welcome. Yes, we might have wished for better. Everything's in the signal streams, of course, but soaking in all the local comms and media traffic of the last twenty-few days is definitely recommended. Worth setting one Mind on that alone, if I may make so bold. My network of sats and such is at your disposal, though of course you may wish to emplace your own. I'd be as happy to advise as to leave you to your own devices.

Are you really so worried regarding the current situation to feel the Delinquents must remain as close guards? I think I speak for the group when I say we were hoping those and more might be available for further use in the current emergency while your own safety might be ensured with your doubtless many other assets.

∞

Let's see how things develop over the next couple of days. For now I'd feel safer with the Delinquents as part of my general defensive mix. I did have to leave some offensive units behind to mop up at Loliscombana. I'm building to replace, but that'll take time.

∞

xLOU *Caconym*
oMSV *Pressure Drop*

What's that big fuck playing at? The next few days are the crucial ones; the *only* ones. We might need those ships *now*.

∞

  It's being cautious and protecting a pop of umpteen bill. When you carry around that sort of responsibility you can't help but become ultra careful. Mostly these big ships pursue a no-risks-whatever policy; I'm mildly surprised it deigned to visit Gzilt at all given the recent excitements.

∞

That's the trouble with ships that size; too big to risk, and also, therefore, to be effective. Terribly impressive, and if all the bios plonk down to Zyse and walk around they can surely make the place look busy for the first time in years, but so what? Couldn't be more of a liability if it had hauled a train of Orbitals behind it and parked them in the local asteroid belt. Anyway, what does that leave us with? The *Mistake Not . . .* is about to hit Xown – again – and the *Passing By . . .*'s two Thugs are keeping remarkably quiet. Wasn't one meant to be shadowing the Liseiden?

∞

  Allegedly. Sending a private request for a public statement; we do kind of need a general update now the big-but-plugged gun has arrived . . . nope; the *Passing By . . .* wishes to remain reticent on the subject. Bet the new boy asks. Anyway, back to listening. Worshipful listening, as I don't doubt it will be interpreted . . .

The reception was muted due to the recent death of the president, but was, nevertheless, still quite entirely splendid.

The enormous central Receiving Hall of the parliament's Upper Chamber had been trimmed everywhere in mourning red, the towering mirror panels reflecting a seeming infinitude of scarlet corridors leading in every horizontal direction.

"Place looks rather good like this," Yegres said, nodding over his glass at the huge central scoop of red marking the covered chandelier cluster hanging from the centre of the space. "We should have lost presidents more often."

"It's a little late, though, isn't it?" Banstegeyn replied.

"Everything is," Yegres agreed. "Oh," he said, catching sight of seven tall figures moving liquidly through the crowd on the main floor. "Oh well, here come the relations. I'd better leave you to your ceremonial solitariness." He chucked back his drink, hitched up his long robes and stepped down from the dais.

The septame watched the arrow-shaped mass of avatars and their hangers-on move towards him, like something aimed. "Solitude," he said, to himself rather than really to Yegres, who was too far away and submerged in the crowd of people behind. "Solitude, not solitariness." Of course, he was careful not to move his lips, in case.

Banstegeyn greeted the seven tall, silver-skinned creatures with all the dignity and politeness he could muster. Solemnity, too, though really it was easy to be solemn; it was the dignity and politeness he was having problems with.

Having dreamt of Orpe on consecutive nights, he'd used the relevant implants to stop himself dreaming over the last two, and had slept well, but now he was starting to feel that he had only displaced the problem, for he had the annoying, irrational and even very slightly frightening feeling– even though he was entirely awake and apparently well rested – that Orpe was just out of sight, just beyond the corner of his eye. It was disconcerting, troubling.

He most certainly did not believe in ghosts or any such nonsense, but – when it happened, catching him out, when he thought he glimpsed her, or thought he'd just missed seeing her, a moment earlier, just as he turned his head or blinked – he felt as terrified as he imagined people must have felt in the old days, when they had been superstitious. He knew it was his own mind, his own brain, acting against him, betraying him, deliberately troubling him, but it *felt* like something other, something supernatural, uncanny.

On a few occasions over the last few days he'd wanted just to scream, for no good reason. Especially at formal ceremonial events when it would have been absolutely the worst, most shocking and disrespectful thing to do. So many aliens arriving, so many different forms and types of creature, so many in exo-suits or things like tiny spacecraft it was like welcoming the contents of a toy cupboard, scaled for giants. How were you supposed to keep a straight face? That was when he most wanted to do it: to laugh hysterically in their faces or scream and shout and swear and thrash about on the floor and tear his hair out . . .

But: just a few more days. A few more days and it would all be over. They could all go to the happy land of good and plenty and never need to bother with horrible, messy, painful real life again.

He couldn't wait. It was the only thing keeping him together.

"Please," he said, smiling too broadly as he half turned to indicate the way through the variously smiling, grinning, tight-faced dignitaries behind him to the scarcely smaller and even more sumptuous room where President Int'yom waited – enthroned, enrobed, befuddled. "This way, please. The president is impatient to meet you."

"Thank you," the leading avatar said. The seven looked

identical: tall, straight, dressed plainly but elegantly and their expressions radiating a kind of severe serenity. At their rear, Ziborlun, the Culture avatar the court had become used to, looked small, plain and homely in comparison.

Just as Banstegeyn turned more fully, to walk ahead of the Culture avatars, he caught a glimpse of – but, no, of course, it wasn't really her at all.

A civilian, she hadn't been backed-up; one of those who believed life was lived all the more sweetly and more sensibly for knowing there was no second chance, while understanding, without ever really needing to think about it, that a society as sophisticated and mature as that of Gzilt made sudden accidental death almost unheard of anyway. So, it wasn't her, and it would never be her.

And only three days to go anyway, he told himself again, so it didn't really matter. He stumbled slightly as he walked in front of the silver creatures to the opening doors of the presidential chamber. He wondered who would have noticed.

Only three more days.

He walked into the hundreds-strong swirl of bizarrely accoutred aliens and milling, red-clad people thronging the presidential chamber.

"Septame, a word?" Marshal Chekwri said, touching him on one elbow to draw him slightly aside from the crowds surrounding the dais where the acting president was greeting the avatars.

"Of course, Chekwri, but I am busy."

"As ever. However. Two things. First: the ships we had see off the Ronte reckon they're heading for Vatrelles. I thought we might let that leak to our new allies the Liseiden."

"What? Why?"

"Distraction. Something to fill the news, and, if they

quarrel, then perhaps another reason to leave this squabbling reality behind, no? Reinforcement."

"Yes, yes, all right. Is that all?"

"No. I did say two things. Some pleasant news."

"Always welcome. What is it?" The marshal's staffers and his own, headed by Solbli and Jevan, had created a space around them so they could talk with a degree of privacy.

Chekwri brought her mouth close to his ear. "We have a major asset in place somewhere it might come in useful."

"Do we? That's good. What, and where?"

"Where, is Xown. What, is the returned *Churkun*. It was off for a while there, thinking about Subliming early following the event at Ablate, but in the end it didn't make the leap; wants to go with everybody else – isn't that nice? – so reported to me, happily – always worth covering such possibilities in standing orders – and asked if it could be of use. So I sent it to Xown, because that was the last place the Culture ship and the absconded Ms Cossont seemed to be interested in." The marshal drew back a little, winked at him. Winked! Had she done this before? Was this some new thing, some fresh loosening of behaviour and discipline ahead of the so-near-now Subliming? "The simulations backed me up, but it was my idea first. Always good to be proved right. Isn't it, Septame?"

"Always," he agreed.

"And I think this time we go in full force, gloves off, maximum strength, if called for, don't you?"

"Yes, yes, whatever you think fit."

"Splendid. So we have a fully equipped, committedly one-of-us combat-hardened battleship ready and waiting at Xown, and that is a very good, a particularly good thing, Septame. May I tell you why?"

"Yes, Chekwri, why don't you tell me why?"

"Because it has just reported that something fast – both

coming in quick and braking very hard indeed – has just about hauled to a stop at Xown, and it's almost certainly going to be the Culture ship."

Colonel Agansu, still undergoing treatments he had come to regard as meaning he was under repair – rather than representing anything as biological as healing – had a dilemma.

"Colonel, the regs are clear. You need to update your avatar down on Xown. It's been plugging along there patiently keeping pace with the airship for nearly ten days but now there's a distinct likelihood it's going to be put in harm's way and it needs to have every advantage we can give it."

"I am aware of that, Captain," Agansu said. "Thank you."

The colonel had been badly injured in the battle at the Incast facility on the Bokri Orbital. The Culture creature – the ship's avatar – had succeeded not only in destroying the combat arbite Uhtryn through the illegal use of anti-matter weaponry within an enclosed civilian space, but had then somehow turned his own weaponry against him, turning a large portion of its own body into a perfectly reflective dish that had bounced his laser pulse straight back at him, crippling both his suit and his body, sending him plunging down the elevator shaft with little or no AG left.

He could still hear his own screams, loud inside his helmet, as he fell, blinded, burning, baked, both legs and one arm shattered, into the shaft, to land with a terrible crushing crash on top of the already wrecked elevator car at the bottom. He'd blacked out then, or the suit helmet's remaining medical functions had put him mercifully under, but he could still hear that raw, inhuman scream in his ears and feel the awful smacking thud of impact, cracking open the suit, splintering his bones and breaking his back.

The suit – its helmet – had saved him. Then the *Uagren* had, too: bringing him back on board, placing him in its medical facility, gently peeling away and removing the blackened, bubbled remains of the suit and slicing away the burned, roasted skin and flesh where it was beyond reusing before it had – coaxingly, almost lovingly – started to knit his bones, repair and regrow his torn, battered organs, and nurture where possible and replace where necessary his bruised, assaulted flesh.

It was a process that was still ongoing. Agansu was many days away from being physically whole again, and would still be largely dependent on the ship when the Subliming happened in three days' time – assuming, of course, that it was still going to take place on schedule.

In its own way, though, even knowing that this body's part in matters was over was itself a kind of comfort. It meant that – having given his all, having been so nearly killed in honourable combat – now he didn't have to leave the healing comfort of the ship again, and could decide at the time whether to Sublime with the *Uagren* and its crew, or not. If not, then he would be left by himself in a medically enabled minor craft, to be delivered to whatever might be left of his regiment, or indeed his civilisation, after the Instigation and the great Enfolding.

But he might go, with everybody, after all. He was thinking of changing his mind, of Subliming despite his earlier decision and still-existing fears. Coming so close to death on Bokri – even while knowing that an earlier, backed-up version of him might be re-wakened somewhere – had been salutary, and had made him think again about his attitude to death, oblivion and the whole issue of Subliming. Also, he had in some way come to feel part of the *Uagren*, and at one with its crew. He liked the idea of Outloading with these already semi-virtualised people. Assuming, of course, that they felt the same way. He worried that he still seemed like an interloper to them; perhaps even a foreign body, an irritant. He was nervous about broaching the subject.

In the meantime, there was the issue of having to update the customised bio-plausible android which the ship had left inside the Girdlecity of Xown when it had set off in pursuit of the Culture ship, nearly ten days earlier. The *Uagren* was on its way back to Xown, but – unable to maintain the kind of speeds it had on that dash, due to engine field degradation – it was doing so at a comfortable cruise rather than a sprint, and would arrive at Xown a full day after the Culture vessel.

It could still transmit the colonel's mind-state ahead and have this new, post-Bokri version integrated into the one that had been left behind, but Agansu had to admit he had been resisting the process, using as his excuse the idea that the longer they waited, the longer he would have to think about what had happened within the Incast facility and learn whatever lessons could be learned from the experience, before transmitting.

The truth was that he was reluctant to hand over to the android left behind on Xown because he was jealous; the android would become the new him, and it – not he – would have the next set of experiences. It would be the one, the version of him that would have the opportunity to engage with the enemy and defeat the Culture ship's avatar. It did not seem fair; *he* wanted to be the victor; *this* version, the original, from-birth Cagad Agansu, colonel of the First, the Home System regiment, and not some quickly customised android formed from a blank the ship had been holding probably since it was first built.

He knew – of course he did – that the android represented a version of him, that it would think of itself as fully being him, but that was beside the point. The action would all happen away from him, and the person, the entity involved, would not be him; he would be lying here, still being carried towards whatever would happen in the Girdlecity, on Xown. Perhaps the experiences the android had could be re-integrated back into his own memory. That was possible, but it didn't always work – it seemed to depend on how extreme and traumatic the experiences had been – but even then, he would always know that in a sense it hadn't really been him there, at the front, at the tip of the spear.

"Colonel?" the captain said, talking to him across the virtual bridge of the ship, where he sat to one side of the arc of officers arranged around their welter of screens, read-outs and controls.

"Yes, Captain," he said. "I think I'm ready. There are no more lessons to be drawn. Please carry out the procedure."

The captain nodded to the data/comms officers. "Proceed."

Agansu seemed to fade away for a moment, and was briefly aware of not being on any sort of virtual bridge at all, but being a broken body, still under repair, held deep in the bowels of the ship, as it read his mind, sorted and arranged the resulting data and encrypted it for transmission ahead to the android waiting on Xown.

"Welcome back," the captain said, smiling, as though, Agansu felt, he was a lone bio who had needed to leave the bridge to obey a call of nature. "And to good news."

"Yes, Captain?"

"We have big guns at Xown," the captain announced. "A capital ship, also reporting to Marshal Chekwri, so on our side no matter how narrowly that's defined." The captain smiled thinly. "And it's already dealing with some of the shit the Culture craft left behind."

The suite of materiel and general sensory assetry the *Mistake Not . . .* had left behind at Xown mostly reported back to a satellite which stowed to about the size of a human fist. Fully deployed, with finer-than-hair-thin tendrils extending tens of kilometres away from it in its geosynchronous orbit, it watched something big and probably military approaching Xown across the skein of space. It was also aware of every piece of free-floating hardware in the system being pinged with signals asking them to identify themselves. This was a bad sign.

It reported this to the also approaching but more distant *Mistake Not . . .* and was told to shut down to passive-minimum awareness. It did so, but it was still found, jolted with a tiny but abrupt gravity gradient that first illuminated it in passing and swept on, then returned, pulsed, and almost immediately plunged it into its own steep, sharp hole in space-time. Its last act was to destruct as chaotically and messily as possible, depriving any focused analytical equipment of the chance to determine much about it at all.

On Xown, scattered about the part of Girdlecity where the airship *Equatorial 353* was moving slowly towards the place it had set off from five years earlier, dozens of tiny bits and pieces of Culture hardware started dropping out of the sky, falling to the floor or tumbling clicking and clacking through the vast piped spaces of the construction. Some burned, or fused, or just glowed, destructing as best they could. Some just had to accept deactivation and likely capture.

A very small number, where able, closed down, closed off or better still ejected all their conventionally discoverable hardware processing and shifted down to back-up bio or atomechanical systems. Even those were vulnerable, through basic triangulation on their last recorded position in the network, as recorded by the compromised components unable to wipe their memories in time, and most succumbed; snapped away by disloc, knocked out of the air with close-range effector weapons or frazzled in mid-flight as they tried to escape by pinpoint bursts of plasma fire like miniature daytime fireworks.

The airship *Equatorial 353*, home of the Last Party, had built up a following of several hundred people over the last few days as it and Gzilt society in general approached the culmination of their respective journeys; however, only a few people noticed any of this small-scale destructive activity, and even they dismissed it as just more random chaotic irrelevance, symptomatic of these final days.

One small device, which had looked like a four-winged insect from the start, suddenly realised that it was probably all that remained of the components the ship had left behind. It sat on the snout of the airship, perched clinging to a thin stanchion supporting a long, dangling, trailing banner, and watched through impersonated compound eyes as another component, a thumb-sized scout missile, plummeted from on high, falling minutely past the bulbous nose of the slowly advancing airship, unwinding a twisting thread of grey smoke as it fell, unseen by any human eye. It disappeared into the dark depths of the huge open-work tunnel beneath.

Some seconds later the giant airship bulged its way through the volume of air the little device had fallen through. The artificial insect detected a faint, disappearing trace-scent of the scout missile's descent.

The insect considered its instructions in the event of such eventualities, waited for a time, then lifted off, buzzing away on a long falling curve, building in just enough erraticism into its course to look convincing as it headed for the nearest point of entry into the body of the airship.

"That's not good," Berdle said.

"What's not good?" Cossont asked.

"Something big and powerful just rolled up at Xown and started blighting all my gear," the avatar told her. They were sitting in the shuttle's compact command space, watching the planet approach as they decelerated from the system edge.

"What gear?"

"The bits and pieces I left behind to keep an eye on whatever's happening there."

Cossont frowned at the avatar. "Do you leave stuff behind everywhere you've been?"

"Pretty much." Berdle looked at her with an expression indistinguishable from genuine incomprehension. "Why wouldn't you?"

"Never mind. This big and powerful something; bigger and more powerful than you?"

"Definitely bigger."

"We still going in?"

"Even less choice now."

"We couldn't just . . . call Ximenyr?" Cossont said. "Could we? You know; just say, Hi, we need them eyes you've got?"

Berdle smiled briefly. "I have been trying to contact the gentleman. I asked Mr QiRia's mind-state if it would co-operate and it said it would, but Ximenyr's been impossible to contact. A direct appeal to him, from Mr QiRia, ought to be our first course of action when we do gain access to him."

"Oh. You might have told me."

"I might." Berdle agreed, looking unconcerned. "I would have, had we been successful."

"Huh. Okay. So: this ship the same one as at Bokri?"

"No," the avatar said. "Can't be. Registering all different anyway. Battleship rather than battle-cruiser; I can outrun it, but that's not much use when we both want to be in the same place at the same time." Berdle shook his head. "Shit in a slather. Pretty much everything's gone or going. I'm losing all my senses down there."

"Think they'll be putting their surveillance in, instead?"

"I suppose. Though, being Gzilt navy rather than special forces or anything, I bet their stuff isn't as sneaky as my stuff."

"What was the last you heard through all this sneaky stuff?"

"Ximenyr was still there on the airship, getting prepared for the latest bout of ceremonial partying. Apparently; that's all according to the airship's own channels. I don't have direct access to him, and he hasn't been heard of for at least seven days. I have – had – stuff inside the airship but nothing in the guy's own quarters after he found that scout missile. Pretty sure he's still there, but not certain. I've found some incidental recording of him still wearing the container round his neck, from the day after we visited him, so – at least initially – we didn't spook him. Also, the whole layout of the airship's been changing, since a couple of days after we were here before; they've created a big new space inside. And they've been bringing in a lot of extra tech, including new field projectors. And water; that thing must weigh a lot more than it used to, but they seem to have balanced it all out with extra AG. None of which would matter if we could see inside it properly, but we can't. Plus now we've got competition, and they know where our attention's been focused, if they didn't before. Not to mention," he said, turning to her, "there's been a guy, walking or jogging ahead of the airship, since we left."

"I thought there were various people doing that?"

"Oh, it's collected lots of people keeping pace with it recently, in air-cars, travel-tube carriages, special trains and ground vehicles, plus there are people keeping pace with it on foot for half a day or so at a time, but there was only one guy who just kept it up all the way through. I had an insectile watching him the whole time and he just never stopped; he hardly even varied his pace. All he did was switch what level and which side he was on, and keep level with different parts of the airship, I suppose so he wasn't too conspicuous. He's got some sort of camo or adaptive clothing on that changes every day, but that didn't throw the bug off; it was still the same guy, walking or jogging day and night."

"Probably not human then."

"Probably not human," Berdle agreed. "Though of course you never know; there are some very odd humans." He frowned at the screen and the giant red-brown, green and blue ball of Xown, as though the planet itself had been responsible for this upset. "Trouble is, he's disappeared now, too."

He awoke.

He was in a military medical facility aboard a regimental fleet ground liaison craft, flying within a subsidiary tunnel space of the Girdlecity of Xown. It was late afternoon on this part of Xown; five minutes off midnight, back on Zyse.

He was lying on a couch, blinking at the ceiling light panels. He was a customised bio-plausible android, waking after having had the latest version of his guest implanted.

He was Colonel Agansu, translated and transplanted into this fresh, tireless, highly capable and perfectly unharmed new body.

It made no difference.

He knew that he had been worried about having his consciousness duplicated in this way, but he had been a fool to torment himself with such concerns. Of course the original of him, lying being put back together and regrown in the bowels of the *Uagren*, would always think of itself as the "real" him – he accepted this without emotion – but he knew who he was, within this body, here, now, and that there was work to be done.

Knowing that there was another iteration of himself elsewhere was mildly comforting, like having another layer of protection wrapped around him, but made little real difference.

A screen on a flex-arm swung over to inspect him. A woman's face looked at him from somewhere remote. The doctor's gaze flicked to one side then the other, doubtless studying read-outs. Then she said, "Well, whoever you are, whatever it is they want you to do, you're as ready as you'll ever be to do it. Good luck and good Subliming, brother."

Agansu swung out of the couch. The screen seemed to flinch, withdrawing towards the ceiling as he did so.

"Thank you," he said.

He felt the aircraft settle on a solid surface; interfaced with the craft's systems, he knew he would be three hundred and ten metres ahead, two hundred and twenty metres away laterally and zero metres vertically from the nose of the airship when he exited. He checked his camouflage clothing, got it to impersonate something civilian and nondescript.

He remembered days of jogging and walking, climbing steps and ramps, descending steps and ramps, in filtered daylight and lamplight and ghostly sat-light and no light, the airship filling his view ahead or a presence at his back or a steady shape at one side or the other or above him or through gratings beneath him as he paced. Sometimes fire-works, lasers and holographic images burst from, lanced out, or enveloped/preceded/trailed the airship, especially at night, and sometimes loud music could be heard playing. Floodlights and running lights lit it every night. Sometimes when he ran behind and above it he could smell food and fumes and detect the spoor of bio-drugs.

He recalled the feeling of being swaddled and protected, within the *7*Uagren*, and remembered talking to the avatar of the Culture ship, and thinking that he had the creature and Vyr Cossont where he wanted them, at his mercy . . . then hurtling broken and screaming down the lift shaft, like a burned insect falling flaming down a tall chimney. He remembered lying broken and burned and taken apart within the ship again, then beginning to be made whole again, while he contemplated how close to death he had come and how the prospect of oblivion within the Subliming had started to seem less terrifying.

Two sets of memories had been formed at the same time, but this made no difference either.

The ground liaison craft carried little weaponry and was only able to equip him with a kin-ex side-arm, but that would not matter for too long. The android body had what was effectively a laser carbine embedded in each forearm, the beams exiting through a skin-disguised muzzle in the heel of each hand.

He jumped easily, seemingly lightly, from the lowered door of the stealth-black craft, then – as it closed itself, flipped over and powered off down the fifty-metre-diameter tunnel – he turned and jogged down a broad, cross-corridor of soaring lattice girders and overarching pipes that led directly to the giant basket-weave of tunnel where the *Equatorial 353* moved. There was an area of open balcony deck ahead. The airship would be just about to pass it by the time he got there.

The *8*Churkun* established contact.

~Colonel Agansu.

~In translation, yes.

~I am captain of the *8*Churkun*. The marshal sends regards.

~Please thank the marshal.

~We have completed the scour of Culture devices from the immediate volume and beyond, though a vessel – I would guess the Culture ship that you encountered at Ospin – is approaching. It was slowing but is now re-accelerating. We are going to attempt to intercept or disrupt any attempt it makes to disloc materiel or personnel into or near the Girdlecity; however, we cannot be certain of success.

~It would help to know the intended location of any such attempted disloc, to help confirm the nature of enemy intentions, Agansu sent, approaching the great open balcony that gave out onto the tunnel which held the approaching airship.

~That is entirely compatible with our own intentions. We'll let you know where any disloc was targeted, whether successful or not.

~Thank you.

There were people ahead. The spaces around the airship *Equatorial 353* had been becoming more populated over the days he had been keeping pace with it. Ground vehicles rumbled slowly past ahead on a broad roadway; they were gaudy, booming with music. Across the gulf of the tunnel he could see a train, trundling, keeping pace, searchlights on it pointing back at the airship, flicking slowly off and on again as they passed behind supporting struts. A smaller airship, like a tiny white cloud made solid, appeared from a side tunnel and drew slowly ahead of the *Equatorial 353*, scattering clouds of sparkling, coloured dust which a rear-facing laser lit up in gyrating abstract patterns.

The skin of the *Equatorial 353* exhibited a series of large moving images, as though projected onto its smooth curvature. There appeared to be seven or eight of these distorted displays covering the airship's surface at any one time. Some of the photographs were stills, most moved, and they sometimes fused together to provide larger images. Some appeared only to make any sort of sense considering the airship as a whole, in other words imagining the form of the display on the other side of the craft. The most common themes appeared to be records of earlier art installations aboard the craft over the last few years, nature in the form of plants and animals, historical and presently existing forms of transport, and pornography.

~We carry four sixty-four-unit platoons of marine combat arbites, the *8*Churkun*'s captain told him. ~They are at your disposal, Colonel. Shall I have my tactical engagements officer ready some or all of them for deployment?

~Please do.

He had to push through a small parade of people – dressed in motley, many dancing as they moved, some singing, some chanting – to get to the edge of the space where the balcony gave out onto the open tunnel of curving ribs and spiralling pipes. There he found the *Equatorial 353*, filling the monstrous tube like a comically slow shell in the biggest, least efficient gun ever made.

Then Colonel Agansu had a sudden, literal flash of memory, and remembered the magnified shadow of his own suited form being thrown out across the elevator shaft within the Incast facility on Bokri as the combat arbite Uhtryn, behind him, was dissolved in a pointillist spray of tiny, fierce anti-matter explosions, blasting a blindingly intense sleet of radiation past him, through him.

~How many of the combat arbites do you need, Colonel?

A chorus of beeps, trills, clangs and musical phrases – followed by some cheers and the start of a fireworks display from the top of the giant airship – announced that it was midnight on Zyse, and the Instigation was only two days away.

~All of them.

Twenty-one

(S -2)

"Because you're liable to get killed."

"That doesn't seem to be stopping *you*."

"Of course not. I'm an avatar. 'Killed' doesn't even mean the same thing for me. You're a bio; I've seen how you guys die and it's messy."

"I meant as the ship. The *Mistake Not* . . . You're liable to get killed. Aren't you?"

"A slightly more weighty consideration, I accept, but even then; I've already transmitted my mind-state to my home GSV and switched to full combat readiness, so I'm kind of ready for death. And anyway, not dead yet."

"This is my fight, though, isn't it? More than yours?"

Berdle sighed. "This is about the Gzilt, but the Culture appears to be all mixed up in it, through QiRia, so it's our problem to sort out."

"It's still basically about us. You can't do everything. You're not our . . . parent."

"You're not even backed-up, Cossont. If you die, you die."

"Can't you back me up?"

"No."

She had a sudden thought. "Did you back-up QiRia, his mind-state from the grey cube?"

"Yes. Also transmitted, with a note it's private and to be wiped if the original survives."

She frowned. "*Why* can't you back me up?"

"You've no neural lace; even starting right now it would take far too long. We're already out of time." Berdle waved his hands, as though exasperated. "Why are you so keen to risk your life anyway? You're a military reservist civilian facing Subliming in a couple of days; why the rush to die? And, I'm telling you: having you present will make my job harder, not easier. You won't be contributing, you'll be jeopardising."

"First of all, on that last point, I don't believe you. I think you're just trying to protect me, being all male-gallant. I'm flattered but there's no need."

"I'm a fucking razor-arsed starship, you maniac! I'm not male, female or anything else except stupendously smart and right now tuned to *smite*. I don't give a fuck about flattering you. The few and frankly not vitally important sentiments I have concerning you I can switch off like flicking a switch."

"Anyway. You can't keep me prisoner on the ship. You're Culture and I'm a free agent. I demand to be set down in the Girdlecity."

"They are *looking* for you, remember? They think you trashed Fzan-Juym with your bare hands or whatever the fuck."

"So you'd better look after me then."

"That's what I'm trying to tell you! I don't need that extra workload! And if you insist on quitting the ship I'll put you down wherever I damn well please, *not* where you specifically demand, so there you are; you can't win."

Cossont, already dressed in the same figure-hugging undersuit she'd worn at Bokri, stood looking levelly at the avatar across the module's lounge. "If you don't give a fuck about flattering me," she said slowly, "and if you can just switch off any sentiments you have concerning me, you can do that down there, on the planet, in the Girdlecity, in the airship. So you don't have to worry about me, and I will help, not hinder."

Berdle stared at her. Then he smiled, and relaxed. His tone of voice changed. "I don't know about you, Vyr," he said, conversationally, "but I'm sort of posturing here." He shrugged. "If you insist on coming, you can, though it's your funeral and I won't risk any part of what I'm supposed to be doing to keep you safe at all, not if it's a trade-off; just nothing." He shook his head. "I thought maybe you were just putting on a sort of good-enough show. You know; so you could feel okay about yourself even though you didn't want to go, or expect to. So, one last chance, in all seriousness: please don't come."

"One last time: I want to. Take me with you."

Berdle sighed. "Okay. You can't say you weren't warned. Put that on." He nodded behind Cossont. She turned round to see a bizarre vision of a man in close-fitting armour – half mirror, half soot-black, headless – marching out of an alcove, growing an extra pair of arms and peeling itself open as it approached her.

"What's that?"

"A better suit. I'm downloading a copy of QiRia's mind-state to it now, so we can access the old geezer's memories direct if we get hold of his eyes without the ship around. Go on; just step in as you are. We've ninety seconds before we snap aboard, so don't take too long."

"I thought we had ten minutes!"

"Not any more; the ship's powering back out again, hoping to lure the battleship away from Xown."

"Shit." Cossont stepped over to the suit and then into it; it flowed closed around her, leaving the helmet component down. "Think that'll work?" she asked.

"Doubt it," the avatar admitted. "Assuming the battleship's been talking to the battle-cruiser, it'll know I've already been moving faster than it can, but it might factor in too much main traction stress degradation after all the dashing about I've been doing lately and think it has a chance. Assuming its engines aren't slightly fucked too, of course. Worth a try."

Pyan, sprawled loosely on a couch all this time, came flapping over and stood on a seat-back, facing her like a small, stiff flag. "Well done you!" it said. "I think you're being terribly brave but I'm sure it'll all work out *splendidly*! And just remember: I've always loved you!"

Cossont was about to say something like, Okay, now I'm worried . . . when her eyes narrowed and she looked at Berdle. "Did you put it up to that?"

Berdle shrugged. "Also worth a try."

"But I do!" Pyan exclaimed, twisting to face Berdle, then back to Cossont. "But I *do*!"

"Yeah," Cossont said.

"Twenty seconds."

*

The ship sent a tiny update of its mind-state to its home GSV, mostly just so there would be a record of Cossont insisting on going with its avatar and other on-planet forces into the Girdlecity.

The ship was a constrained shell of force hurtling across the system now, re-accelerating hard, packaged within its wrapping of concentric fields like something cocooned, engines howling in frequencies no biological living thing would ever sense, a kilometre-long projectile submerged beneath the skein of real space, components of three outer fields lasing in hyperspace to direct the signal to its distant ship-mother, then clicking off again after a nanosecond, while other configurations of fields slid and flicked, stacked and snicked, readying for a series of multiple high-speed, high-accuracy Displaces to a complex-topography target deep in a gravity well; probably opposed.

This was, the ship knew, going to be challenging.

Most serious Culture ships, and all with any pretensions to being warships, possessed burst units: specialised engine components like motive power capacitors capable of providing sudden, brief flares of energy and movement. The *Mistake Not . . .*'s were more powerful and capable than most craft its size, which was kind of a game-giving-away liability if you actually had to use them in the presence of somebody able to spot such shenanigans, but – on the other hand – this was exactly the situation where they might help save the day, so . . .

The ship was already heading dangerously close to Xown's gravity well, having to adjust its course in hyperspace to avoid crashing into the downward curve of skein. It jinked closer still at the last moment, using up all its burst unit energies both to swerve and slow, then focused in on the relatively tiny part of itself that held the module where its avatar and the humanoid were, snapping the two human-shaped forms and the woman's pet away and then the module separately. It loosed the module first, targeting the Displace at a spot just outside the Girdlecity twelve hundred metres above local ground level and ten kilometres back from the current location of the airship *Equatorial 353*.

It was, given the relative velocities involved, one of the most accurate and precisely located Flying Displaces it had ever heard of, snapping the module into the air within an elegantly aligned pocket of vacuum that collapsed at just the right rate to allow the craft to continue on its way – under its own power, now – so smoothly that the ship doubted somebody standing inside the module – had there been anybody – would even have wobbled as the transition was completed.

That the whole craft was almost immediately snatched away again by an almost equally heavy-duty disloc facility – with a most inelegant bang like a sonic boom, caused by the caisson-field collapsing uncontrolled – was, happily, quite beside the point. While the Gzilt ship was busy doing this the *Mistake Not . . .* was merrily zapping all its real payloads – its avatar and Cossont included – into the places it had wanted to in the first place.

That done, within the same millisecond, it was off again, spiralling down under even fiercer acceleration as though intent on diving right under the planet's depression in the skein and aiming for the energy grid far beneath. It steadied, zoomed, sped off, tracked but not targeted by the Gzilt war-craft, which remained stationary, hugging close to the planet.

Pyan was dumped into the ship's last remaining human habitable space, a six-person shuttle.

~Where's this? the creature said.

~New home, the ship sent.

~It's small and boring!

~So are you.

~What! How dare you!

~Would you rather be on the planet?

~Which is safer?

The *Mistake Not . . .* watched the Gzilt ship staying – annoyingly, frustratingly – exactly where it was, singularly failing to pursue it, even though the *Mistake Not . . .* had pretended to be less quick than it really was, just to make it think it had a chance.

~Probably the planet, now, it admitted.

~The planet, then . . . Well? Hurry up!

~Too far. Next pass/approach.

~You're going *back*?

~Of course I'm going back.

~I protest at this behaviour towards me! Why wasn't I—?

~Best you go to sleep now, the ship said.

Pyan flopped inert to the floor of the little shuttle and was tidied, neatly folded, into a slim locker by a small ship drone, which then checked that everything else in the tiny craft was stowed and strapped in case there was any wild manoeuvring. Then it, too, stowed itself securely in another locker.

xGSV *Empiricist*

    oLOU *Caconym*

    oGSV *Contents May Differ*

    oGCU *Displacement Activity*

    oGSV *Just The Washing Instruction Chip In Life's Rich Tapestry*

    oUe *Mistake Not . . .*

    oMSV *Passing By And Thought I'd Drop In*

oMSV *Pressure Drop*
oLSV *You Call This Clean?*

Open question, specifically to the *Mistake Not . . .*: Are you sure you are doing the right thing? It is plausible that the Gzilt craft is an 8*; possibly the ship responsible for what happened at Ablate. It is certainly powerful and may be unconstrained by conscience.

∞

xUe *Mistake Not . . .*

No, not sure at all. But committed, so let's see what happens.

∞

xGSV *Contents May Differ*

I am equally worried re the *Beats Working*. It just transmitted its mind-state.

∞

xLOU *Caconym*

Suggestion? Tell it whatever it's thinking of doing, don't.

∞

xGSV *Contents May Differ*

I have been trying to contact it after the mind-state signal arrived. Nothing. To pass the time while I wait for a reply, I have been trawling the banks for evidence that this is anything other than a bad sign, coming from a Contact Unit. Guess what?

∞

xGSV *Empiricist*

The *Beats Working* is with the largest part of the Ronte fleet, heading for Vatrelles. The Gzilt saw them off but only as far as the system outskirts, then returned, with no known other hostility. That leaves the Liseiden. We have the Thug-class *Value Judgement* with the main squadron, do we not?

∞

xMSV *Passing By And Thought I'd Drop In*
Yes, though the main – the largest – squadron is not the flagship flotilla. They re-dispositioned, bringing various of their separate squadrons together into a more martial meta-configuration following the original decision on preferred Scavenger status going against them. One group of three ships joined the three of the flagship squadron, but three separate groups of three also amalgamated, and as that then constituted the greatest force they had, that is the one the *Value Judgement* was sent to shadow. We have nothing with the flagship squadron commanded by Ny-Xandabo Tyun, and – as that was the force already also converging on Zyse – that is the force most likely to offer any threat to the Ronte attempting to make Vatrelles.

∞

xLOU *Caconym*
  oMSV *Pressure Drop*
Shit. I bet the Gzilt told the Liseiden where it looked like the Ronte were heading. And if the fucking *Empiricist* had let us use those Delinquents we wouldn't be looking at this debacle.

∞

xGSV *Empiricist*
I suggest I send my fastest ship to rendezvous with the *Beats Working* and the Ronte, while signalling the Liseiden to desist from any hostile action they may be contemplating. I am sure we have such a preponderance of forces locally we can prevent any mooted unpleasantness.

∞

xLOU *Caconym*

oMSV *Pressure Drop*

Here we go. Spoken like a ship with no idea of how things actually work. It's not about what forces you've got, it's about what forces you've got *where*. You'd think even a civilian would understand that.

∞

> You may be being too harsh. Agreed, nothing it has can get to the likely volume of combat in time, but it has a point regarding a warning possibly being enough.

∞

That would apply if we had nothing military here at all; we are who we are and we can call any shots at any time. That still might not stop the Liseiden from making a point to the Ronte, just to show who's boss in future.

∞

> Let's hope you're wrong.

∞

Yes, why don't we? That ought to pass the time. Anyway, let's hear what the *Empiricist* thinks we ought to do.

∞

xGSV *Empiricist*

I am despatching the ROU *Learned Response*, the LOU *New Toy* and the GOU *Questionable Ethics* in string formation, ROU leading, to maximum reach and make rendezvous, the LOU to 50 per cent and the GOU 12.5 per cent distance, adjusting to hold at those increments.

∞

xLOU *Caconym*
oMSV *Pressure Drop*

Oh fuck, now it's making pretty patterns.

The/My squadron of six Liseiden ships, led by myself on the pride of our fleet, the Collective Purposes vessel and flagship *Gellemtyan-Asool-Anafawaya*, fell (/ruthlessly*) upon the pitiful/limping/struggling/fearsome* Ronte fleet with resolute professionalism/exemplary courage/heavy hearts**, our *jaws/mouthparts forced* [n.b.: *awkward/over-species-specific in translation; suggest restructure using "given no choice" or equivalent*] by the [?]/ responded to the Ronte fleet's outrageous* provocations/unprovoked aggression**/aggressive intransigence with *the only language they understand***

   * [*n.b.: word choice? potentially hoary*]
   ** [*n.b.: phrase choice? potentially clichéd*]

"Sir?"

"Hmm?" Salvage and Reprocessing Team Principal Ny-Xandabo Tyun accepted the call in his private cabin. It was from his Sensors/Targeting officer. He had asked not to be disturbed unless something urgent came up. "What?" he said with deliberate gruffness, though secretly he was glad of the interruption. He was finding writing what he hoped would turn into one of the more exciting parts of his memoirs rather more difficult than he'd anticipated.

"Sir, we have the Ronte fleet in sight at extended scanner range; thirteen targets."

"Thirteen. So the Culture ship is still with them."

"Appears so, sir."

"Are they aware of us?"

"Doubtful, sir."

"I'd prefer a percentage applied to that doubt, officer."

"Sir. Ninety per cent certain they haven't detected us, sir."

"That's better."

"Also, sir, Comms coming on line with a signal from the Culture GSV *Empiricist*. Shall I—?"

"Yes. Comms, what are they saying?"

"There's quite a lot of it, sir; I've patched it through. But it boils down to them telling us not to attack the Ronte."

"I bet it does. I'll take a look shortly. You have followed my earlier orders and not acknowledged?"

"Yes, sir."

"Good. S/T?"

"Sir," the Sensors/Targeting officer said.

"How long until we have the Ronte fleet in range?"

"A fraction over two hours at current velocities and courses, sir."

"Two *hours*? I thought we expected to have them in range forty minutes after contact."

"Their drive signatures are messier than anticipated, sir, plus the Culture ship with them appears to be hurrying them on; hard to tell from this far away – only about fifteen per cent certain – but it looks like it's encased them in its own field enclosure, highly extended, and is acting like a sort of high-speed tug."

"I see. Engineering?"

"Sir?"

"Can you give us a little more power?"

"Negative, sir. Another step-up from here would imply a seventy per cent chance of serious engine malfunction, probably in one or both of the two Jubunde-class ships."

"Hmm. Very well. Continue to close at current velocity. Combat?"

"Sir?"

"Go to full readiness in one hour, ship-wide. I'll rejoin the bridge then."

"Sir."

"Proceed, all," he said. He cut off the chorus of acknowledgements and resumed his compositional task with a watery sigh.

The insectile drone Jonsker Ap-Candrechenat, representative of the Culture ship *Beats Working*, floated in front of the Swarmprince Ossebri 17 Haldesib, in the command space of the Ronte Interstitial/Exploratory vessel *Melancholia Enshrines All Triumph*.

"This need not be your fight, machine," Haldesib told the drone.

"It feels like it is, Swarmprince. I led you into danger. I thought I might help you escape it, but it would appear we are discovered, so now the least I can do is try to make amends by coming between you and the enemies into whose reach I so foolishly delivered you."

Haldesib flicked one leg in a dismissive gesture. "For ourselves, we do not seek our end; but the hive, the swarm, the race will go on, no matter. You need not presume to share our fate through misplaced guilt."

"I feel I have no honourable choice, Swarmprince."

"You intend to attack the Liseiden ships?"

"I intend to engage with them."

"The distinction might be lost on them. We have dealt with the Liseiden before. They will interpret any 'engagement' as an attack. Or at least claim to, afterwards. Be warned."

"Thank you. I am."

"This is the decision of your human crew?"

"No. It is mine. I intend to get my human crew to safety before matters become critical."

"They concur with this?"

"They have come to accept it. Two wanted to be heroes, and stay aboard. I argued them out of this course."

The Swarmprince flexed his wing plates. In a human, the equivalent might have been a shake of the head. "We may all die out here, machine, but – of all of us – you have some choice. Must *you* be a hero? Can you not argue yourself out of this course?"

"I probably could, Swarmprince, but I'd regret it subsequently. I believe this is the right thing to do and so I am doing it."

"You may steal some of our glory." The Swarmprince's legs flexed as he said this, dipping his body briefly to indicate that it was said humorously, not aggressively.

"I shall engage with them first, independently, Swarmprince, before any action between them and you. If I may, I'll transmit to you whatever I can discover of their ships' abilities, strengths and weaknesses. It may help, if I am unable to stop them."

"We are pleased to accept this kind offer. But what if you prevail? We shall be denied all chance to prove ourselves!"

"Then you will have the benefit of my most profuse apologies, I shall accept any amount of inferred alien cachet value (negative), honorary, you care to bestow, and I shall be grateful subsequently for even the most demeaning and/or minor role in any ship dance within which you care to include me."

Leg-clicks indicated the Swarmprince was laughing. A few other Ronte in the command space joined in quietly. "It has been gratifying to us to witness the knowledge of and respect for our ways you have displayed, ship," the Swarmprince said. "We can only wish you well with your 'engagement'. Fight well. Live if you can, die well if you must."

"Thank you, Swarmprince. It's been a pleasure."

＊

"You look tired, Septame," Chekwri told him as she entered his office in the parliament building.

"I feel tired, Marshal."

"Never mind; not long to go now. You chosen your last outfit?"

"What?"

"Your clothing; whatever you're going to wear for the Instigation. Have you decided how you'll be dressed when you meet your glorious translation into the Enfolded?"

"I . . . I think that's all pre-decided for me. Ceremonial . . . Solbli. Yes, Solbli; she'll be taking care of all that. Umm. You?"

"Oh, I shall be resplendent in all my finery, Septame, medals gleaming," Chekwri said, folding herself into a seat across from the septame. Banstegeyn had noticed that the marshal didn't ask whether she might disturb him these days, or wait to be invited to sit. Before, he might have made some frosty comment and insisted on protocols being followed, but no more. People were going quietly crazy in these last couple of days – in fact some people were going noisily, boisterously, even dangerously crazy. Meanwhile, all across the Gzilt domain, those who had been Stored, some for less than a year, some for a couple of decades or more, were waking up for final reunions, last goodbyes, leaving parties and fare-thee-wells-in-what-comes-next . . .

"I have buffed and polished my medals for decades of steady, dedicated watchfulness," the marshal continued, clasping her hands behind her head as she leaned back and relaxed, legs crossed, "counted and re-counted my medals for outstanding work in simulations and exercises, carefully arranged my medals for heroic bravery under virtual fire, and even found room for my many, many medals for exemplary valour in the face of fellow officers coveting the same promotions as I." She smiled at him without humour. "Shame we haven't had time to strike any medals commemorating our latest exploits: jumping unarmed ships, wasting our own and setting naive aliens on each other. Still, one can have too much of a good thing, eh, Septame? And they do say there's no guilt in the Sublime."

"You seem positively energised by the whole process, Chekwri." He looked pointedly round the room. "And very confident that my office isn't bugged."

"I had my own people make quite sure of that some time ago, Septame," Chekwri said, smiling.

"While planting your own?"

The marshal's smile broadened. "Have you always been so suspicious, Banstegeyn?"

He looked at her, unsmiling. "No, I stumbled into a position of great power quite by accident."

Chekwri grinned, then shrugged. "Our troubles will soon be over, Septame," she said, then frowned. "What?" she asked. Banstegeyn had just twitched and glanced to one side, like he'd seen something alarming from the corner of one eye.

The septame shook his head and bent back to his desk, where he was signing documents on his desk screen. "Nothing," he muttered, scrawling his signature. "Have you only come to discuss matters of ceremonial attire or is there some actual point to this visit?"

Chekwri stood, walked to the window overlooking the stepped gardens and the city beyond the curve of river. "My, I do believe some people have started fires," she said. "I thought that wasn't our style." She looked back at Banstegeyn. "One lot of aliens is about to trash another. The mighty *Empiricist*, no less, has signalled the miscreants telling them to play nicely but the rumour is it's being ignored. I just wanted to be sure you were happy that we let things be and allow what might happen to happen. This is not to say that they'd take any notice of us, either, but in theory we might threaten to withdraw Scavenger cooperation. This has been suggested."

"By whom?"

"Media, Culture, one or two politicos. There'd be more, but of course everybody's distracted."

"You're the brave space marshal. What would your advice be?"

"I'd be indifferent; doesn't affect us . . . save for the fact that our returned bad boy and what sounds like its entire marine force are just about to tangle with a Culture ship, out at Xown. That could get messy. Might require extraneous distractions to keep people from concerning themselves with it." She crossed her arms. "Intelligence has crunched some more numbers and now thinks that particular side-show might all turn on this absurdly old Culture guy, and Cossont, the girl who survived Fzan-Juym and the fracas at Bokri. I think we take no chances and continue to let our assets around the Girdlecity do whatever's needed; does that sound—?"

"Yes. Yes, it does. Do whatever's needed," the septame said, not looking up. "Is that all?" he asked. "Lot of signing required, winding up an entire civilisation, and the president was only too happy to delegate to his trimes and septames. Then I've got the joy of back-to-back receptions for a variety of newly arrived aliens and recently de-Stored self-important political nonentities to attend."

"You should just tell them to fuck off," Chekwri said cheerfully. "Go for a walk. Get laid. Start a fire." She headed for the door. "Why not?"

The door closed, leaving him alone. He brought his head

up, gazing at the closed door for a moment. Then his eyes flicked to one side for an instant, he made a small keening noise and bent quickly back to his task, the nib of the stylo scratching drily at the desk screen.

"Salvage and Reprocessing Team Principal, Ny-Xandabo Tyun?"

"I have that honour. And you?" Tyun had been called back to the bridge from his private cabin half an hour early. It appeared the Culture ship wanted to talk and was falling back towards them, leaving the Ronte fleet to crawl on without it. Tyun watched the representation of the situation on a giant screen stretching right across the forward part of the bridge.

"I am the Culture ship *Beats Working*," the voice said, in perfect, unaccented Liseiden Formal.

"Sir," Tyun's combat officer broke in, "a contact, registering less than ten metres in length and flagging as an unarmed civilian personnel craft, has left the Culture ship. Divergent course; peeling away. Slung and slowing."

Tyun could see the tiny trace, curving away from the approaching Culture ship; a thread from a speck. "Could it be a warhead?" he asked.

"Technically possible, sir," the combat officer said. "Something improvised. Big, though, for such a small craft. They're not supposed to carry any weapons anywhere near—"

"Deploy an HRMP to track it, slow approach. Keep the platform between the new contact and us."

"Heavy Remote Missile Platform launched, sir. Launch authority for the missiles?"

"What would you recommend, officer?"

"Zero automaticity, sir. Our direct positive command."

"That, then."

"Team Principal?" the Culture ship said.

Tyun clicked back to speak to the Culture ship again. "Yes?"

"I take it you've noticed that I have despatched my human crew in a small shuttle craft. Their identities and the craft's course are appended. They and the shuttle are entirely unarmed."

"Why are your crew abandoning ship?"

"I asked them to, and advised them that they ought to."

"Why would that be?"

"In case there are any hostilities."

"Why should there be any hostilities?"

"I believe you mean some harm to the Ronte."

"Not at all. You presume too much. I might as well assume that you mean harm to me and my ships because you have loosed what, for all I know, might be a warhead disguised as a shuttle."

"The shuttle craft is drawing further away from you all the time and its course is set. Also, it is demonstrably unarmed."

"Seven minutes until the Culture ship's in range, sir," the combat officer told him.

"Are we in range of *it* yet?" Tyun asked. He checked the magnification the screen was using, shown as a logarithmically scaled bar on one side.

"Shouldn't be, sir; not a Scree class. They're almost unarmed."

"And you," Tyun asked, clicking back to talk to the Culture ship. "Are you unarmed, machine? And what are your intentions?"

"I have only very limited military capability. My intention is to prevent you engaging with the Ronte ships ahead of you."

"What makes you think we wish to engage with them?"

"You are pursuing them."

"Hmm. I would not care to define it as such. We are merely following them."

"You have targeted them."

"We have illuminated them the better to track their progress."

"This is not fully plausible. I believe you mean them harm."

"Not at all. We may ask them to heave to and submit to our inspection; we are entitled to do so under the terms of our agreement with the Gzilt, as long as the Ronte or any unauthorised military or semi-military forces are in Gzilt space. Which they are, of course."

"You know the Ronte will never permit such a thing."

"That's their problem. Certainly they have proved treacherous in the past and gone back on their agreements with us, so we are unable, sadly, to take their word regarding any questions we may have for them regarding cargo, weaponry and intentions. As I say, our initial approach will be entirely non-violent, simply requesting them to halt and cooperate."

"Such an approach virtually guarantees there will be conflict. I believe you know this."

"I know no such thing, ship. I am acting within my rights according to the recently signed agreement between the Liseiden people and the Gzilt; an agreement which rescinds and cancels any previous agreements your . . . clients might have thought they'd inveigled the Gzilt into signing with them. And I wonder that a Culture ship appears so determined to ally itself with those barbaric ruffians, the Ronte. I wonder, are we suffering from a degree of guilt at having enabled your Ronte friends to encroach so far into Gzilt space? If so, ship, I understand that you might feel some shame, some wounded pride, but our . . . contention at this time is not with you. If it is with anyone, it is with them. I must ask you to break off what is beginning to look like an attack run on our – far superior – force before we are compelled to take defensive action, which may, I'm afraid to say, include interception munitions."

"I intend to continue on my present course, Team Principal."

On the giant screen, the Culture ship looked very close now. Tyun clicked out. "Navigation, prepare to split the squadron in two: three right, three left, to half a light second apart. On my order. We'll let the Culture ship go straight through the gap between. All ships target and prepare to fire on any hostile action from the Culture ship. We can afford to ignore the Ronte for a short while, yes?"

"Maybe five minutes, on present velocities," his navigation officer said.

"Fine. Then make good those orders. And – to be clear – only fire on actual, overt hostile action from the Culture ship; not just targeting. We all got that?"

"Sir."

"Targeting," the combat officer said.

"Split the fleet," Tyun ordered. He could hear and feel the ship around him hauling itself away from its earlier, straight course, starting to curve to one side along with two of the other ships. On the screen, the view swung, keeping the approaching Ronte fleet at one edge as the elongated dot that was the *Beats Working* swept past between the separated halves of the Liseiden squadron.

"Fleet split as prescribed," the navigation officer reported. "Culture ship maintaining – correction: target slowing, rapidly. Target . . . now stopped relative to us. Accelerating. Catching up. Level with us in four seconds."

The screen view swung slowly, keeping the smeared dot of the Culture ship at one edge. The view hazed oddly, as though they were running through a gas cloud.

"Sir, the *Quiatrea-Anang* reports total loss of engine control."

"Sir, the *Abalule-Sheliz* reports total loss of power."

"What?" He had two junior officers from fleet control talking to him at once. The main screen hazed grey then blanked out entirely.

"What the fuck—?" Tyun said, glancing at the display in his own helmet. The helmet display was still working but seemed to be having trouble locking on to his eyes to present a true holo image. A stray flash briefly dazzled him.

"Main screen in shut-down," the damage control officer said, sounding puzzled. "Cause unknown." The screen flashed, shivered woozily, went blank again.

The damage control officer broke in. "Effector attack, on us, targeting engine control and main sensors."

"Sir, the *Quiatrea-Anang* reports total traction loss."

"Culture ship level with us now, sir. Starting to draw ahead. It's not changing—"

"Sir, the *Quiatrea-Anang* reports total sensor loss."

"Engineering telemetry down."

"Sir, the *Laskuil-Hliz* reports total loss of power."

"—velocity. We're slowing. Fleet formation breaking up."

"Sir, the *Abalule-Sheliz* reports it's being targeted by the *Quiatrea-Anang*'s Target Illumination Systems."

"*What?*"

"Our engines beginning stepped disengagement on false telemetry, sir. Trying to head them off and re-initialise but they keep—"

Tyun could hear and feel something alter in the ship; a

single great deep note was deepening still further, like something winding down, while a forward drag stirred micro-currents into the waters around him.

"Sir, the *Abalule-Sheliz* reports it's being targeted by our own TIS."

"That's shit," the junior combat/targeting officer said, voice shaking. "That's just shit, not true. Sir."

"This is an attack!" Tyun said. "This is hostile action! Fire to disable."

"Hard small target, sir. Doubt we can be that accurate."

"Well, just hit it!"

"Sir, the *Fulanya-Guang* reports total loss of engine telemetry."

"No weapon control. All weapons aboard shutting to fail-safe mode, active systems powering down."

"Hit it with something! Disable it, destroy it, I don't care!"

"Nothing to throw at it, sir."

"Sir, the *Quiatrea-Anang* reports total weapon control loss."

"Sir, the Culture ship is within quick strike range of the missile platform launched earlier. Might not have spotted it."

"Can the platform fire? Have we comms with it?"

"Yes, sir."

"Sir, the *Fulanya-Guang* reports total loss of main power."

"Well fire it!"

"Sir, how many—?"

"Everything! All the missiles!"

"Six missiles firing," the combat officer said. "Four sec – one missile gone – two destruct – three, four gone, five . . . five gone . . . Shit!"

"We . . . we hit it."

"Last one got it. Holy fuck."

"We got it, sir."

"The fucker's dust."

"We got it! We fucking got it!"

"Order on the bridge," Tyun said.

"Sir."

"Engine telemetry re-established," the damage control officer reported.

The main screen went into start-up mode, checking itself out with quick darting blocks of colour and sudden scrolls of text and logos, gone too quickly to read.

"Sir, all other ships reporting all controls and telemetry returning to normalcy."

The main screen came alive. It showed a view on medium magnification, looking twenty degrees astern at one edge, of a small cloud of expanding, radiative debris. Dotted alongside, leading away into the darkness, were five even smaller clouds.

"Ronte fleet ahead, sir. Within range. They're targeting aggressively."

Tyun tore his gaze away from the puff of slowly cooling debris falling further away into the night behind them. He switched his attention to the Ronte fleet as the screen view swung back round. The Ronte ships were close now; they had started moving around in one of their odd, forever-changing patterns, as though unsure what formation to fly in. Not that that would make any difference to the targeting AIs. It was even quite pretty, in a pathetic sort of way. Tyun collected himself. "Send the hail."

"Sent, sir."

"All systems aboard at prime, sir. Minimal radiation damage to rear sensors."

"All ships at prime, sir."

"Confirm that, sir. Back to full battle-ready state, zero damage, all ships."

"Positive locks on all twelve Ronte ships, sir."

"Ronte reply in, sir."

"And?"

"Obscene, sir. Absolute non-compliance."

Tyun looked at the message on his now properly functioning in-helmet display. It was indeed obscene; almost inventively so. The Ronte must have been doing their homework on Liseiden physiology.

Salvage and Reprocessing Team Principal Ny-Xandabo Tyun floated back a little in his command bubble. He checked the distance and the time to Vatrelles system, or to any other known ships. Nothing around for light days. They had hours to play with.

"Officers, we are going to fire to disable, targeting their engines."

"Historically, they don't disable too well, sir," the combat officer said.

"Yes. They tend to explode. I know," Tyun said. "Let their high command regard what's going to follow as an incentive to improve their engine design. All combat officers?"

"Sir?" was said in chorus.

"Concentrate all fire, full squadron, flagship combat officer coordinating," he commanded. "Pick them off, one at a time, nearest at all times unless they turn and attack. They probably will. Then each ship to deal with the most immediate threat to it. The flagship will re-send the hail to stop and submit to inspection to all remaining Ronte vessels after each successful engagement. Begin."

The first Ronte ship became an expanding flower of plasma within a minute. The Ronte employed better tactics than had been anticipated and each subsequent ship took a little longer to destroy than the one before; nevertheless, the whole engagement lasted less than a third of an hour. The *Fulanya-Guang* was lost with all hands when what was left of the last Ronte ship, believed to be the fleet flagship, rammed it.

This last development was, Tyun felt – secretly – almost a relief. To overwhelm an inferior fleet with no losses at all made it look like a dishonourably unequal contest; almost a massacre. Losing a ship made everything look a lot better, and would give him an opportunity to sound grave and caring for the dead and their loved ones when he wrote his memoirs.

Besting a suicidal Culture ship gone native – even if it was "just" a Contact Unit, and only tiny – was merely the crustal fronding on the meat-shell, though apparently that phrase, too, was *"awkward/over-species-specific in translation"*.

Twenty-two

(S -2)

xGSV *Empiricist*
    oLOU *Caconym*
    oGSV *Contents May Differ*
    oGCU *Displacement Activity*
    oGSV *Just The Washing Instruction Chip In Life's Rich Tapestry*
    oUe *Mistake Not . . .*
    oMSV *Passing By And Thought I'd Drop In*
    oMSV *Pressure Drop*
    oLSV *You Call This Clean?*

This is all very sad. I especially regret that my own vessels were unable to help in time.

∞

xMSV *Pressure Drop*

I trust the lead ship of your "string" formation, the ROU *Learned Response*, has no thought of revenging the destruction of the *Beats Working*. Our comrade brought its end upon itself. The Liseiden are hardly to be commended, but their principal crime was not offing a semi-civilian craft of ours intent on making amends for earlier over-enthusiasm, but destroying the Ronte ships with all their crews. And even that they had an excuse for, miserable and legalistic though it may have been.

∞

xGSV *Empiricist*

Indeed. I think no immediate action need or should be taken against the Liseiden. Our long-term disapproval, and the implications that this will have for their reputation, might prove most effective. The ROU will continue to the combat volume to retrieve the *Beats Working*'s shuttle with the humans aboard, and check whether any other remains are recoverable, but will not pursue the Liseiden ships.

∞

xGSV *Contents May Differ*

A sealed sub-packet that came with the *Beats Working*'s mind-state just popped. Seems it was so troubled by its own earlier actions that it's requesting that it not be reactivated, save for second-party study, comparative or research purposes. Poor lame bastard doesn't even want to be a ship again.

∞

xLOU *Caconym*
    oMSV *Pressure Drop*

Told you. Five humans: too few.

∞

xLOU *Caconym*

**Meanwhile, on Xown? . . . Reality calling *Mistake Not . . .*,
yes; we're talking about you.**

∞

xUe *Mistake Not . . .*

Yes, hi. It's all getting terribly interesting.

Colonel?

~Ma'am? Agansu replied. The signal-adjunct protocols
indicated he was addressing Marshal Chekwri.

~This is Marshal Chekwri.

~I am aware. An honour.

~Your current status?

~I am walking alongside the airship *Equatorial 353*
awaiting confirmation from the *Churkun* regarding the
disposition of its forces and that of the other side. Media
reports indicate that those in charge of the airship have
undertaken to open the vessel to the public sometime in the
next few minutes. I intend to board then. Or before, should
we find our adversaries are already aboard.

~Permit me awareness through your own senses.

~Of course.

The sensation of manipulating aspects of his sensorium
was a new one for Agansu, and yet one which felt perfectly
natural. He briefly marvelled at all the thought and careful
design that must have gone into making it seem routine for
something like himself – something which felt like a human
– to delve into what was basically its own being and adjust
the settings it found there so that a live link of what it was
experiencing through its senses was now being sent to
another person.

At the same time, Agansu was becoming aware of how

many differences there were between his own, biological body and this one. With the possible exception of being considerably heavier than the bio version – despite being precisely the same volume – all the differences were positive.

How much more powerful, capable and sophisticated this new form was. How much more sensitive where it needed to be – his own bio-body held many augmentations and desirable amendments over the human-basic standard, yet in this new one, for example, he could see in much greater detail and over a far greater spread of the electro-magnetic spectrum than the old version was able to – yet how much less vulnerable it was where it didn't require such sensitivity (this android body felt no pain at all; one's motivation for avoiding harm was knowing that harm reduced one's ability to function, while the indication that harm had been inflicted was no more than that – a sign; something to be noted, taken into account and acted upon, but no more).

~Thank you, the marshal sent.

There had been almost no delay between him agreeing to let the marshal see through his eyes and generally sense through his senses, him setting this up and her beginning to receive the data, and yet he had had time to take a look round inside himself as it were and start to appreciate all the differences between his bio-body and this one, and then to think about all this, all before the marshal had thanked him.

Agansu marvelled at how little time it had all taken. His bio-self would hardly have had time for one completed thought in that half-second or so.

~Right, Colonel, the marshal sent, ~we think the Culture people are trying to get to this Ximenyr guy, because of something he has or something he knows about this QiRia person. You have to stop them. That done, *you* get Ximenyr.

Find out what he has, or knows. You may be as brusque as you like.

~I understand, ma'am, Agansu sent, as he looked about the crowds of chanting, singing, dancing people and gaudily painted, bannered and holo'd machines keeping pace with the giant airship.

~Sounds loud, Colonel.

~Yes ma'am.

He was aware of many different sound streams around him, principally dance music emanating from the various vehicles around him on the broad balcony roadway. More seemed to be joining the throng all the time.

~Kind of crowded there, too.

A burst of fireworks lit up the open-work tunnel around the nose of the *Equatorial 353*. Some set of automatic reactions built into the android he inhabited seemed to be reacting to the fireworks, clenching instinctively as it witnessed nearby mortars firing – nearby mortars which were not flagged as friendly – and their payloads – unguided, highly inaccurately aimed payloads – detonating. Bursts of light were followed by booms, thuds and crackles. A few echoes came back, but most of the sound was swallowed by the huge spaces of the Girdlecity and absorbed within the surrounding patchwork of musics.

Knowing the speed of sound in Xown's atmosphere and the altitude here, he was able to tell exactly how far away he was from each exploding mortar shell.

~Yes, it is, ma'am. Quite crowded.

~Uh-huh. You know, if anything serious does kick off there, Colonel, you will need to limit civilian casualties as far as possible.

~I am aware of that, ma'am, Agansu sent, thinking how typical – and shameful – it was that a superior tried to cover themselves against any unfortunate outcome by re-stating something that was already entirely and properly covered in ambient standing orders and by military rules of engagement. At the same time, if he failed to do as he was required to do by those same superiors because, anxious to avoid collateral civilian damage, he pulled back from using the most destructive weaponry he might have been able to deploy, he'd be blamed for that, too. He had, thanks to her reputation, thought better of Marshal Chekwri, but obviously he'd been wrong to think her any different.

~Marshal, Colonel, the *Churkun*'s captain sent. ~Further on the current situation. We intercepted and re-disloc'd a relatively massive Displace by the Culture vessel and captured what is probably its principal auxiliary craft; however, it was unoccupied and unarmed and probably constituted a diversion. A number of further Displaces occurred almost immediately thereafter, centred on the volume immediately around the airship, but we were unable to intercept or disrupt them. Neither are we able to pin down their destinations further. We are confident they are not actually inside the ship due to the four-dimensional aspect of its construction. It is, effectively, shielded against disloc. This means that the other side must achieve entry to the airship by conventional means. As we have had sensors watching the craft for some time, and discerned no suspicious activity, we are confident that this has not thus far been achieved. Further, the full force of all four of this ships' marine platoons are now available for disloc at instant notice on the colonel's order.

~I see, Captain, Agansu sent. He might have said more, but there would be time later for pinning down the responsibility for the *Churkun* being unable to do more regarding the Culture ship's Displaces. Now was not the time for that. ~So, our adversaries are here, but we don't know where?

~Indeed, Colonel.

~In that case I suggest that you bring in all the marine arbite platoons immediately. Place some ahead of the ship, some behind – say half a platoon in each position – but most in a couple of concentric shells of arbites entirely surrounding the vessel, keeping within tens out to a hundred metres of it but distributed within the structure, with only a squad-level force stationed on the outside of the Girdlecity. Order all of them to keep pace with the airship. Have them stealthed as far as possible, or camo'd to resemble camera drones or other civilian devices.

At that moment, a woman danced out of the crowd of people around him and started trying to get him to dance with her. He shook his head and drew back his hands as she tried to grab them. She persisted, trying to again get hold of his hands, so he turned quickly and walked off, towards the wire parapet at the edge of the roadway, pushing between a couple of people, apologising as he went.

~Suggest we stagger their arrival, Colonel, the *Churkun*'s captain sent, ~or it'll be kind of obvious, popping in that many; you're liable to hear them as well as maybe see them. A second or two between each arrival ought to be okay.

~If you think so, Captain, Agansu replied as another flicker of mortar fire presaged yet more smoky, low-explosive detonations in the tunnel ahead of the airship.

~Captain, Marshal Chekwri sent, ~might I suggest you time more intense disloc bursts to coincide with barrages of fireworks?

~Good idea, ma'am.

Seconds later, Agansu heard a series of additional, dulled crackles sounding all around him, just as the next fusillade of fireworks detonated. He looked around and saw a couple more of what looked like media-cam platforms than had been there before. A few hazy disturbances in the air high over and ahead of the airship – easily missable by the normal human eye – were probably the marine arbites too, camouflaged.

He called up confirmation. Immediately, a picture began to build up inside his mind: a schematic of the Girdlecity around him, showing the tube that the airship *Equatorial 353* moved through at its centre and all the structure around it, along with the positions of all the arbite marines popping into existence.

All that was missing from the picture was any sign of where his adversaries might be.

~Okay, Marshal Chekwri sent, ~I'm at a reception, with stuff that needs to be done. I'll check in later. But let me know if anything dramatic happens, Captain, Colonel.

"You are fucking joking me. We're *where*?"

"We're in the stern ventral waste disposal semi-solids holding tank," Berdle said through the suit. His voice in her ears sounded perfectly unconcerned. She couldn't see him. She couldn't see anything, basically, or touch anything solid.

Cossont was aware of floating in something thick and warm, in complete darkness at normal wavelengths. Her augmented eyes, working in unison with the combat suit's sensors, were happy to relay the fact that the stuff she was surrounded by and floating within was just a little beneath normal Gzilt body core temperature.

"You have literally landed us in the fucking shit?" she said, trying not to sound panicked. Not being able to touch, see or really sense anything very much was, she told herself, worse than knowing what she was submerged within.

"It's ideal," Berdle told her. "This bit of the airship's not shielded with 4D because, I imagine, it gets emptied rather than recycled. Very old-fashioned. Anyway, it means we were able to blat right in. Of course, it's well sensored-up to look out for this sort of intrusion, but the clever bit was Displacing out an exactly similar volume just before dropping us in. Don't think we troubled the header tank or the relief valves at all . . . or caused any blow-back anywhere for that matter. That might have been really messy."

"Thank goodness for that. But, in other business, how the fuck do we get out?"

"Very easily."

"Back to that later, but here's another one; how the fuck do we get *clean*?"

"Also very easily. I'm switching you to sonar. Follow me. Swim."

Cossont suddenly had a view to look at. It was like a drawing rather than a proper picture – everything was white, with fuzzy blue lines delineating edges and a sort of background green wash indicating surfaces.

She could, thankfully, see nothing of what actually surrounded her, but she could see a suited, streamlined version of Berdle a couple of metres away, turning away from her to swim towards the top of the large, cylindrical tank they were in. Beneath and to the side there were hints of tapered supports holding the tank, with further structure sketched in above and below showing where the decks were; these vanished into the distance. Cossont twisted, began to swim after Berdle.

She could feel her hands and limbs contacting semi-solids as she swam. It was like swimming through thick soup. She tried not to think about it. She was doing okay until she remembered the last time she and Berdle had been here on the airship, when they had been met by the strange person with the bowl-of-soup face.

Suddenly, she nearly threw up. Would have thrown up, but something inside her seemed to intervene at the last moment.

"Hey; calm," Berdle said easily as he arrived at the top of the tank. "You're triggering the suit's medical unit." He reached out to something on the under-surface that formed the ceiling.

"*You* be calm," she told the avatar. "I'm swimming through shit here. You're a fucking android, but this stuff is personal to us biologicals."

"Fair enough. But . . . out in a trice," Berdle said, both hands on a circular structure that Cossont sincerely hoped was a hatch. "One more sensor to fool . . . done. And a couple of little expander spheres to emplace, to take up our volume when we get out . . . There." His arms twirled. The circular object swung up and away, hinging. She reached a surface she'd not even been aware was there, her top set of arms and her head suddenly in air. Or at least gas.

She was half a metre below the opened hatch. Berdle pulled himself up through it as easily as though they were in zero-G. Beside Cossont, as Berdle exited the tank, a tiny floating sphere expanded smoothly to over a metre in diameter, pressing against the surface of the tank and then down into the liquid.

Then a hand came down and pulled her up, though the suit made it feel like there was no weight or effort involved anyway. Having four arms probably helped too.

Once she was on her feet, the view switched. Conventional sight again. She was standing under a low, dark ceiling, on a dimly lit gantry facing Berdle – a spotless, conventionally clothed Berdle – across a side-hinged hatchway at their feet. She looked down. Her suit was also spotless, though it had gone back to looking like it was made of liquid mirror and soot again. She heard a tiny plopping noise in the tank beneath and then the suit snapped back to impersonating a normal-enough-looking pants and jacket combo.

"Oh," she said, as Berdle lowered the hatch closed with his foot. Her voice sounded just as it had in the tank, which meant slightly odd. The suit's helmet unit was still covering her face. This doubtless explained why she was being spared any smells she might not have cared for, and why she was still listening to her own voice as relayed through the suit's earbuds.

Berdle nodded. "There you are; clean," he said. "Happy now?" Though *that* was weird too, because his mouth didn't move as she heard him say this.

"Ecstatic. Thanks."

"Welcome. Suit-surface nanofields, Vyr," the avatar said, turning and walking away from her towards a low doorway at the far end of the gantry, where it met a bulkhead. "Zero friction unsticky," she heard him say. He shook his head. "Really."

"Yeah," Cossont said, following him. "Hey, I don't want to disturb you but you were just starting to sound a bit dismissive there."

Berdle was bent down, poking seemingly randomly at the area around the mechanical handle on the door, as though expecting to find a finger-sized keyhole. "Sorry."

She joined him at the door. "Do you think there's *any* field or area where I could make you feel small and a bit slow compared to me, Berdle? Ever?"

The avatar kept poking at the door with his finger. "Well, of course not," he said patiently, his mouth still not moving. "I'm not a person, Vyr; I'm the walking, talking figurehead of a ship." He squatted, staring at the door. "A Culture ship," he added, sticking his finger out and poking again. "A Culture ship," he muttered, "of some intellectual distinction and martial wherewithal . . . moreover." His finger seemed to slip into the surface of the door as though it – or his finger – was a hologram.

Berdle withdrew his finger and stood up. Something clicked and the door swung open towards them. "Me first," he said, conversationally. There was a pause. "Oh," Berdle said. "They really have changed the place."

"Well, we've changed the place a bit," Ximenyr said, walking in front of the reporter arbite with its camera eyes. He was granting an exclusive interview, letting just one media representative in initially before the airship was opened up to everybody else. "The last eight days have been very busy with restructuring. Quite radical restructuring, involving pretty much everybody on board, which has been one reason for keeping people away, though mostly it's just to make it a more exciting reveal." He smiled at the arbite. Ximenyr was dressed in a plain white shift. Five of his fellow partygoers, similarly clad, accompanied him and the arbite along the dark, broad, gently downward-curving corridor. "Many of us have been doing our own personal restructuring too," he said. Ximenyr waved one hand. "I had all sorts of weird shit going on with my body, but I've brought myself back to something much more standard, much more pure, even."

"Do you regret your early excesses?" the arbite asked. It was taking instructions from a panel of bio-journalists spread across Xown and beyond. An AI was collating their queries and producing representative questions.

"Oh no," Ximenyr said, looking almost serious. "One should never regret one's excesses, only one's failures of nerve."

"Is it true your body was covered in over a hundred penises?"

"No. I think the most I ever had was about sixty, but that

THE HYDROGEN SONATA   543

was slightly too many. I settled on fifty-three as the maximum. Even then it was very difficult maintaining an erection in all of them at the same time, even with four hearts. And most of them had to remain dry, or produce only, well, sort of sweat-gland quantities of ejaculate. Though it was very nice ejaculate; sort of slightly oily perfume, and not in the least icky. Unless you thought about it, of course."

"Do you feel you are a more serious artist now?"

"No. I have claimed to be an artist in the past, but really all I've ever been is a sort of glorified surgeon. I would like to think I've been artistic at times and shown artistic flare and so on, but I think that, especially now that we're nearly at the end of things, it's all right to abandon claims and pretensions and just relax a bit. Maybe I've inspired artistry and artisticness in others; that'd be a happy assessment."

"What is the greatest number of people you've had sex with at the same time?"

"About forty-four, forty-five, forty-six? It was hard to be sure, in the heat of the moment. We tried to get to the maximum, of fifty-three, obviously, but even in effective zero-G, all oiled up and most people just sticking their hands in from the outside of this heaving mass of bodies, we just couldn't make it. Too close together. And also, frankly, I think some people got too excited and interested in each other rather than going for this record with me, you know? Still, it was a lot of fun trying. On the other hand, it was an *effort*, too, you know? So much preparation and set-up and planning and briefing. Sex should be about spontaneous fun, don't you think? Anyway, here we are."

Their little party had arrived at the bottom of the gently bowed corridor, where it briefly levelled out and then started to rise again, heading aft. A small crowd of people – mostly dressed in plain white shifts like the one Ximenyr wore, so that they looked vaguely like they belonged to a religious order – were busy gathering up pieces of complicated-looking equipment and wrapping foam and loading everything onto a series of little flat-topped wheeled vehicles; one, fully loaded, was making its own way up the slope beyond, just about to disappear under the curve of ceiling.

Directly above where Ximenyr, his followers and the reporter arbite now stood there was a wide, new-looking circular staircase leading up to a cake-slice-shaped hole in the ceiling, where there was darkness punctured by a few tiny lights.

"Come on up," Ximenyr said, leading the way. He started ascending the fan of stairway, followed by the arbite and the five people who'd accompanied them.

"Lights, please, and enhance," Ximenyr said as he walked out into the space above. The reporter arbite arrived, looked up. The space above was a single enormous space which almost filled the remainder of the airship, right to the top. It was mostly dark, but lit by thousands of small lights pointing inwards at a vast, hazy, cylindrical space perhaps five hundred metres long and four hundred metres across. What looked like a small globular galaxy lay directly overhead, shining. The way the light moved within the space overhead suggested that it was full of water, or some sort of transparent liquid.

The space immediately round the stair-head held stacks and racks of lockers and shelves; beyond, shadows hid any walls. For all its obvious extent, the low ceiling, the darkness and the sensation of a great mass hanging immediately above made the place feel oddly oppressive.

Right in front of them there was one of six small, translucent spheres, each about three metres in diameter, all arranged around the very bottom of the vast container above and looking like hopelessly inadequate supports for its bulk. The dark walls around the vast lit space showed no other form of support, just the tiny floodlights.

"Now, we're playing around with image a bit here," Ximenyr said, reaching up and patting the surface of one of the small translucent spheres, "because you couldn't see through that much of even the purest water, but this is a sort-of-true representation of what you'd see if the water wasn't there."

"So," the arbite said, "what is this?"

"This is a giant water pool; you climb up those steps, get naked, stick one of these breathers in your gob . . ." Ximenyr picked up a stubby tube from one of the nearby shelves and waved it in front of his mouth, ". . . pass through one of these spheres and then float up to the bright lights up there at the top. That's the ultimate party area; that's like heaven, like our own little mini-Subliming. I mean, it's just the usual stuff up there: comfy furniture, drink, drugs and lots of images and music – and dancing, and fucking, you'd imagine – but all a bit more quiet and contemplative, I guess, and all under this lovely clear dome under the top of the ship, and the whole point is this is the only way to get there, and – once you're there – there's no way out . . . but it doesn't matter, because then comes the Subliming." Ximenyr grinned at the arbite's camera eyes. "This was my plan from the start of the Last Party and my original idea was to spend a year or years sort of milking myself for the fluids to go in here, but that proved impractical. Water it is. Perfumed water." He winked at the arbite's eye cameras.

"Fucking typical man," Cossont muttered. "You know what he's done in that water, don't you?"

"Yes, but it's art," Berdle said, looking serious.

He and Cossont were holed up behind some lightweight

furniture in a disused storage space one deck below the curving corridor Ximenyr and the reporter arbite had just walked down. They were watching the arbite's feed along with who-knew-how-many people across Xown and the Gzilt domain; there was no shortage of fascinating screen to watch from all over the Gzilt hegemony in these end-days, for those with time to spare from their own preparations for the Subliming, but the Last Party had achieved a modest level of fame over the years, and allegedly many millions of people were watching.

"Lovely warm perfumed water," Ximenyr was saying, "dosed with cutaneous-contact-hallucinogens, so it'll be quite a crazy ride just getting to the top, and you can't just float straight up either; there are baffles. So it's more of a 3D maze, really."

"So, is this symbolic of our struggle towards enlighten-ment, or a comment on our tortuous route to Subliming?"

Ximenyr shrugged. "Yeah, if you like. I just thought it'd be neat."

"What about pressure?"

Ximenyr snapped his fingers. "Good question. You know, *I* didn't think of that at first either? Just not of a practical or engineering turn of mind, I guess. But it's much smarter than that; there are field projectors and AG units studded all around the cylinder; there are all these exotic matter particles or something dissolved into the water – whatever; don't ask me the technical details – and you pass through these levels of pressure." He slapped the taut-sounding surface of the nearest small sphere again. "The pressure is highest down here, but it's only like being about eight metres down, not four hundred."

"So, Ximenyr, anyone may join you in this?"

"Anyone but not everyone. We'll have to be selective, let

just a few people aboard at a time. We need to balance the extra weight of people coming in with our positive buoyancy . . . factor, or something. Anyway, there's refuse we've got stored up and long-term supplies we're not going to be using, all of which we'll be dumping gradually as we take people on, so we're going to have room for lots more people." He looked up, nodding at the circular patch of bright lights directly overhead. "A few brave guys and gals are already up there, after doing the testing. Couple of panickers when it all took too long and they couldn't work out the maze, but they're fine by now and we've made it all a lot easier, with cheats and guidance available." He smiled dazzlingly at the arbite's camera eyes. "Should be a cool last ride."

"That's annoying," Berdle said.

"Why?" Cossont asked. "Compared to the last tank of warm liquid we were in . . ."

"Yes, but if we have to get through that one, I'm going to show up. I'm too dense. If I support myself with AG or even field, they'll spot me."

Cossont was squatting beside him in her double-layer suit. She had watched the feed from the arbite on a wrist screen after deciding to risk rolling down the helmet parts of both suits. The air, she had been pleased to discover, smelled perfectly nice, though somehow you could sort of tell there had been construction work going on recently.

"Too dense? Like, too heavy?" she asked.

"Yes." Berdle looked at Cossont, nodding at her suit. "And you'll be, too. Those suits mass a lot more than they feel. Outer one especially. Inner might expand enough, though you might look a bit fat."

Cossont shrugged. "I'm not my mother; I don't care. More to the point, though, did you spot that our man doesn't seem to have his necklace on any more?"

"Yes." The avatar nodded. "That could be a problem."

"We don't even know how personal that stuff is for him," Cossont said. "Might have just abandoned it; left it in a bedside cabinet or something. God, he might have thrown it out!"

"Maybe we should look back in the sewage tank," Berdle suggested. Cossont looked at him. The avatar shrugged. "Just kidding; I checked it out as a matter of course when we were in there. Nothing."

"Maybe it's up at his . . . bedroom suite. Where we were when we saw him before," Cossont suggested.

"That's not there any more," Berdle said. "I've found the remodelling plans in one of the airship's data banks, such as they are. Whole volume was ripped out." The avatar shook his head. "Their internal video monitoring is so patchy. There might be some record in here of what happened to all that stuff, but . . . found it. Ah."

"Is that a good 'Ah'?" Cossont asked.

"Partially," Berdle told her. "All his personal effects are more or less where they were; in some sort of chest or locker . . . yes, a big sort of upright wheeled chest thing, in this 'heaven' space, at the top of the giant liquid tank."

"Think Mr Q's missing bits are there?"

"Maybe. Ximenyr's . . . had a temporary cabin near the main medical suite for the last eight days," Berdle reported, still quizzing the airship's systems.

"Probably having all his extra cocks removed," Cossont muttered.

Berdle shook his head. "*Very* suspicious AIs on this thing. I am having to do *so* much track-covering-up as I go along here . . . Yes, he had a locker or something of some sort there too. Going to check that first."

Cossont started to stand up but he pulled her back down again. "I've an insectile on that particular job."

"If they're not there, think we'll have to swim through the big tank?"

"Perhaps."

"Can't we just come in from the top?"

"No. It's all shielded. It looks transparent up there, like a big glass dome, but it isn't; it's a two-way screen, metres thick. Once the ship's back, in about twelve minutes, we have the option of blasting the shielding out of the way and Displacing in, but that's a last resort; wasting 4D without causing horrendous collateral in the associate flat-space is almost impossible. In 4D you think all you've done is kick down a door, and imagine you've done it really neatly, minimum force, but then you look back into 3D and realise you've blown down the whole building. Sometimes the whole block."

"Twelve minutes till the ship's back?"

"Just under. Though how easy the Gzilt battleship will make it for me to do anything as delicate as targeting bits of 4D shielding in the first place is very much open to question."

"Is there going to be a fight?"

"Yeah, could be," Berdle said. "There goes our boy," he added.

Cossont switched her wrist screen on again to see Ximenyr placing his white shift on a shelf and then walking into a vaginal-looking vertical aperture in one of the translucent spheres, a breather tube gripped in his mouth. He was quite naked. Only one penis, as far as Cossont could see. And he didn't seem to have anything else with him that might have contained the pair of eyes.

Some sort of double liquid-lock had allowed Ximenyr to enter the sphere without any fluid spilling. There was a pause while he stood and fluid swirled up around him, then a sphincter valve at the top of the sphere opened and he rose quickly and easily up, out of the sphere and into the liquid-filled tank above.

". . . And so," the reporter arbite began to intone, gravely. Cossont switched the sound off and just watched Ximenyr's pale-looking body as he swam out at an angle into the darkness. The extra lights he'd asked for earlier, or the enhancement, had been switched off, so his shape disappeared into the watery shadows after barely half a minute; the vast tank was now an almost entirely dark megatonne presence hanging over the scene below. The view switched to the other party-goers taking off their own shifts and preparing to step naked into the translucent spheres to follow Ximenyr.

"The locker in the medical suite's got nothing," Berdle said quietly, shaking his head.

"Can I see?" she asked.

"Need a helmet to see properly," the avatar told her. "Use the inner suit." She brought the hood-helmet up. The view darkened, stabilised. A space like a small dark room, one wall edged all round with dim light; quilts on the floor, a small rug, rolled, and a couple of ancient-looking flat screens. "A pair of pants," Berdle announced. "A single sock. The end of a roll of antiseptic splint-bandage patches. A tooth plectrum. A pair of time-to devices. That's all."

"Sure this isn't art too?"

"Fairly certain."

"We're going to have to go up through that fucking tank, aren't we?"

"Looking like it."

Cossont redirected her attention to local reality in time to watch Berdle stand, and then saw what looked like his skin and flesh just falling away, under his clothes, exactly as if his flesh had turned to jelly. She felt her mouth open, had time to wonder if they were under attack from some sort of flesh-melting weapon, then noticed that the avatar was watching this whole process with nothing more than interest.

"Shedding excess weight," Berdle said through her helmet.

He stood in a neatly circular pool of fleshy stuff, reduced to something not far off a skeleton, though one with what still looked like a covering of skin; clothes hanging off him, face like a skull, his knees the widest part of his legs and his elbows the widest part of his arms above his wire-thin wrists, wrinkled skin covering all exposed surfaces.

Then he filled slowly out again, as though his still-skin-covered bones – or what passed for bones – were themselves expanding. His skin became smooth again, his face filled out. Then his clothes fell away too, joining the thick puddle at his feet, all of which turned white and developed folds. The avatar – equipped with a perfectly respectable-looking penis, Cossont was pleased, in a general kind of way, to see – stooped and picked up the stuff that had recently been the equivalent of skin, flesh and muscle and which was now a convincing, if quite thick, white robe, which he let drop on from above. There was another one, still round his feet. He lifted it with one foot, handed it to her.

"Best I can do," he said.

"No, no; bravo."

"You'll need to lose the outer suit; sorry."

"That's okay." The suit split down the front and she stepped out of it. It collapsed and compressed into something that looked like a sort of flattened, elongated black crash helmet.

"We won't have to go out the same way we came in, will we?" she asked.

Berdle shook his head. "Highly unlikely. Just the under-suit would keep you safe, anyway."

The under-suit was changing too; expanding slightly, so that, in most places, its surface was about a centimetre or so out from her own skin. It was changing colour and texture too, coming to look convincingly like skin. A thin layer crept over her face, making her skin feel tight.

"That feels weird."

"Yes, but you're unrecognisable," the avatar told her. Berdle's face had changed too; he looked nothing like he had the last time they'd been here. Still good-looking, but less striking.

Cossont looked down at herself. "Weird," she said. "I feel more naked now than I do when I'm naked." She pulled the thick, heavy shift on over her head. It lay, weighty, on her shoulders. "There's only one set of arm holes!"

Her lower arms had to hang down inside the pale shift.

"Those extra arms are the one thing about you it's hard to disguise," Berdle said.

"Hmm," she said. "Yeah, I suppose it is better if we don't advertise those."

"Take the shift off as late as you can," Berdle suggested.

"Okay. What about Mr Q?" Cossont asked, She recalled the avatar telling her while they'd still been on the *Mistake Not . . .* that QiRia's mind-state had been put into the outer suit.

"I've already transferred him to the inner suit," Berdle told her. "He'll run slower but feel free to wake him up and talk to him if you want; he's functional."

"Maybe later." Cossont used one foot, toeing the compacted outer suit. "This?"

"Stays here unless we need it, when it becomes a drone. Though it'll blow its cover the instant it switches on its AG or a lift-field." Berdle straightened, flexed, looked at her. "Ready?"

"As I'll ever be. Let's go."

~We are quite certain there is no way they could already be aboard? Colonel Agansu asked the *Churkun*'s captain.

~We are reasonably certain, the captain replied. ~Not absolutely certain.

Agansu found this reply inadequate, but chose not to say anything. People were cheering all around him. He looked at the airship. The *Equatorial 353* was displaying a count-down on its hull now; giant numbers three hundred metres high were clicking down the time to zero. There was half a minute to go.

Boarding gantries had swung out from various opened galleries and balconies dotted along the side of the airship, where crew could be seen opening doors and preparing to extend the gantries the last few metres that would let people use them to board. The gantries ended in complicated-looking up-and-over constructions that let them extend over the roadway parapet. Agansu watched the nearest one lower slowly towards the roadway surface, just ahead. A crew-person from the airship stood on the bottom step of the lowering gantry, holding a flimsy-looking gate closed, preparing to open it.

People were already jostling to get close to the steps. Agansu, simply massing much more than any human of his size, had no difficulty in shouldering people out of the way and making his way quickly to the front. He made suitably placatory gestures and muttered, "Excuse me," several times, to avoid unnecessary unpleasantness, though he did hear some complaints. Soon he was walking at a slow stroll with the gated steps facing him and various people jostling him ineffectually at his sides and back.

~Colonel, I'm going to hand you over to our marine operations officer now, the captain sent. ~The Culture ship is returning and showing every indication it intends to pull to a stop here in about ten minutes, and my full attention is required to be focused on this development.

~I see, Agansu replied.

~Marine operations here, Colonel. I've had all units looking for anything remotely like a ship avatar and so far nothing's registering. With this many units in a minimum double-shell configuration we've got really good triangulation and background grain size, so something ought to have shown up by now. I think the person or people you're looking for is/are already aboard. Also, a closer inspection of the airship has identified a few spaces that are not fully shielded. Our surveillance specialist has started putting equipment in there, though it's not proving easy to gain access to the rest of the vessel. Do you want us to look for a place to disloc you aboard?

~That will not be necessary, Agansu replied, looking across to the giant figures displayed on the airship's skin. Just a few seconds left. He could see more galleries appearing on the side of the vessel as portions of the hull folded inwards. Doors were opening. ~I am about to board now, conventionally. Inform Marshal Chekwri.

~Acknowledged, sir. Will do. We've got insect-plausible surveillance devices entering the apertures opening in the airship, though the shielding is going to make keeping in touch with them difficult; we'll need a lot to keep a comms chain open. Also, I'm just getting some civilian feed here from the airship; public channel. Seems this Ximenyr person is heading . . . for the top of the ship, but the only way in is through some big water tank, from the bottom.

~Thank you, Agansu sent, as the countdown shown on

the side of the airship reached zero. A great ragged cheer went up all around and the crew-person on the steps just ahead of him opened the boarding gate.

Agansu stepped onto the gantry, feeling it dip under his weight. ~Continue to monitor me, he sent, ~and have arbites near, ready to lend close support.

~Sir.

He smiled at the crew-person.

Cossont was letting the shift drop from round her shoulders, with Berdle just behind her, sheltering her – "The lady is modest," he'd told the people helping. Just then, right at the entrance to one of the translucent spheres, something happened to several of the lights shining into the giant tank. One in particular, off to the side, flared brightly, then seemed to go out entirely. Most of the rest kept on flickering as they dimmed.

Everybody in the space under the tank was looking at the lights. Cossont, forewarned by Berdle, was almost the only person not distracted. She stepped quickly out of the fallen shift and into the glutinously resisting field protecting the entrance to the sphere. Warm water swirled rapidly up round her almost immediately; she was raised off her feet a little as it reached her neck. She lifted her head, with the breather device clamped in her mouth and over her nose, as the waters closed over her and the valve above opened. She was borne up anyway, but kicked as well, catching a hazy, distorted glimpse of Berdle picking up her shift and walking across the space – beneath her, now – to deposit it on a shelf. The lights seemed to return to normal as the view below disappeared.

"The maze is fairly simple," Berdle said through the suit's earbuds as she bumped head-first into what felt like a ceiling of something elastic and giving, but strong. "The suit will tell you the direction to head in, using this voice. For now, turn ninety degrees to your left, follow the ceiling until you feel a downward current and then swim to your right."

She did as she was told. She could see a couple of other people exiting from other spheres and striking out into the darkness: shadowy forms moving slowly in the darkness like smooth and liquid flames of flesh. She kept her lower set of arms tight against her body as she swam with the upper set until the other people had faded into the darkness, taking different routes. Then she pulled hard with all four arms, and kicked.

She felt a current heading down, and so turned right. "Straight up now," the voice said, and she zoomed, passing into a strange gel-like region in the water where it seemed to grow thicker and press in against her from all sides. Through it, she felt the water pressure change a little, decreasing. The temperature was a little cooler, too. "Just entering the tank now," Berdle told her. "Keep going. I'll stay behind you."

Prevented from speaking by the breather in her mouth, and unable to just think-send speech the way the avatar could, she found herself nodding, and wondered if the suit would transmit the action to Berdle.

She swam on up through the darkness, alone save for the sound of her own breathing and a few dim, wavering lights.

"Firearms are not permitted on board, sir," the crew-person told Agansu. "We're showing that you have a side-arm secreted by your lower back. That will have to be left here, with us."

He had been stopped at the far end of the boarding gantry, on a sort of gallery set into the side of the airship. Two people, both large and dressed in standard-looking private security garb, barred his way. The woman who was talking was in front, her male colleague behind, standing in the open doorway in the hull of the *Equatorial 353*.

"I am a colonel in the Home System Regiment on a special assignment," Agansu said quietly to the woman, aware of people starting to queue up behind him on the narrow gantry. "I appreciate and commend your alertness, however I do require entry to the vessel and I may well have need of my side-arm."

~Marine operations officer, Agansu sent, ~are you reading all this?

~Yes, sir.

~Kindly bring one of your units to bear here, would you? Prepare to stun to temporary unconsciousness the two people blocking my way. Ten minutes should be sufficient. And have . . . four units ready to accompany me inside the vessel.

~Sir. Using AG inside the vessel is likely to make the units obvious to the airship's systems.

~Have them switch to limbed locomotion on entry.

~Sir. Five units switched to your immediate control, now.

~I have them, Agansu confirmed, aware, in a virtual space behind his eyes, of exactly where the five marine arbites were in relation to him and his immediate surroundings.

"I'm afraid our orders make no allowance for that, sir," the security officer was telling him.

~Sir? the marine operations officer sent. ~Getting some data on a person of interest – the Cossont, Vyr, woman – entering the water tank in the airship, sir. Not a definite ID though; small bug, a distance off, and comms link unsteady.

"Hey!" somebody shouted in the queue behind Agansu. "Get moving!"

The security officer glanced behind him, then frowned at him. "Also, sir," she said, "I'm just hearing from our colleagues on board that you are showing as very non-standard physiologically. There is a new policy in force aboard which means that if you're an android or avatar you will need special permission to board."

The man behind her had stepped back a pace and one hand had fallen to a holstered side-arm.

~Stun both, now.

~Sir.

The woman's eyes closed. She collapsed, her knees giving way first so that she just seemed to sit heavily. Then she fell over backwards. The man behind performed the same actions a half-second later, as though in impersonation.

Agansu stepped over the two inert bodies and into the doorway; two marine arbites, visible more as disturbances in the air than as anything physical, darted in before him. They landed on the threshold with audible thumps, the air shimmering as they entered.

"Whoa!"

"Hey, what—?" voices said, inside.

~Stun, Agansu sent, as he looked within.

Two more bodies were folding into unconsciousness, a couple of metres inside the door. Agansu turned and looked back at the faces of the people crowding the boarding gantry. They were all looking either at the two fallen security guards outside, or at him. He smiled. The other two arbites made shimmering shapes in the air and landed in the doorway, slipping inside like shadows, only half seen.

~Close and lock the door, he said, over the channel to the arbite marines. The door swung to, then made clunking, locking noises. The space he was in now was perhaps twenty metres long but only five deep. Various fixtures and fittings, none of them relevant, save that there seemed to be a large number of white tabards or shifts, neatly wrapped and stacked. Another open doorway led into the rest of the ship.

~Show yourselves, please, Agansu said over the marines' channel.

The four marine arbites dropped their camouflage, revealing them as stocky, metallic, vaguely humanoid shapes, crouched on pairs of zigzag legs. Each looked like something crayoned by a child then rendered in gun-metal. Their heads were long, flat, featureless.

~You will be arbites one through four, from lowest to highest serial number, Agansu told them. ~Understood?

~Understood, the arbites said in unison. They even sounded metallic.

She swam up through the layers and corridors of dark, warm water. The suit spoke to her in Berdle's voice now and again, directing her – or Berdle spoke to her, it was hard to tell.

She looked about as she swam, and noticed that some of the tiny, dim lights visible through the fluid had been arranged so as to look like the most familiar constellations visible from Xown. This made the experience like swimming through space. She wondered if the avatar would feel this. She saw only one other person, briefly, some distance off, and below.

She and Berdle had joined the unhurried groups of people heading towards the access spheres from the rest of the airship near the start of the whole process; fewer than fifty people had preceded them into the giant tank. Most of the Last Party-goers would ascend before anybody from outside, though a few would hold back to help guide any stragglers, and there were some who just wanted to be last, or amongst the last, to make the journey.

The other person swam off, away from her, and disappeared. She felt oddly abandoned, almost sad. She hoped the other swimmer would make it to the top of the tank without incident. There were, Berdle had assured her, various viable routes to the top of the tank; she and the avatar were taking the shortest and quickest.

The skin-contact hallucinogens in the water were diluted to deliver a modest dose to somebody swimming completely naked, so they were having no discernible effect on her at all. Still, there was a dreaminess and unreality to the dark swim that – along with the relative simplicity of only having to think to the extent of following an instruction every half minute or so, and the pleasant glow of continuous but unstressed physical effort – allowed her mind to wander, allowed her to think.

What a strange way to be approaching the end of one's life, she thought. Swimming through a vast tank of water and Scribe-knew-what towards a little artificial heaven with no escape, or only one. In search of a man's discarded eyes. With the avatar of a Culture ship following, swimming. And one of her own people's ships seemingly intent on stopping them. She had done a few strange things in her life, she supposed; why not leave one of the weirdest of all till last? To be topped only by the Subliming itself, she guessed.

Her breathing went on, like something apart from her, the whole sound-scape to her steady, paced exertion. Save that, the silence was entire, and she had started to understand something of QiRia's slow-building obsession with immersion, both literal and in sound. Especially in sound; in the waves of compression that took and flowed through the body rather than – like light, like sight – stopping at the surface. She had done something similar in a minor key herself, she realised, every time she stepped into the hollowness of the elevenstring and let that resound around her, through her.

She became slowly aware that, looking straight up, there was a sort of sparkling grey haze ahead of her, spreading to all sides. Lights. Lots of tiny lights. They started to grow brighter, everywhere overhead.

"Not far now," Berdle's voice said.

"Mmm," she heard herself say, mouth still clamped round the breather.

"There's one last turn to your left as it is at present, then straight up," Berdle said through the earbuds. "Take it easy there, okay? Slow down. I'll catch up and we can surface together."

She said, "Mmm," again, and nodded. She wondered why, as an avatar, Berdle couldn't just power his way up to join her, but maybe he was so weakened after having to lose so much mass this wasn't possible, or he just wanted to keep looking plausibly human. The spread of lights was close enough now for her to see the hints of some sort of framework stretched across the whole expanse above her. She thought she could see somebody walking along some sort of pierced walkway, five metres or so overhead.

The two ships faced each other. The Gzilt ship displayed as what it truly looked like inside its nest of fields: a steely clutch of blades like a hundred fat broadswords compressed into a barbed and jagged arrowhead. The Culture vessel projected no image beyond the surface view of its outermost fields. They were absurdly close, by the normal standards of conflict at their technological level, which was generally carried out from real-space light seconds away at least.

To be squaring up to an opponent from just a few kilometres off was pretty preposterous; both ships could extend their field enclosures well beyond this distance. It was a statement of relatively peaceful intent in a way – full-scale conflict was obviously not intended by either, or one of them would long since have opened fire by now – but worrying at the same time, given that both vessels knew their missions and intentions were incompatible.

Relative to Xown, the Gzilt ship had remained almost perfectly stationary throughout, parked in real space directly above the Girdlecity, moving at the same slow strolling speed as the *Equatorial 353*, five hundred kilometres below. The *Churkun* watched the Culture ship draw to a stop, relative to it, still entirely in hyperspace. It was a minor feat of field management to be able to do this so far into the gravity well of a planet, but then, according to the intelligence the *Churkun* had received via Marshal Chekwri, this vessel – the *Mistake Not . . .*, a Culture ship of slightly worrying indeterminate class – had proved itself something of an adept at this sort of thing, at Bokri.

The *Churkun* was keeled into hyperspace, its field enclosure bulging into the fourth dimension like somebody pressing an empty bowl brim-deep into a bath. This let it keep its options open and certainly it was able to watch everything that was happening there, but staying in the Real meant it could react faster to anything happening in the Girdlecity without having to worry about dislocs being intercepted.

The crew of the Gzilt ship were gauging what they could of their potential adversary, which expressed within hyperspace as the usual gauzy-looking silvery ellipsoid. Its current field enclosure topography guaranteed certain physical maxima and strongly indicated some likely limitations. So it was, certainly, categorically, no more than five kilometres in length and a third of that in diameter, and – if it followed conventional Culture field disposition – genuinely, physically, likely to be about twelve hundred metres long and maybe four hundred in diameter. This would make the vessel about fifty per cent smaller by volume than the *Churkun*, though the difference was not so great that it guaranteed the Gzilt ship's superiority.

~Good day, the Culture ship sent. ~I'm the *Mistake Not*
. . . I believe you are the *8*Churkun*.

~Correct. And I am its captain. Might we ask what brings
you here?

~Got personnel inside the Girdlecity, though I suspect
you've already guessed that.

~We are providing support for persons in there ourselves.
Further to that, this is now a zone of operational interest,
so we do have to ask you to leave.

~I see. You still have my module, I believe.

~We do. Though not actually aboard, as it were. Just in
case. We're inclined to treat it as captured hostile equipment,
especially given the way it was delivered. Perhaps we might
return it to you, following your departure, once this is no
longer a zone of operational interest, which, we repeat, we
must ask you to leave. Immediately.

~Ah, keep it if you like. Not that bothered. But I do need
to stick around for a bit.

~It is not going to be possible to accommodate that desire.
Obviously, we have no wish to engage in any hostilities with
you, but, if it comes to it, we are entirely prepared to do
just that if you do not leave, immediately.

~Be a bit close-range. Like nukes in a shed.

~Well, whatever it might take. This is though, sadly, not
open for negotiation. We must ask you to leave immediately.
One Culture ship has already met its end within Gzilt space
in the last few hours. I assume you have heard of the fate
of the *Beats Working*.

~Yes. It's just the kind of thing us Culture ships natter about.

~It would be unfortunate in the extreme if it were not to
remain the only casualty of such status hereabouts. *Please* leave.
And do understand that this is not a reduction in the force of
our demand that you do so – which remains in force and is,

564   IAIN M. BANKS

as of this statement, up to its fourth re-statement. It is, rather, an additional plea from those of us aboard with some respect for Culture vessels that you accede, without delay, to our demand before anything unfortunate occurs.

~Of course . . . not the only casualty, hereabouts, the plucky little *Beats Working*.

~Indeed, twelve Ronte ships were lost as well.

~With all hands. And then, in addition to that, there was that Z-R ship out at Ablate, twenty-two days ago.

~Really?

~Really. Kind of kicked off this whole rolling unpleasantness. Everything was spinning along pretty much fine until that bit of . . . well, how would one characterise it? Illegality? Cowardice? Piracy? Bullying to the point of murder? Just . . . murder?

~How little the differences between these terms mean to those subject to the act concerned. You ought to pay heed.

~Me that spotted it, too. I was rendezvousing with our Liseiden chums out at Ry when it happened. Caught the blink of that particular little atrocity.

~Remarkable. That is some distance away. Well spotted. Now, we really must ask you to leave, for the last time. There will be no more requests, only action. Our patience is, truly, exhausted.

~We could start by sort of tussling with fields. I did that out at Bokri, in Ospin, with your pal the *Uagren*. That was fun. Not something you get to do every day. Bestial, nearly, like locking horns. Actually, more like naked wrestling, all oiled up. I found it quite erotic, to tell the truth. Homoerotic, I suppose, technically, as we're all just ships together and we're all the same gender: neutral, or hermaphrodite or whatever, don't you think?

The *Churkun*'s reply was to attempt to wrap a burst field

all around the smaller Culture ship, an element of its field enclosure pulsing suddenly, nearly instantly out like a loop of a sun's magnetic field flicking, releasing a pulse of charged particles.

~Not even a nice try, shipfucker, the Culture ship sent, already dodged before the field bubble got anywhere near it. ~And now, watch this.

It flickered, shimmering in hyperspace as it fell, powering the trivial distance from where it had been, down the curve of the planet's gravity well, to the Girdlecity. Then it disappeared.

The first sign of alarm had been the warbling of a siren in the distance as he and the arbites had progressed along a broad, downward-slanting corridor. He hadn't noticed at first as he was busy trying to re-establish contact with the ship.

~Marine operations officer? he sent, then waited.

A few civilians walked in the distance. Many were dressed in white shifts similar to those he had seen earlier.

~Captain?

Some more white-clad civilians appeared from an elevator, just ahead; they stopped and stared when they saw Agansu and the disturbance in the air caused by the arbites' camouflage; effectively invisible to the naked eye from as little as ten metres away, the machines weren't fooling anybody this close, not when they moved. Even the blind would know they were there; the machines were marching carefully out of step and treading as delicately as they were able, but there was still a noticeable vibration shuddering along the wide floor of the corridor.

~*Captain?* Still no answer. ~Communications officer?

~Communication with the ship is not possible within this shielded environment, Arbite One told him.

~We have no link to other assets aboard? he asked.

~None at present, the arbite replied.

"Hey!" somebody shouted behind them. "Stop! On the floor, now!"

Agansu turned round to see a helmeted security person, armed with what was probably a stun rifle, running down the corridor towards them. ~Stun, he said to One.

The security guard staggered but didn't collapse.

~Stunning ineffective, Arbite One said.

The guard dropped to one knee and raised the gun.

Light flared, the guard's head flicked backwards and the figure collapsed.

~Weapon aimed, action taken, Arbite One sent, when Agansu looked at it. ~Standing orders.

Now people were screaming; the group at the open elevator were crowding back in. In the direction they had been heading, those who had been walking in front of them were stationary, looking back.

Lights – red, situated every fifteen metres along the corner the walls made with the ceiling – started to flash. Another siren had joined the first.

~I think, to put it in the vernacular idiom, our cover is blown, Agansu told the marine arbites. ~Resume full capacity including AG and field.

The arbites seemed to collapse in on themselves, compacting to the size of bulky backpacks, and hovering.

Agansu thought his own AG on. It was as though an invisible seat rose beneath him, bringing his legs up as he lay back. He had flown like this before in training and simulations; a familiar-feeling virtual glove-control seemed to fill his hand. He held the kin-ex side-arm in the other hand.

~Follow me, he sent to the four arbites. He raced down

the corridor, a metre and a half off the floor, feet first. This was the luge configuration; others preferred the toboggan, though Agansu had always thought such head-first antics both intrinsically more dangerous and a little showy.

The arbites flew in a horizontal square formation around him. They rose very close to the ceiling as they tore over the crowd of people they'd been following earlier, passing overhead without incident, though he heard somebody screaming. They had all dropped to the floor anyway. The piercing sound of the scream dopplered oddly as they swept past above, still following the downward curve of the corridor.

Seconds later, some distance ahead, he could see a crowd of white-clad people clustered around a broad circular staircase leading upwards.

~Insect-plausible device ahead reports person of interest passed this way, up steps ahead, into tank, earlier, Arbite One sent.

There were hundreds there; the steps were packed with people dressed in white.

~Deploy there, he sent. ~Make some noise now; get those people out of the way. Laser area denial bursts too, civilian warning grade.

The two lead arbites deployed tiny blast grenades, producing sudden flickers of light twenty metres in front of the crowd of people. The noise was very loud indeed. More light strobed, turning the whole scene ahead into a bright flare. People dropped, covered their ears, their eyes.

~Make for the aperture, he sent, spotting the large triangular piercing in the ceiling where the steps led.

The two leading arbites zoomed, disappeared. More flashes of light. ~Weapon aimed, action taken, he heard again as he curved up and through to land on the deck above.

It was generally dark. People were scattering. Two guards lay dead, faces gone, stun guns at their sides. This was a dark, very large space, almost entirely filled with a vast tank that looked like water; lights pointed inwards from every side around the enormous space. His enhanced senses mapped out what could be mapped out. One of the insect-plausible devices registered as nearby.

~olonel? somebody sent. The signal protocols were missing.

~Colonel Agansu? It was the marine operations officer.

~Here, beneath this large tank, Agansu replied.

~We're having some problems with the Culture ship supporting . . . The voice crackled, disappeared, came back on another crackle. ~ersons of interest would appear to be up inside . . . It was gone again.

~Units present undergoing effector attack, internal, airship own, Arbite One reported. ~Defending actions deployed.

Agansu was experiencing some problems of his own: the view was hazing over.

~Insect-plau— Arbite Three began.

~Hostile insect-plausible device attached to Arbite Three, Arbite One sent.

Something was glowing brightly on the upper surface of the arbite nearest the triangular hole in the floor.

~Hostile insect-plausible device attached to Arbite Three, Arbite Two confirmed.

~Our insect-plausible device immediately external reports hostile device app— There was a flash outside, where the stairs led down. ~Our insect-plausible device destroyed, Arbite One reported. ~Hostile device approaching registering as knife missile or similar.

~Marine operations officer! Agansu sent. ~Reinforcements, immediately! Use any means—

Something punched through the floor, beneath Arbite

One, spearing it and throwing it upwards to impact against the underside of the giant transparent tank. The glowing thing on the top surface of Arbite Three detonated at the same moment, blinding.

~Destroy the tank! Agansu sent, raising the kin-ex gun. He was able to fire once before he was blown off his feet by the blast from the erupted arbite.

~Destroy tank.

~Destroy tank, the two remaining arbites replied, and began firing upwards and around the walls, filling the darkness with insane, stuttering, flares of light.

She was treading water, revolving slowly and looking down between her slow, weed-waving legs, trying to see Berdle, when he said, "On second thoughts, just get to the surface. I'll join you shortly."

"Mmm," she said, and, after a quick look round, struck out.

"Wrong way, turn about," the suit told her in Berdle's voice.

She stopped. This was the way she'd been heading, wasn't it? Could the suit have got it wrong?

"Wrong way, turn about," the suit repeated.

"Hnnh," she said, then realised she had been twisting round while she'd been looking down to see the avatar. That was why she'd taken the wrong direction initially.

"You're heading the wrong way," Berdle told her. "There's some sort of emergency down there; just turn round, get out as quickly as you can. I'll be there very shortly."

She did a forward roll, started back the way she'd come. "Mmm," she said again, swimming hard now. Suddenly she felt very vulnerable, suit or no suit.

Something flickered deep below, as though from right at

the bottom of the tank. Something very bright. She knew she had seen light that white and intense recently. Her stomach lurched like she'd been punched. She got to where she'd been treading water moments earlier. The light flickered again, brighter still, seeming to reflect off the distant sides of the vast tank.

"Swim up fast *now*!" Berdle shouted.

She was already kicking out as hard as she could when it felt like the whole tank shuddered.

The first kin-ex round from his pistol had hit the lower surface of the great transparent tank and caused a single great torus of white to flash away from the point of impact. Then he'd been knocked off his feet despite the best efforts of the android body to stay upright. Further blindingly bright flashes filled the space as he struggled to kneel, firing upwards. The air shook like jelly around him.

~. . . *onel!* the marine operations officer was screaming at him.

~Unit Four destroyed by enemy action, Arbite Two sent.

The tank burst. It burst raggedly, in many different places; parts and levels of it seeming to stay where they were while other sections tore and fell and the released waters came crashing, hurtling down onto the space beneath. He threw himself to the floor. ~Hold where you are! he was able to send to the remaining arbite before the waters slammed into his back.

Light burst out everywhere below. A series of pulses shivered through the water and through her as Cossont kicked for the silvery, light-flecked surface above.

She had grasped the lowest step of a small ladder extending from the surface-level walkway above and was just starting to pull herself up when the water began to fall away around her.

She spat the breather away and yelled, "Berdle?" as she hauled herself up and out, needing all four arms to pull her own weight and resist the sucking drag of the descending water. A great roaring noise seemed to come partly from below and partly from above, sounding more like a powerful wind than water. The sound from above rose swiftly to a shriek.

Somebody – small, female, wearing a plain dark tunic – was running along the walkway towards her. The water beneath the dripping walkway, no longer lit by the bright pulses of light from below, was five metres down now, swirling in different directions, thrashing like something alive, and lowering everywhere, leaving behind an entire dripping web of walkways a hundred metres across, suspended on swaying chains from a dark ceiling just a couple of metres above, where panels were being torn away and sent spinning, whirling downwards.

"Still making upward progress," Berdle said calmly through the suit's earbuds. "Relatively and . . . now absolutely."

The girl running towards Cossont looked shocked, her mouth hanging open as she glanced over the side. "You all right?" she asked as she knelt by Cossont, having to raise her voice over the screaming wind.

Something burst from the surface of the waters, ten metres beneath, and rose towards them. It was vaguely human-shaped, but too big to be Berdle.

"What the fuck?" the girl said.

The whole airship seemed to shudder; the girl reached out to grab hold of a stanchion. The figure rising from the still falling waters – fifteen metres down now - rotated a little. It was Berdle, holding a naked man, supporting him with his own feet and an arm under his chest.

"Reckoned the time for a stealthy approach was gone," Cossont heard the avatar say as he landed beside her and the girl. "Barely had the AG to rescue this poor fellow." The man he was holding had wide, terrified-looking eyes. He didn't have a breather device in his mouth; he was coughing a lot. Berdle lowered him to the deck and the man clung to it, coughing up water. The girl patted his back.

"Good day," Berdle said to her, loudly, then held a hand out to Cossont. "Shall we?"

Cossont got to her feet. "What's happ—?"

The whole fabric of the airship shuddered once more. Beneath, where the waters roared, fifty metres down, two explosions burst from the swirling waves.

"Time to run!" Berdle said, turning and sprinting off along the walkway for a distant patch of light. "Follow me!"

She raced off after him, vaulting the naked, coughing man and hammering down the walkway behind the avatar. Thin pillars of cerise light flicked into existence, splashing fire from the ceiling. One lanced through the walkway a metre behind Berdle's flying feet; she jumped the resulting fist-sized hole.

"One right turn at the next junction, steps up dead ahead," she heard his voice tell her. "I'll join you momentarily."

Then the avatar put out a hand, caught hold of one of the walkway's supporting chains and was lifted off his feet and spun round, just as another pink bolt pierced the walkway immediately ahead of him. He dropped over the side of the walkway, at first falling, then curving away through the darkness and the everywhere roar of water. Light glittered again inside the tank as two shapes rose twisting though the air beneath, filling the space with hair-thin shining filaments.

She put her head down, pounded along the wildly swinging gantry, skidded round the corner at the junction and saw a short flight of steps leading up through the ceiling.

The storm of air howling down through the hole in the ceiling made it almost impossible to make any headway. She needed all four arms to pull herself upwards on the chain bannister rails, and all the strength in her own legs and the suit's to force her way up the metal steps. Small pieces of debris came hurtling down from above and hit her shoulders or bounced off her head, hurting her even through the thin covering of suit-helmet.

"Ow! Fuck!" she said, though the scream of air tearing around her was so loud she couldn't actually hear anything else.

She made the deck above, threw herself onto the soft, carpeted floor under subdued lighting and rolled away from the torrent of air being sucked howling into the emptying cavern beneath. Around her – in what looked like a very large, complicated, low-ceilinged room – terrified-looking people were staring wide-eyed at her over the top of luxuriously sculpted pieces of pale furniture. A man and a woman were sitting on a nearby couch, feet braced against the floor, causing rumples in the carpet, their fingers clawing into the soft material of the cushions they sat on. The couch itself was jerking and sliding across the floor, towards the hole. The woman closed her eyes. The man opened his mouth in what was probably a scream but there was too much other noise to tell.

Cossont used all four hands to claw her way across the floor. Something white came whirling towards her; she ducked instinctively as a fat square pillow bounced over her and disappeared into the maelstrom around the aperture in the floor. Where it had come from, twenty metres away, part of the floor gave way and a set of couches and chairs holding maybe a half dozen people disappeared, sucked downwards into the darkness.

"*Berdle?*" she yelled. But she didn't even know if he'd be able to hear her – she couldn't hear herself.

*

The first problem was getting all the bits and pieces out of the way, so there would be room for itself.

Actually, who was it kidding? The first problem was all about not blowing up the world, or at the very least not annihilating both itself, fifty horizontal kilometres of Girdlecity, who-knew-how-many lives locally and immediately, and then an additional who-knew-how-sizable number over a significant proportion of the rest of the planet with the resulting fireball, blast front, secondary debris impact events and all the resulting ancillary fire, tertiary impact and ground-shock effects.

Another fucking day at the office, the ship thought, putting all such thoughts to one side and cascade-checking all the available variables, before just doing it.

There were fourteen craft and over eighty individuals in the fifteen hundred metres of tunnel which started one hundred metres behind the stern of the *Equatorial 353*. The first task was Displacing them safely. Or at least quickly. The quickly mattered more than the safely, and one of the larger craft, containing nine or ten people, picked up rather more relative velocity at the far end of the Displace than the *Mistake Not . . .* would have liked, sending the flier flicking forward by a couple of extra metres per second as it bounced in. That might mean broken limbs if the occupants weren't restrained, but that was the worst of it; everything else transitioned relatively smoothly.

The space was clear. The ship went for it, jumping across into real space in a single vast snap, as precisely aligned as possible in the circumstances and the time available, its enclosure fields shrunk, sucked, wrapped as tight as they would go about itself, leaving it with maybe fifty metres all around it between the outermost of those tightly compressed fields and the nearest bit of Girdlecity solidity. There was an important part of the whole process that depended on something called – only slightly misleadingly – the singularity-expansor transfer component. The ship finessed that as well as it could, but this time its own safety – not to mention the safety of the Girdlecity, millions of people, the planet, etc. – trumped technical perfection, so the expansion ended up being relatively rough and ready, and undeniably abrupt.

The ship blew into existence almost explosion-fast, creating a vast pulse of air that tore out through the fortunately dispersed structure of the open-work tunnel and the surrounding architecture of the Girdlecity, bowling people over, sending nearby aircraft tumbling, shattering antique windows and denting cladding panels for hundreds of metres about it.

Messy, the *Mistake Not . . .* would be entirely prepared to concede, but never mind. In the end it had worked and it was where it had wanted to be; in the same huge basket-weave tunnel as the airship *Equatorial 353*, just a hundred metres behind it.

~What idiocy is this? the captain of the *Churkun* sent.

~A fitting idiocy, the ship replied. ~I fit. You won't. And if I need to I can put my enclosure right around the airship from here, so I suggest you leave me be. Out.

The blast of air seemed to have relented a little, if only because more floor panels had given way, providing additional routes for the air to escape through. The two people on the couch that had been slipping towards the hole in the floor had scrambled up and over the back of it, crawling away; the couch itself had stopped moving.

"Berdle!" Cossont screamed. No reply. It was still bedlam but at least now she could hear herself. She saw another stairway, spiralling upwards ten metres away, behind the nearest semi-circle of chairs. She got onto one knee, heaved herself upright and leaned into the still-furious gale, forcing herself forward, straining to see any more debris coming her way.

Another shudder ran through the whole airship, sending her flying. She heard herself yelp as she fell, being blown backwards, caught in the lacerating torrent of air; she dropped to the floor and held on again, cursing.

Agansu pushed himself up against the pummelling force of the water, finally getting to all fours. The android body was gauging, calibrating, allowing for the vast pressing weight surging across it. It could still function, and its AG should still be effective. Walls burst, the floor gave way in a variety of places nearby, letting in a little more light, allowing the surging fall of water to escape.

The remaining arbite reported when Agansu pinged it.

~Holding approximately steady in downward course of water, it told him.

~Attempt to rise, he told it. ~Head for the top of the tank. I shall too.

The suit let him stand, unsteady, shuddering, in the torrent. Agansu saw two broken-looking bodies being swept past, naked.

He activated the AG, lifted off the floor, and began to make his way, quivering, battered from all sides, up through the chaotic swirl of the descending column of water.

He and the remaining arbite burst from the surface of the water into a great dark space more than sixty metres high and hundreds across, buffeted by swirling winds.

High above, just beneath a randomly pierced ceiling, a rig of metalwork gantries hung suspended. Some figures moved up there.

~Avatar-android identified, the arbite told him as they rose, accelerating, together.

~Fire, destroy it, he told the arbite.

Violet bolts seared through the air, sparking explosions from the ceiling; sparks and pieces of glowing debris fell towards them. Two figures were running, overhead.

~Target employing visual camouflage fields, the arbite reported, still firing as they rose. Next thing, the leading figure – a composite haze of images, like a stacked pack of ghosts – fell or threw itself from the gantry and came whirling down through the turmoil of air and falling debris towards them, light glittering from it.

The colonel realised suddenly, only at this point, that he had lost the kin-ex side-arm. He had no idea exactly when or where. This was upsetting. The android body had its pair of forearm-mounted lasers – but he doubted they would prove especially effective after what had happened at Bokri. The arbite fired at the falling figure, seeming to hit it. Agansu raised his arms, aiming at the other running figure, then, in a single staggering impact and a wash of white, was hit by something, and sent tumbling.

He was aware of falling, somersaulting. He steadied himself, or the suit did. He didn't know. When he was floating in mid-air, he looked around and could see nothing of the last arbite or the figure that had dropped from the gantry. Below, in the great swirl of water and dashing, chaotic waves, there were the fading remains of what might have been two large splashes on the dark waters.

~Arbite, report, he said.

"Comms internal only," the android body told him. Agansu felt groggy. And odd: strange, unbalanced. He looked at his right arm, which was not there. He stared. The arm ended at about midway on the upper part. The stump was still smoking.

~Arbite . . . marine oper— he started to say, still unsure regarding what had happened.

"Comms internal only," the android body repeated.

"Yes, of course," Agansu said, looking inside himself to monitor the body's operational state. Severely compromised. AI substrate intact, obviously: AG, conventional locomotion and one arm and one laser left.

~Upwards, he thought, and ascended through the bruising cataract of air.

"Ximenyr? Where's Ximenyr?" she yelled, crouched down by the frightened-looking man in front of her He was clad in one of the dark tunics, and holding grimly on to a desk as the air rushed past. This level, one up, looked like the foyer of some exclusive hotel. Getting up here had been a little easier than her last ascent as the storm of air gradually lessened. It was still fierce enough.

"Where's Ximenyr?" she shouted again over the roaring. The man just shook his head.

She turned away, muttered, "Suit, any idea?"

"Interrogating local systems," the suit said, still in Berdle's voice. "Mr Ximenyr's suite is this way; please follow."

The suit seemed to raise itself. It faced a broad, well-lit corridor. She walked with the suit, then started to jog through the noticeably thinner air. "Switching to supplemental oxygen supply, ten per cent," the suit announced. She felt something connect delicately with her nostrils; a cool draught hit the skin there.

"Still trying Berdle?" she asked the suit.

"Constantly," it told her, in his voice. "Here," the suit said, drawing them both to a stop at a double doorway. "Open?" it asked.

"Yes!"

"Opening," the suit said, and the doors slid apart.

Oh shit, the ship thought to itself.

The *Mistake Not . . .* had lost contact with all of its devices on and in the airship, including its own avatar. It was busily scattering new surveillance stuff all over the place now, as fast as it could, but it might already be too late.

The airship *Equatorial 353* was riding as high as it could go, tearing its upper surfaces to shreds along the giant grater that was the ceiling of the huge open tunnel, shedding panels and pieces of equipment as it ground slowly to a stop, all the while dropping what looked like megatonnes of water from its lower reaches: whole falls, giant cascades of water were issuing from its sides, while further sheets and folds of water fell straight down from its ventral line, taking bulkhead panels and entire sections of hull with them, falling, spinning slowly away in the colossal squall of rain. The airship ground to a stop, trapped against the ceiling of the tunnel. Water continued to gush from its lower hull.

Crushed, broken bodies littered the network of pipes, girders and structure beneath the stricken craft. Not all were dead; the ship Displaced what medical support drone and life-saving equipment it had to those still able to be saved.

There were a lot of drone-like military devices floating about the place – over two hundred and forty of them. They were making a nuisance of themselves; sixty-four had already tried attacking its outermost bump-field with X-ray lasers – though exactly why and with what hope of success, the ship was unable to work out; maybe they'd all gone mad – plus all of them now seemed to be working themselves up to attack it again with some other piece of seed-shootery nonsense, so, once it had despatched all its medical teams, it targeted all of the enemy drones, disabling each with a pinpoint granule of plasma fire and instantly – even before they could explode properly – wrapping them individually in Displace fields and swatting them into hyperspace, directed roughly towards where the *Churkun* was – it assumed they were its.

There might be more of these aggravations inside the airship, it supposed. It still couldn't see within the vessel properly and its devices were taking their time getting inside.

Fuck this, the *Mistake Not . . .* decided, and sliced a tiny cone, less than a couple of metres deep and the same across, off the very stern of the airship with a millimetrically flourished ZPE/b-edged destabiliser field. The cone fell away in a cloud of sparkling grey. No bodies sliced in half, which was good, but there was still 4D shielding ahead. The ship cut again; three metres this time, still with no casualties, or result.

The zero-point energy/brane edging component seemed be handling the 4D shielding well; much less blow-back than it had been led to expect from the simulations. The *Mistake Not . . .* was growing more confident using the weapon. This time it cut twenty metres off the stern of the crippled airship and held the resulting hull section in a maniple field, lowering the conic section to the soaking, pooled floor of the tunnel, trying to avoid laying it on any of the bodies.

Finally.

It was past the shielding. It could see into the interior of the airship. It could already tell there were a lot more dead and dying bodies inside, though no more annoying drone military.

~Berdle? Anybody? it asked.

Ximenyr's suite or not, the man himself wasn't there.

"No persons present," the suit told her.

She looked around. Some sort of sitting or reception room. The place looked banal, in a spacious, luxurious, understated sort of way. Quite different from the sumptuous, over-dressed surroundings she and Berdle had found The Master of the Revels in the last time they'd been in the airship.

"What about that . . . chest, thing, Berdle mentioned?" she asked.

She moved towards another set of double doors. The lights flickered in the suite, seeming almost to fail, then recovering.

"Item fitting description in adjacent cabin, facing," the suit said helpfully just before it opened the doors for her.

Still nobody about. One giant octagonal bed; many curtained alcoves, some holding items of furniture. In one stood the big upright chest Berdle had talked about earlier.

It was about as tall as she was and maybe a metre wide and deep when closed. It had a small wheel at each corner and stood hinged open to about ninety degrees. Clothes on a rail filled most of one side; the other side was all drawers.

She opened the top drawer, going up on tiptoe to see inside. The little cylinder lay on a piece of soft, folded material along with the rest of the bits and pieces that had been on the necklace they'd seen ten days earlier.

She stared at it, picked it up.

Behind their little window of thick crystal, the pair of sea-green orbs that had looked like berries seemed to stare back at her.

"Anomalous pres—" the suit began.

Then two things happened.

She was struck – kicked, it felt like – in the back, very hard, though somehow she and the suit managed to stay standing. At the same time something burst brightly, pink and white, off the drawer-front immediately before her, about level with the middle of her chest.

She was still thinking about turning round, wondering what had happened, when she realised that whatever light had burst against the drawer-front must have come straight through her to get there.

Smoke drifted up from the exit wound in her chest. She could smell roasted meat over the cold, sharp sensation of the oxygen.

"—ence detect . . ." the suit said, as more, individually slightly lighter kicks struck her all over her back and rear. This time she was thrown against the drawers of the chest, and the whole thing nearly tipped over. Then it bounced off the bulkhead behind and she was thrown back again, turning woozily round as she did so – the little trails of smoke made pretty spirals in the relatively still air – before she started to slide downwards. The ruined, ragged back of the suit went stuttering down the set of drawer handles, jolting her as she slumped to the deck.

A one-armed figure was standing in the doorway looking at her, just lowering his one good arm.

"Ship . . . re . . . establish – blish – lish – ish – shh . . ." the suit whispered to her, and sighed to quietness. The faint draft of oxygen at her nostrils faded.

Then the one-armed figure in the doorway lit up brilliantly all down one side, from foot to scalp, and was thrown bodily, hard against the door jamb, pieces flying off it as it rebounded, lit up from the other side now, disintegrating.

What was left, reduced to something like a too-thin, charred, one-armed skeleton, fell forwards, hitting the deck at about the same time as she did.

Twenty-three

(S -0)

Something.
    Somebody talking to her.
Asking questions. A question:
Did she want to keep both sets of arms?
Of course she wanted to keep both sets of arms. What
sort of idiotic, dumb-ass—
. . . back to sleep . . .
This would all be hurried, extemporised, done much more
quickly than the normal guidelines advised, to keep to the
schedule.
She didn't know, didn't care, didn't even know where she

was, in this darkness. Once or twice she woke up – in this darkness – and wondered who she was.

But each time she remembered.

". . . it was all a sociological experiment by the Zihdren. A rogue Philosophariat – the Philosophariat Apposital . . . I think that was their name – they, it – it was all down to one individual in the end – planted everything in the Book of Truth according to some obscure Metalogical hypothesis, to settle an argument between two groups of scholars with opposing theories. Briper Drodj, the Scribe, elaborated on the basics as everybody pretty much knew, but the essence was always what the Zihdren had put there. Of course this whole approach was later discredited and the Philosophariat Apposital was 'Dissolved with Moderate Disgrace' not long after, and this particular experiment – like many similar others – was quietly forgotten. The Zihdren Sublimed a couple of centuries later, decades before the Gzilt even reached space.

"All this became known to a very few people way back at the start of the process which brought the Culture into existence. Happened following contact by Zihdren-Remnanter. They were, I suppose – so they claimed – conscience-stricken. Well, conscience-charged might be a better way of putting it. The Zihdren had felt bad taking this grubby little secret into the Enfolding so they thought they could have the best of both worlds by Subliming without mentioning it but leaving it to their Remnanters to spill the broth at a later date.

"There had been rumours about all this before, of course, but no one who counted in Gzilt society, or not enough of them, had ever really thought it mattered all that much until then, when the whole join-this-new-grouping-or-not thing was in the air. And, by the by, it wasn't even definitely going to be called the Culture at this point; did you know that? A lot of people wanted that we should all call ourselves the Aliens, I remember, but . . . anyway, the vote went to 'Culture'. Though, frankly, I didn't vote for it. Or Aliens, I might add; I abstained.

"Anyway, we knew – the negotiating teams knew – that there was something the Remnanters had inherited – some dark secret or something – that might have a bearing one way or the other on the whole joining issue, for the Gzilt. Maybe even – the rumours were crazy, some of them – for the others too, as in a veto against the Gzilt joining being used, perhaps, by one or more of the other parties. Which was sort of ticklish enough, but, the thing is, the Remnanters still wanted the thing kept secret afterwards, even after it had been factored into the negotiations.

"That caused some head-scratching.

"It was an AI that came up with what looked like the best solution, at which, I recall, we were all quite pleasantly surprised at the time. Huh. That was a sign of the future, if ever there was one. Anyway.

"So, the solution was that one volunteer representative – who at the same time would have to be approved by the others in his or her team, so it wasn't as simple as the first volunteer getting the gig . . . anyway, one of us from each of the relevant civs – should agree to hear this evidence from the Zihdren-Remnanter, vote on it – with a veto – and then *forget* what it was we'd been asked to vote on.

"This was all going to be made possible by preparing each of these rep's brains before they heard the big secret, then – after they had – just, well, wiping that bit of their memories. We were all assured this was all entirely possible, and reliable and not in any way dangerous, and the most we'd forget would be a single day's worth of memories. So we all agreed.

"And it all happened, and we all heard the big, bad terrible secret, but obviously it wasn't *that* big or bad or terrible, because nobody vetoed the Gzilt joining this new cobbled-together civ – we were calling ourselves mongrels even back then, feeling very edgy and radical. And so the Gzilt were cleared to become part of the Culture . . . even though in the end they didn't actually take up the offer and go through with it.

"So. All well and good, you might think. That's what we all thought.

". . . Except one member of the negotiating party, a certain Representative Ngaroe QiRia, from the Buhdren Federality – that would be me – later remembered what it was that he'd heard, what he'd been expected to forget, what he thought, like everybody else, he had forgotten.

"Thing is, I'd always been interested in long-term living, even way back then, and particularly in holding on to memories that might otherwise get forgotten, over-written or whatever. So I'd had some experimental cranial, biochemical brain-chemistry-mangling stuff done, not all of it entirely legal or even medically advisable, but most of it didn't seem to have worked anyway, frankly, so it never really occurred to me it might interfere with this hear-and-forget thing they'd hit us with during the negotiations.

"Turned out I remembered all this stuff I'd been meant to forget due to a fix even I didn't know I had: something the clinicians had added as some sort of experimental after-thought and then either forgot to tell me about – ha! – or decided it might be better to keep quiet about.

"Anyway, the effects have been ongoing, and have stayed and developed, though they've long since been smoothed over and ever-so-carefully incorporated into all the other treatments and amendments and augmentations I've had since.

"At first I wouldn't Sublime or even be Stored or undergo any sort of transitional state because I was afraid this secret would come out, because I don't think I understood that though it was a . . . I don't know; a faith-shaking secret . . . that's just in theory. In practice, people don't believe for good reasons anyway, they just believe and that's it, like we don't love for good reasons, we just love because we need to love.

"Later, even knowing this, and knowing that the Gzilt knowing would make little real difference because they would just ignore the knowledge or find another way of not thinking about it, I still just kept on living, not Subliming with any group and not trans-corporating into a group-mind or into a Mind or anything else because it had become a habit, this going on and going on. It had become so much of what made me who I had become, there seemed no point in trying to change it.

"So I became the man who lived for ever, more or less, because I'd once held a secret I didn't care about any more.

"Well, didn't care about until I heard about the Gzilt Subliming, and, in time, decided that what I knew about them might be dangerous to me. Living for a long time can make you very cautious, cautious to the point of something close to cowardice, frankly . . . and so, anyway, I got rid of the information, had it excised and put it away from me, even though I put it somewhere in Gzilt space, somewhere pointed; with the Last Party, and Ximenyr, where it seemed to me it belonged.

"This amused me at the time. It amuses me still.

"I'd asked Ximenyr to look after what I'd left with him,

and keep it – keep them – close. I didn't tell him what they held, or how important that information might be. I didn't imagine he would wear them, in full view and plain sight. But then, why not?

"That amuses me too."

Berdle had perished protecting her, attacking the android that had held Colonel Agansu's personality before it could target Cossont, who had been running along the gantry above. That had let the arbite accompanying Agansu get in a kill-shot on the avatar. The arbite had then been destroyed by the already half-crippled remains of the outer suit they had left behind earlier, operating, as Berdle had said it would, as a drone.

Ximenyr was dead – he'd been in the tank when it was attacked, helping people confused by the watery maze – but he was being brought back from a Stored version made ten days earlier; he'd always been backed-up.

Hundreds had died in the airship and beneath it: drowned, crushed, torn apart.

The ship had killed Agansu itself, using a Displaced sleet of MDAWS nanomissiles, slaved.

~Your forces have been routed, despatched, the Culture ship had sent to the Gzilt ship. ~No need for you to hang about here now. I'll be going myself, shortly. Probably best you don't try to stop me.

~I have a regimental marshal talking to me – slowly, of course – on another channel. She wishes me to engage you in combat.

~Yes, but I already have what we came here to look for. Unless you withdraw to the system outskirts and make no sudden moves, I'll broadcast the results to the whole of

Xown, and packet it all up to spread through the whole of Gzilt. Let me go without resistance and there's still – I'm guessing – a significantly better than even chance that nothing will come of this, and what I now know will remain buried.

~So all this, so much death, has been for nothing?

~Way it works, sometimes. And *my* conscience is clear; I didn't start this. In the end, though, we're at the place at least one of us wanted to get to. End of run.

~Of course, rather than the choice between what you threaten, and our allowing you to escape, we might engage with you on the instant, to prevent you from carrying out either.

~I never did tell you my whole name, did I?

~You did not. Many have remarked that your name would appear to be part of a longer one, and yet, unusually, even uniquely, nobody has heard the whole of it.

~May I tell you it now?

~Please do.

~My full name is the *Mistake Not My Current State Of Joshing Gentle Peevishness For The Awesome And Terrible Majesty Of The Towering Seas Of Ire That Are Themselves The Mere Milquetoast Shallows Fringing My Vast Oceans Of Wrath*. Cool, eh?

~Such braggadocio. That smacks of smokescreen, not power.

~Take it as you will, chum. But how many Culture ships do you know of that exaggerate their puissance?

~None till now. You may be the first.

~Oh, adjust yourself. You people have spent ten millennia playing at soldiers while becoming ever more dedicated civilians. We've spent the last thousand years trying hard to stay civilian while refining the legacy of a won galactic war. Who do you think has the real martial provenance here? In a fight, you'd have no choice but to try to destroy me immediately. You'd fail. I'd have a choice of just how humiliatingly to cripple you. This is the truth; depend.

~So you say. We might beg—

~Enough. I think I know what happened out at Ablate. I owe you no respect. If you are experiencing a craving to die honourably, feel free to try to stop me when I instigate kick-away, in one millisecond from now. Otherwise, stand aside. Also? I retract my suggestion that you ought to depart. The place down here is a wreck. I'm leaving various drone teams and bits of medical gear behind, but I do intend to leave, and the locals could do with some disaster control. Stepping into that breach would be substantially more constructive than placing yourself across the cannon's mouth. Your choice. Goodbye, one way or the other.

The *Mistake Not . . .* slipped out from under the Real. It left behind a silvery ellipsoid just to the rear of the drained ruin that was the airship *Equatorial 353*. The silvery ellipsoid shrank to nothing and winked out over the course of several seconds in a gentle, orderly fashion, producing no more than moderate breezes as the air flowed in to replace the volume of the departed ship.

The ship itself fell beneath the planet, where the world's gravity distorted the skein of space into a shallow bowl shape.

Then it turned, twisted, aimed and powered away, unmolested.

She felt like shit, and great, and hopeless, and euphoric, all at the same time.

The ship had brought her back to some sort of life.

Normally, that badly injured, that close to death after such major trauma to every single major organ save her brain, she'd have been left in a therapeutic coma for nine or ten days, and even then the change, the difference between her physical state at the beginning and at the end of that time, would have seemed nothing short of miraculous to people of a past age, taking her from good-as-dead to good-as-ever.

Instead, because of the Subliming, she had been repaired bit by bit, detail by detail, almost cell by cell, leaving her body a patchwork of pre-existing normality and dazzlingly fresh new bits, so that she felt jangled, vibrating, bruised beyond belief yet with nothing to show for it, perpetually astounded at being suddenly not dead, not seriously injured to the point of near-death . . .

She had listened in, from her sickbed in a much smaller but still-well-equipped module, to the debriefing QiRia gave on being reunited with the memories stored in the recovered eyes.

"You are, perhaps, the only Gzilt who will ever hear this," the avatar told her.

The ship had made a new avatar. It looked and talked like Berdle had, before it/he had changed to look more like a Gzilt male, the first time they had set foot on the Girdlecity together.

"Sure you should be telling me?" she asked, huskily. Even her throat and lower tongue had taken a puncture wound in that last fusillade of fire from the android Agansu.

"I think you earned it," the ship told her. It had yet to give its new avatar a name. It wouldn't use "Berdle" again; it was sort of a tradition, it said, that when you lost an avatar you gave the next one a different name.

"Huh," was all she would say.

Pyan heard the secret about the Book of Truth too – Pyan, now forever wanting to be wrapped, whimpering and cooing annoyingly round her neck, consoling, seemingly genuinely, honestly concerned for her after so nearly losing her – but the ship, at Vyr's request, made sure that what Pyan heard of this, Pyan forgot again.

She still hadn't managed to lose the elevenstring, either. As part of her personal effects, the ship had thoughtfully transferred it to the smaller shuttle craft before slinging the larger one, the one she'd been staying in, alongside the Girdlecity, to distract the *Churkun*.

It was a relief, albeit a guilty one, that there wasn't room to play it inside the smaller craft.

It still took up an awful lot of space.

xGSV *Empiricist*
  oLOU *Caconym*
  oGSV *Contents May Differ*
  oGCU *Displacement Activity*
  oGSV *Just The Washing Instruction Chip In Life's Rich Tapestry*
  oUe *Mistake Not . . .*
  oMSV *Passing By And Thought I'd Drop In*
  oMSV *Pressure Drop*
  oLSV *You Call This Clean?*

Fellows, colleagues, friends . . . We have our answer. It is much as we expected, though the import of even the most expected news changes when it becomes definite, and fact. The question is: what do we do? What do we say?

∞

xLOU *Caconym*

I'd tell them. I'd swamp their airways with it. I'd announce it so it's the first thing the newly pre-woken hear. But I know we won't. For what it's worth, I'm resigned to the decision we're all about to make, of keeping it quiet.

∞

xGSV *Contents May Differ*
The simulations have been exhaustive but inconclusive; the likelihood is that releasing the information would make little difference, but with the outside possibility that there might be chaos, a partial Subliming with a significant part of the Gzilt populace and AIs changing their minds, further dispute between the Scavengers, and possibly even between the non-Subliming part of the Gzilt and the Scavengers. The chance of things turning ugly is small, but not that small, and the ugly might be very *big* ugly.

∞

xMSV *Passing By And Thought I'd Drop In*
We can't tell them. Those that would most care already know, or guess. Those that might be most affected are those we have the least right to disturb.

∞

xMSV *Pressure Drop*
I can't agree. The truth is the truth. You tell it even when it hurts or it loses value even when it doesn't.

∞

xLSV *You Call This Clean?*
Technically, I agree with that. In practice I agree we say and do nothing. The circumstances, due to the timing, are unique. Yes, you should always tell the truth, unless you find yourself in a situation where it would be utter moral folly to do so. At least now we know the truth. The fevered, speculative potential of it has collapsed to something definite, and not so terrible, after all. To tell it would not be the worst thing ever, either. And one should always tell the truth, unless . . . The point is that we are not automata; we have a choice. I say we exercise it wisely, and stay silent.

∞

xGSV *Empiricist*

So, shall we vote? And/or open it up to others so that more may vote?

∞

xUe *Mistake Not . . .*

If I might.

∞

xGSV *Empiricist*

Please.

∞

xUe *Mistake Not . . .*

We know how this works. If we do nothing then any disaster that befalls the Gzilt over the next few hours is entirely theirs. If we intervene we become at least complicit. This is a truth that has not been asked for; even the original bearers of it, the Z-R, made it clear they were happy it stay unknown. We know, and what we know is – now that we can be sure of what we know – that it is not our business. Whether the knowing was worth the price we and others have paid is another sort of moral equation, at right-angles to this one. I say we do nothing. Vote if you like.

∞

xLOU *Caconym*

Anybody wish to wrest from me my claim for precedence in the awkward customer/dissenting adult/ outright contrarian stakes? . . . No? Thought not. Then when I say that I reluctantly agree with what our colleague the *Mistake Not . . .* has just said, I think we might consider the matter closed.

The *Caconym*, in the shape of its virtual avatoid, returned to the castle-made-of-castles it had modelled within the near-unending recesses of its computational matrices. Its humanoid shape set out from the gatehouse that was made of tens of thousands of already mighty gatehouses, and walked all the way to the high tower which sat like a fat flagpole on top of the great composite tower, many subjective kilometres away into the fractal architecture of the baroque edifice.

It had waited all this time to hear anything from the mind-state of the *Zoologist* – anything at all that might have helped it and its colleagues in their attempts to understand the workings of the Sublime – and, despite being tempted to do so many times, it had not come back here to attempt to force the pace or the issue.

Now that the matter in hand appeared to have been settled – without, it had to be said, any help from the *Zoologist* – it had something to report, and could release the soul of the other ship from whatever obligation to help that it might have felt under. Not that that appeared to be very much, given the continuing silence. At least the instances of weird, ambiguous intrusions into its substrates, maybe from the Sublimed realm, had tailed off to nothing recently. That was a good sign, perhaps.

Or perhaps not. It was starting to worry about that.

It arrived, at last, after a climb of many thousands of steps, at the door to the airy, enclosed lair inhabited by the consciousness of the Sublime-returnee, the abstract of what had once been the Mind of the *Zoologist*.

There was no answer when it knocked. The place sounded quiet. It already felt that it knew what it was going to find. The door was locked, but only at a crude physical level, within the sim. Unlocking it was hardly more complicated than the act of turning the handle and pushing the door open.

The door swung, stuck, had to be pushed.

The *Caconym*'s avatoid walked in and looked around.

The space was, as it had guessed, empty of the *Zoologist*'s mind-state. It was full of almost everything else, including debris, litter and rubbish of every kind, stained glassware, bulbously gleaming electrical gear, intestinal quantities of tubing, foul smells, loudly protesting, unfed animals, and multitudinous ropes hanging from the ceiling, but of the strange creature with the pale red, mottled skin and the long arms with six fingers, there was no sign.

After it stopped looking for the avatoid of the *Zoologist* it started looking for a note. It didn't find one.

"You might have said goodbye," it said, eventually, to the air, in case its departed guest had left some sort of message behind that might be triggered by speech . . . but its voice just disappeared into the clutter and the dust and the hazy sunlight coming through the tall windows, and brought no response.

The ship instituted a full search of its computational and storage substrates, just in case, but with no real hope it would find any sign of the *Zoologist*. Sure enough, there was nothing. Apart from this ersatz, abandoned lab and its own memories of its departed colleague, the *Zoologist* had left without a trace.

The *Caconym* was about to calm the squawking, screeching animals in their cages, but then grew instantly tired of the whole absurd conceit, and with one command abolished the entire castle and everything in and around it, closing down the whole scenario with a single thought.

Twenty-four

(S -0)

In the end he went with everybody else.

There had been a time there when he thought he must have gone mad, for he had been thinking of staying behind, of not going at all, and perhaps – once it had all taken place – of putting himself into the hands of some authority, to be tried and judged and accept whatever punishment might be decreed for what he had done – for all the things he had done, but especially for this last thing.

But that had been just a passing fantasy, a mood, something to be indulged. In the end he knew he had to go, and he told himself that not going, and indulging in this masochistic orgy of justice and repentance, would be the truly selfish thing for him to do. Finally, at long last, it was not all about him. He was, he would be, just another humble Enfoldee, taking his place along with everybody else for the step off the cliff that bore you up rather than causing you to fall . . .

The Presence that had hung over the parliament building for so long had swelled a little, become a dark sphere. In the last few hours, more and more Presences had appeared, sliding into existence throughout the whole of Gzilt space, wherever there were people: in homes and communes and barracks, in ships and sea ships and aircraft, in squares and piazzas, in public halls, lecture theatres, auditoria and temples, markets and malls, sports venues and transport stations and in all the places where the Stored had recently been resting, before pre-waking.

The aliens who had come to wish the Gzilt farewell, and those who had come to profit from their going, had, by convention, withdrawn for the moment, leaving those about to depart to themselves.

Time-to devices and public clocks and displays spread throughout the Gzilt realm ticked down the last few hours and minutes, and people met at pre-arranged places and ate last meals and said last things and, sometimes, told others secrets they'd been keeping. Or decided not to.

Generally, as people tended to, they got together in groups of family and friends, then joined with other groups to form gatherings of dozens or hundreds and – again, as people usually did, though the exact expression of such emotionality depended both on the physical as well as the psychological make-up of the species concerned – they held hands.

Many sang.

Many bands and orchestras played.

And in the end the time counted down to nothing, and, in the presence of Presences, all you did was say, "I Sublime, I Sublime, I Sublime," and that was that. Off you went, just folding out of existence as though turning through a crease in the air that nobody had noticed was there before.

He met up with Marshal Chekwri at the end. She had no more family than he did, and they had come to share much over the last twenty days or so.

They stood in the gardens of the parliament, under an inappropriately squally sky, with showers, waiting to say the words with a few dozen others. They left it relatively late during the hour that was regarded as the optimum period, just to make sure that a respectable proportion of the whole Gzilt civilisation was indeed going.

It was, he reflected numbly, a lot like watching election results coming in. There was a slow start to the Instigation, but the numbers quickly swelled about a quarter of an hour in, according to the news channels still covering events, and by the start of the last third of the hour it was obvious almost everybody was making the transition. The numbers Subliming accelerated again. Those gathered in the garden agreed they could go.

"Traditionally, people tell each other secrets at this point," Marshal Chekwri said to him, in a brief moment when the others were all making their goodbyes and choosing where to stand, and with whom. "Mine," Chekwri said, with a smirk, "is that I failed my officer exam. I cheated. Blackmailed a senior officer to get the pass." She shrugged. "Never looked back." She put her head to one side. "You?"

He stared at her. For an instant he wasn't sure he knew who he was staring at, or why, or that he knew anybody or anything any more. Eventually he shook his head. "Too many," he said, almost too quietly to be heard, turning away from her. "Too many."

Jevan and Solbli, his secretary and aide-de-camp, were there, and he was astonished when it was Jevan who said he had always loved him, not Solbli, whose secret was that she had no secret.

He mumbled something, lost for speech for the first time in many decades.

They chose the end of the just-started minute as the time they would go. They all joined hands and when the time came they all said the words and went, just as a small rain shower began.

In the end he went with everybody else.

He was re-made, and yet he had been destroyed. He knew he would have done all he could, in his additional incarnation within the android on Xown, but still – again – it had not been enough. Had he been successful, he might have stayed behind, with something to celebrate and to live up to. Instead, he could only admit defeat. It was some consolation that nothing calamitous happened in the interval between the failed operation inside the Girdlecity, and the Instigation that was the beginning of the Subliming.

All that mattered now was that the crew of the *Uagren* had accepted him, and he was part of the ship now.

No Presence needed to appear; ship AIs were capable of performing their own Enfolding.

Agansu went with them.

In the end she didn't go, not there and then. She knew what this meant.

"I can't leave without you!" Warib had wailed from the screen, the sea blue-green behind her, the happy voyagers forming up in their last formations, hugging and crying and choosing who to hold hands with.

And in the end all she could say was, "Yes, you can, Mother," and kill the connection, knowing that she could, and that she would.

Twenty-five

(S +24)

At sunset above the plains of Kwaalon, on a dark, high terrace balanced on a glittering black swirl of architecture forming a relatively microscopic part of the equatorial Girdlecity of Xown, Vyr Cossont – Lieutenant Commander (reserve) Vyr Cossont, as she had once been – sat, performing T. C. Vilabier's 26th String-Specific Sonata For An Instrument Yet To Be Invented, catalogue number MW 1211, on one of the few surviving examples of the instrument developed specifically to play the piece, the notoriously difficult, temperamental and tonally challenged Antagonistic Undecagonstring – or elevenstring, as it was commonly known.

T. C. Vilabier's 26th String-Specific Sonata For An

Instrument Yet To Be Invented, MW 1211, was more usually known as "The Hydrogen Sonata".

While she played, and the sun sank beyond the distant, hulking line of the dark, near-totally deserted Girdlecity, a lone Liseiden freighter took off from a part of the great structure just a few kilometres away, close enough for the sound of its relatively crude engines to impinge on Cossont's consciousness.

She was able to ignore this potential distraction. She kept on playing.

Her own flier sat at the far edge of the terrace, twenty metres off, a few lights glowing in the cockpit, where Pyan lay curled asleep, exhausted after an afternoon and early evening spent playing with flocks of birds.

Eventually, almost an hour after she'd started, Cossont got to the end of the piece, and, as the last notes died away, she set the two bows in their resting places, kicked down the side-rest and, flexing her back carefully, stood up and out of the instrument.

She opened her mouth wide, rubbed her face with her top set of hands and massaged the small of her back with her lower pair, through the material of a Lords of Excrement jacket. She hooked her slippers off with her toes, then bent and pulled on her boots. She stood looking at the elevenstring for a while, listening to the quiet harmonics that the evening winds made in the external resonating strings.

She had walked the empty, echoing spaces of the Girdlecity many times over the last few days and evenings, and taken the flier to other places around the planet. You had to fly on manual now; the nav and safety systems were mostly still there, but not to be relied upon.

She had seen nobody at all within the Girdlecity. She had chanced upon the same abandoned school she had walked past that first evening, when Commissar-Colonel Etalde had appeared to whisk her away. It was twice deserted now, with all the Storage units opened, the people they had held departed. Even the guard arbite she'd accidentally activated had gone; maybe taken by the Liseiden. The winds moaned through the vast spaces of the Girdlecity, playing it like some colossal instrument.

In the cities and towns and villages scattered across the planet, she had seen a few people, though only ever from a distance; she was forming the impression that the only individuals left were those who'd always fantasised about having the world to themselves one day.

Most days, though, she saw nobody.

The closest encounter she'd had with anything large and living had been when she'd surprised a wandering skitterpaw late one evening, in a small windswept city on the Dry Coast bordering the Dust; the animal had gone loping off into the shadows after giving her a good long look, like it had been deciding whether to attack her or not. She had a little ten-millimetre knife missile with her – a gift from the ship, and a device not above reminding her whenever she was about to leave home without it – so it hadn't been as frightening an experience as it might have been. Still, it had been scary enough, and it was surprising how quickly the wild had started to colonise the deserted structures of civilisation, and how much difference it made, there being – in most places – nobody about rather than almost nobody about.

The final figures for those making the transition into the Sublime had come in at over ninety-nine point nine per cent, as far as anyone could tell, with little variation between planets and habitats. Xown and Zyse had carried even greater proportions of their populations across into the Enfold. This was, unless you were absolutely determined to regard the whole process as an act of tragic collective insanity, an excellent and satisfying result.

A slightly stronger gust of wind swirled about the platform and the elevenstring made a new, deep, lowing sound, like it wanted to be released back into the wild now, even though there was nothing biological about its construction and it had been fashioned by a Culture ship, twenty years past and a quarter of the galaxy away.

She smiled ruefully in the dusk light, then turned her back on the instrument and walked to the flier, leaving the elevenstring standing, slightly lop-sided, where it was, with its protective case arranged, still open, neatly to one side.

She heaved herself up and into the flier, shooing Pyan out of the way; the creature protested sleepily and didn't wake up properly, finally wrapping itself limply round her neck and hanging there without even bothering to form a knot. She suspected that if familiars had been prone to snoring, Pyan would have been snoring.

She sat in the flier for a moment, letting it check its systems. She gazed at the Girdlecity, focusing on where it dipped to meet the horizon. The sun had not long set, and the red-gold skies were swiftly darkening.

She had thought of looking for the couple with the child again, the little family she'd met inside the Girdlecity on that first evening. The search and successfully finding them would be sufficient, she'd decided; that would be difficult enough. She wouldn't want to suggest that she stay with them or any such foolishness.

In addition, she had an invitation to go with the *Mistake Not . . .*, which would be departing before too long, having helped in the general business of keeping the peace amongst the Scavenger civs as they took stuff, dismantled things, occupied places or studied tech to copy. The Culture ship would be heading out on a long voyage to the planet called Cethyd, on the far side of the galaxy, to attempt to contact the original, biological QiRia, to see if he would like his eyes and his memories back, now that all the fuss was over.

Just getting to him might be interesting, given the bizarre hostility of the locals and not-quite-so-locals, so it promised to be an adventure.

There was no rush, anyway; though the whole Scavenger thing had quieted down, the Culture ships had stuck around for a bit, and were now awaiting the arrival of the last of the ships that had been involved in their recent discussions over what to do about the Gzilt. She'd got the impression they were all quietly pleased with themselves, also that this get-together was just an excuse for some mutual metaphorical back-slapping and whatever passed amongst Culture Minds for nights of drunken revelry and general carousing, and that they were already turning the whole fractious, murderous escapade into something semi-mythical to take its place in the ongoing history of Terrific Things The Culture And Its Brilliant Ships Had Got Up To Over The Years.

Though not one called the *Caconym*, apparently; it had just turned without ceremony and gone back to doing whatever it was it liked doing.

And not the *Empiricist*; it had more important things to do elsewhere. System-class ships always did, apparently.

Cossont strapped in, closed the canopy, took manual control and lifted the little flier away from the terrace, letting the craft rise and bank and pirouette all at once.

First she would go home.

After that, she had no idea what she might do.

The Antagonistic Undecagonstring, caught in the swirling breeze produced by the flier's departure, hummed emptily.

The sound was swept away by the mindless air.

Iain Banks came to widespread and controversial public notice with the publication of his first novel, *The Wasp Factory*, in 1984. *Consider Phlebas*, his first science fiction novel, was published under the name Iain M. Banks in 1987. He is now acclaimed as one of the most powerful, innovative and exciting writers of his generation.

Find out more about Iain M. Banks and other Orbit authors by registering for the free monthly newsletter at www.orbitbooks.net.

An interview with Iain M. Banks

In *The Hydrogen Sonata* you explore the concept of "subliming", whereby advanced civilisations achieve a higher level of existence. You've touched on this theme in previous Culture novels, as well as exploring the idea of digital hells in *Surface Detail*. What is it about these alternative states of being that entices you to write about them?

I guess it's all part of the process of exploring the possibilities the future might offer. The history of technology is largely about wish-fulfilment, even dream-fulfilment: as a species we dreamed of being able to fly, of holding conversations with people on the other side of the world, of exploring and travelling to other worlds ... well, our technology has achieved these things. Historically one of the areas we've been busiest in, coming up with usually comforting but frankly unlikely dreams, is that of existence after death, or just avoiding death in the first place; the kind of stuff, in other words, that religions tend to deal with. Now, while religions tell us next to nothing useful or true about the universe, they do tell us an enormous amount – perhaps an embarrassing amount – about ourselves, about what we value, fear and lust after. It is now those dreams that we might realistically think about fulfilling. And that's fertile territory for a skiffy writer, and relevant, because we stand on the brink of creating things like gods – AIs, we continue to extend our life spans significantly and we seem on the way to blurring the boundary between the real and the virtual to the point of irrelevance. On matters where only religious writing and faith previously seemed qualified to comment, SF is now able to speak with some degree of authority, or – at the very least – propose alternative angles for looking at the same dreams. Though of course there will always be those who choose to disagree, unable to accept that religions are simply part of our wacky narrative history rather than direct, if laughably contradictory, conduits to absolute truth.

The rise and fall of civilisations and empires is another recurring theme in your Culture novels, and *The Hydrogen Sonata* is concerned with the tumultuous last days of a race known as the Gzilt. What is it that fascinates you about the ends of civilisations? In addition, how far is the endless cycle of civilisations in your Culture universe symptomatic of your belief that existence is just – to use your own term – "outrageous chaos"?

I think you'd have to have the heart of a cabbage not to be interested in empires falling and civilisations meeting their ends. We love tragedy as much as comedy, and while we might appreciate, admire and even vicariously glory in the rise to power of somebody or something great, we are certainly capable of appreciating their fall with at least equal relish. Again, SF gives you the opportunity to talk about this kind of stuff, and to custom-build the setting it all happens within to let you better make your point (history has the unfortunate quality of being, generally, pretty much fixed. Even the most zealous revisionism can only take you so far).

I suspect the endless-cycling thing going on in the Culture novels is largely about me trying to reconcile the age and scale of the universe – actually, just this galaxy – with the plausible life spans of both creatures even vaguely like ourselves and the likely duration of their institutions, empires and civilisations. Throughout the Culture sequence especially I've tried to give an impression of the scale of the context beyond the immediate focus of the narrative, both physically and chronologically, and to emphasise that there are lots of different ways for civilisations to interact and develop; with the last three Culture books in particular I've been trying to make it clear that there is a lot more to the galactic meta-civilisation than just the Culture – it's actually a fairly small fraction of the whole.

Beyond that, I might query the "just" in that sentence, "existence is just . . . 'outrageous chaos'": a place within that chaos, that vast unfolding of randomness and pursuance, might be what we're ascending – hopefully and erratically – towards, and what we'll be lucky ever to achieve. I'd argue that you don't even start to become a part of it until you get all your eggs out of the one home-planet basket.

Music is a prominent feature of *The Hydrogen Sonata* and seems to play a significant role in your own life – you've previously reviewed music for a radio show and have admitted that you're "a sucker for a good tune", although an interviewer noted in 2009 that your piano rendition of *Chopsticks* was "faltering". How polished are your musical skills these days, and do you listen to music while you write?

I refute that entirely unwarranted assertion robustly! I've never been able to play *Chopsticks* and I still can't. I can play the first four bars of Beethoven's *Moonlight Sonata*. So well, indeed, that it remains a constant source of surprise to me that the rest of the piece continues to repel my assaults upon it. My conventional musical skills, then, remain quite entirely miserable. However, my skills at putting together pieces of – for want of a better term – music using a terribly clever bit of software called Logic Pro 9 running on a 27" iMac – along with an interface, a few outboard sound modules, a mixer desk and some frighteningly unforgiving speakers – have become sufficient that at least one person is genuinely impressed with the results (though that person would, admittedly, be me).

I listen to music whenever I write. The radio, as a rule: Radios One and Six for pop-rock-hip-hop-neo-folk-whatever usually, though, these days, Radio Three with lots of classical music, too, and occasional dips into Two (can't be doing with talk radio, or radio with adverts). I have multiple playlists ready to go, if there's too much talk on the radio, and Glenn Gould playing Bach as a sort of ultimate resort, for when I really need to concentrate on the words being rattled off the qwerty keyboard and even people singing seems somehow overly intrusive and distracting (distant humming along with the tune is just about acceptable).

With the twenty-fifth anniversary of the Culture series now upon us (*Consider Phlebas* was published in 1987), have you come to regard the series as your life's work? Do you think you'll ever "complete" the series, or do you still have a long list of ideas that you want to explore?

I suppose the Culture series will form the largest part of my life's work; it's unlikely I'll come up with another over-arching structure on the same scale now. I'm perfectly happy with that. I'll keep writing about the Culture for as long as I still feel there are new things to say, new avenues to explore. It's important that I feel able to write SF outside the Culture, but even within it the restrictions are minimal; most of the action in most of the Culture books takes place well outside the Culture itself, and it's been that way since the beginning, with *Phlebas*.

I don't intend ever to complete it; I decided right from the start to resist the temptation to tear it all down at any point, and this has become sort of indicative and symbolic of the nature and demeanour of the Culture itself, now: it means to resist completion and put off Subliming, so that it can keep on going, sticking around in the Real and trying to do good (as it sees it), for as long as it can, and it's already envisaging that when it does finally fade away, it'll be when its going will hardly be noticed, because being something like the Culture – behaving like it – will be pretty much the default state for all galactic civilisations. (Though, in this, it could, of course, be completely wrong.)

I've more than enough material and ideas for another full-on Culture novel, and that has been the case for at least the last decade or so, no matter where I've been in the Culture-novel-writing cycle, as new ideas keep on coming along at a slow but steady rate. At the moment I'm tempted to try something a bit more oblique next time, though I'm also tempted to go with something tighter and more wildly kinetic, too . . . Who can say? We'll see.

You've been writing in the Culture universe for nearly three decades – how do you keep things fresh, and do you still approach new novels with the same sense of excitement? Do you feel you still have anything to prove?

I keep things as fresh as they are – however fresh that may be – by still finding new things to write about. Sometimes these come from brand new ideas – like the Shellworlds in Matter – and sometimes they come from throwaway ideas – sometimes just single words – in earlier novels (like the airspheres first mentioned in *Phlebas* turning up again in *Look To Windward*). The whole Subliming thing in *The Hydrogen Sonata* is another example; Subliming had been mentioned in various culture novels and I'd never really thought much about it – it just gave me an out for civilisations without them having to collapse in the classical, Ozymandian sense. Then people at signings and in interviews began to ask about it, so I started to think about it properly and decided/realised that it was an important part of the whole context of the Culture and the rest of the civilised galactic scene, and could provide an interesting setting in which to tell a story. (This is as close as I ever get, or want to get, to audience participation.) I still needed an idea for a plot, and so the initial idea might have sat on the shelves for years waiting for one, but then, fortuitously, a plot suggested itself and the book was ready to go almost immediately. I can remember where and when the idea came to me: I was lying on a sort of bubble-bed wotsit at the side of a large swimming pool, in the sunlight at a spa complex called Archena, in southern Spain, in October 2011, thinking about an edition of *QI* I'd seen a week or two earlier, in which Stephen Fry had mentioned something called the Great Disappointment. Bang: the plot of *The Hydrogen Sonata* just unfolded in my head.

I guess a little of the excitement I used to feel starting a novel has ebbed away over the years; it's my life, my career, my living, and I've got used to writing a novel more or less every year, so to some degree it's part of a routine, not the dazzling new adventure it used to be. But that's okay, because there are compensations, and the fact that I oscillate between mainstream and SF means that I'm always writing something different from the last book. Plus there is, anyway, invariably a point where the book I'm writing, regardless of genre, sort of takes over and energises the whole process; I get all wrapped up in it and come close to forgetting that I've ever written anything else.

Also, if you have any sort of ambition, pride in your work or even self-respect, in a sense you always have something to prove. I'm getting to the sort of age now when I need to prove there's life in the old dog yet, and fully intend to keep on attempting to do so until it becomes positively embarrassing for all concerned. (In this scenario, the lunch where your publisher takes you somewhere nice but then asks pointedly what your plans are for your retirement represents the equivalent of the smelly mutt's last trip to the vet.)

The Culture is the ultimate utopia: an egalitarian, post-scarcity society, whose citizens want for nothing and do not fear illness or disease, instead being free to live lives of apparent luxury. Yet what power exists in the Culture is firmly in the hands of the Minds, which are artificial intelligences. To what extent are you suggesting that humankind could not achieve a utopia like that of the Culture without ceding control to machines? Is human nature too destructive and corruptible to ever achieve such a utopia otherwise?

In a sense I'm trying to pre-empt objections to the very idea of the Culture. Suggesting that beings much like us can achieve a functioning utopia as though it's part of our plausible, easily envisaged future, our expected and plausible destiny, always seemed a bit wishy-washy to me, too much like just wish-fulfilment. Arguably, we express as too inherently nasty, too prone to become violent, too prone to xenophobia and too easily en-mired in our noxious mythologies of false comfort and dubious exceptionalism for this to make sense (narrative, psychological or philosophical). Taking away the excuse that we need to be mean and selfish to others because, heck, there just ain't enough of everything to go around . . . well, that's one step, but I suspect that while it might be necessary to achieve a hi-tech utopia, it's not sufficient. The Minds – the Culture's high-level AIs – are the other part of the equation. The humans create them and enough of these god-like entities stick around to save us from ourselves. The children create the adults, and behave better as a result. I submit this is no more likely to be wrong than the idea that as soon as we create an AI it'll try to exterminate us is right – that's the us in it talking, if I can put it that way; that's our guilty conscience articulating. The final get-out is that in the end the mongrel Culture, though suspiciously human-like in so many ways, isn't us, so they might just be naturally nicer than we'd ever be in the same situation. Cos that's evolution, that is.

Anyway, one of the side-tracks of the Culture I'm thinking about exploring at some point is one of the parts of it where Minds don't get involved, and people run everything themselves; they'd have computers, I guess, but no Minds. Smart help without any of that concomitant but deeply annoying wisdom. I am not yet sure how this will go.

The tricky thing about claiming we'll ever create a utopian society is that our record up to this point is so lamentable: you can create something as close to utopia as technologically possible at any point in your development once you have a reliable surplus of food and goods: it's not about having rocket-belts, floating cities or even smart-alec drones; it's about having the shared urge, resolve and will to behave decently, altruistically and non-xenophobically towards your fellow human beings, whether your latest invention was the wheel, moveable type or an FTL drive. And in that respect – I humbly submit – we've been heading backwards quite rapidly over the last thirty years or so. It would be pleasant to believe that we're starting to pull up and out of our nosedive into the morass of Greedism and Marketolatry that has characterised our civilisation for the last three decades, but frankly it's still too early to tell yet.

You've mentioned before that you created the Culture as a deliberate response to the science fiction of the time, which was

largely concerned with dystopias. To what extent was your earlier science fiction deliberately aimed at challenging genre conventions, or was your subverting of certain tropes merely a by-product of your desire to tell a ripping story? And is it important for SF writers to strike out into uncharted territory, or is the story all that really matters?

I don't think I saw it as challenging genre conventions as such; I just did what any fan of a genre (who has ambitions to create within that genre) does: look at what's on offer, think "I can do that," and then "But I want to do it differently, I want to do it this way." Especially in SF, it seems right to try to improve on what's already been produced, to take matters forward, to climb onto the shoulders of the giants who have gone before. What I wanted to read – and so to write – was SF with the energy, vitality and can-do attitude of so much great American SF, but which was as well written as so much of the usually more reflective, nuanced and less gung-ho British stuff. What I wanted to avoid was what I saw as the economic – and to some degree political – naivety of the US writers and the sheer god-awful sub-Orwellian miserablism of the Brits. Whether I've succeeded or not isn't for me to say, but either way I'm sure I've managed to introduce my own intrinsic, embedded annoyances that other writers have been, are and will be reacting against for some time. This is entirely right and proper, by the way, and just the way the whole system works. So there.

I think with SF yes, you do, generally, need to strike out into uncharted territory, though there will always be writers for whom the story is all that really matters. Room in the field for both.

The serene image of the Culture hides a dark underbelly: the various agents and AIs that stay in the shadows, working to protect the Culture's existence and future by monitoring and meddling in the affairs of other civilisations. To what extent is this persistent interference a reflection of real-world events? You were a vocal critic of the Iraq war, so is it fair to assume that you are influenced by international politics and that your feelings about world events work their way into your novels, perhaps in some cases even driving them?

It's not a deliberate or thought-out policy, though, as I've always said, even space opera isn't written in a vacuum (repeat until funny . . . thank you Mark and Lard). So events in reality will seep in, I guess. The position implied regarding the use of torture in *Transition* is entirely a reaction to then (and still) current events and effectively my contribution to the debate. Shameful though it is that we should even be having it.

Despite being a pacifistic utopia that promotes tolerance, the Culture's "Special Circumstances" division sometimes resorts to shady practices to defend its civilisation's "moral right to exist". Do you regard any of these practices as ethically problematic, or is any act acceptable when it's geared towards protecting the ultimate utopia?

Very ethically problematic. The Culture itself – both en masse and in the shape of the tiny numbers of people and machines engaged in or in any relevant way connected to that sort of behaviour – is disturbed by the very idea that such actions might ever be justified. That's why they don't do it very often and they're constantly re-calibrating the moral cost-benefit balance through the use of assiduously gathered and honestly deployed statistics (said a Culture spokesperson). Of course, my need to tell a story of even the slightest degree of rip-roaringness means that the novels tend to concentrate on exactly the kind of life-threatening mayhem that the entire Culture is very carefully designed to obviate, both within it and – to the extent that it reasonably and ethically can project its values – around it. The impression the books might give is that this action-adventure stuff is happening all the time all over the place, and that's just not true. (But there we are – that's fiction.) Technically, also, any Mind would tell you that the more often you have to resort to bad behaviour to keep yourself safe, the less plausible your claim to be part of a utopia is. A true utopia implies an inclusivity, a comprehensiveness – limited only by consent – or it's not really a utopia at all. Living in a gated community and employing hired muscle to keep you comfy does not mean that you live in a little utopia. It means you live in a dystopia and happen to be one of the privileged.

A sense of humour runs through all of the Culture novels, whether it's in the form of an eccentric drone or in your famously unconventional ship names – and the humour isn't just limited to humans. If we consider humour to be something of a coping mechanism, how important is it as a prerequisite to a civilisation's development and continued existence? And while we're on topic, where *do* you get those ship names from? Very good question. We'll never truly know until we either meet proper space aliens or create some really high-end virtual civilisations of our own, inside a computer. I suspect – hazarding – it's all-important. Not as a deliberate ploy or strategy you can choose to pursue but as a near-infallibly significant emergent property. I think it's pretty much accepted there is a strong link between what you might call a broad, well-balanced intelligence, and wit. So I'm assuming, anyway. Sadly, being just one very limited human being, I can't make the Minds as cutting, witty and just plain smart as they really would be (did they actually exist – I have to keep reminding myself they don't. This is very annoying).

Ah, the ship names. Sometimes they're a result of me just keeping my ears open, but mostly they come from me trying to think myself into the mind-set of the Minds (or at least a reasonably clued-up human Culture citizen – let's not get too ambitious, given the above and how much I've banged on in book after book about the transcendently ineffable intellectual fabulousness of the Minds). Then I just think about how the Culture would look upon a bunch of barbarians like us, and take it from there.

I am aware this is not a furiously helpful answer. My apologies.

You've created a vast setting where theoretically almost anything is possible. While this gives you an impressively large and expansive canvas to work with, is it important to instil a sense of realism and humanity in your characters? Or is the whole notion of realism (as we understand it) a redundant concept in a world where many people live in hedonistic bliss?
Well, you have to have the feeling that the writer can't just write him or herself into a corner and then do the with-one-mighty-leap-he-was-free! thing. There's no jeopardy, no tension and little interest if you do that. You are allowed to feel that the writer's on the side of the protagonist, but not that they're necessarily going to make sure everything's going to work out all right no matter what (actually that's not true; there are lots of series in lots of media where that's exactly what people want and what they get. Again, room in all the fields for all tastes). And there has to be realism in any depiction of utopia. There is still failure, embarrassment, thwarted ambition, unrequited love and the possibility of suffering a broken heart, even in the Culture. Not to mention existential despair at the utter incorrigibility of one's fellow, less morally developed galaxy-users, almost no matter where or when you care to look.

Ever since *Consider Phlebas*, large set pieces (often involving big explosions, of which you're a self-professed fan) have been a regular feature of the Culture novels. Is writing these epic sequences your favourite part of penning a new story, or do you take equal satisfaction from the interactions of your characters and exploring political and social ideas through their deeds?

It is one of the most enjoyable bits, I do confess. Ultimately, the thing I enjoy most is putting together a good, well-balanced novel; the set pieces, like any other aspect, can't be allowed to play too big a part in that or the whole thing gets out of kilter. Still, I'd love to pack another novel with as many action sequences as *Phlebas*, but then that was the result of sweeping up a couple of decades' worth of such ideas (most of which had been left on the shelf because they were so preposterously over-the-top . . . or under-the-bottom in the case of the fist-fight under the giant hovercraft) and cramming them into the one novel just for the hell of it, so I guess that isn't going to happen unless I stop writing for an unfeasibly long time – even supposing I keep on having that sort of idea in the first place. Still, keeping that kinetic quality in the Culture books is important to me. The characters just have to make their way through the stories and plots as best they can and frankly I pretty much leave them to it. The political and social ideas I touch upon are equally subject to being bundled and tumbled along by the story, rather than ever being granted central stage. Best is when it all comes together and the characters, the story and the ideas all coalesce within a given sequence, producing something – in its own modest way – transcendent. That's the gold standard, that's the longed-for ideal.

Still working on that.

Maybe one day . . .

The Hydrogen Sonata

Names

Individuals:

Agansu, Cagad	Gzilt special forces Colonel, under direct command of Banstegeyn
Aouse	Gzilt journalist
Banstegeyn	Gzilt Septame; in practice Gzilt's most powerful politician
Berdle	Culture avatar of *Mistake Not . . .*
Boyuter	Gzilt Marshal, Commander in Chief of SRPLR-14

Chekwri	Gzilt Marshal, Commander in Chief of the Home System Regiment
Chuje	Gzilt child in Girdlecity
Cossont, Vyr	Gzilt (Lieutenant Commander, reserve), (aka Sister Euphoria)
Diria	Gzilt journalist
Drodj, Briper	Gzilt; prophet; the Scribe
Etalde, Yueweag	Gzilt Commissar-Colonel, SRPLR-14
Folrison	Gzilt parliamentarian
Frix	Gzilt Septame
Gaed	Gzilt Tech Commander, SRPLR-14
Garron	Gzilt relatively young lover of Warib, CC's mother
Gazan'tyo	Gzilt General, SRPLR-14
Geljemyn, Sefoy	Gzilt President
Gerunke, Frex	Gzilt surgeon who sculpted Cossont's arms
Haldesib, Ossebri 17	Ronte Swarmprince and Sub-Swarm Divisional Head
Hassipura Plyn-Frie	Culture drone, acquaintance of Scoaliera Tefwe and QiRia
Iberre	Iwenick mother of Cultural Mission Director Jelwilin Keril
Int'yom	Gzilt trime, later president
Jevan	Gzilt AdC to Banstegeyn
Jonsker Ap-Candrechenat	Culture drone, of the *Beats Working*
Jurutre	Gzilt Septame
Keril, Jelwilin	Iwenick Cultural Mission Director
Kresele	Gzilt journalist
Locuil	Gzilt physician general

Luzuge	Uwanui Docent at Ahen'tayawa Hearkenry, Mt Jamanathrus, Cethyd
Mierbeunes	Iwenick Ambassador to Gzilt
Nyomulde	Liseiden fleet officer
Orpe, Virisse	Gzilt AdC to and lover of President Geljemyn; traitor
Parinherm, Eglyle	android, confused
Pyan	Cossont's familiar
Quvarond	Gzilt Trime
QiRia, Ngaroe	C's oldest human (Tursensa Ngaroe Hgan QiRia dam Yutton) (m) (aka Yutten Turse of Neressi, and Isseren, a Perytch IV leviathid)
Riekl	Gzilt General, SRPLR-14
Sklom	(Sylocule) avatar of Culture ship *Warm, Considering*
Solbli	Gzilt AdC to Banstegeyn
Tefwe, Scoaliera	Culture; friend/ex-lover of QiRia, C's oldest human
Tyun, Ny-Xandabo	Liseiden Salvage and Reprocessing Team Principal (i.e. Admiral)
Ar Uhtryn	Gzilt special forces Ar(bite) drone/bio liaison android
T. C. Vilabier	Gzilt composer [T'krin -] (Vilabier the Younger); long dead
Warib	Gzilt; Cossont's mother
Ximenyr	Gzilt Master of the Revels at the Last Party
Yegres	Gzilt Trime
Yenivle	Gzilt Septame
Ziborlun	Culture avatar of *Passing By* . . .
Zige	Gzilt journalist

Ships:

Gzilt:

5*Gelish-Oplule*	IR-HAS [Indefinite Range, High Acceleration/Speed] cruiser
7*Uagren*	IR-HVW [Indefinite Range, High Velocity/Weapon-load] battlecruiser
8*Churkun*	IR-FWS [Indefinite Range, Full Weapon Spectrum] battleship

Liseiden:

Abule-Anang	Collective Purposes vessel
Gellemtyan-Asool-Anafawaya (First Class)	Collective Purposes vessel
Laskuil-Hliz	Collective Purposes vessel
Quiatrea-Anang	Collective Purposes vessel

Culture:

Anything Legal Considered	Ridge LCU
Beats Working	Scree LCU
Caconym	Troublemaker LOU
Contents May Differ	Atmosphere GSV
Displacement Activity	River GCU
Empiricist	System GSV
Fine Disregard For Awkward Facts, A	MSV
Headcrash	Delinquent GOU
Just The Washing Instruction Chip In Life's Rich Tapestry	GSV
Kakistocrat	GSV
Learned Response	Culture ROU

Mistake Not . . . :	class initially undefined (actually OU/e). Full name: *Mistake Not My Current State Of Joshing Gentle Peevishness For The Awesome And Terrible Majesty Of The Towering Seas Of Ire That Are Themselves The Mere Milquetoast Shallows Fringing My Vast Oceans Of Wrath)* [MNMCSOJGPFTAATMOTTS-OITATTMMSFMVOOW] NB: no ". . ." when spoken.
New Toy	LOU
Outstanding Contribution To The Historical Process	VFP (ex Psychopath)
Passing By And Thought I'd Drop In	Desert MSV
Pressure Drop	Shelf MSV
Questionable Ethics	GOU
Rapid Random Response Unit	VFP
Refreshingly Unconcerned With The Vulgar Exigencies Of Veracity	FP (ex Thug)
Smile Tolerantly	(ex) GCU, ancient; now Zihdren-Remnanter hybrid
Teething Problems	GSV
Unreliable Witness	GSV
Value Judgement	FP (ex Thug)
Warm, Considering	Delta GCU
Xenocrat	Delinquent GOU
You Call This Clean?	Blue LSV
Zoologist	Boulder class Superlifter

Iwenick:

CH2OH.(CHOH)4.CHO

| (galactose - ha ha) | Strategic Outreach Element |
| *Iberre* | personal yacht |

Zihdren-Remnanter:

| *Exaltation-Parsimony III* | Ceremonial Representative Ship |
| *Oceanic-Dissonance* | Adjunct Entity |

*

Ronte:

| *Mansuetude* (gentleness, meekness) | Interstitial/Exploratory vessel |
| *Melancholia Enshrines All Triumph* | Interstitial/Exploratory vessel |

*

Planets:

Ablate	conical planetary fragment (HS-held) deep in blast front of Yampt-Sferde supernova, wrapped in brilliant aurorae: uninhabited ceremonial location
Cethyd	Heluduz system; home of Uwanui and the Mountains of the Sound
Eshri	Izenion system; a Sculpt planet of the Werpesh; moon holds SRPLR-14 HQ
Perytch IV	water world; home of Issialiaya

Tursen	planet Ngaroe QiRia born and brought up on
Xown	in Mureite system; holds Equatorial Girdlecity of Xown
Zyse Gzilt	Gzil system; origin-planet of

*

Orbitals:

Bokri system	Gzilt; microrbital, Ospin
Dibaldipen system	Culture; Angemar's Prime

*

Stars/Systems:

Angemar's Prime	location of Dibaldipen O
Barlbanim	just outside Gzilt space
Gzil	home system of Gzilt
Heluduz	location of Cethyd, planet
Izenion	Eshri
Loliscombana	where smatter outbreak happening
Mureite	location of Xown
Ospin	location of Gzilt Centralised Dataversity
Ry	clinker sun at edge of Gzilt space
Sapanatcheon	star LOU *Caconym* is investigating initially
Taushe	just inside Gzilt space
Vatrelles	where Ronte fleet hides (10 ly from Gzil)
Yampt-Sferde	supernova

*

Species:

Buhdren Federality	humanoid, one of the Culture founder species/civs
Dolstre	mentors to the Oglari
Gzilt	humanoid, nearly Culture joint founders
Issialiaya	water world cetacean
Iwenick	humanoid, agent/PR reps for Liseiden (bland/look "averaged")
Liseiden	eel-like water worlders, Scavenger (Denying; prefer "Enricher")
Oglari	Oglari Jurisdiction; "looking after" the Uwanui
Ronte	GG insectile, Scavenger (Accepting; i.e. agree term)
Sylocule	spikily haired, six-limbed, six-eyed creatures
Uwanui	like dark, angular, tall, multiply-poled tents, complexly folded
Werpesh	long-Sublimed; built Girdlecity of Xown
Zihdren	light-wraith vacuum baskers, Sublimed
+ Zihdren-Remnanter	
eDust	remnant/representative adjunct of Zihdren

✻